# RAIN

## V.C. Andrews® Books

**The Dollanganger Family Series:**
Flowers in the Attic
Petals on the Wind
If There Be Thorns
Seeds of Yesterday
Garden of Shadows

**The Casteel Family Series:**
Heaven
Dark Angel
Fallen Hearts
Gates of Paradise
Web of Dreams

**The Cutler Family Series:**
Dawn
Secrets of the Morning
Twilight's Child
Midnight Whispers
Darkest Hour

**The Landry Family Series:**
Ruby
Pearl in the Mist
All That Glitters
Hidden Jewel
Tarnished Gold

**The Logan Family Series:**
Melody
Heart Song
Unfinished Symphony
Music in the Night
Olivia

**The Orphans Miniseries:**
Butterfly
Crystal
Brooke
Raven
Runaways (full-length novel)

**The Wildflowers Miniseries:**
Misty
Star
Jade
Cat
Into the Garden (full-length novel)

**The Hudson Family Series:**
Rain

My Sweet Audrina
(does not belong to a series)

Published by POCKET BOOKS

# V.C. ANDREWS®

# RAIN

POCKET BOOKS
New York London Toronto Sydney Singapore

Following the death of Virginia Andrews, the Andrews family worked with a carefully selected writer to organize and complete Virginia Andrews' stories and to create additional novels, of which this is one, inspired by her storytelling genius.

This book is a work of fiction. Names, characters, places and incidents are products of the author's imagination or are used fictitiously. Any resemblance to actual events or locales or persons, living or dead, is entirely coincidental.

An *Original* Publication of POCKET BOOKS

POCKET BOOKS, a division of Simon & Schuster Inc.
1230 Avenue of the Americas, New York, NY 10020



ISBN: 0-7394-0783-X



Jacket design by Jim Lebbad

Backjacket illustration by Lisa Falkenstern

Printed in the U.S.A.

# RAIN

# Prologue

My sister Beni and I were jolted simultaneously out of sleep by the explosive sound of a dish smashing against the kitchen wall. We heard the shattered pieces of china rain down on the pale yellow linoleum floor. I lay there, staring up into the darkness and holding my breath. Beni sat up to listen, her braids falling over her eyes so that she had to part them like a beaded curtain.

"What was that?" she gasped.

I was afraid to move, much less speak. The silence was like that moment after you see a streak of lightning and know there will be a boom rattling windows and your own bones. Sure enough, we heard Mama's tear-filled voice wail at Ken.

For as long as I could remember, Beni, Roy and I had called him Ken instead of Daddy or Papa. Calling him by his name instead always fit our lips better. Something in the way he looked at us, especially when we were younger, told all three of us that he didn't want to be known as anyone's father, much less ours.

"Go on, then," we heard Mama cry, "leave. You aren't much good to us here anyway. You never were."

"If that's the way you feel, woman, then I might just go," he roared back at her.

"Go, go, go," she chanted like a high-school cheerleader. The strain in her voice made the strings in my own heart strain to the point of snapping.

"I will," he threatened. "I won't stay where I'm not appreciated. That's for sure; that's for damn sure."

"Appreciated?" She laughed a shrill, thin laugh. "What's there to appreciate? Your spending all your wages on drink and other women? Your coming home and falling on your face? You haven't ever been here for me and the children anyway, Ken Arnold. We aren't even going to know you're gone," Mama assured him.

"Ungrateful bitch! I oughta . . ."

"Lay a hand on me. Go on. I dare you. I'll call the law, I will. Go on," she challenged.

I sat up. It felt like tiny drums of fear were tapping beneath my breast. Quickly, I embraced myself. We had all seen him strike her before. It was ugly and tied knots of fear in our stomachs. Beni moaned in anticipation. She started to edge herself off her bed reluctantly, like someone being urged to run into a burning building.

"Don't go out there," I warned in a loud whisper. "You'll only make it harder for Mama."

She paused. Even in the dark, I could see the abject terror in my younger sister's eyes.

Our older brother Roy came to our door, rubbing his right palm back and forth over his forehead as if he were sanding a block of wood. It took a lot more to wake him than it did us. Mama always said, "That boy proves someone really could be dead to the world when he sleeps."

Roy stopped outside our open doorway. "What the hell's going on now?" he muttered, grimacing as if he had just swallowed some sour milk.

"Don't get between them, Roy," I cried. Once before, he had, and Ken had hit him so hard, he had knocked Roy down and made his lip bleed and swell. Mama kept him from getting up and getting the worst beating of his life for sure.

"Ahh, you deserve me leaving you," Ken muttered.

Apparently, Mama had held up her challenge. She had fixed those hot ebony eyes on him and made him back down. The next thing we heard was the front door opening and slamming shut. It rattled the walls in the small apartment and then all was still for a moment before we heard Mama sobbing.

I got out of bed and Beni and I joined Roy. All three of us entered the kitchen and found Mama seated at the chipped Formica table, her head down on her folded arms, her shoulders shaking.

We had seen her this way many times before.

"What happened this time, Mama?" Roy asked, his eyes blazing with anger.

Mama raised her head slowly and with great effort as if it were made of stone. Her eyes were red and glassy with tears. She deep breath, her small shoulders rising and then falling quickly, sembling some puppet whose strings had been cut. She seemed to s into the chair. When I saw her so despondent, my heart felt like a squeezed orange. My chest was so tight that I couldn't take a deep breath. The tears that had streaked down Mama's cheeks left jagged lines right to the tip of her chin.

She sighed deeply and ran her thin fingers through her hair, hair that had once had a healthy sheen to it and now looked dull, with strands of gray invading like a threat. I hated to see Mama age. Worry and trouble weighed heavily on the hands of her clock, rushing time along. I wanted her to be forever young with a face full of smiles and hope and a voice filled with laughter and song. For as long as I could remember, Mama had to work hard. She hated the thought of being on welfare. No matter how wasteful and neglectful Ken was, Mama wouldn't succumb. She had a steel rod of pride through her spine.

"As long as there's an ounce of strength in these legs and arms," she would tell us, "I'm never going to let the government tell me I'm part of the problem. No sir, no ma'am, no. Latisha Carrol's got a long way down before she hits bottom."

Right now, she looked like there wasn't all that much longer to go. Currently, Mama worked at Krandel's Market stocking shelves and packing groceries like some high-school dropout. She never complained about it, however.

None of us had any kind of job, but when Roy was younger, to earn tip money he would go to the supermarket and carry groceries out to cars for people. Once an elderly white lady gave him a twenty. Mama felt sure she meant to give him a dollar and just made a mistake. She told Roy to wait for the lady and return it as soon as he saw her. Roy didn't want to. That twenty nearly burned a hole in his pocket, but he was afraid to spend it. Finally, he saw the same old lady and told her what she had done. She looked at him as if he was crazy and told him he must be in error. She doesn't make those kind of mistakes. He came running home to tell Mama, who sat back, thought and said, "Well Roy, if that old white lady's so arrogant she can't admit a mistake, then it's honestly yours."

Ken told him he shouldn't have bothered trying to give it back anyway, but Mama always had a bigger influence on us than Ken did. I don't remember exactly when Roy lost respect for our daddy, but I think Ken knew all along that his son didn't look up to him. Maybe that was part of the reason he stayed away from home so much.

ne and left us again," Mama said.

o him," Roy snapped.

like that talk, Roy Arnold. He's still your father the Bible says about honoring your father and

nking of him when he had that written down, Ma," Roy said angrily.

"Don't you go claiming to know what God meant or intended, Roy Arnold," she fired back at him, her eyes filling with the heat and light of her passion. Mama always felt that holding on to her religion was the only glue that held us together. She wasn't a regular churchgoer, nor did she chase us to church on Sunday as faithfully as some other mothers herded their children, but she never let us drift too far from prayer and the Bible.

Roy shook his head and lowered it as he slumped with fatigue.

"I'm going back to bed," he muttered.

"Y'all go back to bed. You've got school in the morning and I don't want to have to shake you girls awake, hear?"

"Are you going to bed, Mama?" I asked her.

"Soon," she said.

I looked at Beni. We both knew she would stay up most of the night tossing and turning with worry. Bills were the ghosts that haunted our home, flashing their numbers on the walls in Mama's room, piling themselves on her shoulders. Ken never worried about our bills. It was always a battle to get him to pay for some of our expenses before he spent his paycheck, when he had one, on his own pleasure and amusement.

Whenever Ken ran off like this, his paycheck disappeared with him and whatever small amount Mama might have gotten from it was gone too. She didn't make anywhere near enough at the supermarket to take care of our needs.

"Beni and I will look for work tomorrow, Mama."

"No, you won't," she retorted so fast it was as if she'd expected my offer. "I want you girls concentrating on your school work."

"But Mama, other girls our age are working part-time here and there," Beni protested. "Why can't we?"

"So when do they do their homework, huh, Beni? They work after school. They drag their sorry selves home late and don't do any reading or writing, and then they work weekends and can't study then either," Mama declared.

"We aren't going to college anyway, Mama. It doesn't matter," Beni said.

"Why can't you try to be more positive, Beni? Rain manages to," Mama said, her eyes narrowing.

Beni flashed an angry look at me.

Mama shook her head and looked at Roy.

"We'll be all right, Mama," he said. "I'm taking that job at Slim's Garage. I'll be giving you as much as he ever did, probably more."

"I don't want you giving up on school, Roy," Mama said, but not with a great deal of insistence. Roy was a man now, eighteen, with broad shoulders pumped with pride, pride she knew he had inherited from her.

"Right," he said and flashed a deep-eyed look at me before he turned to go back to his room.

Mama sighed again and then looked up at me.

"Don't make the same mistakes I did, Rain. You take forever before you hook up with any man, hear?"

"Yes, Mama."

"And don't believe any promises," she warned. "Men are full of promises. They get some well of false hope filled for them the day they can begin to utter their first words, and they just dip into that well every time they set eyes on some unsuspecting female."

"Okay, Mama," I said smiling.

"Look how pretty you are, even woken up in the middle of the night. Come over here and give me some sugar so I can have a good dream tonight," she said and for a moment her eyes were young again, the eyes of the Mama I remembered singing to me, holding my hand, hugging me after bad dreams and kissing me good night.

I embraced her and she held onto me a little tighter than usual, stroking my hair. It put a flutter of butterfly wings in my stomach. I could feel her bones shudder beneath her thin skin. She had lost weight, as if trouble shrunk her by the minute.

"You children are my only hope now," she whispered. "Don't let me down, Rain."

"We won't, Mama."

"Beni's got a bad chip on her shoulder," she said in a tired voice when we parted. "I don't know why. I don't teach her to hate, but she thinks being black means being angry all the time. She needs to smile more. I was hoping you would teach her that, Rain. I was hoping some of your light would spill into her dark."

"She'll be okay, Mama," I promised.

"I know," Mama said, but she looked down when she said it so I wouldn't see her doubt and worry.

"You go to sleep now too, Mama. You know Ken. He'll go off for a while and then he'll come back."

"I know," she agreed. "Go to sleep, Rain. Go on," she urged.

I started out of the kitchen, looking back once to see her take a deep breath, rise and pick up the pieces of the dish she had thrown against the wall. She dropped them into the garbage can and stood there with her back to me, her five feet four-inch frame shriveling a little more. Mama's bank account of hope was dwindling. When do the good get their just rewards? I wondered, and I was positive Mama was wondering the same.

Beni was lying in her bed with her eyes wide open, smoldering like some house that had been set on fire.

"Mama's always going to like you more than me," she snapped at me as soon as I entered.

"No, she's not, Beni."

"No? Why can't you be like Rain?" she mimicked, wagging her head. "That's all I ever hear her say anymore."

She turned on her side so her back was to me.

"She's just worried for all of us, Beni. She doesn't mean you're not as good as I am," I said. I went to her and put my hand on her shoulder. "Don't be like this, Beni. Not now, not with all Ken's doing to her and to us," I pleaded.

She kept her back to me and spoke toward the wall.

"She always had more of you in her eyes than she had of me, Rain. It's like she . . ." She turned to face me. ". . . like she owes you more than she owes me or something."

"That's silly, Beni."

"No, it's not," she said stiffening. "There's something," she said nodding, convinced. "There's some reason."

In the darkness her eyes picked up the small glow of the hallway light and glittered like new dimes.

"I know you know what I mean, Rain," she said in a softer voice. "I know you pretend there's no difference, but I know you know."

I started to shake my head.

"Let's not lie to each other, Rain," she followed. "At least let's not do that."

I didn't speak.

She wasn't really all wrong. I always felt Mama looked at me in a different way. I just didn't know why and I didn't want to find out. I was afraid. I don't know why I had a stream of fear running through the back of my thoughts, but it ran, thin and silvery, like a thread of light I was afraid to touch. It was safer in the dark.

I went to bed and lay there quietly, looking up at the ceiling.

"I hate him," Beni muttered. "I hate him for what he's doing to us. Don't you?"

"No. I don't hate him. I can't hate him. I don't understand him, but I don't want to hate him. He's our father, Beni."

"I don't care who he is. I do hate him," Beni said. "Sometimes, Mama's wrong. Sometimes, hating makes you feel better. It makes you . . . stronger. That's something you oughta learn, Rain. That's something you oughta learn from me."

She was silent for a moment and then she braced herself on her elbows and looked over at me.

"Maybe that's why Mama cares more about you," Beni said, sounding like she was solving her own dilemma, "maybe she knows you're weaker than me and you need more protection. Yeah," she said lying back on her pillow, "I bet that's it."

She liked that idea. I could almost hear her smile of satisfaction. It helped her close her eyes and go back to sleep.

Maybe she's right, I thought. Maybe I am weaker. Maybe Beni had a better chance to survive in this hard world because of the way she was.

I turned over and traveled a different road to the same darkness.

# 1

# The Beginning of the End

For as long as I could remember, we lived in an apartment located in a building complex everyone called The Projects. Even as a little girl I hated the name. It didn't sound like a home, a place to live with your family. It sounded just like the word suggested: some government undertaking, some attempt to deal with the poor, some bureaucrat's program. Beni called it The Cages, which made me feel like we were being treated like animals.

I suppose at one time the buildings looked clean and new. In the beginning there wasn't gang graffiti scribbled madly over every available space creating the Books of Madness, as I liked to describe them. The streets in front weren't dirty and the small patches of lawn didn't look mangy and sick. Now the whole place seemed like someone's ashtray.

Our apartment was on the second floor: two-fifteen. We were lucky because we could use the stairway when the elevator was broken, which was often, and we weren't on the first floor where there was a greater chance for burglaries. Some of the tenants on the first floor actually had bars installed in their windows, which was why Beni named the complex The Cages. It didn't do any good to tell her that bars on cages were meant to keep animals in, not people out. She claimed the government wanted to keep us locked inside.

"We're like some ugly pimple on the face of the capital. I bet the government people don't want foreigners to see us. That's why they don't take them through our streets," she declared, parroting one of Ken's frequent speeches of self-pity.

I couldn't deny that there was a lot of fear and crime around us.

Everyone had some kind of an alarm and often they went off accidentally. It had gotten so no one paid much attention to them. If there was ever an example of The Boy Who Cried Wolf, it was here in The Projects.

Beni, Roy and I had only three city blocks to walk to school, but sometimes we felt we were going through a minefield in a war zone. During the last six months, two people had been killed by stray bullets fired from passing cars, one gang shooting at members of another without regard for innocent bystanders. Everyone thought it was terrible, but went on and accepted it as if it was simply a part of what had to be, like some nasty storm coming through. There wasn't much anyone could do about bad weather and most people had the same attitude about our street crime.

Mama was visibly terrified whenever one of us went out after dark. She'd actually start to tremble. I began to think we weren't living much differently than people in the Middle Ages. When our teacher talked about the fortresses, the moats and drawbridges and the dangers that lurked outside the fortress walls back then, I thought about The Projects now. Beside having alarms and bars on windows, everyone locked his doors three or four ways with chain locks, bolts and bars and did the same with the windows. Many of the elderly sat away from their windows and shivered at the sounds of the night, the screaming in the hallways.

From my window I could just manage to see the lights in some of the government buildings, and when we walked a few blocks east and looked toward the Capitol, we could see the Washington Monument and the Lincoln Memorial all lit up with promises. We were able to take some class trips to the sites and even tour places like the Treasury Building where we saw money being printed, and the FBI building, where we learned about crime labs and fingerprints. We never saw the Congress in action, but we did visit the buildings.

I sometimes felt like an astronaut on these class trips. It was as if we were being transported to another planet. We saw the fine homes, the embassies, how rich and prosperous people were. We heard about all the wonderful hopes these buildings and monuments represented, but we always returned to our reality where it was possible to witness a drug sale on the corner, or see an unattended child wandering near broken glass and rusty metal. What will become of him? I wondered. What will become of us? In school we studied about democracy and we were taught dreams that were apparently reserved for other sleeping faces, not ours.

Recently, someone overdosed on heroin under a stairwell in our building. The police swarmed over the hallway like blue bees and then left as quickly as they had come, none of them seemed surprised or even concerned. I think they, too, had come to accept the horrors the same way we had.

Mama always dreamed of getting us out of here, of course. To me it seemed most of the people who lived here could no longer even imagine that for themselves. Mama wouldn't talk to anyone but us about it because she hated the dark, heavy notes of discouragement. Once, when Ken was doing well, not drinking as much and making a decent wage, we were able to put away enough money to actually consider the possibility of at least renting a small house in a better neighborhood, but then one day Ken went and secretly withdrew the money. I remember how Mama came home looking drained of blood after she had discovered what he had done.

"He killed our dreams," she mumbled.

I thought Mama was going to have a heart attack. Her lips looked so blue and she seemed to have trouble breathing. She had to have a shot glass full of whiskey to calm herself. She sat staring out the window most of the afternoon, sat there gazing down at the streets with a strange, soft smile on her face and hummed an old tune as if she were looking at a beautiful field or majestic mountains. I tried to talk to her, give her something to eat, but she didn't seem to hear me. I was very frightened, afraid for all of us.

Finally, Ken came home. Roy wasn't there at the time. I was glad of that because there would have been a fight for sure. Beni and I were in our bedroom doorway, holding our breath. We expected Mama was going to explode with a fury we had never seen before, but she fooled us. She spoke calmly in the beginning, just asking him to tell her why he had done such a thing without telling her, and what he had done with the money. At first, we thought he wasn't going to tell. He moved across the kitchen, getting himself a beer, wrapping his long, thick fingers around the bottle, opening it and taking a long gulp. He leaned against the counter by the sink.

"I needed it," he finally said, "to pay a debt."

"A debt? What debt? The electric bill that's past due? The dentist bills for Beni and Rain? What debt, Ken?" she demanded.

"A debt," he repeated. He avoided her eyes. She rose slowly.

"Some of that money was money I slaved to earn. Don't I have a right to know where it's gone?" she asked, still remarkably softly for her.

"I had a debt," he repeated.

She seemed to inflate, her small shoulders rising, her bosom lifting. I looked at Beni. Her face was full of anger and my stomach felt like hornets had built a nest inside.

"You gambled away our money, didn't you, Ken Arnold? Go on, tell me. You just threw away all that money, months and months of work, gone!"

He turned to face her, the beer bottle to his lips, his neck working like the body of a snake. Suddenly, Mama slapped the bottle out of his hand and it flew across the kitchen and smashed on the floor.

Ken was stunned. For a moment he couldn't move. He was so amazed at her aggression and her anger, it stopped him from breathing too. For Beni and me the sight of Mama, all five feet four, one hundred and five pounds of her fuming in front of Ken with his six feet five inch, two hundred and fifty-pound body with his massive shoulders and thick neck, was terrifying. He could squash her like a fly, but she stuck her face into his and didn't blink.

"You go and destroy my hope just like that and then tell me it was some debt? You go and spill my blood and sweat in the street and tell me it's just some debt?"

"Back off, woman," Ken said, but I saw he was shaking. Whether he was shaking with his own overwhelming anger or fear was not clear. Suddenly though, he realized we were there, too, and his pride reared up like a sleeping lion.

"What do you think you're doing slapping my beer across the room? Huh?" he roared, his eyes wide. "You're a crazy woman and I ain't standing here and listening to a crazy woman."

He turned and rushed out of the house. Mama stood looking after him for a moment and then she went to clean up the mess. I jumped to help her.

"Watch you don't cut yourself, Rain," she warned in a low, tired voice as I picked up the pieces of glass. Beni was still shivering in her chair.

"I'll do it, Mama," I said.

She didn't argue. She went to her bedroom to lie down. I thought she might never get up, but somehow, Mama found the resilience to fight on, to restore her optimism, to replant in her garden of hope and dream on for all of us.

I think it was Mama's courage more than anything that kept me full of dreams, too. If she could be this way after what had happened to her, I thought, I, who was so much younger and still had so much of a chance, had to be full of heart. I had to hold onto my smiles and not be like Beni. I had to push back the urge to hate everyone and everything. I had to see blue sky and stars even in days of rain, so many days of rain.

Our school was nothing to look at. In fact, I often closed my eyes when I first turned the corner and the tired, broken-down building appeared. It looked more like a factory than a school and all the windows on it had bars. There was a chain link fence around the property, too, with big metal signs warning against trespassing.

Two uniformed guards were at the front entrance when the students first arrived for class. To get into the building, we all had to pass through one of those metal detectors you see at the airports. On too many occasions, students, especially gang members, had slashed other students with knives and on one occasion, a tenth-grade boy was found carrying a loaded revolver. The teachers were adamant about added security. There was almost a strike before the powers that be installed the metal detector and kept uniformed guards patrolling the halls and supporting the teachers.

Mr. McCalester, my history teacher, said all the teachers should be given battle pay as well as their salaries. He made it sound like we should all be thankful if we made it through a school day without being harmed. It was hard to concentrate and care about poetry and plays, algebra and geometry, chemistry and biology while outside the fenced-in area angry young men waited to destroy each other and anyone who got in their way.

Most of my and Beni's friends were battle worn, veterans of the hard streets. Everyone knew about drugs and no one was surprised to find someone using crack, pot or whatever happened to be the flavor of the day. Neither Beni nor I ever used or tried any of it. Roy was the same way. There were times when I was afraid Beni would give in. Girlfriends challenged us, said we weren't being "sistas" and we were acting stuck-up.

Some of the girls resented me anyway because of my looks. Mama always taught me that vanity was a sin, but I couldn't help wondering if I had been given some special gifts. My hair was straighter, richer than most. I had a creamy caramel complexion, never bothered much by acne. I also had light brown eyes, more toward almond, with long eyelashes. Roy once said he thought I could be a model, but I was afraid to even wish for such a thing. I was afraid to wish for anything good. Nice things had to happen to us accidentally, by surprise. If you wish for something too hard, I thought, it was like holding a balloon too tightly. It would simply burst, splattering your dream into pieces of nothing.

When I was younger, Mama loved to brush my hair and hum one of the soft melodies her mama had sung to her.

"You're going to be a beautiful young lady, Rain," she would whisper softly in my ear, "but you've got to know that beauty can be a burden too. You've got to learn to say no and watch yourself more because men will be looking at you more."

Her warnings frightened me. I couldn't help but walk through the school corridors with my eyes firmly fixed straight ahead, not returning a glance, not welcoming a smile. I knew most of the kids thought I was a snob, but I reacted this way because of the tiny hummingbird that fluttered in my heart every time a boy gazed at me with interest. That flutter sent a chill through my spine and down to my feet. I'd almost rather be unattractive, I thought.

I know Beni didn't think she was pretty, even though I thought she had nice features and beautiful ebony eyes. She had a bigger bust than I did and liked to keep a button or two undone or wear tighter clothes, but she was wider in the hips and Roy always criticized her for looking like a tramp. My lips were thinner and my nose was straighter and more narrow than Beni's. Sometimes, when Beni wasn't looking, I would study her face more and try to find resemblances between us. She and Roy looked more alike, although his hair was closer to mine.

Once, I asked Mama about it and she said sometimes your grandparents show up in you more than your parents do. I thought about it and studied the pictures we had of Ken's parents and Mama's parents, but I didn't see resemblances to me in any of them.

Neither Mama's nor Ken's parents were alive. Ken's father had been killed in a car accident and his mother had died of liver damage caused by alcohol. Mama's mother died before her father. She had had a heart attack. I got to meet my grandfather, but he lived in North Carolina and he died of emphysema before I was five, so I didn't remember all that much about him except he smoked so much, I thought it came out of his ears as well as his nose and his mouth. Mama had one sister in Texas. Her name was Alana, and she had a brother named Lamar somewhere in Florida. They rarely contacted each other. I never met Lamar, but I did meet Alana one Christmas when I was seven.

Ken never talked about his older brother Curtis, who was in prison in Oklahoma for armed robbery. A man was killed so he had been given a long sentence.

Aunt Alana was supposed to have had a baby she gave away, but we didn't know any real details about it except that it was a girl. Sometimes, Beni and I would wonder aloud. We imagined she would be about our age and she probably looked a little like one of us. Occasionally, Beni would tease Roy and say things like, "Be careful 'bout the girls you sleep with, Roy. One might be your cousin."

Roy hated that. He hated it when Beni talked about sex. He was always after her to put something on lately, too. She would parade about in her panties and bra and sometimes, she would put on a robe with nothing underneath and not tie it too tightly. Roy would get so angry his eyes would nearly explode. He had Ken's temper for sure, only not for the same reasons.

He was different with me. If he caught sight of me underdressed, he looked away or walked away quickly. I always tried to be properly dressed if I was in the kitchen or the living room.

Despite his gruff manner at times, Roy was as loving and as protective a brother as Beni or I could want. He tried to be right beside us as much as he could be when we were in the streets. Now that he was taking a job at Slim's Garage after school, he was troubled about our walking home without him. He had told us both at least six times to be sure we went directly home and not stop at any of the jukebox joints to listen to hip-hop music. "The worst types hang out there," he warned.

"He just wants to keep us little girls forever," Beni complained. Two of her friends, Alicia and Nicole, were always trying to get her to go out after school. Finally, one afternoon after Roy had started working, she met me in the hallway at the end of the day and said she wanted to go with Alicia and Nicole to hang out for a while at Oh Henry's. It was a dingy luncheonette in one of the worst neighborhoods. Roy always said if all the roaches living in it were harnessed, they'd pull down the building.

"Mama will be upset," I told her.

"She won't know unless you tell. I'll be back before she gets home."

"Why do you want to go there?" I pursued. "You know what it's like."

"I don't know what it's like. I never been there, Rain. Besides . . . there's someone I want to see who goes there," she added with a flirtatious smile. I knew she had been flirting with Carlton Thomas lately; he was in a gang because his cousin was a leader in it.

"If you go, I have to go," I complained.

"No, you don't. I can take care of myself," she bragged, loud enough for Nicole and Alicia to hear.

"I know you can, but Roy will kill me if I let you go by yourself."

"I don't care about Roy. He doesn't run my life," she snapped. "And I don't need you watching over me either, Rain. I'm not a baby."

She spun around and joined Alicia and Nicole. They started for the exit.

"Okay, wait up," I called. "I'll go but we're getting home before Mama," I added when I joined them.

They sauntered along, Beni looking pleased with herself, her eyes full of anticipation, and despite the brave front she put up, a little fear, too.

The music was loud; the room was smoky and crowded and it smelled greasy and sickly sweet, but no one seemed to mind or care. Some people were dancing. Older boys who had been out of school a while were drinking beer and passing the bottles to those who weren't old enough to buy it. I saw some drug deals being made and bad stuff being passed along. Most of it was done out in the open. The owner and the bartender and waitress acted as if the place was empty. If they saw anything, they looked right through it.

I glanced at Beni when we all entered and saw the look on her face was not much different from the look of disappointment and disgust that was on mine, but the moment she caught me staring at her, she acted as if she was still very excited to be there.

"Now that you see what's going on, you still want to stay here?" I asked.

"Of course I want to stay here. Why else would I come?"

She dove right into the crowd with Alicia and Nicole, surrounding Carlton, who was talking to members of a gang. I knew they were gang members because they wore Dickie pants with a blue belt hanging down from their pockets. They called it "flue" instead of blue, which was the color for the Crips.

I didn't see anyone I wanted to talk to so I tried to stay out of sight, more toward the door like someone who thought a fire might start at any moment and it was better to be near an exit. After a while Beni came back for me.

"If you're gonna just stand there like a statue, Rain, you should go home. They're all laughing at you. At least come listen to the music and dance or something."

"We should go home, Beni. Look at this place. Look what's going on," I said nodding toward a couple who were kissing and petting as if they were alone in the back of a car. Across from them, some young man looked like he was in a coma, his body slumped in the chair. The music blasted so loudly around us it was hard to hear.

"Beni," Nicole shouted. "Carlton wants to ask you something."

"I'm not leaving," Beni fired at me and spun around to walk back.

I was so uncomfortable, I considered deserting her. A part of me thought it would be terrible, but another part of me couldn't wait to do just that.

"I ain't seen you here before," someone said, and I turned to look at the heavily pocked-marked face of a young man. He had a cigarette dangling out of the corner of his mouth. It looked pasted there on his wet lips. He had a thin scar over his right eyebrow and his eyes were glassy, red. The blue belt hung from his pants pocket. He looked older than everyone else and was probably in his twenties, I thought.

"That's because I haven't been here before," I said quickly.

"Slummin'?" he asked with a cold smile. He had a gold tooth and when I looked closer, I saw some hairs curled under his chin. Hardened like a prune dried in the hot sun, he looked more purple than black and his lips curled outward with a bruise on the corner of the lower lip. I actually felt my stomach churn at the sight of him.

"I'm not exactly happy to be here," I replied and he laughed a quiet laugh, just his body shaking. He shoved a toothpick into his mouth as soon as he withdrew the cigarette, which he just tossed to the floor and stepped on.

"Come on. I'll show you where it's quieter." He reached for me.

"No thanks," I said stepping back.

"I don't bite. Much," he added with another wide smile. I spotted another scar, this one on the side of his neck. It ran down toward his right shoulder.

"Yeah, well I haven't had a tetanus shot recently," I said, trying to act brave even though my insides were shaking. Come on, Beni, I prayed. Let's get out of here.

He laughed again and two other members of the Crips joined him. He mumbled something to them and they all laughed.

"You want something to drink? Smoke?" he asked me.

"No thanks," I said. I backed up a few more steps toward the door.

"Hey, girl," he said with a look of disgust, "you come here for a good time, didn't you?"

"No," I said.

"Then why'd you come?" he demanded, his face folding deeper into anger, his eyes wider, his nostrils flaring like a wild horse.

"Maybe she likes the food, Jerad," one of the boys at his side muttered, and they all laughed.

"What's your name?" Jerad asked, stepping closer. I looked for Beni, but I didn't see her anymore.

"My sister is here," I said for no reason and I looked harder for her.

"So stick around. What's your name?" he asked, this time more firmly.

His two buddies stepped between me and the door. I hugged my books tighter to my bosom. Looking around desperately, I saw no one who would come to my aid. If anyone was looking my way, it was with a gleeful smile, enjoying my discomfort. It frightened me even more.

"What'cha got under there?" he asked nodding at my bosom. "Some buried treasure?"

They all laughed and the circle they were forming grew wider and tighter as more boys joined them. My heart began to pound. I looked frantically for Beni and saw she was dancing with Carlton.

"I really have to go home," I said.

"So soon? What, are you on parole and got a curfew?" he asked. Every time he spoke, his private audience laughed. I felt their eyes all over me, drinking me up in gulps from head to toe. It made me feel naked, on display. My face felt hot as fear planted itself firmly in my stomach and sent my blood raging around my body.

"Maybe she wants you to walk her home, Jerad," one of the other boys said.

"I could do that. I could drive you home, too," he offered.

"No thank you."

"She's stuck-up, Jerad," another one commented.

"Are you stuck-up?" he demanded. I glanced at him. His eyes looked glazed with anger. "You think you're better than the rest of us because your skin's lighter, girl?"

"No," I said.

"So how come you don't tell me your name?" he followed.

"It's Rain," I said.

"Huh?"

"Rain. My name is Rain, okay? Now leave me alone," I pleaded.

"Rain?" He took out his toothpick and nodded. "I like that. Me and my Rain girl. What'cha think, Chumpy?" he asked a heavyset and much shorter boy.

"Rain's a trouble that will follow you everywhere you go, Jerad," he said.

"Yeah, that's right, Chumpy. You wanna be my Rain girl, Rain?"

"No. I want to get my sister and go home," I moaned.

"Now that's not too friendly," he said. "Come on," he said, grabbing me at my elbow. "I'll buy you somethin' to drink."

"No thank you." I pulled out of his grip.

"No thank you? How polite. Ain't she polite, Chumpy?" he asked.

"I never seen a more polite Rain," Chumpy quipped. Everyone laughed. The circle they made tightened so I couldn't look toward the bar or even at the dance floor.

"I bet kissin' you ain't like kissin' rain, though," Jerad said. He drew closer. I backed up into one of the boys behind me who gave me a small shove forward into Jerad, who then put his arms around me.

"Whoa, take it easy. Don't be comin' at me so aggressively, girl," he said with a laugh, but he held onto me. "I'll be here for you. Don't worry."

They all laughed again. I struggled to get out of his embrace.

"Let me go," I said.

"After I get my kiss. Come on," he urged, bringing his lips closer to mine. "I never kissed no Rain before. Come on."

"No, let me go." I squirmed. He looked at the others and they tightened the circle. Panic nailed my feet to the dirty wooden floor.

Someone from behind seized my arms just above the elbows and pulled them back so hard, my books slipped and fell to the floor. I gasped, but before I could shout, Jerad pressed his thick, wet lips to my mouth, cupping my breasts in his palms as he did so, and the group sent up a cry of glee. It drew everyone's attention because when he pulled back, I could see people looking at us and laughing. Beni stopped dancing and gazed at me with amazement.

"Now that was no Rain kiss," Jerad said, "but that there is some treasure," he added, nodding at my bosom.

I didn't move. I never felt so violated; I was terrified.

"Chumpy," he said. "Pick up the girl's books. Where's your manners?"

"Sorry," Chumpy said. He picked up my books and handed them to me.

I wanted to wipe my mouth, but I was afraid of getting Jerad angry, so I turned away and started toward the door. The boys stood their ground.

"Let her go. For now," Jerad ordered and they parted. I hurried out and into the street. Even the littered gutter felt fresher and cleaner than where I had just been. I walked as quickly as I could, my legs trembling, cold tears flowing down my cheeks.

"Rain!" I heard Beni call and turned before I reached the corner. "What happened?"

"I'm going home, Beni. I don't care if you stay there. I'm going home." I wiped my cheeks and my mouth with the back of my hand.

"Okay," she said, realizing how upset I was. "Wait a minute, will you?" She went back inside and then came out with her books, hurrying up the sidewalk to join me. "What happened? Why did he kiss you?"

"I didn't want him to, that's for sure," I said. "He forced himself on me. I hate that place."

"You know who he is? He's the leader of the Crips here. That's Jerad Davis," Beni said looking as if she was talking about some movie star.

"I don't care who he is. He's disgusting and so are his friends." I walked faster. "I knew something bad was going to happen if I went there. I just knew it."

"Oh, what was so bad?" Beni asked. "He just kissed you."

I stopped and turned on her.

"What was so bad? I didn't want him to kiss me, Beni. That's what was so bad and he touched me, too," I told her indicating my breasts. Her eyes widened.

"He did?"

"He's disgusting and so are his friends and so are most of the people in there," I cried, and walked faster.

Beni mumbled something under her breath and caught up.

"You better not say anything about it to Mama or Roy," she warned.

"Don't worry. I don't want to think about it anymore. You're not getting into any trouble."

We hurried along, Beni looking sullen and frustrated and I feeling completely violated.

It was always difficult for me to look at Roy and hide my thoughts and feelings. He had a way of gazing through my eyes into my heart and mind. No one was more sensitive to my moods than Roy, not even Mama. I was afraid of what he would see when he came home.

As usual, I started preparing dinner for us. If I kept busy, I thought, I wouldn't dwell on what had happened to me. Beni helped some, but was still brooding about having to leave Oh Henry's so quickly. When Roy came home from work, he went right to the stove and looked at the roast chicken. I had small potatoes and onions in with it and the aroma was delicious. He took a deep breath and rubbed his stomach.

"I'm starving," he declared. "Put in a day's work in just four hours. Slim's got himself a new slave, but I ain't complaining."

Beni sat at the table flipping through a movie magazine. Roy stared at her for a moment and then looked at me.

"You better wash off that oil and grease before Mama gets home," I warned him. He nodded, but he didn't change expression. I looked away quickly.

"Everything all right?" he asked. I made the mistake of shifting my eyes toward Beni before replying.

"Yes," I said.

"What's going on, Rain?" he demanded.

"Nothing's going on, Roy. We're just . . . worried and upset because of Ken," I said.

He stared through me in his usual way, those dark eyes fixing so hard and fast, it was easier to shake off fly paper. I had to pretend to check on the chicken.

"You girls come right home after school?"

"Yes," Beni said quickly. "And quit treating us like children. Just because Ken went and run off doesn't mean you're our daddy, Roy Arnold."

"You cause any more problems for Mama and you'll find out who's gonna be your daddy," he threatened pointing his long, thick forefinger at her.

Beni wasn't easily intimidated by anyone, least of all Roy. She flipped her magazine at him as if it was a frisbee and it hit him in the chest. It wasn't that it hurt him. It was that she would do it. He started around the table at her.

"Roy!" I cried.

He stopped, his shoulders up, and looked at me.

"You're headed for trouble, girl," he told Beni.

"It's none of your business," she wailed.

"Just leave her be, Roy," I said. "Mama's going to be home any minute. Please," I pleaded. "I don't want to make her any more upset." He looked at me again, then at Beni, and then left the kitchen.

"Why did you do that, Beni? You know his temper."

"I don't want him thinking he can lord it over us just because he's older and he's a man," she said. "I feel like some trapped bird in here most of the time with him saying don't do this and don't do that, and what are you wearing that for or why don't you wear longer skirts? I don't need any one telling me what to do," she declared. "He never says anything to you."

"He just wants to be sure you're safe, Beni."

"I don't need him to do that. I'm old enough to take care of myself." She stared at me for a moment. "You better not get me in trouble, Rain," she cautioned and went into our room.

Mama came home before Roy returned to the kitchen. She was tired and I saw she was disappointed Ken hadn't returned. I knew she had been hoping he would.

"Dinner looks delicious, honey. Didn't Beni help you?" she asked, looking at our closed bedroom door.

"Yes, she helped, Mama," I lied. A lie to keep Mama from being upset was a good lie, I thought. She shook her head and smiled at me though.

"Sure she did. That girl doesn't lift a finger unless I'm standing right over her. Roy home yet?"

"He's just cleaning up for dinner, Mama."

"Good. I'll do the same and then be out to help," she said.

"There's nothing left to do, Mama. The table's set," I said.

She sighed deeply, smiled at me, and started out, stopping at the doorway.

"Thank God we've got you, Rain. It makes it all a lot easier," she said.

It nearly made my heart crack to see her lower her head and walk with a slight stoop. She was exhausted and full of worry. How could such a tiny woman hold so much grief?

We were all quieter than usual at dinner. Mama tried asking questions about school, but Beni remained sulky and Roy continued to have suspicious eyes. I kept as busy as I could and was actually happy to clean up by myself when Beni complained she had too much homework.

"The teachers don't care how much they pile it on us," she moaned.

"Just do it all," Mama ordered.

"Well, I can't do it all if I don't get started right now," she declared.

"It's all right, Ma. I have most of my work done. I don't need Beni tonight."

Beni rushed off to the phone to call her girlfriends as soon as she saw the opportunity. Mama was at my side and Roy went into the living room to watch television.

"I keep hoping times will stop being hard for us, Rain, but it doesn't seem to change. The first chance you get to leave this hell hole, you take it, hear?"

"I'll never leave you behind, Mama," I promised.

"Sure you will, honey. You're supposed to. You children are the hope."

She put her arm around my shoulders and hugged me to her and then she went into her bedroom. After I finished cleaning up, I started for the bedroom, but Roy came to the living room door. He hadn't been watching television so much as biding his time.

"Come on in here a minute, Rain," he said.

"What?"

"Come on in here," he said more firmly. I lowered my head and walked into the living room.

"I've got homework to do, Roy."

"You'll do it. I want you to tell me the truth, Rain. What happened today?"

"Oh Roy, don't make more trouble."

"That's what I'm afraid's going to happen if I don't know everything. You don't lie to me, Rain. We always tell each other the truth," he said softly. His eyes lingered on my face. They were soft, loving, pleading.

"Beni let her friends talk her into going to Oh Henry's," I revealed. "I went along to be sure she'd be all right, only it was me who got into a situation."

"What situation?"

"Someone named Jerad forced himself on me, had his friends surround me and then he kissed me."

I didn't want to tell him all of it. I could see just being kissed was enough.

"Then what happened?"

"I ran out and Beni followed and we came home. That's the whole thing. It won't happen again. I promise, Roy. We'll never go back to that place."

"Jerad Davis?"

"Yes," I said.

"He's killed people, Rain," Roy said.

My heart was thumping so hard, I had to take a breath.

"If he ever comes near you again, I gotta know, hear?"

"Yes," I said nodding.

"Beni's getting wild," he said looking toward our bedroom. "She's gonna get herself into real trouble someday. I don't want you tagging along. She'll drag you down with her."

"I can't desert her, Roy."

"Don't desert her, but if she's stubborn, don't let her drag you down," he warned. "Promise me." He reached out and took my hand. "Promise, Rain."

"I promise, Roy," I said. His eyes softened again.

"Good," he said. "You're too good for this place, Rain. I've got to get you out of here someday."

"We all have to get out, Roy."

"Sure," he said. He stared hard at me and I tilted my head in confusion. He blinked a few times, then pulled himself up. "Go do your homework," he said like an older brother, "and don't keep any secrets again."

I smiled at him and then I leaned over and kissed him on the cheek.

He was still standing in the doorway looking after me when I reached the bedroom door and looked back. His look stirred that little butterfly in my heart, the one that rang alarm bells when boys fixed their eyes on me in the hallways and in the streets. Maybe Roy felt my butterfly's wings too, because he turned away quickly and disappeared.

Confusion, like static on the radio, jumbled my thoughts. I rushed into the sanctuary of my schoolwork, grateful for the distractions to help me forget the day.

# 2

# Through Thick and Thin

Neither Beni nor I knew it, but after I had told Roy what had happened at Oh Henry's, he got Slim to let him come into work later every day just so he could secretly keep an eye on us when we walked home from school. Apparently, he was always trailing behind us, staying out of sight. He had to promise Slim he would work an extra hour every Saturday for nothing in order to do it, but I didn't learn about that until much later.

Beni continued her flirtation with Carlton Thomas, who was always after her to return to Oh Henry's. We had a big argument about it the following week. She was sullen every day all the way home because I had refused to go along with her return to Oh Henry's. She didn't care if I accompanied her, but I made it clear I wasn't going to lie for her and hide the fact that she was going there if either Mama or Roy asked. I had to tell her that Roy knew about the first time.

"Why did you tell him anything?" she demanded.

"He knew something was wrong, Beni. You know how Roy is. He wouldn't have given up until he found out anyway, maybe from someone else, and then he would have been even angrier," I explained.

She thought for a moment.

"He's got no right butting himself into my business," she declared, but she avoided any argument with Roy that would lead to something worse between her and Mama.

I knew her girlfriends were teasing her about my refusal to cooperate and that was only making her angrier at me. One afternoon, Nicole and Alicia cornered me in the hallway between classes and bawled me out for spoiling Beni's fun.

"Just because you're a snob doesn't mean your sister's got to be one," Nicole charged.

Nicole was a tall, lean girl with a harsh mouth and big eyes. Because she was the star of the girls' basketball team, she acted as if she was someone special. When she got angry, she would put her face right up to the other person's, practically touching noses, and hers was so pointed, she looked like she could stab you with it. She had been in two bad hair pulling, scratching and kicking fights and had been suspended a half dozen times during the last few years. I knew when Beni became friendly with her that there was going to be trouble someday.

"You don't have to be a snob to detest going to Oh Henry's," I replied, trying to hide my fear. She looked like she was ready to slap me silly, but I didn't step back.

"Detest?" She batted her long eyelashes and smiled. "Detest? You hear that, Alicia? You hear her fancy words?"

"It's not really a fancy word, Nicole," I said, and started to walk around her.

She grabbed my arm and pulled, spinning me around. I dropped my books. Some of the boys hurrying by paused to watch, their faces full of smiles, anticipating another fight.

"Don't you go walking away from me, Rain Arnold. You ain't nothing special."

"I'm not going to be late for class," I said pulling away and picking up my books. As soon as I'd gathered up my books I headed down the corridor.

"You're just a frustrated bitch," she called after me. My heart was knocking like a tiny hammer in my chest. I could hear the boys laughing behind me. "Ruining it for your sister 'cause you're jealous."

All the remainder of that day and most of the next, I could feel the derision, the laughter behind my back, and see the sly smiles on the faces of the girls who hung around with Nicole and Alicia. Beni sat with them in the cafeteria and then started to give me the silent treatment in school too, only speaking to me when it was absolutely necessary. She finally broke her silence one afternoon after we arrived home.

"If you liked some boy, I wouldn't threaten to get you in trouble, Rain. Some sister," she muttered.

"That's what I'm trying to be, your sister. That whole crowd's no good, Beni. You're going to get yourself in big trouble hanging around with them."

"I am not. I've got a mind of my own," she said. "You're just scared of growing up," she accused.

She sat on her bed watching me change into a pair of jeans and a sweatshirt. I turned, smiling.

"I'm scared of growing up? Who put that silly idea into your head?"

"Don't laugh at me, Rain. Maybe I don't get as good grades as you, but I'm not stupid. Nobody has to put ideas in my head."

"I never said you were stupid, Beni. People get influenced and sometimes, just because they're where bad things happen, they get blamed or they get in trouble or . . ."

"Stop preaching at me," she cried. "What are you, a schoolteacher?" She grimaced at me. "Don't you ever think about being with a boy? You're older than me and you never had a real boyfriend, Rain. Everyone says you think you're too good for anyone in our school. They call you Miss Prissy."

"That's not true. I just haven't found anyone I like enough or I believe likes me enough," I protested.

"So? Someone likes me. Why do you have to make it hard for me?"

"I'm not making it hard for you, Beni. I'm trying to protect you."

"That's all I ever hear from you and Roy." She kicked the table and folded her arms under her bosom, pouting.

"You can do better than Carlton Thomas," I said.

Her eyes were full of fire.

"He likes me and I like him. And he respects me," she added.

"Sure," I said. "He respects you. Someone like Carlton Thomas doesn't know the meaning of the word."

"Oh and you do, of course. You know it all," she said, her eyes full of fire and tears. "My friends are right about you. I can't talk to you anymore," she declared and went into the bathroom, slamming the door.

Was I wrong? Was I too particular, a Miss Prissy? Was I afraid of boys? Maybe Mama's warnings had too dramatic an effect on me. I wished I could talk to her about it all, but I knew Beni would be even more furious if I revealed any details of her budding romance.

"I'm not trying to ruin your happiness, Beni," I said when she came out to the kitchen. She puttered around, sullenly setting the table. "I mean it," I said.

She slapped a dish down so hard, it almost shattered and then she put her hands on her hips and turned to me.

"Okay, if you mean it then don't spoil my good times," she said. "I want to go to Alicia's Friday night to meet Carlton. She's having a party. Mama won't let me go unless you say it's just a bunch of girls getting together. She won't let me sleep over if I ask but she'll believe you. Are you going to help me or what?"

"You're making a mistake, Beni," I warned.

"If I make a mistake, it's my mistake, not yours, Rain. Well, are you going to help me with Mama or not?"

I was silent for a moment.

"Well?"

"Okay," I said, tired of the bickering. "Maybe it's better you learn things for yourself."

"Good." After I gave in, she became more enthusiastic about getting dinner prepared.

"Just stay away from Oh Henry's. Please," I said.

"Okay, but Carlton said Jerad really thought you were pretty," she revealed.

"What do you mean?" I gasped. "Why were you talking about me?"

"I'm just telling you what Carlton said. Jerad thought you were fine."

"I'd rather get a compliment from Frankenstein," I told her.

She shrugged.

"Everyone's afraid of Jerad around here."

"That doesn't make him some kind of hero. That makes him dangerous and even uglier to me," I said to her.

"At least no one puts him down," she said. "Even the police stay out of his way."

She returned to our bedroom to call her girlfriends with the good news, and I suddenly felt this terrible sense of doom. It was as if a dark cloud had slipped in under the window and pasted itself to the ceiling of our apartment, just waiting to drop its belly of cold rain on our pathetic little world.

Two days later, it almost happened. We were returning home from school. Now that Beni was satisfied that I would support her request to go to Alicia's on Friday night, her girlfriends backed off and there were no more confrontations with me in school. They looked arrogant and pleased with themselves as if they had won some important battle.

I didn't really have many close friends at school. I had never slept over anyone else's house. Boys did ask me out on dates, but like Beni stated, I never had anyone I could call a boyfriend, and just about all of them had stopped pursuing me. I spent most of my time with Lucy Adamson, a girl in my class who was at least twenty pounds overweight. She was very bright and very shy and from time to time we studied together, but I didn't tell her any personal things, and especially didn't talk to her about Beni and me.

On Thursday after school, Beni and I started out for home, as usual. Since I had agreed to help her with Mama, she returned to her old self, pouring out a continuous stream of conversation, telling me about Carlton and his likes and dislikes, his favorite music, even his favorite foods. I realized she was really infatuated with him. In a way I found myself being a little envious. It was as if feeling so strongly about a boy had changed the nature of her world, had put color into the drab grays that surrounded her. Her voice was lighter, running through with excitement, full of bells and music. She talked about her hair and her clothes and wished aloud that she could wear some of my things.

"Wouldn't it be nice if we were closer in size, Rain? Why did I have to be born with such big hip bones and look how dainty your shoulders are. My shoulders belong on a football player," she moaned.

"Oh, that's not true, Beni. You can't have everyone looking the same anyway. You have a nice figure. I know a lot of girls who would like to look like you."

"Yeah? Who? Lucy Adamson?" she asked.

"Exactly, and many more."

"You really think I'm pretty, Rain?"

"Yes, I do, and I'm not just saying that because you're my sister, Beni. You have beautiful eyes."

"Mama never tells me that."

"She does so," I insisted. "I heard her."

"If she did, it was so long ago, I can't remember." She was sad for a moment and then she brightened. "See if you can get Roy to let me wear his leather jacket Friday. He'll let me if you ask him for me, Rain. I look real fine in that jacket. Will you ask him? Will you?"

"Okay," I said laughing. "But I'm sure he'd let you wear it if you asked him yourself."

"No, he wouldn't. He would carry on about me being like some homeboys or something. He doesn't want me looking good."

"Oh Beni, stop being so critical of him. He loves you. With Ken running out on us all the time, Roy feels responsible. It's not easy being our big brother."

She looked at me with her head tilted and her lips pulled back deeply into her cheeks.

"Sometimes you talk like you're twenty years older than me, Rain.

It makes me wonder how we've both been raised under the same roof."

I started to laugh as we rounded the corner, but it ended up being only a brief smile because directly in front of us, leaning against a car, was Jerad Davis. He stood up when he saw us. He wore the same clothes he had worn in Oh Henry's, but he looked uglier and more frightening to me when he smiled and sauntered toward us.

"Well, well, well, look who I bumped into, the Rain girl herself," he quipped.

Beni stopped, her mouth agape. She looked at me in anticipation. I stared at him when I paused, but I didn't speak.

"Can't you say hello? It's not like we don't know each other. Hell, we kissed."

"You mean you forced yourself on me," I accused. He just laughed.

"You were the one who came rushing at me, girl. I've been thinking about you and I decided I'll give you some of my time." He looked at Beni. "I hear you're going to see Carlton Friday night. Why don't we make it a double date, huh?" he asked, turning back to me.

"Excuse me," I said. "We have to get home."

I started around him, but he stepped in my way, holding his arms out.

"Now that's not polite and here I've been telling everyone I met the politist Rain in the city." He laughed.

"Please, let us pass," I said.

"Not until I get another kiss," he declared.

"I'd rather kiss the gutter."

He roared and I tried to walk around him again, but he skipped in front of me, his arms out as if he was going to embrace me.

"You liked it, baby. Admit it."

"It made me sick," I said. "That's all I'll admit."

Beni looked absolutely mortified, the look of terror in her eyes adding to my own fear. Jerad's face hardened, his eyes like stones.

"That's not nice," he said, still blocking my way.

"Let them go by," a voice shouted from behind us. We turned to see Roy come walking from between two parked cars. He had a tire iron in his right hand, gripped like a club. Jerad didn't move, just stared at Roy, his eyes narrowing and the small smile on his lips growing cold and sharp.

"Who the hell are you?"

"Their brother, that's who," Roy said.

"What are you going to do with that tire iron?" Jerad asked.

"Whatever I have to do," Roy replied. He came up beside me. In the silence, I thought everyone could hear my heart pounding like bongo drums.

Suddenly, Jerad's face melted into a smile again.

"Well, that's what I would expect a good brother to do for his sister. You're a lucky girl, Rain. You got a big brother watching over you." He turned back to Roy and looked slyly at me. "You sure you're only watching her like a brother?" he asked.

"What the hell's that supposed to mean?"

"I don't know. It might mean something. It might not. He always trail in the back, keeping his eyes on your behind, girl?"

I looked at Beni, who kept her eyes down, and then at Roy. His face was full of rage. I saw the way he tightened his grip on the tire iron, and I shook my head vigorously.

"Maybe he wants to keep you all to himself," Jerad continued.

Roy glanced at me and then he turned to Jerad, stepping toward him, his body filling up with fury.

"Only a mind grown in garbage would think that."

Jerad laughed. He frightened me because he wasn't in the slightest intimidated by my brother and my brother was so much bigger than him.

"Okay, watch behind her." He stopped smiling and glared at Roy. "But who watches over you, big brother?"

"I watch over myself."

"That might not be good enough."

"I'm okay with it," Roy said, not blinking. Jerad smiled again. It was so frigid a smile, it made his teeth look like pieces of ice.

My heart felt as if it had collapsed like a punctured balloon. I don't think I'd taken a breath from the moment Roy had appeared.

"All right. Long as you're okay with it," Jerad said. He glanced at me. "See you soon, baby," he muttered and stepped back.

I didn't think my legs would work. Beni had her eyes to the sidewalk. We started away.

"Just keep walking," Roy ordered. "Don't look back."

I didn't say a word. I sped up and Beni did the same. That was how we learned that Roy had been watching over us all week. He escorted us to The Projects.

"I gotta get back to work," he said when we arrived. "Just stay off the street for a while. You need anything for dinner tonight, Rain?"

"Mama didn't say," I told him. He stared at me for a moment. I couldn't help it that I was still trembling and I was sure he saw it.

"You okay?"

I nodded and he looked at Beni. She still looked frightened, but she wasn't trembling like I was.

"Maybe we should call the police, Roy?" I asked.

"Naw, they won't do anything, Rain. We have to take care of ourselves. That's why," he emphasized, looking more at Beni than me, "we've got to be careful about where we go and who we see around here."

He gazed at me once more and then he turned and headed back to Slim's. I started for the front entrance, Beni right behind me.

"How come he was there? He must be following us, watching us all the time," she said.

"And I'm glad of that," I said, even though I was more worried for him than I was for myself now.

"He's just lucky Jerad didn't have his gang with him," she muttered. "He probably had a knife or a gun, too. That was crazy. Roy's crazy."

I stopped and turned on her.

"What would we have done if he hadn't come along, Beni?"

"Oh, nothing would have happened," she insisted. Her expression changed, her lips tightening. "You better not back out of helping me with Mama because of this, Rain. You just better not."

"It doesn't frighten you, what just happened and what could happen?" I asked.

She forced a firm face.

"No," she said.

I continued up the stairs thinking Beni was right to wonder how we could be so different living under the same roof.

As it turned out, we weren't so different after all, but that was a discovery Beni would make for herself. That night Beni made her plea to Mama, asking her to let her go to Alicia's and sleep over Friday night.

"Who all's going to be there?" Mama asked quickly.

"Just me and my girlfriends," Beni said. "Can't girls get together and have some fun?"

Mama's eyes were two dark slices of suspicion, especially when Beni shifted hers guiltily away. Mama turned to me.

"That true, Rain?"

"She's been talking about going there all week, Mama," I said, avoiding the question.

"How have your grades been this week?"

"I didn't fail anything," Beni said. She hadn't done especially well in anything, either.

"Which one's Alicia? She the girl whose mother was arrested for being drunk in the movies?" Mama asked.

"No," Beni said. Mama looked at me again, but I really didn't know about that, so I just shook my head.

"We're all going right after school so we'll be there before it gets dark," Beni continued.

"You ain't going anywhere but her house?"

"That's all, Mama. We're going to chip in and order pizza and listen to music. Can I go?" She held her breath.

Mama hesitated. Giving Beni or me permission to do anything at night was a burden to her. I could almost see the turmoil going on in her heart, the fear closing in like a fast thunderstorm. She didn't want to be a monster to her children, but she was so worried for us. Beni couldn't appreciate that now. She was interested only in her own pleasure.

"You better not go to any hip-hop joint after," Mama warned as a way of saying yes. Beni started to swear on a stack of Bibles, but Mama wouldn't listen.

"Just look me in the face and tell me you're not going, Beni Arnold, and that's all I want. I want my children to be honest with me and never lie to me, understand?"

"Yes, Mama."

"When you start lying to your own, you're losing the battle with the devil. Just remember that and carry it with you whenever those other girls try to get you to do something you know I wouldn't want you to do," she told her. "I was your age and I made lots of mistakes, Beni. I know what it's like having all your friends urging you to do what they want to do."

"Oh, Mama," she moaned.

"Oh, Mama, oh, Mama." Mama sighed deeply, her shoulders crumbling under the weight of her worry. Ken hadn't called or returned since he had walked out and the pressures were building on our little world. We were all in a small boat, being tossed and bounced on a sea of trouble.

"All right," she said, "but don't make me sorry."

When Roy came home, he was angry that Mama had given Beni permission to go to the party. He turned to me.

"You aren't going, too?" he asked.

"It's just Beni's friends," I explained.

"Yeah, I seen some of her friends," he quipped and I had to look away or he would instantly know what I knew. For the moment I thought it would be worse to betray Beni than to tell him the truth.

After school Friday, she went directly to Alicia's. Mama actually forgot about it and wondered where she was when she returned from work that night. I reminded her.

"Oh yeah," she said scrubbing her cheeks with her dry palms to revive herself. She looked so tired. "I hope she isn't getting herself into any trouble," she muttered. She thought for a moment and then looked at me closely. "How come you aren't going to any parties, Rain, or asking to go on any dates?"

"I don't know, Mama. I'm too particular, I guess," I said. "That's what all the other girls think about me."

"Good," she said. She stabbed the word at me. "Good. Be particular. Set high goals for yourself. You won't be sorry."

"What if they're too high, Mama? What if they're so high no boy will ever ask me out?" I wondered.

"The right one will when the time comes," she said, full of faith. "You're special, Rain. Always remember that."

"Why am I special?" I asked.

She turned me around so I could look at myself in the mirror as she held my shoulders and gazed at my image with me.

"Look at what you see there, girl. You're special. Anyone can see you have something more in your eyes, in your mind. You're not just pretty. You've got quality and one day, you're going to make me proud," she predicted.

I shook my head. Was she just seeing me through a mother's prejudiced eyes or did she really see something I couldn't see, something her age and experience pointed out for her? I hoped she was right, but I was also afraid she was right. It made me more worried about making some terrible mistake.

When Roy returned from work, the first thing he asked was whether or not Beni actually had gone to the party. He wasn't happy about it and mumbled so much at dinner Mama told him to stop his worrying and go do things boys his age do.

"Why don't you find yourself a nice girl, Roy?" she asked him. "It isn't natural for you to spend all your time trying to be the man of this house. You got a life too. I don't ever want to steal away my children's lives, understand?"

"You're not stealing anything I don't want to give you, Mama," he said.

She smiled and looked at me. Then she grew sad again.

"My children have to grow up faster than most. It doesn't seem right."

"It's too dangerous to be a child and live here," Roy said. "You got to grow up."

"Ain't that the truth. It's what the reverend says too. The precious time of innocence is shorter for us."

Mama was falling into one of her deep depressions. I tried getting her mind off it by getting her to describe her own childhood and her mother and some of the places she had been. She talked a little, but after dinner, she closed her eyes and almost fell asleep in her seat. Roy and I cleaned up and Mama went in to watch television, which meant she would fall asleep in her chair and wake up after the late news to go to bed.

"Why don't we go to a movie?" Roy suddenly asked me.

"You don't have to spend your time amusing me, Roy," I told him. "I have some reading I can do."

"It's no sacrifice. I want to go to a movie and hate going alone," he told me.

"Mama's right, Roy. You should be going on dates, too."

He bristled.

"And what about you?"

"When I find someone I like and he asks me, I'll go," I said.

"That's the way I think too," he said and we both laughed. "In the meantime, we can go to the movies. I got money just waiting to be spent."

I always felt safe with Roy and it wasn't just because he was big and strong like Ken. He was always alert, cautious, aware of what was going on around us in the streets, and he hovered over me like a protective angel. Without speaking, he would take my arm and gently but firmly turn me to cross a street or wait while some gang members passed in front of us. Roy always believed it was easier and wiser to avoid confrontations. It didn't make you a coward; it made you smarter.

Neither of us had spoken a word about the dirty things Jerad had implied when Roy rescued us that afternoon, but I felt he was a little more self-conscious about every look he gave me, self-conscious every time he touched me. Once, I would have thought nothing of him taking my hand when we walked in the street. He was my big brother. Why not? But suddenly, a whole new world of meaning surrounded every move we made, every word we spoke to each other, and every look we exchanged. Even an innocent thing as a big brother asking his sister to go to the movies felt a little uncomfortable, but I didn't want him to feel that way, so I agreed and we went.

The movie had a lot of action in it with special effects that made you jump in your seat, but there was a warm love story, too. The audience was noisy and some boys in front of us got into a fight. The management threw them out. I recognized they were boys from our school.

"Fools," Roy muttered. "They act just the way people expect them to act."

Roy was no activist. He wasn't one to join causes and organizations. He was a private man, really a loner, but he held onto his beliefs about race relations and equality. He never made speeches, but from the things he said here and there, I knew he was ashamed of the way the people in The Projects behaved. It was why he hated the gangs so much and never hung out with boys who belonged.

"As long as we act like they think we act, we'll always be second class citizens," he declared. It was about as much as he would say about the issues. He avoided arguments and never got into discussions about these things. Ken ranted and raved sometimes about the inequalities, blaming his own poor state of affairs on everything from the time of the first slave ship, but Roy never joined in on his complaints and it always bothered Ken that his son didn't parrot the things he said.

"Did you enjoy the movie?" Roy asked as soon as we left the theater.

"Yes. Well, not the car crashes and explosions so much, but I liked the way he broke down at the end and admitted all he ever cared about was her."

Roy laughed.

Above us in an apartment building, someone had their windows open and the sounds of music flowed into the street. Off in the distant sky, a commercial jet rose toward the stars, taking people west, maybe to California.

"You're a sucker for romance, huh?"

"It's nice to have someone care more about you than he cares about himself," I said.

Roy gazed at me and we walked quietly for a while. A gang of teenagers passed by, running in the street and forcing cars to slow down. Some drivers sounded their horns, but that only made the kids more defiant. They disappeared around a corner.

"They're all just bored," I said. "That's why they get into trouble."

"Maybe they're just bad."

"They could be good," I insisted. Roy laughed.

"You're a real sweet person, Rain. You want to know why I don't go on dates so much? It's because I'm trying to find a girl just like you, someone who thinks about other people, too. Most of the girls I know are in love with themselves first and foremost. That's all they talk about when they're with me, themselves, their clothes, their hair, their figures and they're always fishing for compliments. Don't I look nice? Do you like my hair like this or should I wear more make-up? They know the answers. They just want to hear me sound like some fan club."

I laughed.

"What's so funny?"

"I never heard you go on so," I said.

"Well, I can't help it. It gets to me sometimes. You never brag about yourself or put Beni down. I watch and listen to the two of you, Rain. And you're the prettiest girl in that damn school, too," he declared.

"Oh, I am not, Roy Arnold."

"Yes, you are. They know it too. Why do you think other girls are mean to you? They're just jealous, is all."

"You just say that because you're my brother," I told him, smiling.

"I don't say it about Beni, Rain. She's not ugly, but she's not beautiful like you."

I felt myself get warm in the neck and face and looked away quickly. Roy had never said things so directly to me like this before and I didn't know how to respond.

"It's not good for a girl to be so vain. It's a sin, Roy. You've heard Mama say so lots of times."

"You don't have to be stuck-up. Just don't ever feel below anyone, Rain."

"Everyone's got faults, Roy. Me, too. Don't build your dream girl so high you can never reach her," I said. "I don't want to see you lonely. You deserve the best girl."

"Right now, I got her with me," he said. He squeezed my hand and as we walked on home, I wondered if I should dare to believe the things he told me about myself.

Mama was asleep when we arrived, but we were both shocked when we entered the apartment. There was a six pack of beer on the table. Roy glanced at me and then we walked slowly to the living room.

There was Ken sprawled over the couch, his arm dangling. He was home again.

Roy and I looked at each other and he shook his head. We both felt like prize fighters about to start another round.

# 3

# A Terrible Truth

I woke with a start in the middle of the night. She had entered so quietly that apparently no one else in the house had heard. At first I thought it was Ken still drunk and confused, wandering about. I sat up quickly, my heart going like a jackhammer. Someone was standing in the doorway, silhouetted by the weak hallway light. She just stood there staring in at me, not moving, dark and still as a bad dream. For a moment I couldn't find my voice.

"Beni?" I whispered. Why was she home? Why would she just be standing there?

I heard a sob and then she entered and threw herself across my bed, her knees on the floor, her head against my legs. She sobbed louder, harder.

"Beni, what's wrong? Why are you home?"

"Oh, Rain, they put something in my drink. I woke up a little while ago in a bed and I was naked. I had to crawl on the floor to find my clothes. I couldn't find everything. They stole my panties. Someone's got my panties!" she wailed.

I helped her up and she embraced me and hung on as if we were both in a sinking boat. Her tears soaked my cheek. We rocked together. Never had Beni ever held me as tightly. I felt horrible for her.

"What happened, Beni? Tell me all of it."

She choked back her tears and buried her face in my pillow.

"I can't. I'm so ashamed. When I woke up I saw an empty film container on the floor. Maybe they took pictures of me. I'm so ashamed."

"I thought those girls were your friends, Beni. Why did they let this happen?"

She lifted her head and took a deep breath.

"They were all drinking and smoking pot and then . . . then I don't know. The music was loud. Everyone was having so much fun. I didn't watch myself. I just did what they were doing because I thought Carlton liked that. He was drinking vodka in cranberry juice. I was drinking the same thing. I couldn't even taste the vodka. We went into Alicia's bedroom. I remember that. He was kissing me and telling me how much he liked me. We were on the bed and . . ."

"What?" I asked. She appeared to be recalling it as she described it to me.

"The door opened. The lights were bright. I heard lots of laughter and there were other boys. The room started to spin. Then I don't remember, Rain. I can't remember anything. I just woke up and found myself naked. I was naked! They must have put something in my drink!"

"Okay, Beni. Okay. Take it easy. You'll wake Roy," I warned, even though I didn't think so. I had to calm her down.

She took a deep breath and nodded.

"I don't know what all they did to me, Rain. I got stuff on me, on my legs and stomach," she said in a loud whisper.

I held my breath.

"Stuff?"

"I think . . . from boys," she said. "You know, when they get excited."

"Oh, Jesus," I moaned. I couldn't help it. It sounded so disgusting. "You take a hot bath now. I'll go fix it for you, Beni."

She seized my hand, squeezing it so hard it hurt.

"Maybe I'm in big trouble, Rain."

"No, no," I said trying to assure her.

"What if I am? What if I get pregnant or something?"

"You're not going to. Stop thinking the worst. Let me go fix your bath, Beni. Just rest here."

I lifted her arm from my waist and slipped off the bed. She buried her face in the pillow and continued to sob, her cries getting louder.

"Don't, Beni. You're sure to wake Mama. And Ken is back, too," I said.

She stopped crying and pushed herself up a little.

"Ken's back?"

"Yes. Roy and I went to the movies and when we came home, we found him passed out on the sofa. He's probably still there. I don't even know if Mama knows he's back."

"Oh damn. Everything's happening at once. He'll kill me. Ken will kill me if he finds out."

"No one's going to kill you, Beni. You'll take a bath and go to sleep."

"What will I tell Mama when she asks why I came home?"

"I don't know. Let me think, Beni. I hate all these lies," I moaned.

"I don't even know exactly what they did to me," she chanted. She embraced herself and rocked. "Someone's got my panties."

"Maybe you just couldn't find them, Beni." I mumbled and hurried to the bathroom, blaming myself now because I had gone along with her and helped her to get Mama to let her go. I should have known better. I should have done more to stop her. Roy will be so furious at both of us, I thought. And poor Mama, with all she has to bear, now to have this added to the burden. She'll just crumble like some piece of thin clay, old and tired and dried out from shedding all those tears. I had to think, think hard, find a way to keep this terrible secret from her. Even more important than protecting Beni at the moment was the need to protect Mama. And Beni was right. Who knew what Ken would do?

This was one time I was glad Roy slept like the dead. Between Beni's sobs and the noise we made getting her from our bedroom and into the bath, I was sure someone would wake to see what we were doing. Thankfully, no one did. Ken was still snoring on the sofa and Mama must have been so exhausted, she slept right through all the noise.

Once I got Beni undressed, I felt even more terrible for her. Just as she said, boys had done things on her stomach and her breasts. She complained about the aches in her thighs. I got her into the water and helped her wash. She even had to wash her hair. It smelled like someone had poured whiskey on it. Afterward, I wrapped her in a big towel and helped dry her because she suddenly got a violent case of the chills. Her teeth rattled and her whole body shuddered. We returned to the bedroom and I helped her put on a nightgown and get under her blankets.

"My head feels like it's full of pinballs knocking into each other," she moaned.

I found some aspirin for her and had her take two. She held onto my hand as if she thought if I left her side, she would disappear. I sat beside her and waited while she mumbled about what they had done to her until she fell asleep. Then I pried her fingers from mine, straightened her blankets, and went to bed.

But I didn't fall back to sleep. I lay there, thinking, trying to come up with some reason, some way to explain Beni's being home without alarming Mama and causing another family crisis.

However, there was so much commotion in the morning when Mama woke up and found Ken in the living room, I didn't have much chance to prepare her for the sight of Beni.

"So you finally decided to come back, Ken Arnold," I heard her say. "After you ran out of money, no doubt. Just like always."

"Quiet, woman," Ken pleaded. "You'll bust my head open with that mouth of yours."

"I hope I do," she told him.

I looked over at Beni, who was still asleep, her back to me, her face to the wall. I put on my robe and went out to keep Mama from getting into another down and out shouting match with Ken. Roy met me in the hall. We looked at each other and then joined Mama in the kitchen.

"He's back," she told us and waved her hand toward the living room. "Looking like a homeless fool. Go take yourself a bath or a shower, Ken Arnold," she cried toward the living room doorway. "You're fouling up my living room with the stench."

"Leave me be. Make some coffee," he added.

"Make some coffee," Mama muttered. "I hope he didn't go and lose that good job," she continued as she started to make the coffee.

Ken had a job as a janitor in a government building and it would give him benefits if he lasted six months.

Roy scratched his head and turned to go back to his room. He stopped dead in the hallway after gazing through my and Beni's bedroom door.

"I thought she was sleeping over at her friend's house. Why is she home?" he asked.

Mama spun around.

"Who?" She looked at me. "Beni came home last night?"

"Yes, Mama," I said.

She nodded, pressing her lower lip over her upper and sagged her shoulders. Her forehead rippled into folds of worry, her eyes darkening.

"Go on, tell me what."

"Nothing, Mama," I said quickly. "Only, she did what you told her to do. When they were going to leave to go to a hip-hop joint, she left them and came home."

Mama tilted her head with skepticism. I shifted my eyes quickly, only they focused on Roy and that was worse. He was frowning.

"There's more to this," he said.

"There was drugs and drinking," I admitted.

"Beni do any of that?" Mama pursued quickly.

"She drank some, got sick and came home, Mama," I said. It was at least part of the truth.

Mama and Roy looked at each other. If Roy let it go, Mama would, I knew.

"That all?" Mama had to ask.

"It wasn't a nice place to be, Mama. Beni realized that. Most girls in school wouldn't have come home," I added enthusiastically.

"Yeah, I suppose that's true enough," Mama said. "She all right?"

"She's going to have a helluva headache, I bet," Roy said.

"Good. Teach her a lesson. She can go lay in there with her father and they can moan at each other all morning," Mama declared. "What's that they say about the apple not falling far from the tree?"

"I did," Roy said quickly.

"Yes, you did, son. I thank the Lord, too."

"And so did Rain," Roy asserted.

Mama stared at me for a moment and then nodded.

"Go see to her," Mama told me. "I've got a bigger problem on my hands this morning."

She turned back to the coffee. I glanced at Roy, who looked more suspicious than I wanted him to look, and then I hurried back to the bedroom to wait for Beni to wake up. I had to tell her what I had told Roy and Mama or she would get us both in more trouble, I thought.

She didn't appear to be close to waking up, even after another hour had passed and everyone was in the kitchen having breakfast. I had to shake her.

She moaned and turned slowly.

"What?" she asked as soon as she opened her eyes. I told her what I had told Mama and Roy.

"Why did you tell her I got drunk? Now she'll never let me out," Beni moaned.

"She's happy you came home, Beni. I told her most girls wouldn't have, so no matter how she hollers at you, you know she's not as mad as she makes out to be. I did the best I could," I explained.

"I feel terrible," she moaned when she sat up. She held her stomach and then put her other hand over her eyes and moaned. She fell back to her pillow. "Just let me be," she pleaded.

"You better get up and get dressed, Beni. It will be worse if you lay in bed all morning. Mama will be in here soon anyway," I warned.

She narrowed her eyes and stared at me for a moment.

"You're glad, aren't you? You're happy this happened to me. Now you feel so right and perfect."

"That's not true, Beni. I feel sorry for you. I really do."

"Sure," she said. She turned toward the wall. "Jerad was there. He probably got them to do this to me just to get revenge on you and Roy," she declared. "It's true, I bet." Angrily, she threw off her blanket. "None of this might have happened to me otherwise."

"That's stupid, Beni. You can't make excuses for those kind of people and you can't shift blame to me and Roy. So stop it," I snapped at her.

I dressed and came out of the bedroom before she did. Mama had made Ken his favorite breakfast, buckwheat pancakes, despite her show of anger. Roy sat across from him eating sullenly.

"She up?" Mama demanded.

"Yes, Mama. She's coming out."

"What's with Beni?" Ken asked. "She sick?"

"Yeah, she's sick. She caught your disease," Mama told him. His eyes widened and he looked at me.

"What's been going on 'round here, Rain?"

"Since when was that your concern, Ken Arnold?" Mama shot at him.

"Quiet, woman. Rain?"

"Don't yell at Mama," Roy warned him.

Ken turned toward him slowly, his bloodshot eyes suddenly bright as the center of a candle flame. Mama quickly inserted herself, pouring more coffee into Ken's cup.

"Don't you two start fighting now. I don't need that this morning. And don't you worry about him yelling at me, Roy. I can take care of him," she said nodding at Ken. He simmered down and turned back to me.

"What's wrong with Beni?" he demanded.

"She drank some liquor at a party and got sick," I told him quickly.

He stared at me for a moment and then let out a whoop and a laugh, slapping his knee.

"Got sick, huh? Chip off the old block, you say, woman?" he asked

Mama. "I never got sick. She's got your fragile stomach, not mine," he said, as if drinking and eating bad food was an accomplishment.

Mama raised her eyes to the ceiling.

"Lord, give me strength," she said.

Beni stepped out into the hall and we all turned to her. She looked like she had a helmet made of lead over her head. Her eyes drooped like sagging old curtains.

"Well, girl," Mama declared, her hands on her hips, "what do you have to say for yourself this morning?"

"I made a mistake and I don't feel good," Beni replied. She avoided my eyes and Roy's. When she looked at Ken, she shifted her tired orbs quickly and stared at the floor.

"You'd think watching your father all these years would be enough to make you a teetotaler," Mama said.

"What do you mean, watching your father? Why do you blame me for her behavior? You're with her more than me. If she's done bad it's your fault, woman. Not mine."

"Right," Mama said. "You just sire children like some race horse and gallop away," she added.

Beni looked at me, grateful that Mama was directing her anger at Ken and not at her.

"Sit down and put something substantial into your stomach," Mama told her and nodded at the chair.

"I just want coffee, Mama."

"I didn't ask you what you wanted. I told you to eat something, child," she ordered.

Beni did as she was told. After breakfast, Ken went back to sleep and Beni retreated quickly to her own bed. I helped Mama clean the table and the dishes. Roy had to go to work at Slim's, but he paused on the way out when he had the opportunity to catch me alone.

"There's more to her story," he said nodding at Beni's and my bedroom. "Don't believe her."

"At least she's all right, Roy," I said. "She'll think twice about hanging around those girls now."

"Don't bet on it," he said. "And stop protecting her. We're all swimming in rough waters. You let her wrap herself around you, she'll drag you down with her," he predicted and left.

Beni slept most of the day. Mama complained but let her be. In the afternoon, Ken went to meet some of his friends and I finished all my homework. When Beni woke up again, she was even in a more irritable mood. As soon as she stepped out of the bedroom, Mama began to bawl her out and lecture her about her behavior.

"Don't you even think of asking me to let you out of this house at night again for some time, girl," she told her. "I want you home right after school, too. Until you're eighteen, you're my responsibility, hear?"

"That's not fair, Mama. Everyone makes mistakes," Beni moaned.

"Yeah, well, I've got enough problems without you adding more, Beni Arnold. You just make sure you don't fail any more tests, either. I'll be watching you closer than before, hear?"

Beni got up and returned to our bedroom, slamming the door behind her. She glared at me.

"Thanks a lot," she said.

"What do you mean? What did I do?"

"You got me in trouble. If you didn't say anything, I could have made up a better story," she cried. "Now she won't let me do anything. I hate it here."

"That's not fair, Beni. I was only trying to help you. You think I like lying to Mama for you? Well, you're wrong. I'm not going to do it again," I vowed.

"Good," she said and threw herself on her bed with her back to me.

Roy was right, I thought. Beni would sink us both.

It was harder for both Beni and me at school now. Some of the boys who had been at the party teased her and her supposedly loyal girlfriends didn't do much to protect her, either. Every one of them seemed to think what had happened to her was funny and not very serious. Beni looked so lost, I felt sorry for her. I watched her sitting at a corner of her friends' table in the cafeteria, brooding and keeping her eyes down while the other girls laughed and the boys tormented her. Finally, not being able to stand it any longer, I left Lucy Adamson and went to where Beni was sitting.

"Why do you sit here with them?" I snapped at her. "These aren't your friends. Look what they did to you," I said glaring at Nicole and Alicia.

"What's that supposed to mean?" Alicia demanded. "We didn't do nothing to nobody. Anything that happened to her, happened because she wanted it to happen."

"Sure," I said. "With friends like you, she doesn't need any enemies."

"You bitch," Nicole said, rising.

"Just leave it be," Beni told me.

"How can you sit here?"

"She'd rather be with us than with Miss Prissy," Alicia said. "At least she's having some fun with us."

"You call what happened to her fun?" I grimaced. "I really feel sorry for you."

"Shut your mouth," Nicole said. "Or I'll shut it for you."

"Will you just go *away,*" Beni cried. "You're just making everything worse for me."

I looked at her, at the pleading in her eyes. I really felt sorry for her, but I didn't know what to do.

"You're just jealous, is all," Nicole said. "You're dying to have a man put his hands on that precious body of yours, Miss Prissy."

The girls laughed.

"Yeah, it's different than you putting your hands on yourself," Alicia said. They all laughed again.

"You're all disgusting," I said and turned away, leaving their laughter rising like a wave behind me.

"Why are you starting with them?" Lucy asked when I returned to our table.

"I'm trying to help my sister," I said.

"You're just going to get them after you all the time now, and they'll bother me too," she said.

"If you're so afraid, you don't have to sit with me, Lucy," I said.

She looked at the girls and then at me.

"I have to go to the bathroom," she said and left quickly.

Beni didn't want me helping her and now the few friends I had were afraid to be seen with me. How I hated this place, I thought. But home, where I felt like a caged animal, was no better. Mama couldn't do anything to help. Ken was irresponsible, and poor Roy was struggling to keep us above water.

That afternoon when we returned home from school we found Ken in the living room, smoking, drinking a beer and watching television. Why wasn't he at work?

"That you, girls?" he called.

"Yes, Ken," Beni said.

"Good. Beni, get me another beer, will ya. My foot's bothering me today."

She looked at me and went to the refrigerator. I followed her into the living room and watched her hand Ken his beer.

"How come you're home so early?" she asked him.

"Ah, that moron supervisor fired me," he said. "He had it in for me right from the start."

"So why aren't you looking for another job?" I asked quickly, so quickly it snapped his head around.

"Since when did you get such a mouth?"

I felt my heart skip a beat. From the way he was shaking his head, I knew he had already had too much to drink.

"I'm just worried about Mama. She's working an extra shift to make ends meet," I told him.

"What about Roy? He's bringing in a good check. Don't worry," he said waving his hand, "we aren't gonna starve." He stared at the two of us as he drank from his bottle of beer. "You girls ought to find a job, too," he added.

"That's what I told Mama," Beni said.

"Well, that's good. At least you aren't lazy. That's good."

"She won't let us work," Beni complained.

"What? Why not? That's stupid. You're both strong young girls. You can do something until I find another position."

"When's that going to be?" I asked.

Again, he glared at me with those glassy eyes.

"When I find it," he said firmly. "Don't you go being another nag around here," he warned. "You've got no right to talk to me like that. You've got no right to make any demands, girl."

I felt my eyebrows rise. He made it sound as if I wasn't a member of the family.

"None of you do," he added. "Now leave me be. I'm trying to relax and forget my troubles for a while."

"Tell Mama to let me quit school and get a job," Beni told him. "Tell her, Ken."

"I will," he promised, nodding emphatically. "I certainly will. You girls are old enough to help out. I don't see why not." He guzzled more beer. "Comes a time when a man's kids should make things easier for him. Why not?" he muttered and nodded as if he was talking himself into the idea.

Beni looked pleased.

"Don't listen to him, Beni," I whispered when we left the living room. "You can smell the alcohol on him. He doesn't know what he's saying."

"Yes, he does. I hope he tells Mama to let me quit school and work," she emphasized.

I shook my head at her with disgust and went into our room to change. Then I started preparing supper. Mama had brought home some pork chops from the supermarket last night. At least they let her buy groceries at the wholesale prices. Some time back she had shown me how to make stuffed pork chops, which was one of Roy's favorite meals. I began to sauté the onions. The aroma from the garlic and herbs filled the small apartment. Ken peered in to see what I was doing just as Beni came out of the bathroom. His eyes opened and closed and he wobbled in the doorway.

"How come you can't cook like Rain, huh?" he asked Beni.

"I can't do anything as good as Rain," Beni complained with a smirk, "so I don't even try."

Ken's eyes grew smaller.

"Get me another beer," he demanded.

"Don't you think you've had enough?" I asked him.

"I don't need no kid telling me when I had enough. Jeeze, your Mama's turning all of you against me," he wailed.

"I'll get it for you," Beni offered and did.

"Thank you, Beni," he said smiling at her. He glared at me and then returned to plop into his easy chair. Beni smirked at me.

"Ken likes me more, I think," she said smugly.

"I'm glad for you," I told her. She was getting me so angry that I worked harder and faster to keep my mind busy. I had everything simmering by the time Mama came home.

"It smells heavenly," she told me. She heard the television going, but thought it was Beni.

"Why doesn't Beni at least set the table before Ken and Roy get home?" she muttered.

"Ken's home," I told her. "He lost his job."

"No. I was afraid of that. He's just no good." She pulled up her shoulders and straightened her spine for battle.

"I think he's been drinking too much again, Mama. Maybe you should just let him be."

"Damn him," she cried and headed for the living room. I took a deep breath and started to set the table.

Ken had been drinking all day. He had started at one of the taverns when he was fired and then he had come home and had drunk nearly two six packs by the time Mama had arrived. He was nearly passed out when she began on him. I wasn't going to listen. It was like a broken CD, stuck on the same old tune; but they raised their voices so loud, I'm sure the neighbors heard them clearly.

"How could you lose this job? It was one of your better ones,"

Mama said. "If you would have lasted, we would have had some good benefits, medical and dental. Don't you care at all about this family?"

"That supervisor had it in for me. He always did," Ken claimed. "He's a cracker and thinks we're trash."

"That's what you say all the time. Just excuses for your own despicable behavior. That's all that is."

"Leave me be."

"What are we supposed to do, Ken? We have the rent to pay and the girls need things, things we haven't been able to afford. They need clothes. They're outgrowing everything. We're late on the electric and gas and I'm afraid to make dentist appointments for anyone because we still have such a bill. We could get evicted. The manager said so. Then where are we going to be? Out on the street, that's where."

"I'll get a job soon," he promised.

"When? I haven't seen your paycheck for weeks now. How could you waste all that money?"

"I said I'd get work, woman. So lay off of me. Besides, why don't you let the girls get some work? They could bring in some money."

"They're schoolgirls. They don't belong in the streets working some fast-food joint late at night. And I won't have them dropping out to work days. Rain's got a chance to win a scholarship to college," she added. I had no idea Mama knew about the scholarship.

"Well, Beni could work."

"She'll just get into trouble, Ken. She hasn't got as much common sense as Rain does."

"Oh? Why's that?" he demanded. From the way he slurred his words, I knew he was too drunk to listen or make any sense, but Mama wasn't going to let up on him.

"You blame it on me. You think she's just like me, huh? And you know the other one ain't, is that it?"

"It's just how it is," she said. "It's nobody's fault."

"Sure. You think Rain's special. You always did. You care more about her than you do your own. I'm sorry now I did it," he added.

I turned away from the stove and paused near the doorway to the living room. More than your own? What was he talking about?

"Shut your drunken mouth," Mama said.

"You always acted as if you were given some sort of princess," he declared. "She should be working for us. We done enough for her."

"I'm not hearing any more of this," Mama said. I heard her start for the door.

"Just don't throw it up at me that we have all these mouths to feed and dentist and doctor bills," he shouted. "You wanted her and you never complained about the money."

"I never saw the money," Mama shouted back at him. "Now shut your mouth."

"It's time she carried some of the burden here. I ain't as young as I was. I'm tired, too. Let her bring something in. White girls work too, you know," he added.

It was as if a lightning bolt had shot through the apartment. There was that all too familiar silence before the clap of thunder, only this time the thunder was in my head. What was that supposed to mean? White girls work too? I waited.

"Please Ken, lower your voice," Mama cajoled.

"I'm not lowering anything. This is my home, hear? I'm the man of this house and I got rights. We did plenty for them." He was quiet for a moment and then I heard him say, "We didn't get enough the first time. We should get more. Yeah, that's what I'm going to do. I'm going to get us more."

"Don't you even think of it, Ken."

"Why not? It's like you said, there are more bills now. We didn't know at the time just how expensive it was going to be, see? We weren't given enough so it's only right that we get more."

"Just sit there. Don't you move. Don't you do anything stupid, Ken Arnold."

"I'm tired of you bossing me around, Latisha. Get outta my way. I got business."

"Stop it!" Mama cried.

The next thing I heard was her scream and the sound of a crash and splintering wood. I rushed into the living room. Beni came out of the bedroom, too. When I reached Mama, she was lying on the floor beside the table that I imagined she had fallen on top of. Ken stood over her, his hands clenched in fists. He gaped at me.

"Did you hit her?" I demanded.

"Don't you stand there accusing me, girl," he said.

Mama reached up. Her right eye already looked swollen.

"Let her be, Ken," she moaned.

Ken stepped around me and headed for the door.

"Don't do it, Ken," Mama pleaded, but he was out the door.

"Get me some ice," Mama called to Beni. She turned to me. "I don't want Roy hearing about this, Rain. It will be bad."

"Your eye's swelling up already, Mama."

"I'll tell him I fell. You back me, Rain."

"When are we going to put an end to all these lies, Mama?" I muttered, more to myself than to her.

Beni brought Mama some ice wrapped in a washcloth. She pressed it to her eyebrow.

"What did he mean before, Mama?"

"Mean?"

"I couldn't help but hear. When he said white girls work too? What did he mean by that?"

"Who knows?" she said shrugging as she pulled herself up onto the sofa. She lay back, holding the ice to her eye. I looked at Beni, who was embracing herself and looked like she was about to burst into tears, too.

"Where's he going?" I asked. Mama didn't answer.

"What did he mean, you didn't get enough from them? Enough from whom, Mama?"

"Stop asking so many questions, Rain," she snapped at me. "See about the dinner before something burns."

I rose slowly, looking from Beni to Mama.

"You always tell us it's a bigger sin to lie to each other, Mama. You always say that."

"Oh Rain, please. Don't we have enough trouble already?"

"Where's Ken going, Mama? Who does he expect will give him more money and what does it have to do with me? Please, Mama. Tell me." Mama never avoided my questions. The way she was acting now scared me more than Ken's violence had.

"Oh Lordy, Lord, help me," she wailed and rocked herself.

"Mama?"

She raised her eyes to the ceiling. I knew she was praying. I looked at Beni, who looked as frightened as I felt as she stood there, practically holding her breath.

"Mama?"

She looked at me, her lips pressed hard together.

"This isn't the way I wanted you to find out, Rain. This isn't right."

"Please, just tell me, Mama."

My heart pounded. I held my hands against my stomach. Tears clouded my eyes.

"Why can't you just let it be, child?"

"Mama, please, just tell me," I cried. I felt Beni step up beside me.

Mama took a deep breath. She seemed to reach down into her very soul for the strength.

"He's going to try to get your real mama to give him more money," she said.

And it was as if the ceiling of our apartment had come crashing down around me.

That long awaited thunder roared through my ears, and then, silence.

# 4

# All I've Ever Known

I glanced at Beni; her eyes were whirlpools of confusion and her jaw hung open as if she was in the middle of a scream. Mama looked like she was on fire. Her face was filled with that much pain. I felt as if I had gone deaf. All the usual noises around me had died. I heard no footsteps, no shouts from the hallways, no clanging pipes or wailing car sirens from the street below. The only sound was the rumble following the rush of blood from my face down into my neck.

Without saying a word, I turned and ran out of the living room and then out the front door.

"Rain!" Mama shouted, but I let the door shut off her voice and I charged down the stairs, my whole body thumping with every step.

I didn't even remember leaving the building. One moment I was standing there looking at Mama and Beni and the next I was on the street, walking so fast I was practically running. I didn't hear or see anyone or anything, including cars. Horns blared, and people shouted at me when I crossed against the light. One automobile's brakes screeched so sharply and loudly, my ears stung. However, I kept walking as if I knew where I was going. Tears streamed down my face and flew off my chin. My chest felt as if it was going to explode, but I didn't stop even though the world in front of me and around me was a blur.

Latisha Arnold wasn't my real mother? The woman I had called Mama all my life wasn't part of me and I wasn't part of her? Who was my real mother? Was Ken still my real father? More important, who was I? Ken had called me a white girl. How could that be? What did he mean?

Suddenly, in one quick moment, my name, my family, all of my history, my memories, everything, was like soap bubbles popping all around me. The whole world had been turned upside down, pulled out from under me. I felt like I was dangling in space.

I stopped to look at myself in the window of a shoe store. The image I saw seemed like the image of a stranger. My hair looked wild, my eyes frantic. It made me laugh a mad laugh. I put my hand over my mouth to stop it and then, I started to cry again and walked on, faster, harder. Vaguely, I was aware of people staring at me, including people who knew me.

My tears were hot and zigzagged down my cheeks burning a path over my skin. After another ten minutes or so, I tightened my arms around myself and stopped, finally feeling the ache in my legs and my stomach. For a moment I just stood there on the street corner looking at the park directly ahead of me.

Now I realized I had walked blocks and blocks. I was in a much nicer section of the city, a neighborhood of small houses, town houses, brownstones occupied by middle class families. Their children were in the park playing around the seesaws and sliding ponds. There were mothers and nannies nearby. The laughter and shouts of small boys and girls was constant, a flow of underlying music as if happiness were a song sung only here.

I checked the traffic and crossed the street to stand by the fence and look in at these contented children. One little girl was crying and her mother had knelt down to comfort her. She wiped back the strands of light brown hair from her forehead and what she was saying, the softness in her voice, the love that flowed from her eyes and her smile, drove away the unhappiness quickly. They hugged and the restored child returned to the merry-go-round, laughing and moving as if nothing sad or horrible had happened or ever would.

Mama had been that way with me, I thought. She could wipe away my tears, fill my heart with hope, sing me to sleep and help me back to candyland dreams. She had never once given me the feeling she wasn't my real mother. How did she do that? Why did she do that?

What Beni always said was true, too. I often felt Mama cared more for me than she did for Beni. How Beni must hate me even more now, I thought, to know I wasn't even Mama's real daughter and still, Mama treated me with more love and care. It was all so confusing and so unfair.

A boy no more than nine or ten chased after a red ball that settled near the fence. He picked it up and looked up at me with curiosity.

"Hi," I said.

He smiled with the most dazzling and joyful cerulean blue eyes I had ever seen.

"Hi," he replied, widening his smile.

He turned and ran off, his legs going so fast and awkward, they looked like they were wound up with rubber bands. He glanced back to beam another smile at me. Was I ever that happy? Would I ever be again?

I walked on. The afternoon sun had fallen behind the buildings, and shadows long and deep oozed across the sidewalks and over the streets like maple syrup over pancakes. Lights were going on in apartments and homes. Families were sitting down to dinner. I thought about the pork chops I had left simmering and for a moment I wondered if everything that had happened had only been a dream. Would I blink and find myself standing in front of the stove? I would even welcome back our hard life over this, I thought.

Exhausted, I sat on a bench at a bus stop. Two elderly black ladies arrived and sat beside me, waiting. I didn't really listen to their conversation, but I heard bits and pieces about grandchildren and looking forward to the holidays. Without a family, there were no holidays, I thought. There was no Christmas, no presents to get or presents to give, no Thanksgiving to celebrate.

I guess I moaned out loud because the two old ladies turned and gazed at me.

"You all right, baby?" the one closest asked.

I didn't reply. The bus arrived and they got up, gazing back at me curiously when I didn't get up too. They boarded and the bus left. It grew darker and colder. I embraced myself when I felt myself shiver and tremble. Traffic flowed by, people crossed in front and behind me, but I didn't notice anything. I stared ahead, my thoughts frozen.

Finally, I rose and just walked, not thinking of direction, not thinking about any destination. I had my head down, but I vaguely noticed a car full of boys slow down, pass by, stop and then turn around. They were in a beat-up vehicle with a smashed rear window. It looked like the sort of car Roy called a Lazarus, something raised from the dead. When it went by this time, all the boys looked my way. The driver whistled and that was followed by catcalls. I ignored them and turned down another street.

However, they followed and were cruising very slowly right behind me, hovering like some large cat about to pounce. My heart started to pound when I finally looked around and realized I was in a more depressed, run-down neighborhood. I had made something of a circle and had come back to my own neighborhood. I knew I had put myself into danger and I was very frightened, but instead of thinking about myself, I thought about Mama and how afraid for me she must be back in our apartment.

But I couldn't help being angry too. I should have been told the truth long ago. My whole life was a lie and Mama hated lies. Why did she keep this one alive so long? Would she ever have told me the truth if Ken hadn't blurted it in one of his drunken rages?

"Hey, baby, need a ride?" the driver in the beat-up car called out to me.

I walked faster, but I still wasn't getting any closer to home; in my panic I must have taken a wrong turn. In fact, there seemed to be less traffic where I was heading and practically no one in the street. Darkness was falling like a lead curtain and residents hurried to get behind locked doors.

"Don't be shy," one of the boys said.

The car pulled up closer and was now moving alongside me. I glanced at it and saw there were four boys inside. They looked like members of a gang. The car pulled ahead. I thought they were going to leave me be, but it stopped and one of the boys in the rear stepped out, holding the door open.

"Step right in, honey," he said. "Your limousine has arrived."

I stopped.

"Leave me alone!" I cried.

"We're just trying to help."

"I don't want your help," I said.

The car began to back toward me, the boy walking along with the door open. I turned and walked faster in the direction from which I had come.

"Hey, where you going? That ain't polite," the boy cried after me.

I heard the car's tires squeal and the door close as the car spun around. I looked back and saw they were going to pursue me. I broke into a run, but I was unsure of where to go. Every side street looked darker and more desolate than the street I was on. In moments they would be right beside me again, I thought. I looked back and saw the car charging after me, pulling closer. Gasping for breath, I ran faster, not even looking where I was going until I hit somebody hard. He kept me from falling, but held onto me. All I could think was I had run into a trap.

I looked up into the face of an elderly black man who still appeared firm and strong. He had wide shoulders and a thick neck, but his hair was thin, wild and smoke white. He wore a flannel shirt rolled up to his forearms, jeans and a pair of old sneakers. He had been carrying a sack over his shoulder and set it down quickly.

"Whoa," he said. "You'll knock over a building running that fast."

The boys in the car gaped out the windows at us.

"She's too young for you, Pop. Give her to us," the driver said.

"Get the hell outta here," the old man told them.

"What are you gonna do, call the senior citizen police?" one of the boys teased.

They all laughed.

The elderly man released me. I thought he was going to walk off and leave me, but instead he reached into his sack, fumbled around and then brought his hand out with a revolver clutched in it. I was close enough to see how rusted and old it was, but the boys couldn't tell. He pointed it at them.

"Jesus!"

"Take it easy, Pop. Point that someplace else."

"Take *yourselves* someplace else," he ordered and pulled the hammer back.

The driver hit the accelerator and the car shot off. We watched them turn a corner and disappear.

"Thank you," I said.

He looked at me with disapproval and shook his head.

"What are you doin' walkin' 'round here by yourself, girl?" he asked me. "You just lookin' for trouble or what?"

"Oh, no sir. I got lost," I said.

"This ain't no place to get lost." He gazed back up the street. My heart was still pounding. Were they waiting around the corner? He might have been thinking the same thing because when he looked at me again, his face was softer, kinder.

"Come on," he said. "I live in the basement over here. You got any money for a taxi?"

"No sir," I said.

"I got a phone. You got someone to call to come fetch you?"

"Yes sir," I said.

He smiled.

"Go ahead then," he said nodding. "Just after that next building. See that stairway going down? That's my place," he told me and put his old revolver back into the sack. He lifted it over his shoulder and waited. I couldn't help being afraid.

"You don't want to go walkin' 'round here anymore, Missy," he said, "and it's getting cold. I'd like to get into my home, as little as it is," he said.

I nodded at him and followed, looking back once to be sure the boys were gone.

What he called his basement apartment was barely bigger than Beni's and my bedroom. He had a little nook on the right with a sink and a hot plate and a small table. There was a tiny refrigerator on the floor. The room itself had an old sofa, an easy chair, a beat up wooden table, one standing lamp and an oval throw rug with holes in it.

"The bathroom's in there," he said nodding at a narrow door on the right.

"I'm fine," I said.

He grunted.

Where did he sleep? I wondered and then thought the sofa might be a pull out.

"There's the phone," he said nodding.

At first I didn't see it. Then my eyes nearly popped. Under the table was a toy phone!

"That's not a real phone," I said softly.

He looked at me and then at the phone.

"Sure it is. My boy calls me once a week on that phone," he told me. "Go on, use it."

I stood there, not knowing what to do. He went to the makeshift kitchen and began to unload his sack. Producing potato chip bags with a few chips left, cans, some old rusted tools, a cracked glass and empty beer bottles, I realized he had obviously been foraging in garbage cans and dumpsters. He treated everything as if it were gold. Finally, he put the old revolver on the table and looked at me again.

"Did you call?"

"Yes sir," I said.

"Good. I can make you some tea. Didn't get any coffee today," he said.

"That's all right. Thank you," I said inching back toward the door.

"I got a television," he said and reached behind the sofa to produce an old, small black and white set. He put it on the table and turned it on. He played with the knobs until he was able to get a picture and sound. "You can sit on the sofa and wait and watch television, if you want," he said.

"Thank you, but I said I'd wait outside."

"It's gettin' cold out there."

"It really isn't that cold," I said backing toward the door. "Spring's here."

"Yeah, and the cherry blossoms," he said smiling. "My son should be calling soon," he added suddenly and sat on the sofa staring ahead.

"Where is your son?"

"Oh, he's up north in Rochester, New York," he said. "He's a manager in a restaurant."

"That's nice. What do you do?" I asked.

"Me? I'm retired. I used to be maintenance man here. Now, I'm . . . retired. I'd go out and wait with you," he said, "but I got to wait for my son to call. You stay right nearby and come back if them hooligans bother you, okay, Missy?"

"Thank you." I opened the door. "Oh, I'm sorry," I said. "What's your name?"

"I'm Norris Patton," he said. "I was a light heavyweight champ when I was in the service." He showed me his closed fist. "They used to call me Sledgehammer." He laughed and I saw he was missing quite a few teeth in the rear of his mouth.

"Thank you for helping me, Mr. Patton," I said.

"You're quite welcome," he said and then his face burst into a smile of great joy. "That's him," he said and reached under the table for the toy phone.

I watched him for a moment and then stepped out in the street. Would that be my fate? I wondered. Without a real family, would I just imagine one, too?

I had a general idea of which way to go, but I was a lot more timid about walking now that it was really dark. As I approached the corner, however, I saw a familiar vehicle turn down the street, moving very slowly. A street light illuminated the side panel on the passengers' door. It read, SLIM'S GARAGE. Roy was at the wheel. The moment he saw me, he sped up and pulled the truck to the curb. He jumped out and came around the front quickly.

"Rain, thank God I found you. Why the hell did you go and run off for? Mama's in such a panic she had to lie down. What are you doing here?" he asked looking around. "This is a crappy neighborhood. Huh?" He stared at me. He was about as angry at me as he had ever been.

I was so happy to see him, but I didn't know what to say or do.

"Don't you know why I ran off?" I asked.

"Just get in the truck, Rain. I have to bring it back to Slim's. I took off with it as soon as Mama called and Slim doesn't even know."

"Now, I'm just trouble," I said moving to the truck. He opened the door and I got in.

"You're never just trouble, Rain, but you shouldn't have done this. I've been riding all over looking for you. Pete Williams said he thought he had seen you make the turn up there, so I tried this neighborhood. Man, Rain, Mama's all broke up."

"So am I," I said. "She's been lying to me all these years."

He looked at me and shook his head.

"I don't know anymore about this than you do, Rain, but Mama isn't one to want to lie. You know that. You should know that," he said. "There isn't a better woman in this city," he added.

"Don't you know what happened?"

"Yeah," he said softly. "Beni told me."

I looked down.

"She's not my real mother," I said softly.

"That doesn't mean she doesn't love you as much as a real mother would," Roy asserted.

"It's still very painful, Roy. Maybe I would never have found out. Maybe she never would have told me."

He didn't say anything. He drove directly to The Projects.

"You just go up to see her, Rain. I have to return Slim's truck and I'll be right along."

I hesitated, staring at the apartment building.

"That there is the only home you've got, Rain," Roy said nodding at the building, "and in it are the only people who love you."

I stared at him for a moment, my eyes glassy with tears. Then I opened the door and hopped out. He watched me head toward the front entrance before pulling away.

Beni was the only one at the dinner table. She sat there picking at her food and glared up at me as soon as I entered.

"Where'd you go?"

"For a walk," I said.

"A walk?" She smirked. "Mama's been crying. She didn't want to eat anything and went to bed."

I stood there.

"What are you mad at her for?" Beni demanded.

I looked up, my eyes hot with tears of anger.

"I should've been told long ago. How would you like to find out about yourself like that?" I asked.

Beni shrugged. Then she stared up at me looking furious.

"So you've got white blood. I always thought that about you, Rain. I don't know why, but I did."

"It doesn't change anything," I said sharply.

She smirked again.

"Rain," we heard. It was Mama calling. "Is that you, sugar?"

I looked at Beni who gazed at me with such disgust, I had to look away.

"Sugar," she mumbled.

"Yes, Mama."

"Come in here, honey. Please," she begged.

I entered the bedroom. Mama had a cold wet washcloth over her forehead. She looked gaunt in the dim light from the small table lamp. I felt a shiver in my heart. Mama was more fragile than any of us thought. She had been straining under the weight of this family for too long.

She reached out for me and I took her hand.

"The last thing I want to do is hurt you, Rain, honey. I never meant that," she said.

"I know, Mama."

I couldn't help but continue to call her Mama. I didn't know her as anyone else.

"There were many times when I almost told you all of it, and times when I thought you realized something was different. Not to mention the hundreds of things Ken said in the past that might have raised your suspicions. I warned him that if he ever hurt you that way, I'd kill him.

"Funny thing was," she said smiling, "when he first came to me with the idea of taking you into our lives, I nearly hit him over the head with a frying pan. How were we going to take care of someone else's child, even for all that money?"

"How much money was it, Mama?" I asked.

"What do you need to know that for, child? Ken, he wasted it on drink and gambling anyhow," she said.

"How much?" I demanded. I wanted to know what sort of a price my real mother had placed on my head. She stared at me. "How much?"

"It was twenty thousand dollars," she said. "I wanted to put away some of it in a savings account and use it for your college, but Ken got his big paws on it and before I knew it, it was all gone."

"Will you tell me all of it now, Mama? No more lies," I added.

"I didn't lie to you, child. I never thought of you as anything else but my own and I loved you as much as I could love any daughter," Mama claimed.

"You lied about family, Mama, about me taking after grandparents. There were lots of stories you made up, Mama," I reminded her.

She smiled instead of looking guilty.

"I only wanted you to feel you belonged, Rain. I told those stories so much, I believed them myself."

"Now it's time to tell the true story, Mama," I said.

She nodded, moved the wet cloth off her forehead and sat up in the bed. Beni stepped into the doorway and leaned against the door jamb.

"Is this Rain's secret?" she asked, "or do I have a right to know, too?"

"That's up to Rain," Mama said.

"Of course you have a right to know, Beni. You're in this family," I told her.

She came farther into the room. Mama looked at both of us, sighed deeply and began.

"Your real mother got pregnant with you in college. She was the daughter of wealthy people, but she was rebellious and involved in protests and causes. She got herself in trouble with a young black man—no, honey, it wasn't Ken—but she didn't tell her parents until it was too late and I guess there was quite a hullabaloo."

She paused and I took a deep breath. So Ken wasn't my real father. I couldn't help being relieved about that. I was afraid he had had some affair with a white girl and brought me home, forcing Mama to bring me up as her own.

"Anyhow, Ken was working for her father and he came to Ken and made the proposal that we take the child, who was you, of course. You were to be born in secret somewhere. 'Course, Ken got excited over the idea of so much money just for taking in another baby. What did he care? He was never home much anyway."

"You could just take in a baby, just like that, and pretend it was your own?" I asked skeptically.

"I was angry and I didn't want to do it, but Ken he just brought you home and I wasn't going to throw a baby out into the street, so I mothered you and here we are. It's long over and done, Rain. I swear I don't even think of it. We all love you, honey. I'm hoping you can just accept things as they are now; we *are* your family," she said.

"Did my real mother ever come to see me?" I asked.

"Oh no, honey. We haven't seen hide nor hair of those folks since the day they brought you here. Not even a phone call," she added.

It gave me a sick feeling to hear that. How could anyone give away her own baby so easily and forget her forever?

"They made us promise not to contact them, ever," Mama added.

"They didn't want to set eyes on you because you had a black father," Beni said gleefully.

"Hush up, Beni. That's putting salt on a wound."

"Why are you always protecting her, Mama? Even now you're more worried about her feelings than your own. Jesus, Mama, she ran out on you. She thinks you're a liar," Beni insisted. "Why are you taking her side and yelling at me?"

"I'm not taking anyone's side, Beni."

"Beni's right, Mama," I said softly. "I shouldn't have run out on you and made you sick. It wasn't your fault my real mother gave me away."

I looked up at her, my eyes burning with hot tears.

"You gave me more than I deserve. I was wrong to be angry at you, Mama. I'm sorry."

"Don't you start crying now, Rain," Mama said sniffling herself.

I stepped forward when she held out her arms and embraced her. When I gazed back at Beni, I saw her look of pain.

"I hope you'll still think of me as your sister, Beni," I said stepping back.

" 'Course, she will," Mama answered for her.

"Do I have a choice?" Beni quipped. She walked out of the bedroom.

I turned back to Mama.

"I'm worried about what Ken's doing," she said. "I think he's going off to try to blackmail those people and they aren't people you blackmail."

"I'd like to know who they are, Mama," I said.

"It will just bring you more pain, honey."

"Does my mother still live in Washington, D.C.?" I asked.

"I really don't know for sure."

"Can't you tell me her name, Mama?"

"I was hoping you wouldn't want to know, Rain. It's like going to those fancy stores and looking in the windows at beautiful things you can't have. It makes it harder to accept who you are and what you've got."

"I'll always wonder, Mama. I can't help it," I said.

She nodded and rose slowly from the bed. She went to the closet and brought out an old shoe box. After she opened it, she sifted through some papers and then found what she was looking for. She gazed at it for a moment.

"She's probably married with a different name now," Mama said handing the slip of paper to me.

I gazed down and read the name Megan Hudson. It was all I had of my real mother, her name.

"Can I keep this, Mama?" I asked.

She nodded.

"I'm sorry about all this, honey," she said, "but it's never lessened my love for you."

"I know, Mama."

We hugged again.

"You go get yourself something to eat," she said, "and see what Beni's done to the food. Your brother will be home any moment and he'll be starving, I'm sure."

"Okay, Mama," I said and went into the kitchen.

Beni hadn't taken the pork chops off the stove quickly enough. I tried to salvage as much as I could and warmed up some new vegetables. She heard me working and came out of the bedroom. She stood there staring at me with her arms folded under her breasts.

"Did you have enough to eat, Beni?"

"Did you have enough to eat, Beni?" she mimicked.

"What's wrong with you?"

"Nothing," she said. "You never do nothing wrong. Now I know why Mama always treats you so special. Bet you're going to be even more stuck-up."

"That's silly, Beni. Of course I won't and I'm not stuck-up now."

The door opened and Roy entered. He paused looking from Beni to me.

"How's Mama?" he asked.

"She's just fine," Beni replied sharply. "Now that Precious has returned."

"Huh?"

"I'm going down to see Alicia," she said moving to the front door.

"You better not leave this building," Roy warned.

"Why? What's Mama going to do to me when I come back? Is she going to hug and kiss me and call me Sugar?" she replied and left, slamming the door behind her.

"What's wrong with her?" Roy asked.

"I don't know," I said. "She's more upset by all this than I am."

"Is Mama really okay?"

"She's fine, resting," I said. "I did the best I could with the dinner. Sorry about the burnt chops."

"I'd eat chunks of charcoal tonight," he said. "Be right out."

He crossed to the bathroom while I finished fixing the table.

"We hear from Ken?" he asked sitting down.

"Not that I know," I told him.

"He'll probably end up in jail like his brother," Roy predicted. He really had a voracious appetite, eating everything in sight. I ate as much as I could, which was nothing more than a few bites because my stomach still felt like it had been beaten on by a heavy-metal drummer. Roy looked in on Mama after dinner. I cleaned up and then took a shower, lucky because for once the water remained hot until I was finished. After, wrapped in a large bath towel, I sat in the bedroom and finished drying my hair with another towel. I heard a knock on the door.

"Yes?"

"Want some company for a while?" Roy asked.

"Sure," I said.

Roy opened the door, but paused in the doorway.

"Oh, I'll come back if you want."

"No, it's all right. I'm done," I said fluffing out my hair.

He walked in and sat on my bed, his head down.

"Mama all right?" I asked.

"Yeah. She's asleep." He looked up, his eyes full of pain. "That woman's been through hell. She doesn't need any more trouble," he said.

"I'm not going to cause any more, Roy."

He didn't look convinced.

"Do you think I'll be different, too, Roy? Like Beni thinks? You think I'll act as if I'm better?" I asked him.

"No," he said. "I can't imagine you treating anybody bad, Rain. Beni will get over it," he assured me. "She's always trying to get someone to feel sorry for her."

"She needs your love, Roy. She needs to feel wanted," I said.

He looked away for a moment and then he sat forward, bringing his hands to his lap and slowly lifting his head, his ebony eyes fixing on me so intently that it made my heart flutter.

"What?" I asked.

"You know how I felt when I first heard about you?" he asked.

"Confused and upset, I guess."

"No," he said. "I got this overwhelming feeling of relief; I was glad, Rain. It made me feel better about myself," he said.

I shook my head. "Now, I'm the one who's confused."

He looked down again before he looked up at me with the softest eyes.

"I used to think there was something terrible wrong with me, Rain. As long as I can remember, I had feelings toward you that made me sick sometimes."

"Sick?" I turned more toward him. "Why?"

"Because I was looking at you in a way a brother shouldn't look at his sister. I couldn't help myself. I tried not to look at you more than I should. I even tried not to touch you. And if I did . . ."

"What?" I asked, my breath caught in my throat.

"Well, I was feeling more like a man than a brother. You understand?"

I did, but I shook my head because I didn't want to understand.

"I was even jealous of the idea of you having a boyfriend. I was glad you were so particular. And I'd hate myself for being like that. I even thought about going to see the minister. Sometimes, I'd lay awake just listening through the walls to hear you and Beni talk, to hear your voice.

"I didn't want to be that way. I hated myself and once . . . once I poked a pen into my leg to stop it," he said.

My eyes must have grown so big so fast, it scared him.

"I didn't really hurt myself that much," he quickly added.

"Stop what, Roy?" I asked.

He looked away and then back at me, his face angry.

"The feelings I had for you, the heat in my body. It isn't right, I kept telling myself. It's ugly. It's sinful. But I couldn't help it and the older and prettier you got, the harder it was for me to stop it. When that creep Jerad made those remarks in the street about us, I thought I would kill him with my bare hands, but not because of what he said. Because I felt as if he saw what was inside me and I hated him for that and hated myself for showing it.

"So," he continued with a small smile on his lips, "when Beni told me what happened and the truth about you, I felt this weight lift off my heart, Rain. I thought, I'm not bad, after all. I know this is painful for you, but I can't help it—I'm *glad* you aren't my blood sister," he finally admitted.

Suddenly, as if for the first time, I realized I was sitting there with just a towel around me and Roy was in the same room. I never thought much about it before, but now I actually began to tremble in my seat, uncertain, wondering what I should say or do that wouldn't make him feel horrible. He was big and strong, but he looked as vulnerable as that little boy I had seen in the playground, desperate for a smile and some reassurance.

"You don't hate me for telling you this stuff, do you, Rain?"

I shook my head.

"No, I just don't . . . I mean, I'm not sure what to say, Roy. After I came home and Mama told me the whole story, it didn't make me feel different about her or Beni or you. Family has to be more than just having the same blood running through your veins. There are lots of brothers and sisters who never talk or see each other. Mama doesn't see her sister or brother and Ken hardly ever mentions his."

"Oh, I know that," Roy said quickly. "I don't expect anything to change overnight."

"I don't know what could change, Roy," I said softly and reached for his hand. "All my life you've been my big brother. I've loved you that way," I said. "I hope you'll always be my big brother."

He looked sad again, the pain that I had seen in his eyes returning, but he tried his best to disguise it.

"Sure," he said, nodding and forcing a smile. "I know that. I'm always going to be here for you, Rain. Nothing's changed that way."

"I have a lot to sort out now," I said. "I'll need your help."

His smile widened and warmed.

"Right. You know, in time, when everything settles in, the whole world will look different to you," he said hopefully. I knew he meant himself, but I couldn't begin to think of him as anything else but my big brother Roy.

"Well, isn't this cozy," Beni said entering.

The blood drained from Roy's face. He let go of my hand as if it was on fire and stood up.

"You shut your dirty mouth," he charged.

"Don't you be the one calling me dirty, Roy Arnold. You hear she isn't really your sister and you're in here holding hands before the day's over?"

"We're not holding hands that way. We're just . . . talking things out," he stuttered.

"Sure," she said. "Just talking things out." She smirked. "I'm tired. I'm going to bed." She started to undo her blouse.

Roy glanced down at me and then hurried out of the room, pausing in the doorway to look back at Beni.

"You better not make any filthy remarks or—"

"Or what?" she fired back at him, her hands on her hips. "I'm all you've got now. I'm your *real* sister. She ain't," she said, jabbing her forefinger at me.

Roy's mouth opened and shut and then he turned and slammed the door closed behind him. Beni smiled, happy with herself. I watched her move around the room, getting herself ready for bed.

"That was cruel, Beni. You have no reason to be so angry at us."

"Oh please," she said. Then she stopped and turned on me. "I might as well have been the adopted child. That's the way I've been treated."

"Beni—"

"Let's just go to sleep," she said, "and make believe we're sisters."

"We are sisters. We'll always be sisters, Beni. Nothing about that has changed," I said.

She looked at me as if I was saying the dumbest things and then gave me one of her annoying, condescending smiles.

"Why sure, Rain sugar, we're as thick as water." She laughed and went to the bathroom.

I put on my nightgown and crawled into bed. Beni had nothing more to say. She went to bed herself and put out the lamp on the table. It was dark and unusually quiet in the building. I lay there with my eyes open, thinking about Roy, on the other side of the wall, surely staring into the darkness, too, and maybe listening for the sound of my voice.

It frightened me, but in a confusing way because I couldn't help being flattered, titillated, maybe like Eve reaching for the forbidden fruit, terrified and excited at the same time.

I was almost afraid to fall asleep.

I was almost afraid of my dreams.

# 5

# Exposed

Ken came home very late that night. I fretted in and out of nightmares, tossing and turning on my bed as if I were in a small boat caught in a storm. I didn't hear him come in, but I heard raised voices, Mama's cries and her voice cracking with sobs, and then all was quiet. I looked over at Beni to see if she had been listening, too, but she was fast asleep. I lay awake for a long time before drifting back to my own restless sleep. Beni actually woke the next morning before I did and slammed the bathroom door to wake me. It sounded like a firecracker under the bed and I woke with a start. I hurried to wash and get dressed.

Roy was at the refrigerator, Beni was sipping coffee and munching on a sweet roll, and Mama was hovering over her own mug of coffee when I finally came out. Everyone looked at me, but no one spoke. There was a deep ominous silence like there would be if someone was in the next room dying. Finally, Beni smiled and said, "The princess has risen."

"If anyone thinks she's a princess around here, it's you," Roy charged.

Mama groaned at the prospect of early morning arguments among us and lowered her head some more. Her moan seemed to come from deep within her, from somewhere near the bottom of her soul. Roy and I exchanged a look of great concern and even Beni looked a little remorseful.

"What is it, Mama?" I asked.

She shook her head and then took a deep breath.

"He's gone and done something bad," she said. "I don't know what will come of it."

"What did he do, Mama?" I asked breathlessly.

She looked up slowly.

"He went to those people and demanded more money. At least, that's what he says he did," she added.

"What people?" Roy asked.

"Rain's people, who do you think?" Beni said. Roy scowled at her and then turned to Mama.

"He's just blowing air, Mama. He wouldn't try to blackmail those people," Roy said.

"Oh, there's no telling what he'd do, Roy," she said with a voice dripping with fatigue. She sat back and gazed at her bedroom door. "He's a wild horse that won't rein in. I've tried, goodness knows, I've tried."

"Why'd you marry him, then?" Beni demanded rising. She dropped her cup into the sink so hard it almost shattered.

Mama looked from Roy to me and then laughed at Beni.

"Why did I marry him? Look who's sitting in judgment. Haven't I told you a thousand times, girl? Judge not that ye be not judged," Mama recited.

"I'm not afraid of being judged, Mama," Beni cried, her eyes tearing over. "No matter what you hear." She looked at me.

"Beni's not a bad girl, Mama," I said.

"I don't need you sticking up for me, Rain," Beni snapped at me.

"Why shouldn't she stick up for you? And you should stick up for her. You're kin," Mama said. "Never think different. You hear me, Beni? Beni?" she snapped when Beni looked away. "You hear?"

"Yes, Mama. We're kin," Beni repeated, but with a face she would have if she had bitten into a rotten apple.

"Good. Good," Mama said. She took a deep breath. "Just remember," she advised, "there's someone like that man I married waiting for you around some corner. Don't trust so quickly. Don't let yourself get into any more situations you'll regret, Beni."

Beni gazed at me again with her head tilted and her eyes slits of suspicion. I busied myself with my own breakfast. However, on the way to school, when Roy was far enough away, she asked me if I had ever told Mama what really had happened to her at the party.

"Did you tell Mama the truth about what happened at the party behind my back, Rain?"

"No, of course not," I said. "How could you think that, Beni?"

"You get along with Mama better than me. Lots of times you talk and I don't know what's said, Rain. You might be making yourself out to be better than me."

"I wouldn't do that, Beni. You should know me enough to know I wouldn't."

"I don't know nothing about nobody," she mumbled as if I had been the one who had kept the secret of my birth hidden all these years.

As soon as we arrived at school, she left me for her friends, even the ones who she knew had betrayed her. Could we ever be sisters again? I wondered.

I couldn't help feeling different about myself. It was like being born again or like I had slipped into another person. I kept gazing at myself in the mirror, thinking about my features, wondering how much I looked like my real mother and my real father. I felt so changed I was sure others saw it, too.

Even before all these revelations, I thought other students looked at me suspiciously. I knew from what Beni often gleefully told me that many thought I was too stuck on myself as it was.

"Even the white girls complain that you look down on them, Rain," she said with a laugh.

I did have what I thought was a good sense of myself. I confessed to an air of confidence. My teachers praised me when I spoke and complimented me on my schoolwork. I thought it was good to be a little proud. But now, after what I had learned about myself, I couldn't help feeling even more alone. I wasn't white and I wasn't black. I was a mulatto, but to me that sounded like a disease and not an identity.

With whom did I belong, the white girls or the African-American girls? Would either want me? Maybe it was all in my imagination, but as the day continued, it seemed that everyone was even more standoffish than before. In class I felt as if everyone was staring at me more intently. As it turned out, I had good cause to be paranoid.

For reasons she would later regret, Beni had revealed my secret to Alicia and Nicole. I think she was looking for some sympathy, but she just as well could have gone to the devil himself. It was as if she had given them a gift, shown them the weakest part of my fortress, a way to get in and revel in my downfall. I had stood up to them one too many times. They were the sort who just lay in waiting, hoping for just such an opportunity. And Beni, my sister, had given it to them.

Before the day ended, they and some of their friends cornered me in the girls room between classes. Unbeknownst to me, they had been watching for the opportunity. Moments after I went into a stall, they gathered in the bathroom. At first I didn't realize so many girls had gathered, but the sight of all those feet and the subdued laughter and muttering caught my attention.

"How's it comin' out in there, Rain, white or black?" Alicia shouted. They all laughed.

When I opened the stall door, I confronted half a dozen girls, all looking at me with twisted smiles on their faces.

"Bet you think you're something now, huh?" Nicole threw at me.

"What do you mean?" I asked.

"Now we know why you act so haughty all the time. You think you don't belong with us lowly black folks," she said imitating some stereotypic black slave from some old movie.

"That's not so, and I wish you'd stop trying to make it seem so," I told her.

"Oh you do, do you? Girls, you hear that? Miss Prissy wants me to stop telling lies about her."

All the girls smiled, their eyes full of excitement and anticipation. My heart began to pound.

"I have to get to class," I said trying to push between Alicia and Nicole. They didn't move. I stepped back.

"I have to get to class?" Alicia mimicked. "Why?" she demanded angrily, "to show off your pretty face and shake your booty in the hall to tease the boys?"

"No," I said. "I don't tease the boys. I leave that all up to you and your friends. Are you going to get out of my way?" I asked, trying to hold up a brave front while inside my stomach was doing flip-flops.

"No, I don't think so," Alicia said. "How about you, Nicole? You going to get out of Miss Prissy's way?"

"No, I don't think so either. I kinda like that blouse you're wearing, Miss Prissy. I think it'd look better on me."

"That's ridiculous," I said. "It wouldn't even fit you."

"I can make it fit, can't I, Alicia?"

"Sure you can, Nicole."

"Take it off," Nicole ordered.

"What?"

"You heard her, take it off," Alicia said.

"I will not."

"If you don't take it off, I'll rip it off," Nicole threatened. I looked toward the doorway. The other girls were blocking it. All I could do was back into the stall.

"Leave me alone," I cried.

"Why, cause you got a white mother?" Alicia asked.

It weakened me in the knees to know Beni had told them. I couldn't keep the tears from my eyes.

"Oh, look she's crying," Nicole said, with laughter in her voice.

"Black or white tears?" one of the girls asked.

"Can't tell. They're gray, I think."

They all laughed.

Nicole reached out and seized the collar of my blouse. I dropped my books and grabbed her wrist to pull her fingers away, but she held tight and we struggled like that for a moment.

"Stop it!" I screamed.

The girls started to cheer. The first button of my blouse popped and then another and another. I screamed again when Alicia took hold of the back of my blouse and pulled it so hard it sent me back against the cold metal wall of the stall. Nicole tore the blouse down.

"Now I want that bra, too," she demanded. When she reached toward me, I kicked out and caught her in the stomach. It took her by surprise and backed her up, but that made her even more furious. After she straightened, I knew I was in for great trouble.

Just at that moment, Beni came into the bathroom.

"What's going on?" she asked. The girls cleared a view for her and she saw me squatting, holding my blouse together, and crying in the stall. She looked at Nicole and Alicia. "What are you doing to her?"

"Just trying to borrow some of her clothes," Alicia said. The girls laughed.

"Leave her alone," Beni snapped. "Leave her be!" she shouted. The laughter stopped. "I didn't tell you to do this. Get away from her."

"What are you worrying about her for?" Nicole asked. "She ain't your real sister. You said so."

"She isn't my blood sister, but she's my sister. Get the hell away from her," she ordered the girls around her. Glaring at them, she hoisted her shoulders and raised her fists.

They backed off.

"Whose side you on, girl?" Alicia demanded.

Beni gazed at me and then stepped up to her.

"You shouldn't have done that, Alicia. My mother's going to be upset and I don't want my mother to be upset. It makes me mad," Beni added, her eyes filling with fire. She clenched her hands into fists again. Alicia looked at Nicole and a deep moment of silence passed. Beni wasn't backing down.

"Let's get outta here, before we get in trouble for nothing," Nicole said.

They sauntered past Beni and out the door, the other girls following as if they were a tail to Nicole and Alicia's comet.

I sat down on the toilet seat.

"You all right?"

"No," I moaned. "Look at me. Do I look all right?" I shouted hysterically at her.

She hurried to pick up my books.

"They just don't like you," she muttered. "They never will."

"Yeah, well, it didn't help to tell them about me. Why'd you do that, Beni?"

"It just came out," she claimed. "I was upset and I said it before I thought. I'm sorry."

We heard the bell ring.

"Now we'll both be late for class," I cried.

"You can't go anywhere like that anyway. I've got a sweatshirt in my locker. I'll go get it. Stay here," she commanded. She turned to go and then paused. "I'm sorry," she said.

I just looked down at the floor, angry at her, angry at Mama again, angry at the world for putting me here. I sucked back my tears and thought seriously about running away. I'd be better off anywhere but here, I thought. Here, I was going to only be trouble.

Beni was back quickly. I took the sweatshirt and peeled off what remained of my blouse.

"They're nothing more than a bunch of animals," I said. "I don't know how you can stand being with them, Beni."

"They're the only friends I've got."

"You're better off with no friends. I'm not going to class," I told her after I put on her sweatshirt and picked up my books. "I'm going to the nurse."

"I didn't tell them to do this to you," Beni assured me.

I just stood there, looking down.

"Mama's gonna hate me more now," she added.

"Mama doesn't hate you, Beni."

She held her lips tight as her eyes watered with tears.

"She wishes you were her real daughter, not me," she said. "You're everything she wants in a daughter. I stink in school and I'm always in trouble. That's why she kept it a secret all these years from us and from you. She just wanted you to be her real daughter and not me," Beni concluded.

"That's not true, Beni. There's nothing stronger than bonds of blood. You're really a part of her. She carried you and gave birth to you and nursed you. I was just dropped on the doorstep, brought in like something you buy in a store. And now look at me. I'm nowhere. Who wants me? Where do I belong? How do you think it feels knowing your real mother gave you away as easily as she'd give away an old dress or something? You're the only family I have and you hate me, too," I added.

"I don't hate you." She paused, looked down and then up at me with sad eyes. "I'm sorry," she said. "I just have a big mouth. It always gets me in trouble. Look at your blouse."

We gazed down at the torn garment in my hands.

"Mama bought me this for my birthday last year," I said.

"I'm going to kick the guts outta that Nicole."

"No, you won't, Beni. That's just going to make more trouble for both of us. Ignore them."

"What are you going to tell Mama?"

"Nothing," I said. "She has too many burdens to carry and you and I aren't going to add any more, okay? I'll just hide the blouse. She won't know. Okay?"

She looked down so I poked her in the shoulder.

"Okay?"

She smiled at me.

"Okay. Maybe I should go to the nurse, too," she thought aloud. "Otherwise, I'll be in trouble for being late to class and get detention."

"What do you think the nurse is going to think about both of us going to her at the same time?"

She laughed.

"She isn't going to believe this face anyway. That's for sure. I'll see you later, much later," she added and headed to class. I took a deep breath and followed her out.

I wasn't one to use the nurse as a way of avoiding things. In fact, this was the first time I had ever gone to see her. She took one look at my face and asked me to lie down. She took my temperature and then concluded I might be coming down with something.

"Is there someone at home to come for you?" she asked.

"I'll be all right," I said. "I can get home myself. My mother's at work."

Nevertheless, she tried phoning, which was a big mistake. Ken answered and when she told him what was wrong, he said, "What can I do about it. I ain't no doctor."

She was so shocked, she had to repeat what he'd said to her.

"He lost his job," I explained, "so he's very depressed."

"Parents," she muttered and wrote the release note.

When I got home, Ken was already gone. I was grateful for that. I took a quick, hot shower and crawled under the covers. Roy had found out that I had left school sick and instead of going to work at Slim's right away, he came home to look in on me. Beni had gotten detention, just as she expected, and wouldn't be back for another hour and a half. I was already in bed when Roy entered the apartment. I was surprised to see him.

"What's wrong? Why did the nurse send you home?" he asked, his eyes full of concern. I wondered how much he already knew.

"I just had this terrible headache, Roy."

If he found out what those girls had done, he'd go after them, and the situation would continue to fester like a bad sore. Right now, I dreaded the thought of going back to school.

"You sick?"

"I'll be fine," I said.

"Beni's in detention," he muttered. "Late for class. She wouldn't tell me why. I bet she was smoking in the girls room."

"She doesn't smoke, Roy," I said.

"Sure," he said, twisting his mouth. "She's a little angel."

"You have to stop riding her so much, Roy. She feels picked on."

"She needs to be."

"She needs to feel loved and wanted, Roy. You can't just see the bad things or she'll believe there aren't any good. And she really isn't a bad person, Roy. It's not easy for anybody in this family," I added.

He laughed.

"I swear you'd see the good in the devil if he stopped by for a beer with Ken," he quipped. I laughed.

"I bet he has."

"That's better. I like it when you smile and hate it when you're unhappy, Rain."

We stared at each other, his eyes holding onto me so firmly, I felt my heart skip a beat.

"Shouldn't you be at work, Roy?" I asked softly.

"I'll just stay an extra half hour or so. Slim's cool about it long as the work's done." He came farther into the room and sat on the bed at my feet.

"I don't recall you ever leaving school, Rain. Even when you had that bad cold, you stayed and sniffled and coughed until that teacher asked you to stay home rather than make him sick, too. What's his name, Ketchum, something like that."

"Mr. Kitsman," I said smiling.

"Yeah. Must be some helluva headache," he said looking harder at me, drinking in my face with scrutiny. "I bet it's because of all this craziness around the house, huh?"

"Yes," I said.

"Well, maybe something good will come from it." He looked down and then he moved his hand toward me and put his large palm over mine.

"Roy," I said just over a whisper.

He turned to me, his eyes so full of love, I couldn't speak.

"Maybe if you gave it half a try, Rain, you could think of me as not being your brother. Maybe you could look at me different."

"I don't know if I could, Roy," I said as honestly as I was able.

"I never touched you or kissed you except as a brother, Rain. Things change when that happens."

I started to shake my head, but he moved his hand off mine and let his fingers glide softly up my arm as he leaned toward me.

"I remember once when you were only about thirteen, I was walking by your door and I gazed in when you had just taken a shower. You were standing there naked and I know I should have turned away, but I couldn't. It was like my eyes were metal and you were a magnet."

I felt the heat rise up my neck and into my cheeks.

"You were already on the threshold of being a beautiful young girl, Rain. I can still see you now as if it happened minutes ago. You aren't mad about it, are you?"

I shook my head, afraid that if I tried to speak, my voice would crack or get caught in my throat.

"Your skin's like one of those mocha cream puffs," he continued, his hand reaching my bare shoulder.

I lay there trembling under the blanket, uncertain, wondering what to do that wouldn't make him feel hurt and angry. He did seem like a stranger, but he also seemed weak, dazed, perplexed. I held my breath and it felt as if the hands of the clock froze as well. The tips of Roy's fingers were just under the edge of the blanket, inches from my naked breasts. I couldn't stop the tingle of excitement from whirling about in my stomach, but I felt guilty for it, embarrassed.

His fingers began to move the blanket down.

"Don't, Roy," I stammered, trembling more. I brought my right arm around to hold the blanket up.

"I know I shouldn't, Rain, but I can't help wanting to look at you. You've grown so lovely. I felt like a cloud hovering above a garden in which you blossomed. We've got to begin, to try and see if we can do it," he added.

My fingers, as if they had a mind of their own, relaxed as he moved the blanket to the crest of my bosom and then, after looking into my eyes, down over my nipples that stood erect to welcome exposure. I felt glued to the bed, unable to move, even to stir.

"You're beautiful, Rain."

Slowly, ever so slowly, his eyes on me until he couldn't look at me anymore, he lowered his lips to my breasts and kissed me so softly, I wasn't sure he had. Then he nudged my bosom with his nose and kissed the side of my breast before raising his face to bring his lips to mine. It wasn't a long kiss, but it was one that sent a tingle down my spine. When he lifted his head, his eyes filled with confusion.

"Why you crying?" he asked.

I hadn't even realized tears were streaming down my face.

"I can't help it," I said. "I can't help feeling this is very wrong, Roy."

"We haven't done anything bad." He reached for my chin to turn me back so I had to look up at him. "I haven't done a single wicked or unholy thing. You and I don't share the same blood. We could have met someplace else and this would be okay, right?"

"But we didn't meet someplace else, Roy. We've been living as brother and sister for all my life and almost all of yours," I said pulling the blanket over me again. "I can't help how I feel."

"It was different though, wasn't it? Just now, it was a whole other thing, right?"

"Of course it was different."

He nodded, serious.

"Maybe it will make you think different, too."

"I don't know, Roy. I'm afraid," I said.

"Sure," he said patting my hand. "Sure, that's understandable. Truth is, I'm afraid too, but I can't help the way I feel about you, Rain, and how I always felt."

"Mama would be very upset, Roy."

"Maybe at first, but not afterward," he said, sounding more like someone trying to convince himself more than me. He smiled and stood up. "I have to get to work. You going to be all right?"

I nodded, even though my heart was still thumping so hard and fast, I thought I might just pass out.

"Good. Everything is going to be just fine," he assured me. "You'll see. You want anything, need anything?"

"No thank you."

"See you later," he said and started out. He paused in the doorway to look back. "Don't blame me for my feelings," he begged, and then he was gone.

Who should I blame for my own feelings? I wondered. I couldn't help wanting someone to love me as much as Roy did. Was it possible that his love for me was so strong, so powerful and overwhelming that it could wash away years of being brother and sister? Can someone love you so much that you can't help but fall in love with him?

Maybe this was why I never became interested in anyone at school? Maybe, like Roy, I had something deep within me telling me there was more between us or could be more between us. Lots of girls want a boyfriend as nice as their big brother. Maybe I was lucky. Mine could be my big brother.

Or maybe this tingle inside me wasn't a tingle of excitement so much as it was a tingle of fear. Roy was right. Blood was blood and we could have just as easily met someplace for the first time and fallen in love, but we hadn't, and all my life I thought we had the same blood in our veins. It wasn't something I could forget in a moment, even after a thrilling kiss. And maybe, maybe it wasn't something I should forget?

The more I learned about myself, the more twisted and entwined my life became. I felt like someone trying to unravel strings only to get things more knotted and confused. I had the strong sense that I wasn't anywhere near all the important discoveries. Something else loomed out there, some other dark truth that would make even all this seem like nothing.

All the turmoil and emotional tugs of war within me exhausted me. I fell asleep and was still asleep when Beni finally came home. Mama, fortunately for Beni, had not yet returned from work and Ken was probably still in some run-down bar. Roy had to work late so it was just the two of us. I heard her sobbing and woke. She was standing there, looking down at me.

"What is it, Beni?" I cried and sat up quickly.

"More trouble," she said. "More trouble I caused."

"You mean being in detention?"

She laughed through her tears.

"Hardly," she said. "I been in detention many times before this and Mama knew it."

"Then what is it, Beni? Did you get into a fight?" I asked, thinking that if she had, she didn't do badly. There wasn't a scratch on her nor did her clothes look a bit rumpled.

She took a deep breath and held something out in her closed right hand. I looked closely and saw it was a photograph. She opened her fingers and I gasped.

It was a picture of her sprawled on her back, naked, her legs apart. She started to cry harder.

"They did do it," she bawled. "What I was afraid they'd done at the party. See?"

"Oh Beni, throw it away. Tear it up and throw it away," I said unable to look at it.

"What good's that?" she said, even though she did rip it up.

"They've got more. They've got the negatives."

"Who gave it to you?"

"Carlton," she said with a bitter smile. "He claimed Jerad had it and gave it to him to give to me."

"Why?"

"They want two hundred and fifty dollars for the negatives. I have to bring it to the old mattress warehouse on Grover Street tomorrow night at eight or they swear they'll give out the pictures to everyone at school. I'm just going to die, Rain. I'm just never going back to school and Mama will hate me. I'll have to run off like you did, only for real," she said.

"Don't talk like that, Beni," I said.

"What else am I going to do, huh? Mama's going to find out that I lied about the party. She'll *want* me to run away," she said.

I sat there, staring at her for a moment.

"We'll just have to get the money and see if they'll give us the negatives," I said.

"Where we going to get that much money?"

"How much do we have together?" I asked her.

"I have twenty-two dollars put away in my drawer," she said.

"And I have fifty-seven saved in the old shoe box." I threw all my change and extra money in it to save for Christmas presents.

"That isn't nearly enough."

I thought for a moment.

"I'll pawn my bracelet," I said. It was the most valuable thing I owned, a real gold bracelet with real diamond chips. Mama had scrimped and saved on things she needed herself just so she could buy it for me on my Sweet Sixteen. I practically never wore it for fear I might lose it.

"You would do that?" Beni asked, amazed. She always coveted it and envied me for having received something so valuable from Mama. Ken supposedly kicked in some money, but I always thought Mama had made that up.

"Mama will find out and then—"

"She won't know for a long time, Beni, and by then, this might all be over."

"What about after?" she asked.

"We'll buy it back," I said.

"How we going to get so much money if Mama won't let us work part-time?"

"We'll find a way."

"How?" she pursued.

"I don't know right this minute, Beni. We've got to deal with one problem at a time," I said sharply. She winced.

"Why do you care about helping me anyway? Look what I did to you today," she said.

"You're my sister, Beni. You'll always be my sister, blood or no blood."

She nodded.

"I know," she said. "I tried to act as if you weren't my sister anymore, but it didn't work."

"We've shared too many laughs and tears in this room," I said.

She smiled.

"I really don't have any friend but you, Rain. I make believe I've got a whole lot of friends, but I don't have one like you."

We hugged.

"Let's get dinner going before Mama comes home," I said and she jumped to help me for the first time in a long time.

I rose, got dressed and then went to my dresser drawer and looked at my precious bracelet. How proud and excited Mama was when she gave this to me, I thought. How beautiful it was and how beautiful it looked on my wrist. I recalled Roy saying I had the fingers and the wrist for precious stones. It was the best birthday of my life and gazing at the bracelet now brought back all those smiles and kisses. Mama could look so young when she was happy and she was never so happy as she was for me that day.

How could she be like that knowing I wasn't really her daughter?

How could one small lady have so much love inside her? My real mother couldn't be half the person she was. How I wished it was all untrue. How I wished I was my adoptive mother's real daughter.

I put the bracelet back. I'd take it with me in the morning. Right after school, Beni and I would go to the pawn shop. I wasn't comfortable doing things like this behind Mama's back, but what was the alternative? Beni was right: it would break Mama's fragile little heart to learn about this disgusting and terrible mess. Beni would be convinced that Mama would hate her forever. I had to help her.

I hoped I was doing the right thing. I hoped and prayed I wasn't just buying back my sister's love.

# 6

# A Family Shattered

Roy didn't say anything about Beni's being in detention and neither did I, of course. Fortunately, Mama was too tired when she got home from work to ask us much about our day at school. The trouble with Ken the night before had left her drained and she barely had enough energy to eat dinner. Ken came home after we'd finished eating and demanded to be served. Often, when he drank too much, he was belligerent, blaming us for his own failures. We had heard it so often we barely listened anymore. Even Mama behaved as if he wasn't there.

He babbled through his litany of complaints.

"You're all a burden. None of you appreciate me. You should all be doin' more for me now. Roy shouldn't be thinkin' he's something special for workin'. I had to work when I was only ten years old and I didn't resent my father. Latisha should stop naggin' me."

On and on he went, slipping into his diatribes about the government and race prejudice.

"Now that you know you got white blood," he told me with eyes of accusation, "you're probably going to pretend you don't know us."

"I won't," I insisted.

"Believe me, Rain, you're going to lean on your white side more than your black. I bet deep down you're glad you got white blood."

"That's not true and I'll never deny Beni, Roy and Mama. Never," I vowed.

You I would deny, I thought, but I wouldn't say it.

He smiled with that irritating disdain I had learned to despise.

"We'll see," he said.

I warmed the food and served him, hoping a full stomach would quiet him down and put him to sleep early. I couldn't help feeling uncomfortable with him since he had revealed the truth about my origins and what he hoped to do. His eyes followed me about the kitchen, his gaze making me so nervous my fingers trembled and I nearly dropped a dish. Roy had gone to his room right after Ken arrived. I knew he was brooding about everything and was especially furious at Ken. What Mama didn't need right now was a full-blown fight between the two of them. Roy was smart enough to realize that was exactly what would happen if he remained in Ken's presence.

I hated seeing father and son competing like two lions for the same territory, each needing to be recognized as master, circling each other, eying each other, ready to roar. Since Roy was bringing in the checks now and Ken was just wasting what little we had, Roy was seeing himself as more the head of the family and Ken knew it and resented it. With Beni's problem now, our little home was so full of tension, you could practically see it crackle like lightning in the air.

Beni was very anxious and afraid about tomorrow. She withdrew as soon as she could, not even wanting to watch any television. Mama fell asleep on the sofa while Ken finished his dinner. After I poured him a cup of coffee, he pushed back on the table and gazed up at me with his bloodshot eyes.

"I'm not sorry I let out the truth about you," he said. "Your Mama was the one who wanted it kept hid all these years."

"I wish I never knew," I said and began to clear away his dirty dishes.

"Yeah, well, you do and you should know you owe me. I took you in when your own folks didn't want nothin' to do with you," he said.

"You got paid well for doing it," I snapped back at him. It was like having a scab torn off a healing wound to have him remind me that I had been discarded, given away and forgotten.

"That wasn't enough. Now it's up to you. You're a grown up woman."

"What do you want *me* to do?" I cried at him.

He shrugged.

"Nothin', except when you do get some work, be sure some of it goes to me. Payback. Both you girls oughta be workin'," he started again. "Help tide me over until I find something new. Maybe not Beni so much as you," he added, which just made me feel that much worse. "No one appreciates me," he chanted like some member of his own private cult.

I sucked back all the words that wanted to go flying off my tongue and finished cleaning up. Ken nearly fell asleep in his chair sipping his coffee and finally did get up and go to the living room. I heard him try to start a conversation with Mama and then give up. Less than a half hour later, he was fast asleep.

Beni lay in bed with her Walkman earphones over her head, her eyes closed. I knew she was trying to shut out the world. How often lately I felt like doing the same thing, but after a while, you have to open your eyes and take off the earphones. Reality wouldn't go away.

She jumped when I touched her hand.

"Sorry," I said.

She lifted the earphones and sat up.

"How are we going to get out tomorrow night, Rain? It's a school night. Mama won't let us go anywhere," she fired at me quickly; obviously she'd been brooding about the problem.

"I thought about that. You know how I hate lying to her, but in this case, I don't see any way out of it."

"So?"

"We'll pretend we have to study for math. It's exam time. You're going to work with Alicia Hanes and I'll be going to study with Lucy Adamson," I said. "We'll ask them to cover for us later if Mama should ask. She won't, I'm sure."

She nodded, surprised I had thought it out.

"I know how much you hate doing this kind of thing. I owe you big, Rain," she said.

"You don't owe me anything. We're sisters," I told her firmly.

She smiled.

"Yes," she said. "We're sisters."

Even so, my conscience was bothering me so much after I went to bed that I lay there feeling like a coiled fuse attached to a time bomb. As soon as that clock struck seven and we got up, it would just explode. But maybe I was still the cockeyed optimist Roy accused me of being. I looked forward to going through the turmoil and freeing Beni from the chains of humiliation and scandal she had wrapped around herself. By this time tomorrow, I thought, it would all be over and we could get along with our lives. How I longed for that. It was funny how the life I thought was so terrible before looked so desirable now.

In the morning I planted the seeds for our story about the need to study in the evening. Roy didn't look like he had gotten much more sleep than Beni and me. He sat with his eyes half shut and didn't question anything I said. Mama looked a little skeptical about Beni wanting to study, but I explained how important the tests were and how it might make the difference between passing and failing the quarter. Every time I looked at Beni's face, I had to look away. Despite her experience at it, she was a poor liar. Her face was a window pane. Anyone could gaze into those eyes and see right past the untruth.

Ken never got up before we left for school, not that he would have cared about anything I had said. I couldn't recall a time he had ever asked any of us about our school work. Even when we were little and we would show him our pictures or stars on homework papers, he would glance with barely any interest, grunt and move on to something else.

On the way to school, I learned why Roy was so tired and why he'd had so much trouble falling asleep himself. When Beni pulled ahead to talk to Dede Wilson, Roy practically lunged to my side, taking my arm to slow me down.

"Are you all right?" he asked.

"Just a little tired," I said thinking he might suspect something now.

"I'm sorry about what happened yesterday. It was too fast and it wasn't fair to you. It bothered me all night thinking about it. I couldn't sleep much and you know how unusual that is for me," he added with a smile.

"I know." I smiled, too.

"I don't want you to hate me, Rain."

"I could never do that, Roy," I said growing serious.

He nodded and then Beni fell back and he drifted away from us.

"Roy suspect something?" she asked.

"No."

"He looks upset. I'm so scared, Rain," she said.

"Me too," I admitted, which widened her eyes. "But we'll be fine," I told her.

It was just as hard for Beni at school as I expected it to be for me. Because she had come to my rescue the day before, her hot and cold weather friends were running ice water through their veins and shunned her as well. At lunch, she and I sat together for the first time in a long time. We could see Alicia and Nicole mocking us across the way, and I knew it bothered Beni so much she couldn't eat.

"You ought to think about what a friend really is supposed to be, Beni," I told her. "Those girls are just using you for their own amusement. The fact is they would do the same thing to each other that they're doing to you."

She nodded, but she didn't look convinced.

"I won't have any friends in school. The other girls don't like me," she said.

"They will when they see you're not with those nasty girls anymore," I assured her, but Beni didn't think that was much of a solution. To Beni, most of the other girls were boring or immature. Once you go speeding along recklessly and are excited by the adventure and the danger, it's hard to slow down and cruise with the careful, ordinary folks. Despite what had happened to her and how she had been abused, she couldn't help but be attracted to those who lived on the edge. I knew I should have felt happy my sister was spending so much time with me, but I couldn't help feeling sorry for her too. She had to make great changes in her style and her thinking and I was afraid she wasn't capable of it. What was even more frightening was I was afraid I couldn't really help her.

After school she and I went to the pawn shop. We knew of other kids who had gone there—many of them to fence stolen items. In fact, the short, balding, pasty looking man behind the counter gazed at us suspiciously when I produced the bracelet. He had skin that was dry and wrinkled, and dull, watery gray eyes that peered at us with vague disgust. The shop itself smelled rancid, like a room that had been flooded. The wooden floors looked damp, as if they were rotting, and there was enough dust to choke ten vacuum cleaners. The lighting was dim, maybe deliberately so because it made everything you put before him appear plain and worthless. He put on thick glasses and turned the bracelet around in his short, fat fingers that were stained with nicotine at the tips.

"It's real gold," I said. "You can see where it's stamped 18 karat right on the snap."

He raised his light brown, bushy eyebrows, looked at the bracelet and put it down.

"Where'd you get it?" he asked moving only the right corner of his thick lips.

"It was a birthday present. My sixteenth," I added to impress him.

"I can give you a hundred and . . . . twenty-five."

"Oh, we need more than that!" Beni exclaimed.

"It ain't worth more to me," he said.

"I know it cost close to five hundred," I said, "and that was nearly a year ago."

He laughed. It was more of a grunt with a half smile, jerking his shoulders.

"If you paid that, you were robbed."

"It has real diamond chips on it!" Beni pointed out. "You have to give us more!"

He stopped smiling abruptly.

"I'll go one-fifty," he said, "but that's final."

Beni and I looked at each other, mentally adding our own funds. With the one-fifty, we had a total of two hundred and twenty-two dollars. I thought for a moment and then reached up and undid the clasp around my cross necklace.

"Can I get twenty-eight dollars for this?" I asked him putting the cross in his palm. He smirked, but turned it around in his fingers. "It's a real gold chain, too."

"Gold ain't worth what you think," he said. He sighed. "All right. I'll give you twenty-eight."

"Rain!" Beni said. "Mama's going to notice you don't have it."

"We'll get it back. This is supposed to be just a loan, right?" I asked him. "You won't sell it."

"Not right off, but most times, you people don't come back and I get stuck with this stuff," he said.

"We'll come back," I swore. I turned to Beni. "Afterward, I'll get Roy to loan me the twenty-eight."

"You'll need more for the interest," the pawnbroker said.

"How much more?"

"Depends how long it takes you to come back."

"I'll be back fast," I vowed.

He shrugged and put everything in his counter. Then he opened his lock box and counted out the money. I re-counted it to be sure and we left.

"I'm going to throw up," Beni declared. "I'm so scared of Mama finding out."

"Just don't think about it," I told her.

"How am I supposed to do that?"

"Make believe it's all just a dream," I told her.

She laughed at me.

"How come you know so much about lying to people?"

"I don't, Beni, but I know a little bit about lying to myself," I said.

The idea was like a small bird too fast and too high for her to grasp. She just shook her head in confusion and walked on, stepping over the sidewalk as if we were both barefoot on ice.

Roy called near dinner time to say he had to stay at work and finish a job for Slim. They had promised a customer he would get his car in the morning. Slim had done him so many favors lately that Roy felt obligated. He said he and Slim were going to send out for a pizza. Actually, I felt a little relieved that Roy wouldn't be there to hear me tell Mama my lies. I was even afraid he would follow us out to see if we really did go to study with friends.

Mama was occupied with some bills that had come due and she pounced on Ken the moment he entered the house. He flailed about like a man being chased by bees and promised her he would get work soon and start paying off some of the debt, but he continued to curse the family that had given me to them.

"They won't even talk to me," he declared. "I just get this nosy secretary who keeps asking what's it about."

"I don't blame them," Mama said. "If I had a choice, I wouldn't talk to you either."

That set him off on a tirade about all he had tried to do for our family and how no one appreciated his efforts. They carried their arguing into the living room and Beni and I prepared to leave.

"Don't stay out too late," Mama called to us. "Getting a good night's rest is just as important for a test."

"What would you know about that, woman? You never even finished high school," Ken told her and they were at it again, clacking their tongues like two angry chickens, neither really hearing what the other said. What would become of them? One day Ken would surely leave and never return, I thought. Surely once they had been happy and hopeful. What had changed?

Beni and I looked at each other and slipped away. Neither of us spoke as we made our way out of the building and into the street.

"You let me do the talking when we get there, Beni. What they're doing is blackmail and if they don't give us those pictures, we're going right to the police. We've got to get them to believe we'll do that," I said.

She nodded, too frightened to speak. I talked because I was too frightened not to hear the sound of a voice, even if it was only my own.

The neighborhood where the warehouse was located was in a dark, dingy area. It was a run-down industrial block with empty store fronts, their windows either smashed or boarded over. Some had notices and posters pasted on the doors. No one cared to repair the broken streetlights. The vacant warehouses and buildings were taken over by homeless people or the gangs. If Roy knew we were here, I thought, he would be so angry, the top of his head would turn as red as a thermometer in boiling water. As we walked toward the warehouse, we drew closer to each other. It was quiet, deadly quiet. There was little reason for any traffic or any pedestrians on these streets.

The old mattress warehouse was a five-story building. It had a facade the color of rusted metal. Most of the windows were smashed and the sign dangled ominously on wires over the chipped and broken sidewalk below. I was surprised no one had done anything about it, but like so many of the dilapidated and depressed places in our city, government officials were satisfied pretending it simply no longer existed. They had more important areas for their attention and money.

There were three cars parked in front, but there was no one in them or on the sidewalk.

"What time is it?" Beni asked me.

"It's just past eight," I said. I took a deep breath like I would if I were about to go under water. "Let's get this over with."

The front door hung loosely on its hinges and was partly open. I stepped up to it and gazed inside. I could hear music coming from within and saw a lighted area. Then I heard some laughter.

"Maybe we shouldn't do this," Beni muttered. I was frightened, too, my brave face evaporating like a mask of wax at the sight of the deep shadows and the large, empty room before us. I felt like we were about to step into hell itself.

Some heavy metal object clanged and then there was more laughter. I stepped farther in. What I was sure was a big gray rat scurried by, only inches from my feet. I gasped and stepped back.

"You're late," someone said above us. A flashlight was turned on us, the beam blinding me for a moment. I put my hand over my eyes and gazed up. Carlton was standing on a ramp. "You brought your white sister?" he asked Beni.

"Shut up, Carlton," she threw back at him. He laughed.

"We have the money," I announced.

"Wait down there."

He turned off his flashlight and then we heard his footsteps on a metal stairway. Seconds later he was in front of us.

"Come on," he said.

"Why don't you just give us the negatives and the pictures and we'll give you the money?" I asked, not eager to go too much farther inside.

"Because I don't have them," he barked. "You want 'em or not?"

I hesitated and gazed back at the partly opened front entrance. For the rest of my life, in my mind's eye, I would gaze back at that door. I kept thinking about the Robert Frost poem we read in English class, the one about the two roads that split and the choice that made all the difference. Beni was wilting at my side. They would destroy her with those pictures. I had to go forward, I thought. I had to be brave and strong for her.

"Well?"

"We're coming," I said sharply.

He led the way deeper into the warehouse. There were cobwebs everywhere and more rodent sounds coming from the darkest corners. By the light of a few lanterns, we could see a group of about five boys and two girls, who were sitting and sprawling on old mattresses. They were drinking whiskey and vodka and cheap wine. Wrappers from fast food hamburgers and fries, some still holding food remnants, were on the floor beside them. Cigarette smoke spiraled into the darkness above and from the aroma, I knew that some of it was smoke from marijuana. They stopped laughing and talking when Carlton shouted.

"She's here!"

At first I didn't see Jerad anywhere and I was happy about that. We would pay the ransom for the photographs and go home quickly.

"Who's that with her?" I heard from a dark corner. Moments later, Jerad emerged. I could just make out a girl lying on a mattress behind him. "Well, well, it's my old girlfriend, Rain," he announced as he buttoned his shirt and fastened his belt. "This here's a nice surprise." There was a little laughter. He drew closer. "Why are you just standing around like that, Carlton? Get these girls something to drink. Where's your hospitality?"

"We don't want anything to drink. We have the money," I said. "Give us the negatives and we'll go."

"That's not a very friendly attitude, now is it?" he asked his group. Some said no. "After all, we're doing you a favor. You could at least be friendly and show some gratitude."

"We're giving you two hundred and fifty dollars," I said. "That's all the money in the world for us and all the gratitude we can afford."

Jerad laughed.

"Two hundred and fifty . . . hell, girl, I have that much for pocket change. Hang around with us and you'll see a lot more than two hundred and fifty."

"I'd rather stay poor," I said.

His cold smile slipped off his face like a thin sheet of melting ice.

"All right," he said. He snapped his fingers and held out his right hand. The heavyset boy he had called Chumpy in Oh Henry's leaped to his feet and put an envelope into his palm. Slowly, Jerad reached into it and came out with a row of negatives. He held it up and then another against the dim light. "Yeah, these are them," he said with a leering smile.

He looked at us again and stepped closer.

"But how do I know this is the girl in the pictures?" he asked looking at Beni.

"Huh?" Beni said.

There was a ripple of laughter. My heart, which had felt as if it had stopped, suddenly began to thump heavy warnings against the inside of my breast. I took a deep breath and reached down for my fistful of courage.

"Very funny," I said. "You know those are Beni's pictures and you know how disgusting they are and how terrible it was for her. We could just as easily go to the police and tell them what's happening, but I'd rather just end it here, please," I said.

"Is that so? Go to the police, huh? What do you think of that, bros?" he asked his followers. They responded with more catcalls and laughter, even the girls, whom I didn't recognize. I imagined they were school dropouts.

"What you are doing is blackmail," I said. "It's a crime, a serious crime. A felony."

"Oh, so you're a lawyer, too. I heard you were the smart one." His lips twisted into a bitter smile. "If you're so smart, why didn't you tell your sister to be careful and not get into trouble?"

"Leave her alone," Beni said, suddenly stepping forward. "It's not her fault. It's mine." She reached for the money in my hand and held it up. "I have what you want, so give me my pictures."

He drew closer as if he was going to hand over the envelope and then hesitated.

"Now that I see you better in the light, I don't think you look like her."

"What are you being stupid for?" Beni asked bravely.

"You don't look like the girl in the pictures. Does she, bros?"

"No," they resounded.

"That's ridiculous," I said. "We've seen one of those disgusting pictures. There's no question what was done to her. Do you think we would be here if she wasn't the one in the photographs?"

"Nope," he said shaking his head. "The more I look at her, the more I think these here might be pictures of someone else. There's only one way to be sure," Jerad said.

I felt my heart fall down to my stomach. I gazed back at the dark path to the entrance. We had better just retreat, I thought, while we had the chance.

"What do you mean?" Beni asked, not understanding. "What do you want?"

"You'll have to get undressed so we can compare," he said. The others laughed harder, especially the girls. How could they just sit there and let us be ridiculed like this? I wondered. Would either of them like it if it happened to her?

"Just step into the light and take off those clothes."

"Like hell I will," Beni said. "Give me those pictures now, you bastard."

"Whoa . . . eee. This here's a nasty-mouth girl," Jerad declared. "I said if you want these pictures," he said holding up the envelope, "you take off your clothes and stand in the light. We'll inspect and decide."

"Let's go, Beni," I said backing up. "This is a matter only the police can handle."

"We're the police here," Jerad declared angrily. "This is our territory. We decide what's to be done, hear?"

"C'mon," I said reaching for her hand, but Beni was nearly hysterical with anger and fear. She lunged forward to snap the envelope out of Jerad's hands and he pulled back and caught her around the waist.

"That's an assault!" he cried. "You all saw it."

She struggled to get out of his grasp.

"Let her go!" I demanded.

"She committed a crime. She has to be tried and punished. We're the police, judge and jury here," Jerad said. "You want to be her lawyer? Okay, start pleading her case."

Beni tried to kick herself free. Jerad passed the pictures back to Chumpy and put a choke hold on Beni to stop her from resisting. Then he pulled the envelope with our money out of her hand and shoved it into his pocket. She started to gag. I panicked and screamed.

"Stop it! You're hurting her. Let her go now!"

"Only way I can let her go is if you agree to take her place as the defendant. We allow that sometimes," he said.

Beni gagged again. Her eyes bulged with her effort to breathe.

"Okay," I said. "Let her go."

He loosened his grip. She went to her knees, choking and spitting.

"You're horrible," I said. "How can you do this to her? Does it make you feel big and strong in front of your friends to bully a couple of girls?"

His eyes lost their glee and became cold again.

"I think you have a big mouth and someone's got to teach you a lesson," he said. "Tonight's your lucky night, girl. Step up here and let a man make you a real woman."

Beni looked up at me. I saw something in her eyes and started to shake my head, but she moved too quickly. She turned and with her closed fist, she swung her arm up between Jerad's legs and hit him hard where it hurts a boy the most. He gasped, seized his stomach and fell to his knees. Beni slammed her open palm into his nose and he fell onto his back. The others just stared in disbelief.

"Run, Rain!" she cried rising to her feet.

I turned and ran, expecting her to be right behind me. I ran with all my might toward that doorway. I heard the shouts, but I didn't look back. I banged into something hard and nearly fell when it spun me around. Somehow, I managed to keep my balance and keep going. Moments later, I shot out into the street. I ran a few yards and turned, waiting for Beni to appear. She didn't. Instead, I saw Carlton in the doorway.

"Come on back here," he called.

"Beni!" I screamed.

"Come back here. She ain't going nowhere."

I looked behind me at the empty street and then at Carlton.

"I'm going to get the police," I said.

"You better not," he threatened. Another boy came up beside him.

My feet felt glued with fear to the sidewalk, but I had to do something and do it fast. I turned and I ran without looking back. When I rounded the corner, I saw a car and ran out onto the street, waving my arms. The driver stopped. It was a black man about Ken's age.

"What's wrong?"

"They've got my sister in an old warehouse. Please, take me to the police," I begged.

"Who's got your sister?"

"Gang members," I said. His face wrinkled with fear.

"I ain't gettin' involved with no gang."

Before I could plead, he accelerated and pulled away. I thought I heard voices and footsteps behind me and ran harder. I ran until it felt like knives in my side and I had to slow down. I had reached a busy street and saw a police patrol car on the corner. I was afraid they would pull away before I reached them. Somehow, I managed to find more energy and strength and broke into a run. When I reached the police car I practically fell against the door on the driver's side. The policeman, a dark-haired white man, and his partner, a shorter but more burly black man, looked up with surprise. They had a pizza on the seat between them.

"My sister!" I gasped.

"What?"

"My sister . . . is trapped back in a warehouse."

They looked at each other and then the driver put down the piece of pizza he was eating and stepped out of the car.

"Take it easy, miss," he said. "What are you saying?"

I blurted as much of it out as I could as fast as I could. Finally, they decided to go to the warehouse. They put me in the rear of the car and called their station, asking for backup. I directed them to the old mattress building. When we arrived, I saw that the cars that had been parked in front were gone and there was no one in sight. My heart had been pounding so hard, my chest ached.

"This is the place?" the black patrolman asked.

"Yes. I'll show you."

"No, you just stay here," he said. "We'll check it out." Another patrol car arrived and parked behind us. The four policemen gathered and then went to the door of the warehouse. I waited, my face pressed to the window.

To me it seemed like at least an hour went by. I couldn't get out of the car, however. There was no handle on the inside. Another patrol car arrived and parked in front of the one I was in. The two officers, one of them a woman, got out quickly and hurried to the warehouse. I tried to get their attention, but they didn't hear my screams or didn't want to.

Finally, the policeman who had driven the vehicle I was in emerged. He walked slowly toward the car and opened the door for me.

"Is she all right?" I asked as soon as I got out.

"What does she look like?" he asked and took out a small notepad.

I began to describe Beni and I described what she was wearing as well. Another patrolman emerged and then another.

"Give me your name and telephone number. Your mother or father home?"

"Yes, they're both home," I said. I gave him our phone number. I wanted to answer all his questions quickly so I could get some answers, too. "What about Beni? Was she in there? Did they take her somewhere else? Tell me!" I screamed.

He looked at his partner and then at me. I saw by the expressions on their faces that it wasn't good.

"Beni!" I cried and lunged toward the door. The policewoman stopped me and held me back.

"You don't want to go in there, honey," she said.

"Why? What happened to my sister? Is she all right? Tell me."

"The girl in there is dead," she said. "She was stabbed, cut real bad. I'm sorry."

I looked at her, but I never really saw her face. I can't recall anything about it to this day. I felt her arms around me and then I felt my legs disappear as the darkness that filled the warehouse poured out and enveloped me, washed over me like a flood.

I sank and went under and when I came back up, I was back in the rear of the patrol car again. A paramedic was hovering over me.

"Take it easy," he said as soon as my eyes opened. The smelling salts made me gag.

It took me a moment to remember where I was and what had happened.

I started to sob uncontrollably, my whole body shaking.

"Hey," he said. "Take it easy."

I shook my head.

"It's my fault," I said with my voice cracking. "I ran and left her. It's my fault."

# 7

# Farewell

If Beni could see the way Mama reacted to her death, she would never have had any doubts about Mama's deep love for her. I had only to look into Mama's eyes to start crying hysterically again and again. At first Mama looked like someone so confused she thought she was still trapped in a nightmare. She listened when people spoke to her, but I didn't think she heard a word. Her eyes were more like tiny mirrors reflecting back the images, preventing them from entering her mind. From the moment she realized that Beni was gone, her brain shut down, slammed a heavy iron door closed and refused to accept another devastating message.

Whenever she did look at me, it was with an expression filled with pleading. I could hear her even though she didn't speak. "Rain, tell me this isn't happening. Tell me this isn't true. Tell me you never took Beni to that warehouse. Not you, Rain. Not my reliable, precious Rain. Please. Please wake me up. Shake me hard. Throw off the sorrow and the tragedy from my shoulders. Sweep it up and dump it back into the gutter where it belongs. Rain?"

My own heart felt shredded. I cried so hard, my ribs ached. The police brought Mama, Ken and Roy to the morgue to identify Beni. The sight of her was so horrendous that Roy was reduced to a waxen image of himself. He looked bloodless, hollow, so crushed his shoulders sunk and his neck weakened until his head could barely be held up.

Even Ken was stunned into silence. He didn't speak until we were all home again and he could fit the events into his particular twisted view of the world. Somehow, he managed to turn it around so it was a blow against his own personal future.

"Just when a man raises his kids to the age where they can kick in and help him in his time of need, something like this happens. Where's the police when you need them? No one cares about us folks."

He began to drink heavily and spew out his dark rot about society and how he was part of the deprived and persecuted class of people. It took only seconds after we walked in for him to get on his soapbox. Mama, near collapse, went to bed. Roy helped her. I trailed along in a daze, afraid to touch anyone or say a word. Mama, Ken and Roy had been told bits and pieces by the police, but no one had confronted me directly yet to hear the grisly details.

Mama didn't have the luxury of sleeping pills or a doctor to prescribe them. She asked Roy for some whiskey. I stood in the doorway, waiting to speak to her, unsure as to how I should begin, terrified of what I would sound like. Ken ranted to his imagined audience in the kitchen as Roy hurried to pour Mama a half a glass of hard liquor. She always said she was a cheap date because it took only one drink to put her to sleep. For her sake, I hoped it was true.

Roy brushed past me on the return and handed it to her. She took a long gulp, coughed, dropped her head to the pillow and looked up with eyes of shattered glass.

"Where's Rain?" she asked Roy.

He turned to me. He had yet to say anything to me, even to ask how I was.

"I'm right here, Mama."

"Tell me all of it," she commanded and I approached the bed. Roy continued to glare at me with two dark pools of pain and confusion.

I began, first describing the terrible things that had happened to Beni at the party and how she was so devastated and embarrassed, she didn't want anyone to know.

"She wasn't trying to hide her own failure, Mama. She was afraid of upsetting you and making you sick. She made me promise to keep it as secret as possible. She hoped nothing more had happened and she promised to behave."

I swallowed hard before going on to describe the blackmail and how once again, Beni and I tried to protect Mama from bad news.

"You really thought you could deal with scum like that?" Roy asked me. Anger rattled his words. "You really thought you'd get what you wanted from them?"

"I thought all they wanted was money and once we showed them we had it, they would give Beni the pictures and we could put it behind us."

"Oh Lord," Mama moaned. "My little baby. Oh Lord, what they did to her."

"I told you they were dangerous," Roy said. "Why didn't you come to me?"

"We were afraid you would get yourself in trouble or get hurt," I said.

"Afraid I'd get hurt? Look what happened to Beni," he cried, his arms out. "I thought you were the smart one."

I started to cry again and Mama reached up for me.

"She had only good intentions in her heart," she said.

Roy looked away and then left when I took Mama's hand and let her draw me down to hold and hug her. We both cried hard and then I rose and went to my own room to let Mama get some sleep.

Ken was still babbling like a man who had been struck in the head. He had started on the bottle of gin and I knew that he would grow worse because of the hard liquor. Roy came out and told him to be quiet.

"Mama needs rest," he said.

"Mama? What about me?"

"You need to go to hell," Roy told him.

"What did you say, boy?"

Oh no, I thought. They're going to fight. Not now, please, not now.

"You came riding along on your horse and swept her off her feet with promises," Roy began. "You had a family and you just didn't care what that meant. Why are we here, Daddy?" Roy asked, calling him Daddy for the first time in a long, long time. "Why are we living in this . . . this project, huh? Why are we living where we're surrounded by gangs and crime and dirt, huh? Why is Mama working in a supermarket like some kid? Why do we have all those bills in the drawer? Why did Beni end up dead in some deserted, rat infested warehouse, huh?"

"You blame all that on me?" Ken asked, his voice filled with surprise and self-pity.

"You ever look in the mirror? You ever look in the mirror and see what everyone else sees?"

"Don't you talk to me like that. I'm . . . I'm . . ."

"You're what? You can't even say it. You aren't anybody's father. You don't even know what it means to be a father. Have another drink. Have a lot of drinks," Roy said and walked away from him, only he didn't go to his room. He came to mine and closed the door behind him.

I was on my stomach, my face pressed into the pillow. I turned slowly and looked up at him.

"She was so afraid of everyone finding out, Roy," I said. "She just wanted to get out of it and start new. I hoped I could help her do it. You have to believe me."

"I believe you," he said. "I'm just disappointed you didn't come to me."

I nodded.

"You're right. I should have gotten more help."

"How could you go alone to that section of town? You think you've got some special guardian angel now since you found out your real mama is some rich white lady?" he asked.

His question drove a bee sting of pain straight through my heart. I saw the anger in his face, the fury in his eyes. It was the way he wore sorrow and pain most comfortably.

"No," I said softly. "I never thought I was anyone special and I certainly don't think so now."

"I'll get that Jerad," he vowed. "I'll tear him apart with my bare hands."

"Just leave it for the police, Roy. If something happens to you because of all this, it will be my fault, too," I told him.

"It's too late for any of us to feel sorry for ourselves," he said harshly.

He gazed at Beni's empty bed, at her posters and her Walkman with the discs beside it. And then he looked at me and shook his head before leaving, closing the door behind him.

If I had any tears left, I would have cried on and on. But my well of sorrow was bankrupt. All I could do was lie in pain and stare at a picture of Beni and me when we were younger and we still thought the world was Disneyland. Beni and I never talked much about death even though there was so much violence around us. I recalled once when we came upon a shooting and saw a body covered with a blanket on the sidewalk. The police were there and some curious onlookers. There was even some blood visible on the concrete.

Someone had taken pictures, but everyone was standing around and talking quietly as if this was nothing special. The dead were anonymous, statistics, short sound bites and reports on local television news. People ate and drank while they watched and listened. Sometimes, they shook their heads or commented, but most of the time, the words and the pictures were lost in the mixture of scenes and stories that were woven to form another day in the city we called home.

We almost felt as if the dead would rise, wipe off their clothes, ask how well they had performed, and go off to return for another day's reportage. When reality was so harsh, you turned to make-believe to help swallow the daily doses. But there was no make-believe for me in Beni's and my room. I could close my eyes and wait expectantly for her to come through that door, but I knew she never would; she would never come in again. It made me wonder if I had truly been a good sister.

Should I have done more, tried harder to get her away from the nasty girls? Should I have worried less about myself, about my grades and my looks and helped her improve herself? If I had worked more diligently, would I have prevented her from ever getting into the trouble that led to her death? Had I been too selfish, too prudish, too prissy and stuck up to get my hands dirty?

Poor Beni had thought so little of herself. She tried so hard to get people to like her. She thought if she could be in with the hard crowd, she would gain respect. I remembered how excited she had been when Carlton had shown her attention—the sound of her voice, the music in it as she described her budding new romance.

I knew when it came to Mama and Roy especially, she was always measuring herself against me. She wanted me to be more like her, but in her secret, put-away heart of hearts, she really wanted to be more like me. I knew she resented me and loved me at the same time. That was why she sat with those horrible girls, why she pretended not to know me in school, and yet, she was there when I needed her the most.

The truth I couldn't even voice was that Beni sacrificed herself to protect me. Maybe if she hadn't struck Jerad and fought back, I wouldn't have had the opportunity to escape. Should I have run? Was I a coward? Or, if I hadn't, would I have wasted her effort and put us both in harm's way? I could imagine her face full of anger if I had remained behind. It almost made me laugh. I gazed at her bed and imagined her lying there as usual, lecturing me on being too good.

"It's not your fault; it's mine. You just tried to help me. Stop taking on my sins as your own. Everyone's going to end up feeling more sorry for you than for me," she would moan.

I did laugh thinking of her saying those words. I sat back and gazed at everything that was hers. I couldn't help but think about all the secrets and dreams we'd shared in this room. The walls held tightly to the fantasies we'd created when we were much younger. As we grew older, we drifted apart. We were like two boats floating beside each other. Suddenly, waves came to bounce us and separate us more and more and no matter how I reached out, how I stretched and strained, I couldn't quite grasp her hand in mine again.

She was carried away.

And now she was gone.

All of us dreaded the funeral. I remember thinking on the way to church that funerals are horrible because they confirm what you hoped was just a bad dream. I would wake up in the morning and gaze over at Beni's bed, expecting to see her turned to the wall, the blanket wrapped awkwardly around her, her braids poking out from under the covers. Even when I didn't see her there, I would lie and listen for the sound of water running in the bathroom. Maybe it was one of those rare days when she rose before I did. Maybe she wasn't dead. Maybe everything was really just a nightmare.

I listened.

The silence pounded down the coffin lid, closing itself around my heart.

Friends and neighbors arrived to offer condolences. Many brought homemade cakes and baskets of fruit. Ken's acquaintances brought beer and gin and before long, they were gathered in the living room, raising their voices to overcome each other with prophetic pronouncements about the day of reckoning that was coming for the rich power structure. Justice for the poor and the downtrodden was just around the next corner. Soon, the reason for their arrival here in the first place disappeared and their conversations twisted and turned back to their usual topics. They all drank too much, made too much noise and eventually drove away the people who really could have comforted Mama.

Roy couldn't stand being there. He left as soon as people arrived, especially Ken's friends. I was afraid he was prowling the streets, looking for Jerad. We expected the police were searching for him and for Carlton, but neither had been found. I could only describe some of the other gang members and the girls there. I didn't know any other names, except the nickname for the fat boy Jerad called Chumpy.

Late in the afternoon of the second day of mourning, Alicia Hanes arrived and quickly approached me. Ken and his friends had taken over the kitchen and Mama's friends sat with her and me in the living room. Most of the time, I sat there like an amnesiac, gazing at faces and listening to conversations without any understanding or recognition. People shook their heads at me, pitying me, but those who knew something about the story inevitably made comments like, "How could you go to a place like that at night? What were you thinking?"

Behind their masks of pity, their faces wore condemnation. Blame like fog rolled into our home and settled around me. I could see it in their eyes, in the way they stole glances at me and then whispered, and in the way they shook their heads and pressed their lips together. The steel ball of guilt bounced inside me and eventually settled on my heart, making it harder and harder to breathe. The room was stifling.

"I've got to talk to you," Alicia whispered, gazing fearfully toward Mama. "Alone."

I lifted my drooping eyelids with a modicum of interest.

"Why?"

"I have to give you something and tell you something," she continued.

Usually, I sat on the sofa almost all day, barely rising to go to the bathroom. Mama's friends did all the serving and cleaning and feeding of the mourners. It was as if no one wanted me to touch their food or their silverware and plates anyway.

I got up and led Alicia to my room. She closed the door and I turned to her.

"What do you want?" I asked. None of Beni's other so-called friends had stopped by, not even the girls who lived in the building.

She unbuttoned her blouse, reached in and brought out the envelope of those horrible negatives. Recognizing it sent a bolt of lightning down my spine and then left me feeling numb and cold. I felt like my blood had frozen in my veins. I tried to swallow and speak, but I could only gaze at the envelope in her hands.

"I was told to give this to you," she continued.

I reached down to find the strength to talk.

"How did you get it?" I whispered.

"A boy. Someone I never saw before," she added quickly, "came up to me in the street out front and handed it to me. He said I should bring it right up to you and tell you there is a note for you inside and you better read it right now." Her eyes went wide for emphasis.

Slowly, as if I was putting my hand into fire, I reached for the envelope. I gazed at Alicia to see if she had looked inside, but I didn't think she had. I could tell by her grimace of fear and terror that she was glad to be rid of it.

I opened the envelope and took out the note. Alicia stared at me as I read what was written.

It simply said, *Open your mouth to the cops anymore about who was there and what you think happened, and your brother's next.*

My legs wobbled. I pulled up a row of negatives to confirm that they were the photos of Beni.

"Who gave you this?" I demanded.

"I told you, a boy I never saw before."

"What did he look like?"

"I don't know," she said backing toward the door. "It happened too fast. He just shoved it at me and told me to bring it up to you. I gotta go," she said grasping the doorknob.

"You have to tell the police what he looked like. You have to, Alicia."

She shook her head.

"Not me. I didn't even want to bring that to you," she said, "but he told me if I didn't, I'd be sorry. Don't ask me any more questions. If you tell the police I brought that to you, I'll deny it. I ain't getting killed."

She turned and rushed out.

"Alicia!" I screamed.

She was out the front door before I could call out to her again. Ken looked up from the table where he was holding court with two of his drinking friends. They were all staring at me.

"What's that about?" he asked.

I looked at them.

"Nothing," I said.

"Most everything is around here," he quipped and his friends laughed.

I backed into my room and closed the door softly. What should I do? I wondered. If I didn't tell Roy about this, he'd be even more angry at me, if that was possible. Yet once he saw this, he'd be furious. I sat on my bed and held the envelope in my hands. I might as well have chains wrapped around myself, I thought. That was how helpless and trapped I felt. I remained there, pondering and worrying most of the afternoon until I heard a knock on my door and Roy appeared.

"What's going on?" he asked.

I looked up surprised.

"Ken says some girl came here and you were acting strange and screaming after her. For him to even notice is amazing, so it must be something." His eyes went quickly to my hands. I didn't realize I was still holding the envelope. "Who was the girl who got you so upset?"

"It was Alicia Hanes," I confessed. "She said someone told her to bring this to me. She wouldn't tell me who or even describe him."

"What is it?"

I shook my head and started to cry. He closed the door behind him and approached.

I hesitated and then I handed it to him. He opened the envelope and read the note. Then he looked at the negatives. His face turned ashen.

"You tell anyone else about this?"

"No, not yet. We should call the police," I said.

He smirked.

"What for? You think they're going to find Jerad and even if they do, you think there will be enough evidence to convict him of anything? You know how people get away with things around here, Rain. They get away with it because we're only killing our own most of the time," he said bitterly.

"You sound like Ken," I said.

"Yeah, well, sometimes, he isn't wrong."

"What are you going to do about it, then, Roy?"

He thought for a moment.

"Come on," he said.

"Where?"

"You need to get out a little anyway. Come on," he urged and started out. I rose and followed.

Ken and his friends had left, but Mama was still talking softly in the living room with some of the other women from the Projects. Roy glanced at the living room and then went to the front door.

"No one's going to miss us. Don't worry," he said.

I followed him out. It did feel strange leaving the apartment. I felt exposed, vulnerable again. While I was surrounded by grief and condolences, I was in a cocoon, wrapped in my own misery, but shut off from the prying eyes of the curious. Sounds of life seemed awkward and incongruous. Why wasn't everyone as sad and gloomy as we were? Why were they all so unaffected by Beni's horrible death? Wasn't it close enough to them? It was painful to be out in traffic and noise, to hear laughter and see people smiling and enjoying themselves.

Roy walked quickly, his shoulders hoisted about his neck as if these sounds and sights stung him as well. We went around the building and then across a street to a vacant lot. It was filled with debris, rusted metal, bags of garbage, old tires, even pieces of old furniture. He stood there for a moment looking over the site like a general inspecting the aftermath of a battle scene. He spotted what he wanted and marched to it.

I watched him set a few pieces of broken furniture in the center of a tire. He added some paper and found a smashed and battered gas can. Apparently, there were a few drops of gasoline left. He let them drip on his little pile and then he dropped the envelope of negatives on top of it.

"You're going to burn them?"

"Damn right, I am," he said.

"Isn't that evidence though, Roy?" I asked.

He shook his head.

"You want people looking at that, even police?"

"No," I said thinking about it, about some strangers leering at poor Beni naked. "I guess not."

"Me neither."

He knelt before the tire and lit the little pile. We both watched the flames lick the envelope and finally ignite it. The negatives curled as the small, dark puffs of smoke rose. How I wished the entire event, the beastly things that had been done to Beni, could be burned away and turned into nothing more than smoke. Roy remained kneeling, watching it burn. I gazed around, suddenly feeling fearful, feeling as if someone might be watching us. Every vacant building, every broken window, every cavernous structure looked ominous. The sky itself had darkened with an impending rainstorm. The breeze strengthened and lifted some debris, sending papers, boxes, and garbage bouncing around us. I embraced myself.

"Let's go back, Roy," I urged.

He acted as if he didn't hear me and then he stood up and stomped on the little fire, crushing what remained into the ground. He kicked the tire and turned away. I saw the tears that glazed his eyes. It knocked the breath out of me for a moment. Then he nodded and we started back. A police car with its siren screaming and its bubble lights spinning shot down the street to our right. We watched it pass through the neighborhood.

"They'll catch them, though, won't they, Roy?"

"What if they do? They've gotten away with something like this before," Roy said. "There's only one way to stop someone like that. . . ."

It was quiet when we returned to our apartment. Mama's friends had all left. They had cleaned up nicely, even taking care of the mess Ken and his drinking buddies had left. Mama was lying down.

"You want something to eat, Roy?" I asked.

"Maybe," he said. "I'll wash up."

I looked in on Mama. As usual, she was able to sense me around her, no matter how quiet I was. Her eyes opened and she gazed at me.

"Tomorrow," she said, "I have to bury my baby. There isn't anything worse for a mother, Rain. Nothing the devil himself could create," she said.

I ran to her and wrapped my arms around her. She stroked my hair and gave me comfort, even though it was I who should be comforting her.

Guilt was a disease invading every part of me more than ever on the morning of Beni's funeral. It started in my heart and trickled around my body in my blood, infecting my legs and my arms, my neck and my shoulders. It made my eyes ache so that I had to keep them either closed or fixed in a downward gaze, avoiding anyone else's eyes. When we sat in church, I could feel the heat of condemnation at the back of my neck, and when we rose to leave, I was afraid to glance right or left. There weren't that many people at the funeral, and even fewer at the cemetery. Those who kissed and hugged Mama, hugged Roy and shook Ken's hand either just nodded or glanced at me. I had left my sister in the valley of death. That was what I believed they thought.

The rain that had begun the day before still fell, but sporadically. We were actually able to get through the service at the grave site before it began to pour. The rain chased everyone back to his or her vehicle and we left the cemetery faster than I had anticipated. It was so final.

When we got home, the dreariness invaded our apartment and our hearts. Ken's solution, of course, was to drink more and faster. He eventually drank himself into a stupor and collapsed in bed. Roy withdrew and fell asleep in his room. Mama tinkered in the kitchen, made herself some tea and sat with me for a while before trying to sleep herself.

"We all just have to get back to living," she said finally. "Nothing we do will change things."

It seemed an impossible task to me, but somehow Mama managed to get herself up and back to work the next morning. Her strength gave me strength. Roy and I walked to school, unable to ignore the emptiness around us. How much we would have given to hear Beni arguing with us about something silly. Roy told me he was returning to work right after school.

We had yet to hear a thing about Jerad or Carlton or the others. For now it seemed Roy was right. Nothing would be done. It would just go away like most of the terrible things that happened around us. Returning to school, however, was far worse than I had imagined it could be for me. Some of the kids I knew told me how sorry they were, but Beni's crowd went after me with a vengeance. It was almost as if they thought Jerad and his gang were innocent bystanders, just doing what came natural to them.

"If you hadn't left her behind," Nicole charged in the hallway between classes, "she would be fine. They were just joking with you."

"You don't know what you're talking about," I said.

"Yes, I do. Your white blood showed itself," she declared. "And you ran. You're no sister, not to us."

Her friends nodded.

"That's stupid. You don't know how stupid you sound," I snapped back at her. I was tired of her, tired of all of them.

" 'Course, we're stupid," Alicia declared sarcastically. "Meanwhile, you're alive and Beni's dead."

"She wouldn't have gotten into trouble if you hadn't played that horrible trick on her at the party. You're the ones who should feel guilty, not me," I cried. "You were some sisters, betraying her like that, making her feel too embarrassed to show her face."

"Just listen to this girl," Nicole said. "What are you trying to say?" she asked, putting her face into mine. "You trying to put the blame on us, girl? Huh?" She poked me in the chest with her long, bony forefinger. It hurt, but I didn't retreat.

Instead, something inside of me finally exploded. I hated them for what they had done to Beni and I wouldn't let them twist and distort everything to make themselves look good and me bad. Using my books as a club, I slammed them into her side so hard, she fell down and the girls screamed around us. She was stunned for a moment, but she lunged like a panther and seized my hair. I dropped my books and grabbed her at the waist. We both spun, and she hit the lockers hard and then pulled me down. A crowd quickly gathered.

Before she could come at me again, Mr. McCalester and Mr. Scanlon grabbed her. She kicked and swung her arms, but they held her back and forced her to turn away. She cursed and screamed at me as they continued to drag her down the hallway. More teachers came out of their classrooms. The uniformed guards came running up the hallway and the crowd was ordered to disperse. I was led to the principal's office behind Nicole, who let loose a string of curses from her mouth like dirty bubbles meant to float back and splatter on my face.

They made her sit in the outer office and brought me into the principal's main office. All I could think of was that on top of everything else, I had brought new grief to Mama's door.

Our principal, Mr. Morgan, was a burly man who had been an outstanding football player in college. We were told he nearly played pro ball, but opted instead to continue his education and go into the field of education because he liked working with young people. He had a deep, resonant speaking voice and sang in the church choir. I admired him because he seemed to be able to be firm whenever he had to be firm, and yet friendly and interested in students as well.

I was greeted by his look of astonishment and then disappointment when he was told what had occurred.

"All right," he declared. "Take a seat."

He thanked the teachers who then left his office.

"Well," he continued after he sat behind his desk, "do you want to tell me exactly what happened?"

"They all attacked me in the hallway," I cried. I touched my scalp and looked at the blood on the tips of my fingers.

"Why?"

"Because I told them they're to blame for my sister's death," I said. I had to look away from his steely eyes. "I hate them. I hate all of them and they hate me. They always have."

"Why have they always hated you?"

"They just do. Because I don't think much of them and because I tried to get my sister not to hang out with them. They call me a snob," I added.

"Did you think fighting in the hallway would change anything?" he asked softly.

"No, but I was tired of their nastiness," I said. "Tired of them pushing me and poking me and mocking me."

"You know about our strict rules against violence. Little spats grow into serious ones very quickly around here. I can't tolerate them; they must be dealt with seriously," he said.

"I know. I'm sorry."

"If someone is bothering you, you come to me," he lectured.

"I wasn't thinking," I admitted and then I looked up at him. "It hasn't been exactly an easy time for me or my family."

"I understand that and I'm sorry about it, but I have to think of the whole school. I'll have to suspend you for three days. Your mother and/or your father will have to come in to see me before you can be readmitted. When you return, I hope you'll think hard before fighting again and if you're bothered, you'll come to me."

"They'd only hate me more," I said, "and make things worse for me."

"Let me see about that," he retorted. "Is there anyone home in your house?"

"Maybe Ken," I said.

"Who?"

"I mean, my father. He's out of work."

"I'll have Mrs. Dickens call. If there's no one home, I'll have the truant officer take you home. I'm very disappointed, Rain. You're one of our better students."

"It's not something I wanted to happen, Mr. Morgan," I fired back at him.

He nodded, his face now showing some sympathy and even some pain. I knew it would be difficult if not impossible for him to let me off and punish Nicole. He really didn't have much choice.

"It won't happen again," I promised.

Ken wasn't home so the truant officer had to take me. I couldn't hide the incident from Mama since she had to go to school with me. She would have to get out of work and that made it even worse. Roy found out what had happened and came home before he went to Slim's. I told him the whole story.

He smiled.

"I heard you gave her a huge lump on the forehead."

"It's no great accomplishment. Look how much trouble I've created."

"They better not pick on you anymore," he said, his eyes blazing with anger.

I closed mine and looked away. Was I going to get everyone in some trouble? Was that my destiny?

Mama was upset, of course, but she was more concerned about my being attacked than she was about my being suspended.

"It isn't safe here for any of us," she muttered. She complained to Ken, but there was little he could do or would do. He didn't even have a new job yet, much less any options for moving the family.

Three days later, Mama accompanied me to school and met with Mr. Morgan. She lost two hours of pay, but she was feisty, demanding that the school do more to protect me. In the end there wasn't much the school could do. What happened to me next, happened off school grounds.

Nicole was too afraid to bother me in school. Mr. Morgan had threatened to have her expelled next time she got into trouble, but she wanted her revenge so badly, I could see the longing in her eyes whenever she gazed at me. I should have been more cautious, but I was almost indifferent to my own fate.

Nicole and her friends waited for their opportunity. They followed me home one afternoon about a week later. I didn't hear them coming after me until they were right upon me. All I heard was my name and I turned to be splashed with a small canful of gasoline.

I screamed and then Nicole nonchalantly walked to me and threw a lit match at my dress.

"Let's make you darker, Miss Prissy," she cried.

My dress caught on fire and I ran, hysterical. It drew everyone's attention and a security guard at an office building across the street shouted at me to roll on a small patch of lawn. I did what he instructed, but my thighs were burned enough for me to have to go to the emergency room. The hospital called Mama at work and by the time she arrived, I was bandaged and lying comfortably on a gurney in one of the examination rooms. They had given me something for the pain.

The policeman outside told her what had happened and the emergency room doctor explained my injuries. There was a possibility my legs would be scarred.

When she came in to see me, she was crying. She rushed to my side and held my hand.

"I'm all right, Mama. I'm fine."

"You could have been killed!" she cried. She shook her head. "They aren't going to stop. I know them. They run on hate." She pulled herself upright and made her lips firm. "I'm not losing you to the streets, too," she declared. "They aren't going to get any more chances to hurt you."

"What do you mean, Mama?" I asked.

"I lost one child here. I'm not losing two. No ma'am, no sir. No."

"You won't lose me, Mama," I said.

Her expression didn't change. I had never seen her look as determined. Her eyes were cold gray stone. She brushed my hair out of my face and stared down at me, shaking her head softly.

"I know you won't ever stop blaming yourself, Rain. You aren't ever going to be safe here now, child. And you aren't ever going to look at yourself in the mirror and feel good about what you see as long as you're here."

"Well . . . what are we going to do, Mama?" I asked, my heart thumping.

"It's not what we're going to do, Rain. It's what you're going to do."

"Me? What am I going to do?"

"You're returning to your blood. You're going back to a safer world. I'm going to see to it," she asserted.

I was sure my heart stopped and started again. I shook my head.

But no was not in Mama's vocabulary anymore. She had been to hell and back with the loss of Beni. She was determined not to travel the same highway again, no matter what the cost, even if it meant losing me. She was like the mother in the Bible when King Solomon threatened to cut the child in half. She would rather lose me than see me harmed.

I wanted to hate her for even thinking about it, but deep in my heart I knew her thoughts were like flowers springing out of a bed of love.

I could hate this place. I could hate the girls who had done this to me. I could even hate myself.

But I could never, ever hate Mama.

# 8

# Face-to-Face

The burns made it hard for me to walk so I remained at home for nearly a week after the attack. The police arrested Nicole, but because of her age, she was treated as a juvenile and put on probation. Roy thought it had been a waste of time even to make the complaint. Nicole was already back in school and being treated as a heroine by her followers while I was recuperating at home and missing school.

Roy was still very angry about it and about the police's failure to arrest Jerad and his gang. This just added to the winds of frustration that fanned the fire in his heart. Jerad was sighted at a number of places, but the police never seemed to get there in time to capture him. There were so many problems and other crimes for them to address, Roy was positive they had put the case at the bottom of their smokestack-high pile. Mama and I knew that Roy went out from time to time on a hunt combing the hip-hop joints, hoping to run into Jerad. We were like two people watching a movie, holding our breaths at a dangerous moment. Both of us lay in our beds with our eyes glued open until we heard him come home.

And then, one night toward the end of my week of recuperation, we heard the news that Jerad had been found dead in a vacated building, a victim of a drug overdose. His friends suddenly came out of the shadows, willing now to admit that Jerad was totally responsible for Beni's death. I thought Roy would be pleased, but he was even more frustrated by the news. He hadn't gotten his chance to level his own justice and revenge on Jerad, and now the others, whom we all knew were probably just as guilty, were going to get off scot-free.

I never saw Roy wrapped more tightly, all of his nerve endings like wicks on dynamite sticks, just waiting to explode. Whenever he spoke, he ranted about the degeneration of our neighborhood and the indifference of the government, sounding more and more like Ken. His temper was short and for the first time, I saw him drink hard liquor. Mama was very troubled and walked about with deep lines of worry etched in her forehead.

And then, the inevitable clash of titans finally occurred. Roy and Ken got into a bitter argument because Ken had not found work and was spending all of his time in the taverns, drinking up the unemployment checks. The quarrel broke out late one night. Both Mama and I had gone to bed. I had just gotten to the point where I could walk without any pain and I was looking forward to getting out and returning to school, despite Nicole and her gang.

I woke to the clatter of Ken's and Roy's loud voices. Soon after I heard a bottle break and a chair fall over. I leaped out of bed and went to the door just in time to see Roy toss Ken over the table. He landed on a chair and shattered it. Wobbling, Ken rose slowly, blood trickling down the side of his head. He shook his fist at Roy, and started to go back at him. Mama screamed from her doorway and Ken turned on her.

"This is a fine way to treat the man of the house. The hell with you all!"

He rushed out the door, not even closing it. Mama put her fist in her mouth to hold back her moans. Roy, gasping for breath, looked at her and then flopped in a chair. His face was beaded with sweat and his eyes were as wild as a trapped alley cat's.

"You're becoming just like him," she said. She pointed to the door. "Go watch him walk away so you'll know what's in store for you."

Then she turned and went back to her bed. Roy looked up at me, his face filled with remorse.

"I couldn't help it, Rain," he said. "I . . . . just couldn't take any more of him and his complaints about the rest of us."

From the way he shifted his eyes, I wondered if some of Ken's complaints weren't directed mainly toward me.

I went to Roy and put my hand on his shoulder. He put his hand over mine and looked up at me, his eyes bloodshot from his drinking and fighting.

"You won't be like him, Roy," I said. "No matter what Mama said, I know you won't."

"I will if I stay here," he said. "But I'm not staying."

"What do you mean? What are you going to do?" I asked, frightened at the thought of his leaving us.

"I'm going into the army. I decided yesterday, Rain. It's a way out for me and I need time . . . . time away from you," he said softly.

"Roy—"

"No, you don't understand. You just don't know how painful it is for me to come home every night and go to sleep just on the other side of that wall. I can't help but listen for every sound you make. It's no good." He gazed toward Mama's bedroom. "She's got too much tearing her up right now for me to add something like this."

"But Roy, the army? Are you sure?"

"Yeah. I can get trained in something worthwhile. I'll still be able to send you some money from time to time. I won't need much and with me gone, there'll be fewer mouths to feed."

"Mama's not going to like this, Roy," I said.

He smiled.

"She's the one who suggested it," he revealed.

"Mama?" I started to shake my head.

"That's one great woman," he added nodding toward her bedroom. "She never thinks of herself, only of us." His face hardened. "That's why I hate him," he added. "He's never thought of anyone but himself. Good riddance to him. If I never see him again, it will be too soon."

How could I bear the thought of Roy leaving? With Beni gone, it seemed like the end of our little family. I started to cry softly. He turned and wrapped his arms around my waist and put his head gently against my hip. He held me for the longest time and then he rose and went into his own room, leaving me without saying another word.

I straightened out the chairs and cleaned up the mess the best I could before returning to bed.

By the time I woke the next morning and washed and dressed, Mama was at the table, her hands around a mug of coffee. She looked like she had been there for hours and she looked so tired and thin. The events of the last few weeks had aged her. Her hair was grayer and there were dark bags under her eyes.

"Good morning, Mama," I said.

She lifted her eyes as if they were heavy as lead and gazed at me while she took a deep breath.

"Where's Roy?" I asked.

"Gone to work," she said. "He didn't want breakfast. He said he'd get something at the garage."

"Last night, after the fight, he told me he was going to join the army. He said it was your idea. Was it, Mama?"

She nodded.

"If he stays here, he'll die. You saw what happened last night. It was bound to happen sooner or later. I'm only glad it wasn't worse."

"Did Ken come home?" I asked looking toward the bedroom.

"No," she said straightening firmly in her chair, "and if he does, I'm throwing him out," she said. "I've made up my mind about that. Get yourself some orange juice and something to eat, Rain. I want to talk to you," she said.

Her voice seemed to have the ring of doom in it. My heart started to beat quickly, and my fingers fumbled and nearly dropped the container of orange juice. I sipped some and sat across from her.

"I'm better, Mama," I said. "I'll be returning to school on Monday," I added, thinking that was what was upsetting her too.

"I hope not," she said.

"What?"

"I hope you never go back to that school, Rain. The trouble's never going to end there. Never." She sipped some coffee.

I hadn't thought much about the dire comments Mama had made at the hospital because she never mentioned them during the week, but suddenly those words came rushing back like words spoken in an old dream, words you wanted desperately to forget and never hear again, but words that lingered in the darkest closets of your memory.

"You and I have a lunch date today," she continued.

"Lunch date? With whom, Mama?"

"With the woman who is your real mama, Rain. I've been calling her all week and finally, I got to speak with her. She wasn't jumping for joy when I told her what I wanted, but I could hear the curiosity in her voice. She wants to have a look at you. It's only natural."

"Natural?" I spit back. "What would she know about being natural? She sold me, didn't she?"

"Well, she didn't have much choice, I imagine. That's a story she going to have to tell you herself. I can't speak for her. I never spoke with her before or her daddy. Ken did all the talking in those days. I told you, I wasn't for it in the beginning, but once I took a gander at you, I wasn't going to turn you away."

"You want to do that now though, don't you?" I charged. The anger that rose and put fire in my eyes stung her, but she didn't flinch.

"I don't want to, no. But what I do want is for you to be safe and healthy. I want you to have the best things and I want you to become someone, Rain. You've got something up here," she said pointing to her temple. "Why, there's nothing you can't become if you set your mind to it, I bet."

"But Mama . . ."

"But what, honey? Look around you," she said holding her arms out and nodding at our run-down apartment. "What can I give you, huh? What's here? I know what's waiting for you out there and it scares me to death to think of it. I got your brother set on leaving and I'm glad. In my heart I'm glad even though I hate to see him go. I need to do something for you too, Rain, before it's too late."

"I can't leave you, Mama. You're throwing Ken out. Roy will be gone. Beni's dead. You'll be all alone," I said shaking my head.

"No, I won't. I'm going to go live with my aunt Sylvia in Raleigh. She's all alone now with Uncle Clarence gone and she would welcome my company," she said.

For a moment I couldn't speak. Mama had been planning all this? Could she really leave me? Leave Roy?

"You're just saying that," I said smiling. "You know you wouldn't get up and go somewhere else."

"Yes, I would, Rain. Yes," she said firmly. "I'm tired of all this, tired of the battling and the hardships. I'm tired of worrying myself to death. I told you before. I'm not losing you to the streets, too."

I started to shake my head.

"You want to be a burden to me all my life, the little I have left of it?" she asked.

Tears burned my eyes.

"I'll never be a burden to you, Mama," I wailed.

"Yes, you would. Yes," she said. "If we stayed here and I had to worry myself sick every day you went off to that school and walked these streets, yes, yes you would."

"I'll get a job. I'll quit school."

"Oh, that would be just fine. I'd really feel good about that," she said smirking. "My one great contribution to your life is to make you someone's waitress or maid or maybe you'd get a job alongside me in the grocery, huh? Maybe you could stack cans, too, and mop up when some child knocks a bottle of sauce off the shelf?"

"We could move, Mama. We could go somewhere else and I'll start school in a better neighborhood," I suggested.

"Move? Where? How? Aunt Sylvia's barely got enough room for me. You know how silly you sound, girl, and you aren't a silly girl. You have a real head on your shoulders, Rain. You just sit there a moment and you give all this a real think and I'm sure you'll agree I made the best decision I could."

"What do you expect will happen at lunch, Mama?"

"I expect the right thing will happen," she replied. "Finally, I expect the right thing. Now, after you have some breakfast, you pick out your Sunday best, Rain, and you make yourself look the prettiest you can. We're meeting her in Georgetown and you know that's the ritzy area. Lots of well-to-do folks will be around us and we aren't going to be embarrassed for ourselves. No ma'am, no sir, hear?"

I looked down at the table. I could feel the tears filling behind my eyelids.

"Some day maybe, you'll thank me," she said sadly.

Then she rose and with her shoulders slumped, she went into the bathroom to shower and make herself as presentable as she could.

What did it take more of, I wondered, a great deal of strength or a great deal of fear to hope someone else will become the mother of your child?

I was her child, blood or no blood. There was no way I could love the woman who gave birth to me the way I loved Mama, but Mama had a deep faith in the power of heritage and family. She thought blood would overtake everything.

I thought it would do nothing more than drown me in my greatest sorrow.

Mama put on her Sunday church dress and I put on a dark-blue cotton skirt and blouse. I didn't really have a nice jacket so I put on a cardigan sweater. My nicest shoes were flats, but they were a little scratched and scuffed.

As I sat before the mirror brushing out my hair, I felt a little steel ball of nervousness begin to roll around the bottom of my stomach. I was hurt and angry and very anxious, but I couldn't keep back the rush of curiosity either. What was my real mother like? What did she look like? What would she say? What would she think of me?

How could I face her or speak to her knowing she had been willing to give me away? Mama had too much hope, I thought, and it wasn't like her. She wasn't a dreamer. Maybe there was a time when she was just like the rest of us, but the disappointments and the tragedies had soured all the cotton candy fantasies and put clouds forever and ever in her blue skies. What did she really think would happen? Why was she doing this?

"You ready, Rain?" she asked from my bedroom doorway.

Getting to Georgetown wasn't going to be easy. We were going to walk and take the metro.

I looked up at her. She tried to smile and when she did there was a flash of what once had been her youth and beauty in her eyes.

"You look very nice," she told me, but when I stood up and finished buttoning my blouse, she gasped. "Rain, where's your chain and cross?"

I hesitated. With all that had happened since Beni and I had gone to the pawnbroker, I had forgotten.

"Oh, Mama," I said.

"You lost it? Someone take it from you?"

"No, Mama. I had to pawn it along with my bracelet to get the money for Beni. I'm sorry," I said.

She was silent a moment.

"The only thing we have left to pawn is our souls," she said, "and we aren't ever going to do that. Let's go," she said with even more determination.

I put on my cardigan quickly and followed her out of the apartment. I couldn't remember the last time Mama and I had gone anywhere together. When I was little, Mama would take me and Beni with her to go shopping. She took all of us to a fair once. Roy was too bashful to hold hands but Mama made him anyway. I smiled at the memory.

It was a beautiful spring day, which made our walking at least pleasurable. I was surprised at how spry Mama was considering how tired she had been lately. There was a purpose in her steps and her eyes rarely wavered from the direction we were heading.

I had never really been to the Georgetown area. I knew it had many upscale restaurants and shops and the population was mainly professional people. Mama had the address written down. We were going to the three thousand block of M Street N.W. Neither of us were seasoned travelers in the city. Mama was very nervous, but she hid it well and maintained the look of someone who knew exactly where she was going and how to get there. When we got to the station, I read the map on the wall and we were off.

"How did you get her to meet with us, Mama," I asked, "if Ken couldn't even talk to them?"

"Mothers speak a different language," she muttered. I smiled to myself and she looked at me. "If you heard Ken on the phone making demands, would you want to talk to him?"

"No," I said laughing.

Mama squeezed my hand for reassurance. We rode on, neither of us saying much more. Our thoughts were too cluttered and our nerves too jumpy.

"Where are we meeting her, Mama?" I asked when we arrived at the station. She looked at her note paper.

"Café St. Germain," she replied, only she pronounced it Café St. German. Then she asked, "What in blazes is it?"

"A French restaurant, Mama."

"French? I don't think I've ever eaten anything French, except fries," she quipped.

I laughed. It eased the tension between us and I took a deep breath and looked about the street. There were fancy shops with their windows stocked with expensive looking clothing and shoes, gourmet food stores, chocolate shops, and restaurants and cafés with people sitting on patios, talking and eating. Everyone looked happy and successful. How different it all was from the streets around our apartment.

"Which way?" Mama wondered aloud. She turned a bit frantically. "We're going to be late."

"This way, Mama," I said noting the numbers. A few minutes later, we stood before Café St. Germain.

Through the large front windows we could see a very elegantly dressed crowd. Most of the men were wearing jackets and ties. The women wore so much jewelry they glittered like Christmas trees. All of them had styled hair. Their clothing looked even more expensive than the jewelry. I imagined every famous designer was represented by someone in there. Even the waiters looked rich in their black slacks, white shirts and black bow ties. A hostess who might have been on the covers of yesterday's fashion magazines stood near the entrance talking on the telephone.

Mama looked as though the sight had nailed her feet to the sidewalk. She swallowed hard and clutched her pocketbook. Now she seemed ready to turn and sprint back to the trains.

"Do you know what she looks like, Mama?"

She shook her head.

"Well, she doesn't know what we look like," I thought aloud.

"She told me to just ask for Megan Hudson Randolph's table," Mama said.

I looked through the window again, searching for a woman sitting alone.

"Well, we're not late," Mama said. "We're right on time. Let's go, honey."

She gathered her courage and hoisted back her slim shoulders before stepping through the door. I followed right behind her. The hostess looked up with an expression of half amusement, half disdain. It seemed to me that everyone in the restaurant paused in their conversation to look our way. Suddenly, my cardigan felt like a rag and I was never more self-conscious about my battered shoes. Mama kept her eyes focused on the hostess.

"Can I help you?" she asked before we reached her. It was as if she thought her words would stop us or put up some protective wall.

"We're here to meet Megan Hudson Randolph for lunch," Mama said.

The young woman's amused smile hardened into plastic. She shook her head slightly, maybe to replay the words in her diamond studded ears.

"Mrs. Randolph?"

"Yes, that's right," Mama said firmly. "We're not too early and we're not late," she added.

"Oh." She gazed at her chart. "Yes. Mrs. Randolph has booked a table for three at one o'clock. She's not here yet," she added. There was a pregnant pause, one that could give birth to a scream if my anxious lungs had their way. I stepped forward.

"You could seat us at the table," I suggested. "Mrs. Randolph might appreciate that."

"Oh. Yes," she said. She turned and signaled to a waiter. He hurried over. "Daniel," she said, "would you show these ladies to number 22, s'il vous plaît."

"Oui, Mademoiselle," the waiter replied.

Mama's eyes widened. She turned to me as we started behind the waiter.

"They speak French, too?"

"It's just part of the act, Mama," I said.

The women and men we passed along the way all gazed at us with quizzical smiles. One woman looked upset, however, and whispered to her lunch date, who laughed aloud. Number 22 was a table all the way in the rear of the restaurant. I was positive Megan Hudson Randolph had asked for it to be less conspicuous. That was also why she was arriving late.

The waiter pulled out the chair for Mama and she sat. He did the same for me. Mama ran her hand over the tablecloth.

"It's good cotton," she said.

I had to smile.

"I'm sure this is a very expensive restaurant, Mama. The customers expect the best."

She nodded and looked up when the busboy set a basket of warm French rolls on our table. Another busboy poured water from bottles of Evian. Mama watched everything with the eyes of someone who had just been let out of prison. The most expensive restaurant we had eaten in was Joe Mandel's Beef and Ribs Diner, and not that often either.

Now that I was actually here, my nerves grew even more frazzled. Every time a single woman entered the restaurant, I felt a terrible pounding of panic. Although we were seated, people were still stealing glimpses at us. I imagined every whisper, every laugh was about Mama and me. Finally, a brunette in a dark blue pin-striped suit entered and approached the hostess. I saw her turn and nod in our direction. It made me wish I could shrink into that small hiding place in my brain where I could feel safe and unafraid.

Mama was studying the menu, complaining about the French words. "How are we supposed to know what everything is?"

"Mama," I said nodding toward the front of the restaurant.

She turned slowly. As the woman who might have been my mother drew closer, I held my breath. She was about my height, but she was wearing high heeled boots. Her hair was styled and the length was an inch or so above the nape of her neck. She was slim and small boned. I thought she was very pretty. I saw immediately that we had the same color eyes and practically the same shape jaw. Her lips remained taut until she was only a few steps away. Then, her eyes rested on me and her lips quivered in the corners, almost forming a smile. It was as if they wanted to, but something stronger held them back.

She turned to Mama.

"Mrs. Arnold?"

"Yes," Mama said.

For a moment the two women just drank each other in. To Mama's credit, she didn't appear intimidated or insecure.

"I'm Megan Hudson Randolph," my real mother said. She turned to me.

"This here's your daughter, Rain," Mama said. "Say hello to your real mama, honey."

"Hello," I said, my throat so tight, I thought I would gag.

My mother put her jeweled purse on the table and waited for the waiter to pull out her seat.

"Good afternoon, Mrs. Randolph," he said.

"Please get me a Chopin vodka and club with a twist of lime, Maurice," she commanded with the tone of someone who desperately needed a drink. She looked at Mama. "Did you want to order something to drink, some wine perhaps?"

"We've got water," Mama said nodding at the glass of water.

"Fine. That will be it, Maurice."

"Merci, Mrs. Randolph," the waiter said and hurried off to do her bidding.

Although I knew I was being rude, I couldn't take my eyes off her. She had perfect skin, rich with a tint of apricot in her high cheekbones and a slight dimple on the left side of her jaw. Gold teardrop earrings hung from her lobes, each earring with a tiny diamond in the center. When she put her hands on the table, I saw the biggest diamond ring I had ever seen. From advertisements in magazines, I knew her watch was a Rolex.

"Let me begin by telling you, Mrs. Arnold, that if you called me as part of what I'm sure was your husband's attempt to extort more money from my family, you're . . ."

"I don't want any of your money. I curse the day we took one cent and the truth is, I never saw much of it and neither did Rain," Mama shot back at her. "I didn't need a bribe to take in this child," she added nodding at me.

My mother looked at me again, this time permitting herself a longer gaze. Her lips softened.

"You're very pretty," she commented, finally addressing me directly.

"And very smart," Mama said. "She gets A's all the time."

My mother's smile widened. She looked down at the table and shook her head.

"Well, there's no genetic resemblance there. I barely got through my Bachelors of Arts program," she said. She took a deep breath.

The waiter brought her drink and she seized it and took a long sip. Then she nodded at the menus.

"Let's order something to eat."

Mama finally showed some lack of confidence.

"What are you going to have, Rain?" she asked.

"You'll like the crevettes au safron, Mama," I said.

"I will?"

"Do you know what that is?" my mother asked.

"Shrimp in saffron sauce," I replied.

Her eyebrows lifted.

"I took French as my language elective," I said.

"I told you she was smart," Mama bragged.

"I'm not sure about the entree below it," I admitted. "I know canard is duck but the rest . . ."

"That's a raspberry sauce. It's my favorite," my mother said. "Is that what you'd like?"

"Yes," I said.

She called the waiter and gave him our order.

"Well," she said sitting back and contemplating Mama, "you got me here, Mrs. Arnold. You have the floor."

"The floor?"

"She means tell her what you want from her, Mama," I said softly.

"Oh." Mama looked at me and then at her. She shook her shoulders and straightened her back like a proud hen, something she usually did when she was about to make some dramatic statements. "I know you don't know anything about us and about what kind of life Rain's had all these years. I did the best I could with what I had. I had two other children, a son and then after Rain came to us, a daughter. Beni," My mother said. "Named after my mother Beneatha."

"Is that so?" my mother said squirming with boredom. She nodded and smiled at someone across the room and then took another sip of her drink.

"Yes, only my Beni was murdered a few weeks ago," Mama shot back.

My mother nearly choked on her drink. She put the glass down and wiped her mouth quickly.

"Murdered?"

"Where we live, that isn't so unusual," Mama said. "Lots of times it doesn't even make the newspapers."

"I'm sorry. What a horrible thing. Was the killer caught?"

"No. He died himself from drugs, but that doesn't matter. It didn't bring Beni back. Anyway, my son Roy, he's going into the army, and Ken, the man your daddy paid, the man who's never been much of a father or a husband, lost his job again and gets drunk most of the time. I'm throwing him out."

"I see." She shifted in her seat as if she were sitting on a pea. "I'm sorry about all this, but I don't see . . ."

"I can't do it any more," Mama wailed. "With my husband gone, my son in the army, my youngest murdered, I can't do it any more," she concluded, raising her voice enough to make my mother look around to be sure we weren't attracting undue attention.

"Please, Mrs. Arnold. Let's keep our conversation at this table," she said.

"I don't care who hears me," Mama snapped.

"Well if you don't want any money, then what is it you want from me?" my mother asked petulantly.

"What I want?" Mama sat back. "What I want? I want you to take responsibility for your own flesh and blood. That's what I want," Mama said sharply.

For a moment my mother just stared at her. She gazed quickly at me and then back at Mama.

"Take responsibility?" She shook her head. "I don't understand."

"What's there to understand? She's your daughter. You're the one brought her into this world. It's time you took over."

"You expect me to take her into my home?"

"Don't you care? Look at her," Mama said nodding at me. "She's your real daughter. Doesn't blood mean anything to you people?"

My mother started to speak and then stopped as the waiter arrived with our food. She sat back and watched him serve us. Mama gazed at her food and looked up at me with a confused smile on her face.

"This sure doesn't look like any shrimp I've eaten before," she said.

"You'll find it delicious," my mother commented with a twist of her lips.

"Will there be anything else, Mrs. Randolph?" the waiter asked.

"No. Merci, Maurice," she said. She leaned forward on her elbows, glanced at me and then at Mama. "Let me understand what you're saying, Mrs. Arnold. You want to give her back to me now, after all these years?"

"She's a good girl and a beautiful girl. Anyone would want her for a daughter. She hasn't ever given me any trouble," Mama said.

"I believe that. However, this is . . ." She shook her head and smiled. "This is incredible. How do I even know she's who you say she is?"

"Mama, let's go," I said. Those words stung.

"No," Mama snapped. "How do you even know?" Mama smiled coldly. "You know. Look at her. You know," Mama said firmly, nodding. "I'm not a stupid woman, Mrs. Randolph. I'm poor but I'm not stupid. There's medical ways to prove it and you know there is. If we have to do that, we will," she threatened.

"Mama."

"Now just a minute, Mrs. Arnold . . ."

"What do you want me to do, make some announcement in the papers, embarrass all of us?"

"This is blackmail," my mother said angrily.

"I told you I don't want any of your money. I'm trying to save this girl's life. You think you'd be glad of that. If she stays where she is now she'll get into some trouble sooner or later. I made up my mind I'm not going to let that happen. Are you going to tell me all these years, you never wondered about her, never thought about her?"

My mother sat back and looked at me. I couldn't help but fill my face with the same question.

"It's not that I don't want anything to do with her," she said in softer tones. "Of course I've thought about her, but my husband doesn't even know about this. When he asked who your husband was and why he was calling and asking for me or my father, I told him I had no idea."

"How come he didn't ask your father then?" Mama wondered.

"My father died two years ago," she said.

"Well, then maybe you should tell your husband now."

"I can't do that. We have two other children. My husband's an important attorney. He's going to run for political office in the near future. This would just break him. No," she said shaking her head emphatically, "it's all out of the question. I can get you some money, perhaps."

"Money," Mama spit. "You people use it like Band-Aids. Don't you ever think about the pain you're causing? Money," she said. Mama looked at her food and then she rose from her chair and stood as firm as a statue while she gazed down at my real mother.

"I don't have anything compared to you, Mrs. Randolph. What you're wearing might pay our rent for a year. That fancy pocketbook probably cost as much as we spend all year on food. I'm ashamed of where I am now. I'm ashamed of my life and I'm afraid for this girl your daddy handed over to us like some sort of packaged goods. I was hoping you had an ounce of charity or love in you. This girl doesn't belong in a ghetto. She doesn't belong in harm's way, and not because she has your blood. Your blood isn't any better than mine. She's a real good girl, smart and pretty. She deserves better than I can give her. I was hoping once you set eyes on her, you'd see that too and you'd feel something in here," she said putting her hand over her left breast. "I guess you aren't the woman I hoped you'd be. Come along, Rain," she ordered and I stood.

I gazed once at my beautiful mother. She was a stranger and yet there was something in her eyes that attracted me, some warm flow of energy that made me hesitate for a moment before starting away with Mama.

"Wait," my mother said.

Mama hesitated.

"Please, sit and have your lunch. I have a possible solution," she added. "Please," she pleaded when Mama still hesitated.

Mama lifted her chin and looked down skeptically, but then she returned to her seat. I noticed how we had attracted the attention of almost every table around us.

"That shrimp is really delicious. You should eat some of it."

"I'm not really hungry," Mama said but she poked a fork into one and tasted it. She couldn't hide her pleasant surprise. "What's your possible solution?" she asked finally after a few more bites.

"As I told you, my father died recently. My mother needs someone to live with her. She's not very well. My younger sister Victoria and my mother don't get along and Victoria, who isn't married, won't live with her. Mother is a stubborn woman and insists on being independent anyway. She barely tolerates the maids and I'm usually replacing them regularly because they can't deal with her. I'd like someone to be there with her.

"It's a big house with plenty of room," she continued. "I'll even put her in private school nearby. It's all just outside of Richmond."

"You want her to live with your mother instead of you?" Mama asked, incredulous.

"She'll be out of the world you call hell."

"What are you going to tell your mother?"

"My mother knows the truth. She'll understand and keep discreet. However, as I said, no one else in my family does. Victoria knows nothing and I'd like to keep it that way for now," my mother added.

"Even your husband?" Mama asked. "You'll still keep him in the dark, too?"

"Yes," my mother insisted. "It's best, believe me. I mean, she's a beautiful girl and I can see she's bright, but it's not something he would understand."

"And then what?" Mama asked. "What about after?"

"We'll see. Let's just take it a step at a time. I'll get the information to you and send someone around to take her."

I wanted to scream. Not once had my mother asked me a question directly, or even called me by my name. I was supposed to put my life in the hands of this woman?

"Mama," I said softly, shaking my head.

"She's right, Rain. It's a way out for you, child."

"I don't want to go to some snobby school," I said. It was as if Beni had whispered in my ear.

"Hush up, child. It may be a snobby school but it will be clean and safe."

"I don't have the kind of clothes I need to go to school like that, Mama."

Mama looked troubled by that and turned to my mother.

"I can fix that. Meet me at Saks tomorrow and I'll get you what you need. I'll be there at three. Here's the address," she said opening her jeweled purse and plucking out a card. "I have a personal salesperson. That's her name. Just ask for her if you get there before I do."

I stared at the card she held toward me.

"You really want me to live with your mother?" I asked, still shocked by the speed with which events were occurring. My mother didn't look at me.

She turned to Mama to reply.

"It's the best I can do," she said.

"I'm sure it is," Mama said shaking her head. "And that's the pity of it."

My mother put the card down in front of me. Then she rose and grasped her purse.

"I'll take care of the bill on the way out," she said. "I'll see you tomorrow, Rain," she added, turning to me.

We watched her walk away.

"I want to stay with you, Mama," I said immediately. "Not with some strange old lady even if she is my grandmother."

"You go where your blood takes you," Mama muttered. "At least I'll know you'll be safe and out of hell's kitchen; and you know you'll get the best. If you can't do this for yourself, at least do it for me."

She took another bite of her entree.

"This isn't all that bad," she said, "but why don't they just name it what it is instead of using all those fancy words?"

"Mama. Who named me Rain? Was that her doing?"

"No," Mama said. "She never give you anything before this, honey. Not your name, nothing. Except the blood running through your veins, and whether she knows it or not, or you know it now, someday, that's going to count for something.

"Someday," Mama said, her eyes filling with some deep wisdom I might never understand.

Or maybe, I'd never want to understand.

Only time itself knew that answer.

# 9

# A Whole New World

Defeat like some dark blue liquid stain darkened Roy's face when he heard what Mama had arranged for me. He listened, his head bowed, his eyes haunted with pain. When he spoke, his voice was merely a whisper.

"That's good," he said even though I knew his heart was being shredded. "I'm leaving in a week and I won't be around here to protect you."

"There," Mama said as if that was all the confirmation she needed to be sure she was doing the right thing.

"These people are strangers to me, Roy," I said. "My real mother still wants the truth kept secret. What kind of an alternative is that?"

He raised his head and gazed at Mama before looking at me. I had the suspicion they might have discussed this plan before Mama even told me.

"Just think of it like you're going away to school or something," he said. "I'll come by first chance I get and someday soon we'll all be together again."

"Sure," Mama followed, practically jumping on his optimistic words. "That's a good way to think on it. You listen to your brother," she ordered. "He's a sensible young man, always was. The only thing he inherited from that no-good father of his is his good looks. Ken was a handsome man once," she added reluctantly. She was at the point where she didn't want to say anything nice about him.

"I'm far from handsome, Mama," Roy corrected.

"Don't you tell me what's handsome and what isn't. I'm not that far gone yet," she quipped. Roy laughed. She was doing her best to keep up all our spirits.

"When are you leaving?" Roy asked me.

"She's going shopping with her mama tomorrow and then the day after they're coming for her," Mama volunteered.

"I'm never going to think of her as being my mama," I vowed.

"That's something she'll have to face and change," Mama said. "If you want, you'll find a way to give her a chance."

"No," I fired back. "Roy's right. I'm going to think of this as just going away to school and nothing more," I insisted.

Mama shrugged.

"Long as you're gone from these here streets, you can call it what you want," she said.

Then she started cooking as special a dinner as she could manage for us, her stuffed pork chops. Both Roy and I watched her try to drum up good feelings and happiness at the events that were about to take charge of our lives. We both knew she was battling inside herself, the sadness rushing at her dam of happiness and relief, threatening to sweep over it all and send her into a deep depression. Roy smiled at me when Mama turned on the radio and sang along with the music. For a few moments of time, we were thrown back to happier days, a time in our lives when there was still hope and we were all dreamers. Back then we even permitted Ken to draw up fantasies and listened attentitively to his plans of starting his own business, moving us to the suburbs, buying a new automobile, taking vacations, becoming part of the America we saw every night in television commercials, an America with healthy children and happy-go-lucky families. For us television was a window on a Wonderland, the place where dreams come true.

At dinner Roy talked about where he was going to boot camp and what he hoped to accomplish.

"I want to get into electronics so when I come out I can get a good job," he said. "I hope I get to travel a little too, and see something else beside dumps and slums."

"You just don't volunteer to go into any fighting," Mama warned.

Roy laughed.

"You don't volunteer in the army, Mama. You're *ordered* to volunteer."

He talked about some of his friends who had joined and what they had told him about it. I never saw him talk so much, in fact. I thought he was doing it to keep us from having those long periods of silence when we were left at the mercy of our own bleak thoughts. Music, conversation, good food and the clatter of preparing, eating and cleaning up kept the three of us from talking about all the scary tomorrows that were about to begin. Once in a while, we heard footsteps in the hallways and paused to see if Ken was going to come through the door. Mama had a frying pan she vowed she was going to use to drive him back out.

"Once you two are gone," she said, "he can have this pleasure palace all to himself, for I'll be on the train to Raleigh."

That set Mama talking about Aunt Sylvia and some of her memories from her own youth. For a while it seemed like we would never leave each other. We would stay around the kitchen table until the first light of morning. Suddenly though, Mama sighed deeply and scrubbed her cheeks with her palms.

"I don't know about you two, but I'm thinking about going to sleep. This seemed like a day with forty-eight hours, not twenty-four."

"I'm tired," Roy admitted.

"What's Slim say about your leaving him to join the army?" I asked.

"He's upset, but he told me to come around every time I get leave and work for him. I told him I don't exactly see myself spending leave time back here. Not with Mama down in Raleigh and you just outside of Richmond. At the end of the day, he told me he was happy for me and said he would do the same damn thing if he was young enough. He's been robbed twice this year, you know," Roy told us.

Mama shook her head. She rubbed Roy's head like she used to when he was much younger and then all of a sudden, as if by reflex, he seized her hand and pulled her to him. He held her in his arms tightly. She fought back her tears as hard as she could, but it was a battle she was doomed to lose.

"Get on with you," she muttered and turned away quickly. We watched her go into her bedroom and then we looked at each other, sadness making both our faces long and hollow eyed.

"I'm going to pack some things," I said in a voice only a shade above a whisper.

He nodded and I went to my room. I stood there for a long moment just gazing at everything, at all of Beni's things, at all of our memories. What would I take with me? I had to take something of hers, of course, all our pictures together, some birthday cards we had given to each other and saved for years, her charm bracelet and her favorite ring. Nothing was very valuable. It was all imitation stones and fake gold, but it was hers.

I sat on the floor and went through a carton of memorabilia, laughing at the funny recollections, growing thoughtful at some of the others.

Roy knocked on the door and peered in.

"I want to give you something," he said.

"What?"

"This." He slipped off his tiger-eye ring. He had saved and saved to buy it for himself and was as proud of it as anyone was of any jewel ten times its value.

"Oh no, Roy. I can't take that."

"Sure you can, Rain. It's something I want you to have. Whenever you get lonely, pick it up and twirl it in your fingers and think of me. Come on," he urged, handing it to me, "take it. Please."

I reached up and took it, closing my fingers around it.

"Mama's done the right thing," he said. "I'll be able to sleep nights knowing you're both out of this place."

"We'll be together again, Roy. I know we will," I chanted. It was like a prayer.

"Sure," he said forcing a smile. He started to turn away.

"Wait," I said. "Sit with me a while and help me go through some of these pictures."

He looked at the carton and then at Beni's empty bed.

"I don't think I can do that, Rain. I've got to get some sleep. I promised Slim I'd help him finish some jobs before I took off. I'm leaving for the garage earlier than usual tomorrow morning."

He stared at me a moment and then, as if he was battling invisible steel chains to escape, he turned slowly and left.

After breakfast the next morning, Mama gave me some money. I knew she couldn't afford it, but she insisted I take taxis to and from the department store.

"You aren't going to ride any buses and such with your arms full of new things, Rain. Chances are you'd get robbed or something."

I couldn't help being nervous about meeting my real mother, this time without Mama along. I wasn't sure how we would even talk to each other. I was at the department store just a little before three and found the salesperson whose name was on the card my mother had given me, Autumn Jones. She was a pretty woman in her thirties with highlighted blond hair and green eyes. My mother had called in the morning, so Autumn was prepared for me.

"Oh yes," she said when I appeared, "Mrs. Randolph told me to tell you she would be a little late but we should start. From what she says, you need a complete wardrobe to take to your new school. Let's start from the inside out," she suggested and took me to the lingerie department. She appeared to know exactly how much of everything I should have. An assistant, a young, dark-haired thin man, trailed along and collected whatever was chosen or made notes on a pad.

After pantyhose and socks, I was shown nightgowns, robes and slippers. When I questioned a price, Autumn informed me that I was not to be concerned. Finally, my mother appeared, rushing down the aisle to join us in the skirt and blouse section.

She looked very stylish in her man-tailored black velvet suit. I thought she even looked somewhat sexy with her shirt undone, beaded high-heeled pumps and tousled hair.

"Sorry, I'm late, Rain," she said. "It's been one of those days," she added with a wave of her hand as if I would immediately understand. Every day to me was one of those days. "How far along are we, Autumn?"

Autumn told her what we had already picked out and then my mother directed us toward a leather skirt outfit that had immediately caught her eye.

"She certainly has the figure for it, Mrs. Randolph," Autumn said surveying me from head to foot.

"Yes, yes she does," my mother agreed.

They sent me in to try on the skirt and blouse with a matching jacket. I looked at the tags that dangled from the sleeve and nearly fainted at the price. When I stepped out, they both nodded with satisfaction.

"Alison wanted this suit," my mother muttered, "but she doesn't look good in skirts this short. She has her father's bone structure, unfortunately, wide hips, bony knees."

"Who's Alison?" I asked.

"My daughter," she said and then after a moment added, "your half-sister. She's three years younger than you. You have a half-brother, too, Brody. He's a junior and a shoo-in someday for a football scholarship. They're both good students, but Brody's straight A's, honor society, the whole enchilada, as they say. He takes after Grant and was so bright Grant got him into an accelerated program. After second grade, they advanced him two grades and he went into an accelerated program in high school. He's two years younger than you, but you could never tell. Alison does well, but it's like pulling teeth to get her to work at it. She's too easily satisfied with C's. It drives her father crazy."

I looked at Autumn who was across the aisle putting together a few more outfits, blouses and a pants suit for me.

"Who does she think I am?" I asked, nodding at her.

"Oh. I told her this was an act of charity, don't worry."

"Charity!"

"Keep your voice down," she ordered.

"I'm nobody's charity," I said.

"All right. Let's not make a federal case over it. I had to tell her something," my mother said.

Still, I couldn't help but fume. She avoided my eyes.

"Autumn, please show Rain some coats and a raincoat," my mother said. "She'll need a short leather jacket, too."

"As you wish, Mrs. Randolph. Rain, would you step over here?" Autumn said.

"I'm no charity case," I emphasized. My mother directed her attention to a pair of slacks and pretended not to hear.

After a coat, jacket and a raincoat were chosen for me, I was taken to the shoe department. My mother bought me boots, flats and a pair of high heels to go with my formal outfit.

"How am I going to get all this home?" I asked her.

"It will all be packed for you in luggage I'll buy and placed in the limousine. What point is there in your taking it back to . . . wherever and then having to pack it again?" she asked.

I had intended to show it all to Mama, but neither she nor I had any conception of how much my mother was going to buy for me.

"I can't send you to my mother's house without a decent wardrobe," she continued. "I'd only hear about it."

"So then, you already told her about me?"

"Sort of," she said.

"Sort of? What does that mean?" I asked.

"It means . . . sort of. Why do you have to ask so many questions?" She stared for a moment and then relaxed her shoulders. "All right. My mother's a problem. She can be a terrible pain in the ass, and my sister doesn't help the situation much," she muttered.

"Did you tell her I was going to live with your mother?"

"I just told her I found someone to stay with Mom. She knows we had to do something and she doesn't want to live with her."

"Why not? It's her own mother, isn't it?"

"When you meet Victoria, you'll understand," she said, frowning.

"Don't you like her?"

"Boy, you do ask lots of personal questions, don't you?"

I stared, barely blinking. I wanted to say why shouldn't I? It's my family too, isn't it? I think she heard my thoughts.

"Look, my sister and I don't exactly see eye to eye about things. We're . . . different. We have different needs. Victoria is content being single, being . . . Victoria. She spent a lot of time working with my father, and she was very good at what she did and valuable to him, managing his accounts and overseeing the budgets on his projects. He was a developer. He appreciated her, but she always thought he favored me over her."

"Did he?"

She looked like she wasn't going to answer and then she smiled.

"Yes, as a matter of fact, he did. He was a real ladies' man and he wanted women to look and act like women. Victoria can come off hard, unfeminine. She's more comfortable with a balance sheet than she is with a bed sheet."

She paused and looked around.

"What else? What else?" she muttered. "Oh, let's just take a break. I need a cappuccino. Come on," she commanded and started for the elevator. "I'll call you about all this in a little while, Autumn," she sang as we walked. "Just get it all ready for packing."

"Yes, Mrs. Randolph."

We stepped into the elevator and she pushed the button for the floor that had the coffee shop.

"What about your husband?" I asked as the doors closed.

"What about him?"

"Won't he ask questions about me, about these bills?"

"He doesn't ask questions about my bills. I have my own money."

"But what about my living with your mother? He'll know about that, won't he?"

"Yes," she said with great effort as the doors opened.

"Well?"

She stopped and turned to me with frustration.

"I don't have all the answers just yet. I'm planning on telling him you were recommended by friends of mine who are involved with charities. He'll think it's a nice thing. I'm doing something for Mom and I'm finding a home for a needy young girl at the same time," she concluded.

"Won't he still ask a lot of questions about me, though?"

"He has too much on his mind these days to be distracted by my problems," she said as she continued walking.

"Problems. Is that how you see me?"

"Oh Lord," she said gasping and putting her hand on her forehead. "Look," she said turning back to me. "I know this isn't easy for you, but you've got to think about me, too. I don't know you. I don't know how to talk to you. I don't even know if I'm doing a good thing. Give me a break, will you. Teenagers," she muttered. "As if I didn't have enough at home."

"I can go back to Mama," I threatened.

"Oh sure. No thank you. That's one woman I don't want mad at me," she said.

I couldn't help but smile to myself at that.

"Let's just relax for a few minutes. Please," she pleaded. "My head feels like it's being used as someone's bowling ball."

I followed her to the café where we were seated in a booth.

"What would you like? They have a great ice mocha with whipped cream," she suggested.

"Just coffee," I said.

She shifted the menu and looked at me.

"Just coffee? Well, I feel like a rich cappuccino." She ordered for us and ordered chocolate biscotti, too. Then she sat back and contemplated me. "Tell me about yourself," she said.

"What do you want to know?"

"What are your interests? What do you want to do with your life? Do you have any boyfriends? Is there someone you're going to leave behind?" she catalogued. "Jeeze," she said, sitting forward, "I thought you were smart. Figure it out."

I didn't know whether to be angry or not. There was something I really liked about her. She was rich and elegant and even snobby, but she had an edge, an offbeat way about her that brought smiles to the faces of my most critical thoughts.

"No, I don't have a boyfriend, but I'm leaving Roy behind. Actually, he's going into the army anyway," I said.

"Roy is . . ."

"My brother," I said. I looked down. "Well, not really, I know, but that was how I was raised."

"Are you really a good student?"

"Yes."

"Do you play an instrument? Were you in school plays? A cheerleader?"

"No to everything," I said. "The school I attend isn't exactly conducive to all that."

"Conducive?" She smiled, acting impressed. I had to smile myself.

"I read a lot. That's a big interest. I like music, but not hip-hop."

"Hip-hop?"

"You know, rap."

"Oh." She fixed her gaze on me a little more intently and for the first time, I felt she was looking for something or someone in my face.

"What about my real father?" I asked.

The waitress brought our order. I waited for my mother to respond before sipping my coffee.

"What about him?" she countered.

"I thought you were smart," I served back to her. "Figure it out."

She looked at me without much expression for a moment and then started to laugh.

"I guess we are related. Okay. I don't know where he is or anything about him now. We met when I was in college. I was not exactly the perfect little rich girl then. In fact, there were times I resented my family, my father and mother, their wealth and position. I felt as if I was part of some oppressive power structure and so I hung around with rebels and protestors, poets and singers. To tell you the truth, they were a lot more interesting. One of them was a handsome African-American man who looked like he could be the next Sidney Poitier. We had a hot and heavy passionate romance. I got pregnant and the rest you know."

"What was his name?"

"Why? Are you going to search for him?"

"I'd just like to know. Wouldn't you?" I demanded.

She softened.

"Larry Ward," she said.

"What happened after you became pregnant?"

"Daddy took me out of college and sent me to a Midwestern school. I met Grant while he was in law school and we became engaged and married shortly after I graduated. Daddy helped Grant set up a practice here. He introduced him to influential people, politicians, and Grant built himself a significant firm and reputation. Now he's thinking about getting into politics, maybe someday becoming Attorney General. He's ambitious and he'll probably do what he sets out to do."

"Weren't you ever curious about my father, what happened to him?"

She sighed, dipped her biscotto into the cappuccino and then nodded.

"Yes. I did hear that he had gone to England. He was very creative, a writer, and he wanted to teach. He always talked about immersing himself in the Elizabethan age, Shakespeare, all that," she said.

"And that's all you know?"

"I'm different now, a different person with an entirely new lifestyle. I don't resent my wealth and position anymore. I don't choke on the silver spoon. I have to erase him from my memory, pretend those years never happened."

"Then you must hate the sight of me," I concluded.

She froze for a moment and then shook her head.

"I don't hate you. How can I hate you? I don't even know you. Maybe after a while, I will hate you," she offered.

She kept doing that, unfreezing my face, cracking my ice with her quips.

"I just can't . . . acknowledge you the way you would like me to," she continued on a serious track. "Please try to understand. Believe me. It will make it easier for all of us."

Mainly for you, I wanted to say, but I drank down the words with a sip of coffee.

"Let's get this shopping done," she declared. "I see you don't wear much make-up, not that you need it. You could do something more with your hair, though. Ponytails are coming back into style, you know. You know what else would look nice, a French twist. Your ears aren't pierced, I see. Don't you want that? It will make it so much easier to wear earrings.

"You need some costume jewelry and you don't have a nice watch, I bet. Do you? Doesn't matter," she said before I could respond. "Let's get you one."

I had a hard time not laughing at her. She seemed to enjoy shopping for me. As we paraded through the perfume department and she experimented with colognes and lipsticks and scented lotions, she grew more enthusiastic and energetic, whereas I was beginning to feel exhausted. Finally, she stopped and turned to me, noticing the look on my face.

"I'm sorry," she said. "I didn't mean to do so much at one time, but I never get a chance to do this with Alison. She hates my taste and doesn't enjoy shopping with me. She's at that stage, you know, when it's poison to be seen with your mother."

I couldn't imagine why. Despite myself, it was impossible not to enjoy someone who knew about all the styles and the latest fads buying you things, and buying without any worry about cost, too. Mama and I never had the opportunity to do this sort of thing. We made a single visit to a discount shoe store or the lower end department stores for an item or two from time to time, but to spend an entire afternoon in a department store, talking about clothes and hair and cosmetics was a fantasy come true. Before long, my mother was laughing at me and I couldn't help but smile back at her.

"Well, that's a start," she declared after she had chosen a silk scarf for me and had it placed with everything else.

"A start? I think we bought more today than I've bought in my entire life," I said.

"Let this be my first mother-daughter lesson," she lectured with a small smile on her perfect mouth. "When you buy clothes, it's always just a start. We're made to be pampered and spoiled. That's our destiny ever since Adam picked out a leaf for Eve."

"He didn't pick it out. He just paid for it," I said, "in more ways than one."

She paused and then she broke into a real laugh. I had to laugh too.

She stared at me a moment.

"You laugh like him," she said.

Her face grew serious, pensive, and then she smiled.

"This could work out," she said. "Come on. Let's get you a taxi. I'll have the car come around for you about ten tomorrow morning."

She confirmed the address.

"This is one of those developments, those low-income projects, isn't it?"

"Yes," I said.

"I don't blame your mama for wanting to get you out of there. If I was in her shoes, I'd probably do the same thing or try to. I don't know if I could have pulled it off like she did. She's a tough lady."

"Yes, she is," I said.

"I want to get to know you, Rain. I'll never be the mother she was to you, but I hope we can be friends at least," she said. She looked back at the department store. "This was fun."

"Fun? I thought it was work," I declared and she laughed again. Then, impulsively, surprisingly, she hugged me and quickly got me a cab.

After I got in, I looked back and saw her disappearing down the sidewalk. I took a deep breath. The day had been a whirlwind and it had left me twisted and confused inside. I felt dizzy, twirled about in a kaleidoscope of emotions, attracted to my real mother and repulsed by her almost at the same time. She was so beautiful and confident and alive. I wanted to be like her, yet I hated myself for not wanting to be like Mama. Like some rubber band, I was stretched to the point of breaking, but I already knew that Mama was going to be the first to let go.

Mama wasn't completely sure it would all happen the way she had planned it, however. She was waiting for me when I returned home. She had gone to work as usual, but had come home early.

"Where are your things?" she asked the moment I came through the front door.

"There was just too much, Mama. She decided to have it all packed into luggage and put in the car coming for me tomorrow. You won't believe how much she spent, how much we bought," I said breathlessly.

Mama sat at the table while I catalogued it all from start to finish, barely pausing to tell her about having coffee in the café and discussing my real father. She listened with a half smile on her face, her eyes dark and sad at times, and happy for me at others.

"Good," she said when I finished. "She's doing the right thing. Good."

"I don't think she has the happiest family, Mama," I told her, and described some of what my mother had told me about her daughter Alison and her sister Victoria.

"Every family, rich or poor, has problems, Rain. It's just easier to handle them when you don't have the rest of it to worry your head over like we do. Well," she said rising, "I'll see to supper. Your brother's going to come home with a big appetite. He's put in a long day today. He doesn't want to leave Slim with anything undone. If only his father had half his sense of responsibility, we wouldn't be where we are," she moaned.

I set the table and then went into my room to complete my packing. I wasn't going to take much, I thought, but every time I debated over something, I ended up deciding it belonged with me. Mama worried that I was taking too much.

"You don't want to go and bring a lot of old clothes and things to a new life, honey. Just leave it be. I'll give some of it away. I already have most of Beni's stuff packed to give to the thrift store for charity."

I reconsidered and took out nearly half of what I had packed. In the end I had only one suitcase and a small bag to take with me.

"I wish I had more to give you, honey," Mama told me.

"You gave me more than my real mother could ever give me,

Mama. Money can't buy what you gave me and still give me," I reminded her.

She smiled and hugged me and then we finished preparing dinner and waited for Roy. He came home about a half hour later than usual.

"I worked as fast as I could," he said, "but we got interrupted a lot today with minor repairs."

"Just wash up, son. We've got everything warm and ready," Mama said.

It didn't occur to me until he came out and sat across from me that this might very well be our last dinner together for a very long time, maybe . . . forever. Whatever appetite I had, evaporated. I picked at my food.

"We all have to wipe the sad faces off," Mama declared. "We're all going to do something better, hear. It's going to be all right. No one's saying good-bye forever. Don't make me feel like I'm not doing the right thing," she pleaded.

Roy smiled.

"It's not that, Mama," he said looking about our run-down apartment, "I'm just going to miss the roaches and the noise so much."

Mama laughed and I smiled. It broke the cloud of doom that hovered over us and we talked with more energy and excitement about the things we were planning to do. Then Roy said he had heard something about Ken.

"Charlie over at the Big Top Hamburger said he saw him the other day with Greasy Max and Dudley. He said they looked like they were planning something he called not kosher."

"He'll end up like his brother," Mama predicted, "in some lockup." She shook her head. "Sad to see it happen. You kids can't remember him the way he used to be, maybe, but there was a time when he was full of hope and strength and just bursting with good energy. I suppose that's what attracted me to him the most," she thought, "his beautiful dreams. I couldn't imagine someone with so many good dreams not making at least one come true.

"Be careful about your dreams," she told us. "When they get too big, dump them."

"I don't plan on dreaming much in the army, Mama," Roy said laughing. "I'll be too tired."

"You'll dream," she said. "And you'll make yours come true."

None of us wanted to go to sleep. We were afraid of the dark, of our own thoughts, and especially of the morning. Mornings were always beginnings to me before this. Now, morning was an end.

About an hour or so after I went to bed, I heard my door open and looked up to see Roy standing beside me. He was so quiet, I thought for a minute that I just imagined he was there. Then he knelt and took my hand in his and held it for a long moment.

"Don't fall in love with anyone too fast, Rain," he begged. "One day I'll come strutting into your life again and I'll be different. I'll be older, a man, and you'll think of me as someone else, just like I told you you would."

"I won't fall in love with anyone fast," I promised, "but you promise me that you won't stop yourself from falling in love with someone else, Roy. This is too high a mountain for us to climb and it just might not be meant to be."

"I'll always love you, Rain, and it will always be more than the love a brother has for his sister." He was quiet for a moment and then he looked up through the darkness and added, "Maybe that's why I hate Daddy. He brought you here and he made you my sister. It was wrong and it wasn't natural. He put us in this place."

"We might never have met otherwise, Roy," I pointed out.

"Yeah, maybe. Maybe not. Maybe there is something magical about people who really fall in love. Maybe they can't help it from happening. Just don't forget me," he said. "Twirl that ring from time to time."

He leaned over and kissed me on the cheek. A moment later he was gone. It had happened so fast, I couldn't be sure I hadn't just dreamed it.

In the morning, by the time I rose, washed, dressed and came out, Roy had already left for work.

"He didn't want to say any more good-byes," Mama told me.

"Was he all right?"

"He was fine. Don't worry none about that boy," she said proudly.

She and I ate breakfast, although I couldn't swallow much. We watched the clock and when it drew close to ten, I got my suitcase and bag and she and I went out to the front of the Projects.

It was a cloudy day with rain threatening from the northwest so the wind was stronger. My hair danced around my face. Mama embraced herself. We both gazed at the street, the traffic and the noise. We saw a homeless man crawl out from under a bench and start pushing his grocery cart full of dirty bags down the sidewalk. In the distance a siren wailed.

"You have to feel good about leaving this hell hole," Mama said. I knew she was trying to keep up her determination and keep the tears down. I nodded. "It's a good chance, Rain. You'll make me proud, I'm sure. I only wish I could have done more for Beni."

"I know, Mama, but don't blame yourself for that."

"And don't you blame yourself. You had nothing but love for your sister. You hear me, Rain? Don't carry away any more baggage in your heart, honey. Don't let anything stop you from becoming something."

"Okay, Mama. When are you going to Aunt Sylvia's?"

"In two days," she said.

"You're really going, right?"

"Of course I'm going. You've got the address. You write and I'll write back," she promised.

Suddenly, like a black shark, cruising in the sea of traffic, the limousine emerged. It was such a rare sight in this neighborhood, there was no doubt in our minds who it was for. It pulled up in front of us and the driver got out quickly.

"Rain?" he asked. He was a man about fifty with thin, graying hair and friendly blue eyes.

"Yes," I said.

"Let me take that for you," he said reaching for my suitcase and bag.

Mama came around to the trunk of the limousine and saw all that had been bought for me the day before. She gasped for joy, the tears rolling down her cheeks.

"Just look at all that. You're going away like some princess," she said.

"I don't feel like a princess, Mama."

"That'll change," she predicted. "Okay, don't keep the man waiting here. Get along with you. It looks like it might rain any moment."

"Mama . . ."

"It's going to be fine, honey. It's going to be real fine. I'm giving you back, but I'm not giving you away, darling. No sir, no ma'am," she recited.

I hugged her tightly, so tightly I know she thought I would never let go.

"Go on," she whispered, her voice raspy. "Get what's coming to you, child. Go ahead."

I pulled back. Her face was locked with all the determination her little body could muster. It was cruel to linger.

Into the limousine I went and the driver closed my door. Mama stood on the sidewalk, smiling through her tears. I pressed my face to the window and then we started away. She held up her hand, watched me for a moment and turned to go back into the building.

As we rounded the corner, I looked to my left and I was sure I saw Roy standing there just behind a car, his face soon lost in the darkness that dropped from the thundering clouds rolling in.

Seconds later, the neighborhood and the only life I had ever known was behind me and I was on my way.

# 10

## No Turning Back

Once when I was in the fourth grade we had a terrible fire drill at school. The principal had bawled out the student body just a week before because we took too long to evacuate our classrooms and the building and there was a great deal of talking.

"This time it was just a drill," he warned, "but next time it could be for real and if you take as long as you did this time and make as much noise, some of you will surely die."

I didn't think he wanted to put panic in our hearts so much as he wanted us to take it all more seriously. Nevertheless, when the alarm rang the next week, there was an air of frenzy. Someone swore she smelled smoke. The next thing I knew, we were all rushing out and our class ran smack into another class in the hall. There were two classes already crowding behind them. The orderly way we were supposed to exit broke down when another student cried, "It's a real fire!"

The kids around me screamed. My heart felt like it had melted in my chest. Someone pushed someone else and then all of the classes began to run toward the exit despite the protests of our teachers. I was numbed. Panic had put glue on the bottoms of my sneakers so I didn't move fast enough. However, the momentum was behind and around me as waves and waves of swinging arms and legs rushed by. Bodies pushed on mine and I found myself being carried along, moving fast whether I wanted to or not. We burst out of the building like drowning people gasping for air. I have never forgotten my sense of helplessness, my inability to oppose the power that was sweeping me along.

It was just how I felt in the limousine as the world I had known fell away behind me. Once again, I was being carried along, swept away, rushed over highways, unable to stop. In a real sense, I thought, I was escaping a burning building, a fire. At least that was what Mama truly believed. I saw the relief in her eyes when the door of the limousine was closed and I was sealed in this plush vehicle that moved with the glitter and sharpness of a needle through the shroud that had once covered me in this city.

The driver said little to me during the trip. About an hour after we were on the road, he asked if I wanted to hear any music. He explained that there was a radio above me on the ceiling of the limousine. I wasn't in the mood for music so I just thanked him, and I didn't push any buttons or turn any knobs. He glanced back at me once and then ignored me until we were closing in on what would become my new home. He muttered, "Not much longer now."

Instead of bringing relief, his words sent a finger of ice sliding down my chest, between my breasts and over my ribs. I tightened my arms around myself and sat frozen in the corner of the limousine gazing out the window. When the driver had left the main highway and we were moving through the countryside, I began to see the large estates with beautiful grounds. It was hard to believe that a single family owned so much. The houses looked larger than embassies. Everything was clean and spankingly new, the hedges and flowers brilliantly dressed in their greens and reds and yellows. The water gushing from magnificent fountains sparkled like liquid diamonds in the late morning sun. Uniformed gardeners and grounds people manicured the landscaping. They resembled an army out to conquer ugliness. The opulence was so great it frightened me. Anyone could take one look at me in this setting and know I was an immigrant from poverty, fleeing the dirt and the crime. They'd wonder how I ever got here.

Fear actually made my teeth chatter along with the electric chills in my bones. This was a horrible mistake, I kept thinking. I should go back and I should return all the beautiful things my real mother had bought for me. I was too awkward, too unrefined. I would be a total embarrassment to my real grandmother and she would send me packing almost minutes after I had arrived.

Convinced of the impending disaster and full of dread, I found it hard to breathe when the driver finally announced, "We're here!"

He turned up a long circular driveway toward another one of those large houses I had seen along our route. This mansion was two stories with four large, tall columns holding up a front-gabled roof that made the house look like a Greek temple. This impression was reinforced by the stone steps running the width of the entry porch.

The lawn and gardens seemed to go on forever to the right and to the left. I saw a three-car garage on the left with what looked like a vintage Rolls Royce parked in front. Someone had just washed it. The hose and the pail of soapy water were still beside it.

The driver got out and then opened my door.

"This is it," he said with a small smile.

I stepped out slowly and looked up at the house. There was a breeze, but nothing moved, not even the leaves on the small trees or hedges. Everything was so still, I felt as if I was about to enter a painting. Suddenly, a cloud slipped over the sun and a dark shadow washed across the front of the mansion. On the second floor, a curtain moved, but I saw no face. The driver began to unload my luggage.

"You can go on inside," he said. "I'll bring everything."

I had half expected the front door to open and my grandmother to step out, anxious to greet me, but there wasn't any sign of life. Even the birds that flitted from tree branches to fountains and benches seemed to keep their distance, eying that front door nervously.

I started up the steps. The stone looked pristine beneath my feet. I imagined the steps were swept and washed as vigorously as the very floors inside. I found no doorbell button, just a brass knocker in the shape of a ball hammer with a brass plate beneath. I let it fall once and then, thinking it wasn't loud enough of a knock, did it again, holding it back and pushing it down so that it sounded louder.

Moments later the grand door opened and I was facing a maid who looked no more than twenty, if that. She had short blond hair trimmed with precision to the length of her ear lobes. It was brushed straight and sat over her temples and forehead like thin wires, devoid of softness, dry, almost painted on. Her eyes were a dull brown set back too far from the bridge of her nose. She squinted as the cloud moved off the sun and some light was reflected off the cold white stone floor of the portico. I didn't imagine she was outside much. She had a pale complexion with a prominent birthmark on her narrow forehead.

Her apron was knee length over a dark blue skirt and her blouse was buttoned tightly at her neck. She was small busted, but somewhat wide in the hips. Sad and dumpy, she looked like someone destined to go unnoticed, to be forever a menial servant. The reality of her situation had planted a dark depression in her eyes. I imagined a smile was as rare as a diamond in her life. She glanced at me and then shifted her body to look at the limousine and driver.

"You're Rain?" she asked. She seemed surprised. What had she been told? I wondered.

"Yes."

She grimaced as a look of annoyance and disgust washed through her face.

"This way," she said and turned her back on me quickly.

I hesitated. This was my greeting? I glanced at the driver who was starting toward the steps and then I stepped into the large, long entryway with creamy marble floors. To my right was a tall, wide mirror in a rich oak frame. It nearly reached the ceiling. On my left was a matching oak antique table with what looked like a pewter vase now full of jonquils.

The maid continued toward the stairway and then paused to say, "I don't have all day."

I hurried along, gazing at the paintings on the walls, glimpsing the richly furnished sitting room to my left and the large dining room down on my right. I just managed to catch sight of the table that looked like it went on into the next state.

The maid started up the thickly carpeted steps. Along them ran the dark gray marble balustrade and above us was a huge crystal chandelier. I was taking in everything so quickly and with such big visual gulps that I stumbled on a step and nearly fell flat on my face.

"Watch your step," the maid said in a mechanical voice. She sounded as if she was programmed to say it. There wasn't the slightest sense of real concern for my welfare. I straightened up quickly and hurried to catch up, but she didn't wait for me when she reached the landing of the second floor. She acted like she wanted to get all this over with as quickly as possible.

The hallway was wide and also furnished with antique chairs and tables, beautiful vases, a bronze statue of a cherub, and oil paintings on every available wall space. Most of the pictures were of colonial scenes, some simply of men and women who had that aristocratic, superior glare as if they were looking down upon the artist who painted them. I felt as if I was walking through a museum.

The maid stopped in a doorway.

"This is your room," she declared and stepped back. I turned and gazed in at a room the size of our apartment back in D.C. There were two windows facing the east and two facing the south. The bed was a large canopy with thick carved posts and a pink and white spread bordered in lace. Everything in the room looked brand new, from the light pink, marshmallow carpet to the vanity table and mirror, the curtains on the windows and the desk on the right. I saw there was a walk-in closet on the left and just past that a bathroom.

My own bathroom!

The look on my face finally brought a reaction from the maid. She nearly smiled, gazed at the room herself and then turned to me.

"This used to be Miss Megan's room," she said. "Mrs. Hudson told me. So take good care, y'hear?"

My mother's room. How appropriate, I thought. The driver came up behind us.

"Where is Mrs. Hudson?" I asked.

"She's not up to meeting anyone yet," the maid said. "She told me to get you settled in your room and get you some lunch. I got some chicken salad prepared. If you want anything else, you'll have to wait."

"Chicken salad is fine," I said. "Thank you. Is she sick?" I asked.

She stared at me for a moment.

"I don't talk about people. I just do my job," she remarked with a twist in her lips. "You got everything you need in the bathroom," she added. "When you're ready, come down to the dining room and I'll serve lunch."

"Excuse me," I said as she started away.

She turned, her eyelids fluttering with confusion.

"Yes?"

"What's your name?"

"I'm Merilyn," she said.

"You're the cook and the maid?" I followed.

She did smile this time, but it wasn't a warm grimace. It was more like I had asked a stupid question.

"There's only me and Mrs. Hudson," she said, "and now you. I don't think we need anyone else unless you're going to be a lot of trouble," she added dryly as she turned away.

If you're an unhappy person yourself, I thought, you can't help but make everyone around you feel unhappy, too. If I had any room left in my suitcase of sympathy, I'd pack some pity in it for her as well as myself, I thought, but right now, I couldn't fit in another tear.

The driver placed my luggage on the floor and left to get the rest of my things. I watched him and Merilyn descend the stairs and then I entered my room, took a deep breath, and swallowed down my anxieties like a child forced to eat something horrible, but told it would do her a world of good.

After all my things had been brought up, I unpacked my clothing and put everything away in the dresser and in the walk-in. Even with all my mother had bought for me, my wardrobe looked pathetic, barely taking up a tenth of the space available. It would take a fortune to stock this place, I thought.

The mattress of my bed was firm, but my pillows were gigantic and as fluffy as clouds. I ran my palms over the soft comforter. Everything smelled new and fresh. Had it all just been bought for me or had it been here forever and ever?

I looked in the bathroom and found the hair dryer, the make-up mirror, the large pink tub and stall shower, everything scrubbed spotlessly. The towels even looked brand new. I realized I had an electric toothbrush and when I opened the cabinet, I saw it had been stocked with everything from Band-Aids to shampoo and conditioner.

It was the same at the vanity table. There were new brushes and combs, scissors and tweezers, creams and perfume. When I smelled an open bottle, I recognized the scent as the one my mother had been wearing. It couldn't have been left here from when she lived here. Either she or my grandmother had bought it, but how did either of them know whether or not I would like it? Perfume is so personal, I thought.

I went to the window and gazed out at the grounds. Not far off I saw a large pond. It looked like it had a dock and two rowboats tied there. From this height and distance, the water resembled a sheet of clear thin ice, so still, glittering in the sun. What a beautiful place this is, I thought. How I wished Mama could see it. Maybe someday she would.

I suddenly realized I was very hungry and hurried out, pausing before I started down the stairs. I had the strange feeling I was being watched, but when I turned and looked at the doors to the other rooms, I saw they were all shut tight. I listened for a moment and then bounced down the steps. Merilyn must have been waiting for me because the moment I rounded the stairway, I heard her say, "Finally."

I saw her disappear through a door. I felt funny and awkward just sauntering in and sitting down at the long, polished wood table by myself. A setting had been placed for me on the other end. I walked to it slowly, gazing at the large mural on the wall. It depicted a country setting with a brook and hills, animals and small cottages. There was something about it that made it seem like a faraway place. I continued to stare at it after I sat.

Merilyn came through the doorway from the kitchen carrying a silver tray upon which she had a platter of chicken salad, crackers, and small dinner rolls. She placed the tray on a server and then brought the dishes to the table.

"What would you like to drink?"

"Just water is fine," I said nodding at the pitcher already set before me.

After she set the food down, she poured a glass of water for me. Then she took a step back and waited as if she wanted to see whether or not I liked the chicken salad. I glanced at her and tasted it.

"This is very good," I said.

She didn't smile. She just turned and started back to the kitchen.

"Excuse me," I said before she left the dining room.

She turned.

"Yes?"

"What is this picture?" I asked nodding at the mural.

"It's a place in England where Mr. Hudson's family lived is what I was told. Don't ask me where. I wasn't told exactly, and I wouldn't know anyway. I've never been to England," she said and left before I could ask anything else.

After I ate, I walked through the house. There was a very formal living room with furniture that looked like it had rarely been used. All the tables were polished to the point where I could see my face reflected in the wood. There were paintings everywhere, all the same style and period and all rather dark, I thought. Whenever the sun was blocked by a cloud, the rooms took on a melancholy gloom since there were no lamps lit and the furniture was all dark wood. Everything looked impersonal to me.

Finally, when I gazed around the office, I saw some evidence of family. There were pictures on the large oak desk. I recognized my mother and imagined that the other young woman was her infamous sister Victoria. There didn't seem to be much resemblance between them. Victoria's hair was light brown and in all the pictures cut very short. Her facial features were harsh, her nose wide, her mouth masculine. She looked to be at least four inches taller than my mother. There were only a half dozen pictures of the two of them, but in all of them, Victoria's figure was lean, almost boyish, and in all of them she barely smiled. Her eyes were deep, her expressions firm and far more serious than my mother's.

In many of the pictures there was a handsome gentleman I imagined to be my real grandfather. His jaw was nearly square and his eyes were set deeply under his wide forehead. In the pictures that included him, I could see the way he hinged the right corner of his mouth in a sort of flirtatious smile. There was only one picture of the woman who had to be my grandmother. It must have been taken when she was in her late twenties or thirties. I saw the remarkable resemblances to my mother, only she looked stronger, her eyes so focused and firm, I imagined her to be a woman with steel in her bones. In the picture her hair was in a tight chignon and she wore a beautiful diamond necklace. This was a woman who could advertise for the concept of style and elegance, I thought. What would she think of me?

The shelves of the office were filled with the classics, many bound in leather. In the far right corner there was a table with what looked like a model of a housing development, including the landscaping and streets, as well as the streetlights. It even had tiny cars and human figures placed in driveways and walkways. At the base of the model was a metal tag with the words HUDSON ACRES carved across it. Each of the houses was different in style and architecture.

"Don't touch that!" I heard Merilyn warn from the doorway. "Mrs. Hudson don't want nobody even in here. I should have told you. She barely lets me in here to clean it. You can go anyplace else," she said.

"Oh. I didn't touch it. What is it?"

"It was Mr. Hudson's dream is all I know. Better come out of here," she added, looking terrified herself. "She'll be angry if she finds out I didn't tell you not to go in here."

"Okay," I said and left the office.

"How long have you worked for Mrs. Hudson?" I asked her.

"Just three weeks. I'd like to try to keep the job," she added, "so I'm trying not to make any mistakes or let anyone get me in trouble."

"I'm sorry," I said seeing how serious she was. "I didn't mean to get you into trouble."

She tucked in her lips.

"Why don't you go outside," she said, "it's nice outside and you'll be out of my way."

"Is Mrs. Hudson coming out at all?" I asked sharply.

"She will probably come down for dinner. She thought you could find enough to amuse yourself until then," Merilyn added, sounding like she was parroting my grandmother.

"I'll try," I said petulantly and walked out of the house. She knows I'm her real granddaughter, I thought, but she's not breaking her neck to meet me. I guess I know where I stand in her eyes, I concluded, and stood fuming for a few moments on the front steps.

The sound of a car trunk being closed hard drew my attention to the garage where I saw a tall, lean, balding man wiping his long hands with a rag. He wore a dark blue shirt and dark blue pants and smiled at me.

"Hello there," he said. He folded the rag as neatly as he would an expensive towel.

I walked down the stone steps toward him. The sun was behind him, making it seem as if he had a halo around his head. Actually, the bald spot glittered. When I drew closer, I saw his eyebrows made up for his loss of hair. They were bushy and thick over his dark brown eyes. He had a narrow face with a slightly cleft chin and a nose that was just a little too long and too thin, but his smile was warm, friendly. He looked amused as I approached.

"Hi," I said.

"You're the new roommate, huh?" he said with a laugh in his voice.

"Excuse me?"

He laughed.

"I heard from Mrs. Hudson that a young lady was coming to live with her. I'm Jake Marvin," he said extending his right hand. It felt silly putting my tiny hand into his because it disappeared and looked like he was shaking my wrist. "I take care of her car and drive her places whenever she wants to go anywhere, which isn't often these days."

He leaned toward me and winked.

"It's an easy job. Actually," he said straightening, "I'm only part-time. What's your name?"

"Rain Arnold," I said. He nodded with that same small smile as if he had expected it.

"You meet her yet?" he asked nodding toward the house.

"No."

He laughed.

"She doesn't do anything until she's ready and willing," he said. "Don't take offense. She's not treating you any differently from the way she treats every other human being."

"You don't sound like you like her much," I said.

"Oh, on the contrary. I like her a great deal. She's an extraordinary woman. Few left like her. She was liberated before women's lib was a gleam in what's her name's eye," he said.

"Gloria Steinem?"

"Something like that. So, you make yourself at home?"

I nodded.

"It's so big," I said.

"That it is." He turned to look out at the property. "My father owned all this once."

"Your father? But—"

"Oh, he lost it all in the market crash and Mr. Hudson came along and bought it up. That was years and years ago. Here I am, back again," he said.

"Were you always Mrs. Hudson's driver?"

"Oh no. I was in the navy for nearly twenty-two years. I've seen the world," he declared, "made a full circle. I worked in radio and advertising for a while and then drove for one of the big hotels. That's when Mrs. Hudson came along and asked why don't I come by and drive her around and take care of her car. Her husband was gone and she hated even the thought of driving. I was ready to become semiretired, so I took her up on it and here I am. Full circle," he said and gazed toward the pond.

He was silent for a moment and then smiled at me.

"You'll like it here. It takes you over, romances you. Wait until you see the sun go down over those trees in the west and the ducks come back and camp out on the pond. You're a city girl, I hear?"

"Yes, from Washington, D.C."

He nodded.

"Well, the nights are considerably quieter here. You made a wise choice," he added. He opened the car door. I wanted to say I didn't make a choice; it was made for me, but I let the words crumble on my tongue. He got into the Rolls and drove it into the garage. Then he pulled down the door.

"My Rolls is just over here," he said indicating the side of the garage. I followed him as he walked around to a late model Ford.

"You don't live here, too?" I asked.

"Oh no. I come when she needs me to. I live in Jessup's Gap, hardly much of a town about ten miles southwest. Mrs. Brown's rooming house. Been there about seven years now," he said squeezing his chin between his thumb and forefinger. He smiled at me and got into his vehicle. I watched him start the engine and roll down the window. "She tells me I'll be driving you over to the Dogwood School for girls and back," he said, "so we'll have plenty of time to get to know each other, unless you're the type who doesn't like to talk early in the morning.

"Me?" he said shifting into drive, "I never shut up, morning, noon or night. At least, that's what she's always saying," he added nodding toward the house again. "Welcome." He saluted and started away.

I watched him coast down the driveway. He was funny, I thought, and made me feel a little welcome at least.

I walked on with my head down toward the pond. The birds seemed to get louder around me and flit along as if I was of great curiosity to them. In the distance clouds thickened and rolled toward the west, chasing the sun. Two large black crows came off the lake toward me and then veered sharply to my left and into the trees. The breeze picked up. I felt my hair dancing over my forehead. The air did seem cleaner, fresher here and the songbirds replaced the sounds of traffic, horns and squealing brakes. I could smell the perfume of wildflowers and plucked a blade of tall grass to hold between my teeth.

Jake was right, I thought. The land romances you, but would I be comfortable here? Could I be so alone and be happy? Beni would hate it here, I thought with a smile. She'd complain about the distance to hip-hop joints and how boring it was to just walk and look at nature. She'd hate the quiet and moan about the absence of boys.

But Roy would probably like it here. He hated the city and he was alone so much of the time that the solitude wouldn't make his nerve ends twitch the way it would make Beni's.

I stood on the dock and looked out over the water. The strong breeze made it lap against the shore. The rowboats knocked gently against the side of the dock. One had a little water in it, but the other was bone dry. There were no oars. I wondered if my grandmother would ever let me go in one. Beni might like this, I thought. Roy would love it.

"Hey!" I heard and turned to see Merilyn standing on the lawn gesturing.

"What?"

"You have a phone call," she cried. She gestured emphatically.

"A phone call?" I hurried back toward the house. Who was calling me? Mama? Roy?

I broke into a trot. Merilyn went into the house but was in the hallway when I entered.

"The phone's in there," she said pointing to the less formal living room.

I hurried in and picked up the receiver.

"Mama?"

"No, it's only me," my real mother said. "How are you doing? Has my mother said anything nasty yet?"

"Oh. No. I haven't met her yet. She's in her room, I think."

"Figures she'd pull one of those. All right, listen, don't argue with her. Don't talk back. Don't challenge anything she says or tells you to do. You don't have to fall in love with her. Just live there, follow her rules and you'll be fine."

"When am I going to see you?" I asked.

"I can't come there for a few days yet. Just . . . make the best of things, okay? I have to go. I just wanted to be sure you arrived all right."

"I've arrived all right," I said dryly.

"That's half the battle," she replied. "I'll call you soon."

She hung up without saying good-bye. I plopped on the leather chair beside the phone and sat staring at the brass figurine of an eagle. It looked like it was glaring back at me angrily.

"Don't ask," I muttered. "I don't know why I'm here either."

"Really?" I heard someone say sharply and turned to see my grandmother standing in the doorway. Immediately, I jumped to my feet and we confronted each other.

She was taller than I expected and still very stately with posture as perfect as could be. Her Confederate gray hair was cut and styled to frame her face, the prominent feature of which was her tight, strong jaw line. I saw my mother's eyes and nose, but my grandmother's mouth was fuller.

The wrinkles at the corners of her eyes were deep, perhaps because of the way she squinted at me. Other than those, there weren't many lines in her face. She didn't appear to be wearing much make-up, if any.

She wore a turquoise velvet robe with a gold fringe on the collar and the sleeves. The robe reached her ankles. Her feet were in velvet slippers that matched her robe.

"I am absolutely positive you know why you are here," she continued. "Sit," she ordered and waved at the chair I had been sitting in. I did so quickly.

She crossed to the leather sofa and pulled her robe tightly around her as she sat. She leaned back, resting her right arm on the arm of the sofa and stared at me. I saw the way her eyes shifted, studying my face, pausing, softening and then hardening again as she drew her shoulders up.

"Megan tells me you're a good student. I hope that's not another one of her exaggerations. She's prone to do that . . . she has exaggerationitis," she remarked.

"What? I never heard of such a thing."

"Nevertheless, she has it. Well?"

"Well what?"

"Are you a good student?"

"Yes. I've been on the honor roll ever since the seventh grade."

"And what happened before that?"

"There wasn't any honor roll," I said dryly.

She stared, her lips relaxing in the corners for a moment and then stiffening.

"You understand that I am not in favor of your living here. I've never mollycoddled Megan or made excuses for her behavior. When she was pregnant and showing, I had her sent away. She had none of her family with her when you were born and my husband handled the arrangements," she said sternly.

"Do you want me to leave?" I countered.

"Don't be stupid," she commanded. "I said I wasn't in favor of your living here, but I didn't say you couldn't do so. Under the right conditions, of course," she added quickly.

"Which are?"

"One, we don't admit to anyone who you really are. At this stage of your history, it would be an insufferable embarrassment. I am known for my philanthropic works. I serve on the boards of various charitable and nonprofit organizations. It will not be considered unusual for me to take in someone such as yourself under the guise of doing something for the downtrodden," she proposed. Her voice was deeper and thicker than my mother's and she cracked a whip on her consonants and vowels like someone practicing for speech class.

"You are to always address me as Mrs. Hudson and when Megan comes here, which will be rarely, I expect, you address her as Mrs. Randolph. Is that understood?"

"Yes," I said, my eyes beginning to burn with the tears that filled underneath my lids. How would she like to feel as if no one wanted to claim her?

"Good."

"You said one so there must be a two," I said after swallowing back my pain. I didn't disguise the fury in my voice. She looked amused rather than upset, however.

"Oh there's a two and a three. Two . . . I understand from where you come and how you've lived. You're to leave all that outside the door. No smoking, no messing up the house, no leaving clothing strewn about your room like teenagers are so prone to do these days. I don't want the phone ringing off the hook with calls from new boys you've met and you are not to invite anyone here without my permission first. And definitely no loud music!"

She paused as if trying to remember something she had memorized and then continued.

"I want you to maintain a clean and presentable appearance at all times. I often have important visitors and now that you are here, you will represent me as well.

"I hope you will always maintain decent standards of language and the moment I see evidence of drugs or drinking, you'll be asked to leave. Am I clear?"

"My family is poor and we lived in the ghetto, but I know right from wrong," I shot back. "Mama didn't tolerate bad language. We didn't have much, but we were always clean and I never as much as touched any drugs."

"Good," she said. "Let's hope all that's true."

"It's true," I said firmly. "I don't lie like some people."

She gazed at me, her lips relaxing for a moment and her eyes filling with an amused twinkle. Then she returned to her stiff and formal posture.

"I have already made the necessary arrangements for you to attend Dogwood. My driver will take you to and from the school. I expect you to be on your best behavior there as well as here. Whatever you do there will again reflect on me. It happens to be one of the most prestigious private schools in the Southeast. Elizabeth Whitney, a descendant of Eli Whitney, the man who invented the cotton gin, is the headmistress and a dear friend of mine."

She sat forward, her eyes fixed on me more intently.

"It's been a long time since I've had anyone as young as you under my roof. My grandchildren, Megan's other offspring, don't come around that often."

I wanted to say maybe they don't feel welcome, but I kept my lips pasted.

"Teenagers are almost another species these days," she quipped. Then she rose. "We dress for dinner. I understand your mother has bought you the beginnings of a decent wardrobe?"

"I suppose," I said. "I don't spend money I don't have on fashion magazines."

She formed a wry smile.

"I'm sure she spent a lot of money and bought you the most up-to-date styles. Megan never worried much about spending. She was spoiled and she spoils her children."

"Why did you spoil her if you think it's so wrong?" I asked.

"I didn't. Her father did. Anyway, it's too late for regrets. I don't wallow in the past. If you have grit, you step over your hardships."

Yes, I thought, if you have grit and money, lots of money, you can step over them.

"I hope you will have a similar attitude. Dinner is at six-thirty tonight," she added and started out. She paused in the doorway and looked back at me. "The things you have to do for your children," she muttered, shaking her head.

Wonderful, I thought. I just love feeling like someone's burden. I was tempted to just run out of the house, leaving all the new things behind. Maybe that's what she hoped I would do. Then she would be comfortable with her beliefs. She could go on and say I was just what she had expected and I behaved just the way she had predicted.

She was my grandmother and she did have steel flowing through her veins, but her blood had been passed on to me whether she liked it or not, I thought.

I'm not running.

I'm here, Grandmother. I can't call you that, but soon enough, yes, soon enough, you'll know I'm your granddaughter, and all the lies and phony smiles in the world won't change that one iota.

I turned and looked back at the eagle.

"I was wrong," I admitted. "I do know why I'm here. I'm here to teach that rich, important woman what family means."

The eagle looked impressed.

# 11

# The Ties That Bind

As I sifted through my small but expensive wardrobe, I felt like a frenzied moth madly circling the flame of a candle. Which was the correct dress or outfit to wear to dinner? What did my grandmother mean by "We dress for dinner?" I wanted to make the right choice just to prove that my background and upbringing didn't mean I had no style and no taste. Like the moth, I started toward what attracted me and then I pulled back as if I thought I might burn my fingers, sifted through the garments, and started to choose something else, only to hesitate. If I dressed too formally, would my grandmother laugh, call me ridiculous? If I put on this beautiful blouse and skirt, would she turn up the corners of her mouth and snap, "Didn't I tell you we dress for dinner?"

Why, I paused to ask myself, was pleasing her suddenly so vital? She hadn't thought I was important enough to greet me as soon as I arrived, and she certainly didn't do much to make me feel welcome when we finally did meet. Usually, I despised someone as conceited and as condescending as she appeared to be. What would I gain by pleasing or impressing her? Could I ever do either to her satisfaction anyway? I was her daughter's mistake, a living example of the burden children lay upon their parents. She practically told me so to my face.

I stood back from the clothing, my arms folded under my breasts, fuming for a moment, and then, impulsively, with as much of a devil may care attitude as I could muster, I stabbed out and plucked the leather skirt and leather vest outfit. I chose it because I liked the way it looked on me and not because it would be what my grandmother would choose. It was something my mother had muttered when we were snaking our way through aisles and displays of garments in the department store: "If you please yourself first, you'll be happy and your happiness will make others feel good about you."

At first I thought that was a very selfish attitude, but after I thought about it awhile, I realized it made some sense. Whenever you were unhappy about yourself, you weren't good company, right? Look at Merilyn, for example. She was so sour on herself that she curdled everything around her.

I put on the cream silk blouse my mother had chosen to go with the leather outfit, found the matching shoes, and then concentrated on my hair, making sure it was primped and neat. When I gazed at myself in the mirror just before leaving my room to go down to dinner, I felt my heart thump in loud, quick beats. I looked fine, I told myself. I looked better than ever. She has to be impressed.

Merilyn had set the table with what looked like the most expensive china in the world. I was afraid to touch the paper thin crystal goblet for fear it would shatter if I pressed my fingers around it too hard. The plates had gold trim and pink roses at the center. The silverware was so heavy, I thought my trembling fingers might drop a fork or a spoon on a dish and shatter it, and there were so many forks, even one with another spoon at the top of the plate. What were they all for?

My setting was placed where I had sat to have my lunch and my grandmother's was at the head of the table. She wasn't there when I arrived, and I had arrived on time.

"What are we having, Merilyn?" I asked when she came out of the kitchen with a pitcher of ice water. I was too nervous to just sit quietly and watch her work.

"It's Tuesday. Mrs. Hudson has fish on Tuesdays. Poached salmon," she added with a tone of voice that added "whether you like it or not."

The tick of the dark hickory grandfather clock in the corner of the dining room seemed louder than before, especially while I was sitting there alone, waiting. I stared at the mural, wishing myself in that scene. It looked so peaceful, friendly and, unlike my present circumstances, so uncomplicated. Finally, I heard footsteps in the hall and then my grandmother entered the dining room.

Once, when I was very young and walking with Roy, we saw many rich and elegantly dressed people arriving at what looked like a major social event in Washington, D.C. It was at one of the finer restaurants. Limousines stopped to empty their affluent passengers in front and out stepped lavishly adorned women, their hair styled and glittering with jeweled hairpieces, their necks roped in diamonds, their bodies encased in furs and black cashmere fur-trimmed capes, and their gentlemen all in tuxedos. They glowed under the lights and I had to stop and drink in all the glamour and wealth. They looked like royalty to me. I imagined them coming from some magical kingdom where skin blemishes were forbidden, where everyone was born with perfect features, where laughter was musical and smiles fell like rain upon their blessed faces.

"Who are they, Roy?" I had asked my brother in a loud whisper.

"Them," he replied, not without a little bitterness in his voice.

"Who's them?"

"Them's them," he told me looking back as we continued on. "There's us and there's them. That's them."

It made no sense to me, of course. I wasn't very class conscious at nine years old, and it wasn't something that haunted me as much as it haunted Ken, Beni and Roy. Mama seemed aware of it, but resigned to the division of the world, and I tried to be more like her. What good did it do to walk about with green eyes and a stomach churning up unhappiness?

However, when my grandmother entered the dining room, her diamond necklace so prominent, her matching earrings sparkling under the light of the chandelier, her beautiful, black velvet dress making her look even more stately, I had to catch my breath and remind my heart to beat. She was definitely one of *them,* which reinforced the fact that I was not.

She did seem like royalty. She moved like a queen, head high, posture regal, pausing before she had come halfway to her chair.

"It's proper for young people to stand when their elders enter the room," she said through her nearly clenched teeth. "Especially in the dining room."

I rose quickly. She looked me over intently; checking my hair, my make-up, and of course, my clothing. Once again, I saw that tiny gleam of warmth in her eyes before they turned indifferent.

"Who chose that outfit for you? Your mother or you?" she demanded.

"We both did, I suppose," I replied.

She shook her head and continued to her seat.

"Megan has such a difficult time being the wife of a conservative man. The little rebel in her like some persistent ember won't go out. Are young people back to wearing skirts that short?"

"It was what the store featured," I told her.

She sat and nodded at me and I sat.

"You look like you do take care of yourself and know how to wear your hair," she admitted with a little surprise echoing behind her words.

Merilyn hurried in to pour her a glass of water and then filled my glass as well. Then she rushed out with a look of abject terror on her face. Despite her coolness to me, I couldn't help but feel sorry for her and wished that I could just get up and help serve the dinner. I would have been glad to prepare the salad or something instead of waiting around for the sacred dinner bell to ring or my grandmother to make her grand entrance.

"Why shouldn't I know how to take care of myself?" I asked self-defensively. I couldn't help but sound like Beni with a chip on my shoulder. Some people just made it appear, people like my rich and conceited grandmother.

She didn't answer. Instead, she unfolded her napkin carefully and placed it on her lap. Then she gazed at me. I quickly did the same with my napkin.

"From time to time," she said, "you will be present at the dinner table when I have important guests. Of course, they will know you come from unfortunate circumstances, but they will nevertheless expect a show of proper etiquette simply because they will know you are under my roof and I would demand nothing less. I expect you to look presentable, even at breakfast."

"I'll always be presentable, but I'm not going to be a phony," I said.

She laughed coldly, shaking her head. Then she sighed, lifting and dropping her shoulders as if they were of great weight.

"What is that saying, 'The more things change, the more they stay the same?' Megan used to tell me something similar." The smile evaporated and she leaned forward. "Mealtime manners have nothing to do with being a phony. Good manners are part of what makes the experience pleasurable, for others as well as for you. Sprawling posture, elbows akimbo, or talking with a mouth full of food are simply unacceptable. It's simply a matter of courtesy toward other people at the table.

"Besides," she continued, "tomorrow you will register in a prestigious school. You will eat in their cafeteria with young people who come from the finest homes and backgrounds. You wouldn't want to look foolish, would you? Unless, of course," she added with a tiny smile on her lips, "being foolish is who you really are."

"I'm not foolish," I insisted.

"Good. You have good posture. That's a start," she said. "To this day, Megan slumps. Sometimes I think she does it deliberately just to be defiant."

I didn't remember my mother slumping at the French restaurant in Georgetown, but I was so anxious about meeting her, I could easily have not noticed.

"I know something about good table manners," I said. "I know you're not supposed to put your elbows on the table."

"Well, that's not always the case," she said and hesitated as Merilyn brought in our salads.

My grandmother watched me. I was waiting to see what she would do, which fork she would take. Again, a small smile crinkled her lips.

"The fork and the spoon above your plate tonight are for our dessert. I had an English trifle made, not by Merilyn, of course. She doesn't have that skill. When it's served, I'll explain how you use the fork and the spoon. For now, just remember that you use your silverware from the outside in, so the fork on your far left is your salad fork," she added and reached for hers.

"Why did you say not putting your elbows on the table was not always the case? I always thought that was rude. Mama told me that."

She chewed her food, swallowed, touched her lips with her napkin and then sat forward supported by her elbows on the table.

"A woman is far more graceful looking like this than like this," she said taking her elbows off and hanging over the table. "With my hands in my lap, leaning awkwardly like this, I look like I have cramps now, don't I?"

For the first time, I smiled, but she didn't mean to be funny.

"Well, don't I?"

"Yes, I suppose."

"Just don't put your elbows on the table when you're eating, only when you have to speak to someone across the table, understand?"

As the meal continued, she continued to lecture me as to how to hold my silverware, how to ask for things, and how to eat different foods properly. I never realized how complicated proper table manners could be. After dinner, when the English trifle was served, she showed me how to use both the fork and the spoon to eat it.

"Did your mother teach you all these things?" I asked her.

"My mother? Hardly," she said a little bitterly. "They sent me to a private preschool, a private school and a finishing school. I was away more than I was home, but if I didn't behave properly at their dinner table, I was sent to my room without supper."

"Do you have any brothers or sisters?"

"I have a younger sister Leonora who lives in London. No brothers," she added. "Leonora is married to a barrister. Do you know what that is?"

"Yes, a lawyer," I said. "I think he's the kind who actually argues cases in court."

"Very good," she said, her eyebrows rising. "I guess you are a good student. How did you manage that living under the conditions Megan describes?"

"I don't know what my mother told you, but Mama always wanted us to do well in school. She wouldn't permit my sister Beni and me to work part-time jobs after school because she thought it would hurt our school work, and we could really have used the money," I said.

"I see. Well, your Mama does sound like a wise person."

"She is, and a loving person, too. What's happened to us isn't fair."

My grandmother's eyes grew narrow and cold.

"Why was she so eager about giving you up?"

"She wasn't eager about it," I countered sharply. "She wants only the best for me and she was afraid for me after Beni was murdered," I said.

"Tell me about that," she commanded.

I briefly described what had happened and what sort of things had been happening to me afterward. She listened attentively, sipping her coffee.

"Tried to set you on fire?" She shook her head. "From the way Megan described your Mama, as you call her, it sounded like she was blackmailing us. Now that I hear more detail, I can appreciate her sacrifice. I would do anything I could also to get you out of there."

I smiled, relaxing. Could I have a good relationship with my real grandmother after all?

"However," she continued, "even though I am presenting this . . . arrangement to the public as an act of charity, I don't want you to think that I don't expect you to respect all my wishes and demands. If at any time you betray my trust, you'll be on your way faster than you can blink. Am I understood?"

"Yes ma'am," I answered, my heart thumping again. She was like the faucets in our old apartment that could run hot and then unexpectedly turn cold.

"You're well-spoken. I like that and I deplore these profane and dirty expressions children use these days. My grandchildren constantly spew that garbage. They think they're being cute or what do you say, bad, cool?"

"I don't know what I would say. I never met them."

"You will, although as I told you, not often," she admitted, which made my eyes widen with curiosity. "I'm not exactly their favorite person to visit."

"Why not?" I asked, too quickly and too vehemently perhaps, but I couldn't hold back my curiosity.

She stared at me for a moment and then lowered her coffee.

"It always amazes me how young people today have no sense of decorum. When I was your age, I wouldn't dream of cross-examining my elders, but in this day and age everyone is almost proud to talk openly about their weaknesses. You turn on the television set, which I rarely do, and all you see are people revealing their most intimate secrets. Disgusting. No one has any self-respect anymore.

"I imagine," she went on, "that some other grandmother would announce you to the world, parade you about, maybe even get on a talk show. If you take anything away from your stay here, I hope it will be discretion," she concluded.

She sipped her coffee and a silence fell between us. Minutes later we heard a loud rapping at the front door and Merilyn came hurrying out of the kitchen.

"Are you expecting anyone, Mrs. Hudson?"

"It might be Victoria," she said. "It's like her to arrive just as we've finished dinner," she muttered.

Merilyn went out to the front door.

"You know who Victoria is, don't you?"

"Your younger daughter."

She didn't reply. She sat back and watched the doorway. I turned when Victoria followed Merilyn back. Merilyn stood to the side.

"Good evening, Mother." She turned to me. "And this is Megan's charity case?" she added.

In person my Aunt Victoria didn't look much different from the way she looked in the photographs in the office. Her hair was still as short and dull, her figure just as lean and bony. She was somewhat taller than I had envisioned from the pictures, and her eyes were a darker brown, if not just as coldly analytical. She wore a light tweed skirt suit and a frilly collared blouse. Her shoes had thick, wide heels, which were what gave her an extra two or three inches of height. As the pictures indicated, her features were harsher, and her complexion paler than my mother's.

She wore a rather big-faced, manly looking wristwatch and what looked like a school ring.

"If you are referring to the young lady seated at the table, her name is Rain Arnold," my grandmother said. Her eyes moved toward the ceiling, ordering me to stand, which I did promptly.

"How do you do? I'm pleased to meet you," I said extending my hand.

She looked at me and then laughed.

"Have you been teaching her manners already, Mother? I would have thought you would give it a day or two."

My grandmother's shoulders stiffened and her eyes turned hot with indignation.

"Obviously, I've done a poor job with you when it comes to that, Victoria. The girl offered you a proper greeting."

"Yes, yes, she did." She reached out to take my hand, touched it, muttered a hello, and then moved around the table.

"Were you intending to have dinner with us? When I spoke to you yesterday, you told me you didn't think you'd be here in time and—"

"No, I had something to eat at the office," she said. She looked at Merilyn. "However, I will have some coffee, Merilyn, please." She sat across from me.

"Very good, Miss Victoria," Merilyn said and went to get a cup and saucer. She paused in the doorway. "Will you be having any trifle?"

"Trifle? My, my, we are out to make a good impression on our new little guest, aren't we? No, thank you, Merilyn. It's always been too rich for me.

"So," she continued turning her attention back to me. I sat. "Do you have any idea of how lucky you are?"

I glanced at my grandmother. Something in her eyes told me that Victoria knew absolutely nothing about the truth.

"Yes," I said. "Not being born into all this, I'm hardly one to take it for granted."

My grandmother laughed. It was the first full and sincere laugh I had heard in this house.

"I believe the expression is touché, Victoria," she told her. "This happens to be a very bright young lady."

"Really?" Victoria said dryly. "How did Megan ever become involved with such a person?"

"Megan does her own good charity work from time to time, which is something you should think about, Victoria. Working like a Wall Street businessman all day and all night is not all there is, you know. It doesn't leave you any time for any sort of social activities, charitable or otherwise."

"We've had this discussion ad infinitum, Mother, must we have it again in front of a stranger?" Victoria said in a tired voice.

Merilyn brought Victoria a cup and saucer and poured her some coffee.

"Will there be anything else, Mrs. Hudson?"

"No," my grandmother said sharply. She kept her gaze locked on my Aunt Victoria, who sipped her coffee and peered across at me.

Did she know everything anyway? She looked smart enough to figure it all out, I thought. It made me very nervous.

"My daughter Victoria," my grandmother said, "has taken over my late husband Everett's business enterprises. Usually, she only visits me to have me sign documents or lecture me about the cost of things, especially this home."

"I don't see why you insist on keeping all this, Mother," Victoria said with a wide gesture. "You're by yourself. You don't need the overhead heating and air conditioning all this space, and keeping it clean, and these grounds—"

"I think I'm the best one to decide what will be over my head and what will not," my grandmother fired back. "Besides, what will become of all my money if I simply accumulate interest upon interest and dividends, Victoria? It will only be left for you and Megan and her children to squander."

"I don't squander money, Mother. I'm only giving you prudent advice. I'm not after any inheritance or trying to make it bigger."

My grandmother shifted her eyes back to me and in them I saw her skepticism.

I couldn't help but be fascinated with how the really rich talked among themselves. Despite their wealth, money seemed to be an ever present concern, a subject that found its way into every discussion. I tried to imagine a similar conversation about inheritances between Mama and me or Beni or Roy. It nearly made me laugh out loud.

"So," Victoria said putting down her coffee cup, "what do you and Megan hope to accomplish with this bright but poor young girl? Is she back to her causes, her days of protests and rebellion?"

"Why don't you ever call her and ask her those questions yourself, Victoria?"

"She never bothers to call me," Victoria replied, slipping into whining, which suddenly made her look younger. It wasn't hard to see there had been some significant sibling rivalry. Would I get into the middle of all that now? "Whenever I send them any information about the business, she has one of Grant's accountants call me."

"Megan was never one to understand or care about money," my grandmother said.

"I wonder where she gets that from," Victoria mumbled.

"That's enough," my grandmother snapped. "Rain has lots of time to smell the dirty laundry. She doesn't need it waved in her face her first night here."

"Oh, excuse me, Rain," Victoria said, smiling and bowing her head with about as phony a grimace as anyone could muster, "I didn't mean to upset you." She turned to my grandmother. "Where is she sleeping?"

"In Megan's old room."

"Really? Not one of the guest rooms? That's a surprise," she commented.

For a moment my grandmother looked like she would stammer, but she pulled herself back quickly and shook her head.

"It really doesn't matter where she sleeps and Megan's room has everything all set up for her."

"Isn't that where you usually put Alison, though? Won't your granddaughter be upset?"

"When was the last time Alison stayed overnight with me, Victoria? I don't even think she would remember where she slept," my grandmother said.

"You're sending her to Dogwood?" my Aunt Victoria asked, looking at me disdainfully.

"That's correct."

She spun around in her seat to fully face my grandmother.

"Do you know what the costs are at that school? I happen to know that they've gone up considerably since Megan and I attended and—"

"Why don't we leave that worry up to my accountant, who gets paid plenty to worry," my grandmother said.

"I just don't see why she can't attend the public school here as well. You pay enough taxes. You could send her there with no difficulty and it wouldn't cost you anything."

"Yes, well, that's not your decision to make, Victoria."

Aunt Victoria glared at me as if I had forced my grandmother to send me to the private school.

"I don't understand all this," she said shaking her head. There was a deep moment of silence. Grandmother Hudson glanced at me and I looked at her, then down quickly.

"But then again," Aunt Victoria said, "I don't understand half the things Megan does and three quarters of the things you do, Mother."

"Isn't that unfortunate?" my grandmother said in the same tone of dry understatement Victoria had used earlier.

Victoria shook her head, sighed and then sat forward, turning away from me and to my grandmother again.

"I have a few business issues I want to discuss with you, Mother," she told her. "Can we excuse Rain or go to the office?"

"Can't it wait, Victoria? I'm exhausted today."

"Did you see the doctor this week?" Aunt Victoria followed quickly.

"No. I'm not running to the doctor every other day. There isn't much he could tell me that I don't already know."

What was wrong with her? I wondered.

"Still, I think—"

"Actually, I didn't expect you to be coming around at all tonight, Victoria, and I had intended to go to bed with a book and relax. Call me tomorrow and we'll make arrangements to have a business meeting. I'll call my accountant."

"I wish you wouldn't involve him at every meeting we have, Mother. I think by now you would agree I have proven myself quite capable of handling things. I don't expect Daddy would have given me as much responsibility if he didn't think I could manage it."

"Yes, well, I can't manage it," my grandmother said rising. "That's why I need someone like Philip Gassman." She turned to me. "Be ready by seven-thirty to be driven to Dogwood," she said. "My driver will be waiting outside. Merilyn already knows to have breakfast prepared for you by six-thirty. That should give you sufficient time."

She started out of the dining room.

"You're going up to bed now, Mother?" Victoria asked, astonished.

"I thought I made that quite clear, Victoria."

"But—"

"I wouldn't advise you to stay up too late, Rain," she told me, shifting her eyes toward Aunt Victoria and then quickly back to me. "You'll need to be as fresh and ready as you can for the challenges that lie ahead." She glanced again at Victoria and left me alone with her.

My heart paused and then pounded. Aunt Victoria glared at me for a moment and then sat back with a wry smile written across her lips.

"Exactly what do you expect you'll get from my mother?" she asked.

"Pardon me?"

"Oh please," she said, stabbing her fury at me with cold, sharp eyes, "you're not the first person to come around here hoping to con my mother into something or other. I don't know what Megan promised you."

"First of all, I didn't come around here, as you say. I was asked to come here, and second, I have no intention of taking anything from your mother other than what she wants to give me herself. I'm not a thief. I'm not going to fill a pillowcase with the family jewels and disappear into the night, if that's what you're afraid of, and Mrs. Randolph didn't make any promises to me."

She stared quietly for a moment and then sat back.

"How did you meet Megan?"

"I don't know why I have to sit here and be cross-examined like a common criminal," I said. "I don't mean to be disrespectful or rude, but if you have any questions about me, you should do as Mrs. Hudson suggested." I stood. "Call your sister and ask her. I'm tired, too. Please excuse me," I concluded, turned, and with my heart thumping so hard, I was sure she could hear it as well, walked out of the dining room.

I was shocked to see my grandmother waiting just outside the doorway. She had been listening to the conversation. She stared at me with a strange, tight smile on her lips and didn't say a word. Then she turned and walked to the stairway. I watched her go up. As I started for the steps, Aunt Victoria emerged, gazed angrily my way and went into the informal sitting room to use the telephone.

There was a phone in my room on the desk. I thought about it for a moment and then picked up the receiver and dialed Mama.

The phone only rang once. Then there was a tiny bell sound and I heard a mechanical voice declaring the phone had been disconnected. My heart sank. I had hoped to at least speak with Roy. Where were they? It hadn't taken her long to pack up and leave. Roy must have gone too, I thought. I imagined neither of them wanted to be there when Ken came around, especially if he found out what Mama had done with me and how he would never get any money out of it.

But when would they call me? When would I hear from them again? Already I missed Mama so much it broke my heart, and I needed to hear her voice more than ever.

Maybe loving each other and caring for each other was a luxury in my poor home, but it was a luxury we shared. These people were rich, but they were a family in name only, it seemed to me. I once heard it said that people could love each other without liking each other. It was as if love was something that came included with being born into a family. It was expected, part of who and what you were. Mothers and daughters, fathers and sons, everyone was expected to love everyone, but when it came right down to it, personalities were so different and there were so many resentments floating around that liking each other was a real challenge sometimes.

This family was a perfect example, I thought. There didn't seem to be much love lost between my grandmother and my Aunt Victoria. No two people seemed more different. They were barely even civil to one another.

What would my place be in all this? I felt like someone who had to tiptoe on thin ice all day and night for fear I would say the wrong thing and crack the fragile floor that held up this artificial relationship.

I sat on my luxurious bed and gazed around at my wonderful room. Most of the girls at my school would imagine they were in heaven, but I felt I had entered a different sort of cage.

There weren't bars on these windows, Beni, I thought, recalling how she used to think of the Projects, but believe me, the people who lived here and who live here now are just as trapped as we were. I hope I haven't exchanged one prison for another.

I went through my wardrobe and chose the garments I would wear to my first day at this new school. Then I got into bed and watched television on the small set in the armoire until my eyelids felt too heavy to keep open. When I turned off the set and the lights, I lay there listening to the silence.

How different it was from my room at the Projects where Beni and I could often hear the sounds of other people either in the hallways or through the floors and ceilings. There were no sirens screaming outside, no car horns blaring. I could see the half moon peeking between two large clouds and I saw some stars. The stars did seem brighter and bigger here. Being able to see so much of the sky made me feel smaller. I imagined I looked tiny in this large bed.

There was so much here, so many reasons to be happy and content, so many weapons with which to battle depression and sadness. These walls should be tall enough to keep out unhappiness; these hallways should be resounding with laughter and the mirrors should be worn out with smiles. How lonely my grandmother must really be, I thought, locked up in her room. The gap between us was as wide as oceans, but I couldn't help believing that when she gazed at me in the distance, she saw something she missed, something she needed, something she wanted very much to have.

Just as I did.

The clocks moved their hands, their ticks like drops of rain falling on our ears, reminding us that we could wish all we wanted, but we couldn't keep tomorrow away.

# 12

# In the Spotlight

The moment I woke the next morning, it felt like my stomach had been turned into a popcorn maker. My electrified nerve endings kept exploding with little bursts of nervous energy. The sun was pouring through my window brighter than I expected. I glanced at the clock, realized I nearly had overslept, and then flew out of bed. I took a quick shower, dressed in my new black skirt and cashmere sweater set, and did the best I could with my hair with the time I had before hurrying downstairs to breakfast. When I entered the dining room, I found my orange juice already had been poured in my glass. The moment I sat, Merilyn appeared in the kitchen doorway like a figure in a cuckoo clock.

"What would you like for breakfast?" she asked without saying good morning. "Eggs, cereal, toast? We also have sweet rolls and bacon."

"Oh no, Merilyn. I couldn't eat much this morning. Just some toast and coffee."

"Butter and jam?"

"Yes, please."

She went back into the kitchen. I sat impatiently. Why couldn't I fix my own breakfast? I had been afraid of even suggesting it for fear I would violate another unwritten rule of the house or that Merilyn would think I was trying to undercut her. I might as well be sitting on a car fender, I thought, as I shifted my weight uncomfortably and drummed my fingers on the table. I was so eager when Merilyn finally brought the toast and coffee that I gobbled it down before she cleared off the empty juice glass, poured me a cup of coffee and returned to the kitchen.

"I thought you said you weren't hungry," she remarked, the corners of her mouth sagging.

"I'm not. I'm just nervous," I said.

"About going to school?" She laughed through her nose. "What's there to be nervous about? You can't get fired," she moaned, gazing at the doorway. "I thought I did a good job last night."

"You did," I said amazed.

"Mrs. Hudson called down to tell me I had overcooked the fish and dried out the potatoes." She glared at me sharply. "Did you complain?"

"No," I said. "I thought it was all just fine."

"So did I, but my opinion don't count," she moaned and returned to the kitchen.

I sat there sipping my coffee. Grandmother Hudson was really a very unhappy woman, I decided, and Mama always says unhappy people are fertile ground for complaints. In their garden complaints grow like weeds.

The grandfather clock boomed on the half hour and I was up like a jack-in-the-box hurrying out the front door. I stopped after I closed it and turned to face the beautiful, warm day with clouds looking like dabs of white paint on a blue canvas. When I shaded my eyes, I saw Jake Marvin standing at the opened rear door of the Rolls Royce. He was dressed in a snappy, gray chauffeur's uniform with black trim on the cuffs and collar and he wore a cap. I didn't realize until this very moment that I was going to school in the Rolls Royce. Me, being brought to school by a chauffeur! I actually froze for a moment, my feet feeling as if they had become part of the portico floor. I know my mouth was open wide enough for me to look like I was trying to catch flies with it, as Mama would say.

Jake laughed.

"Let's go, M'lady," he said with a dramatic bow. "You don't want to be late for your appointment with the headmistress of Dogwood or you'll be in the dog house on your first day."

I laughed and hurried to the car. As we pulled away, I looked up and thought I saw Grandmother Hudson between the curtains peering out of a window.

"So, how was your first night at the Hudson castle?" Jake asked.

"Very quiet," I said, "after I met Victoria, that is."

"Oh, Victoria was here? So what do you think of her?"

"I've been taught not to say anything if I can't say anything nice, so I'll wait until I can," I told him and he roared.

"Her bark's worse than her bite," he promised. "Boy, everything's got to do with dogs this morning, get it? Bark? Bite?"

"I got it," I said smiling.

"So what was your previous school like?" he asked.

"Like a prison. We have metal detectors and security guards in uniform," I said. "There's a chain link fence around it and some of the windows actually have bars on them."

"Well, you're in for a pleasant surprise," he said. As we drove along, he lectured like a tour guide about the flowers and the trees, houses and farms. He told me all about the Dogwoods and why the school was named for them. He was right when he warned me he talks a lot, I thought, but I really didn't mind it. I needed to keep my mind off what was just ahead.

And there was no way I would ever be prepared for what lay ahead. In fact, I didn't know we had entered the school's grounds until Jake pointed out the riding ring.

"Riding ring? What do you mean? What's a riding ring?" I asked.

"That's where you practice riding horses," he said.

"Horses? In a school?"

He laughed again.

"All the girls become equestrians. It's part of their training here," he said.

"I never rode a horse. I never even saw one except under a policeman, in the movies or on television," I said with trepidation.

"Don't worry about it. They have a beginner's class, I'm sure. Only thing is, you'll have to have the right outfit. Maybe Mrs. Hudson took care of that," he mused.

"My mo . . . Mrs. Randolph never mentioned it," I said, staring back at the ring as we continued.

"There's the horse barn, the hay barn," Jake pointed out. "On the left are the classrooms. The main building's coming up."

"What's that other big building just past the classrooms?"

"That's the gymnasium and pool."

"Pool? There's a pool in there, too?"

"Didn't nobody tell you anything about this place?" he asked, amazed.

"No. Just that it was a private school for girls."

"Yeah, that it is, and that school across the pond there," he said nodding to the right at an even more prestigious looking stone structure, "is Sweet William, a private school for boys, the brother school, I guess you'd call it, although Sweet William is older. The two schools combine to have dances and to do some activities and they also compete with each other in debates and such. There's the ballfield and that's the cafeteria building," he continued as we turned and passed under a half-moon sign held up by two round posts. The sign read DOGWOOD SCHOOL FOR GIRLS.

School? I thought. This is more like a small city. My eyes felt like they were popping and my head moved like a windshield wiper from side to side as I tried to take in everything at once: the beautiful trees and flowers, the small fountains and the pond, the athletic field and tennis courts, the chapel and a separate building called the Dogwood Theater.

Jake stopped the vehicle in front of the administration building. He got out and quickly opened my door. I hesitated. If I ever felt like turning and running before, I certainly felt it now.

"It'll be fine," Jake said, seeing the anxiety in my face. "You just go in that door and you'll see someone immediately at a desk on your right who'll help you along."

"How do you know so much about this place, Jake?"

He blinked rapidly for a moment, looked up at the building and said, "I just do."

I stepped out, took a deep breath and started toward the door.

"Good luck, Rain," Jake called. "I'll be here at the end of the day to scoop up what's left of you," he added with a laugh.

"Thanks a lot for the encouragement," I said and he laughed again.

Mama, I thought, as I opened the large glass door, you had no idea, no idea at all.

The lobby had a dark marble floor and a large mural that went to the ceiling. It depicted angels rising toward a heavenly light. On the right, just as Jake said, there was a young woman at a desk and a computer. She turned as I approached.

"My name is Rain Arnold," I said. "I'm here to see Mrs. Whitney."

She studied me for a moment as if she was the first line of defense, deciding whether to let me take a giant step forward. Her eyes moved across my face, looked over my clothing, and then turned to a folder on her desk.

"Just take this through that door," she said nodding at the door on the left, "and go to the first door on your left. That's Mrs. Whitney's office. Her secretary's name is Susan Hines."

"Thank you," I said taking the folder.

She returned to her computer so quickly it was as if she were part of it, her fingers plugged in along with the other wires. I started for the door, conscious of how my feet clicked on the marble floor and echoed off the walls of the big lobby. I couldn't imagine it being any cleaner, even the day it had first opened.

The corridor was shorter than I anticipated and Mrs. Whitney's office came up immediately. The outer office wasn't very big or elaborate. Susan Hines was a woman who looked to be about thirty with light brown hair and dark brown eyes that were a little too large for her small face, pug nose and thin mouth. She looked like someone who was in a continuous battle with the calorie monster, buxom and wide in the shoulders, her chin drooping as if she had swallowed a small balloon.

Her smile was friendly and warm, however.

"Hi," she said quickly.

"Hi. I'm Rain Arnold," I said.

"Yes, Mrs. Whitney is expecting you." She took my folder. Why couldn't the girl out in the lobby have left it with her to start with? I wondered. Everyone here must have his or her little job, I thought.

"Just have a seat," she told me and rose to go into the inner office.

I sat on the leather sofa and gazed at the Dogwood yearbook from the previous year. Aside from the obvious richness of the book production itself, the pictures weren't all that different from any other yearbook I had seen, except for the fact that there were only girls in almost all of them. I saw how many clubs and activities there were, how the girls competed against other all girl schools in just about every sport, including horseback riding, swimming, and fencing. Fencing? This was like training for the movies.

The theater looked so big and professional. They had done a musical last year, *The King and I.* I noted that the boys in the production were from Sweet William. They had also done a production of *The Diary of Anne Frank.* I knew that book and loved it. I recalled reading passages to Beni, who pretended she wasn't interested but listened anyway and finally asked so many questions, I made her read it too.

"Mrs. Whitney will see you now," Susan said from the doorway.

I rose quickly and walked into the office. This one was quite large, but very neat and organized, one wall covered with plaques and awards, citations with pictures of important politicians and benefactors, and another with two oil paintings, each depicting Dogwood from a different perspective, revealing the pond and beautiful gardens.

Mrs. Whitney looked trapped behind her large, maple wood desk. I was surprised at how small she was, maybe just an inch or so taller than five feet. I didn't imagine her to weigh an ounce more than one hundred pounds. Her blue-gray hair was brushed and styled with a slight wave through the center, but her hair was thinning so that her scalp was clearly visible in spots. She wore simple gold teardrop earrings, a dark blue suit and an expensive looking gold watch. I noticed she wore a wedding ring, but no other rings.

What she lacked in physical size, she made up for in stature and voice. There was a strong, no-nonsense demeanor about her, a firmness in her eyes and face that telegraphed about as much grit and strength as I had seen in any woman. I thought her to be in her sixties, but later found out she was seventy with no intention, not even a passing thought, of retiring. She was, I would soon learn, the personification of Dogwood. It was her school to give over to a new headmistress and she was in no mood to even consider it.

"Please have a seat," she said, directing her dark blue eyes toward the chair in front of her desk. I took it quickly. "Thank you, Susan," she said, nodding at the secretary who then closed the door.

For a long moment, Mrs. Whitney simply contemplated me. I was almost ready to ask her why she was staring at me so hard, but I didn't have the nerve to utter a syllable. She had a way of commanding with her eyes, dominating with her firm posture.

"I am fully aware of your situation," she began. "Mrs. Hudson and I are close friends and Mrs. Hudson is a significant benefactor of Dogwood."

Mrs. Whitney wore only a trace of lipstick and some powder on her cheeks. Her chin was sharp and the skin was taut up to her ears, so that the very bones of her face seemed to rub when she spoke. Her forehead was as wrinkled as one of Ken's shirts and the lines at her eyes and around her mouth were like sharp, dark slices, but if her face was aging, her mind was not. She looked like she could leap out of her old body anytime she wanted and challenge anyone to anything.

I was truly impressed.

"The moment you walk out that door today, this part of our conversation is buried and forgotten unless Mrs. Hudson herself resurrects it. You understand?"

"Yes, ma'am," I replied, afraid my voice would crack or that I wouldn't get up enough air to make a sound.

"Good. Now to the school and you," she began opening my folder. "We already have your transcripts and you do look to be a worthwhile academic candidate, although I have my doubts as to the quality of your education up to this point. We'll see," she added cautiously. "Maybe I'll be pleasantly surprised.

"Dogwood is one of the oldest private institutions of its kind in this state. We are dedicated to offering not only a rigorous college-preparatory program, but a well-rounded education. Our girls leave here fit for the intellectual, ethical and emotional challenges of life. We instill confidence, leadership, independence, self-esteem. Recent studies strongly suggest that girls who attend single sex institutions possess more positive attitudes toward academics.

"At the same time," she continued, "we recognize that young women need to become aware of different viewpoints and have to learn how to work with young men in a variety of settings. That's why we encourage our girls to participate in the cooperative ventures between Dogwood and Sweet William.

"You've been given a wonderful opportunity, my dear. I hope you appreciate it and will make every effort to live up to our standards of behavior and excellence.

"I won't take up your time now to go over these rules," she said, handing me a small pamphlet, "but I do expect you will read this and commit them to memory. I know you will find vast differences in the level of expectation here and what you were accustomed to in the inner city. We are proud of the fact that we have never had a single instance of drug abuse, vandalism or violence at our school. We won't tolerate even a suggestion of such a thing."

"Neither would my Mama," I said sharply.

She raised her thin eyebrows, but I was tired of everyone who looked at me and knew where I was from assuming I had been either a member of a gang, a girl with loose morals, or a thief just because I had darker skin and came from a low income neighborhood. People rose above their problems and situations, didn't they?

"Good," Mrs. Whitney said. "I don't want to waste the precious time you'll need to get accustomed to your new surroundings. Just be assured that I will take a personal interest in your progress as a favor to Mrs. Hudson."

I was going to say, "Thank you, I think," but I just said, "Thank you."

"Susan will personally escort you to your academic adviser, Mr. Bufurd, who happens to be our dramatics instructor as well. In fact, he has casting today for our final school production of the year, *Our Town.* Do you know it?"

"Very well," I said. "It's one of my favorites. We read it in tenth grade."

"That's very good," she said, obviously impressed. She rose and started around her desk, which was when I noticed she had a very bad limp. I guess I had a surprised look on my face. She paused.

"This isn't from an injury," she said. "I was born with a defect, one leg shorter than the other. It obviously reduced my chances to be in the Olympics," she added. For a moment she kept her face serious and then smiled and I laughed. It was like cracking a wall of ice between us. "That and my height and size informed me at an early age that I would have to compensate in other ways, so I won a Fulbright, got my doctorate in education before I was thirty, wrote two well-received books on educational philosophy and became the headmistress of Dogwood.

"As I think you can appreciate and understand, Miss Arnold," she said with a sharp twinkle in her eyes, "disadvantages can be a good thing if they serve to motivate us to overcome them."

I think I like her, I thought, and suddenly, I was no longer afraid of this place or the people in it.

The walk from the administrative building to the classroom was through a beautiful garden setting. The sunlight was still elbowing aside any cloud cover and bringing out the vibrant colors.

"You're from Washington, D.C.?" Susan asked as we walked. "Born there, I mean?"

"Yes, ma'am."

"Oh, you don't have to call me ma'am, honey. I'm just hired help," she said with a laugh. "I'm from Richmond, never got far away," she said.

"How long have you been working here?"

"Three and a half years. Mrs. Whitney's wonderful to work for, an elegant lady. I hope you like her," she said. "Everybody here's pretty nice. My mama was hoping I'd meet a handsome professor and get married, but that hasn't happened yet," she said with a small giggle. Outside of the office, walking along with me, she suddenly didn't look all that much older.

A group of girls burst out of the classroom building and walked quickly toward the horse barn and ring, all seemingly talking at once. They were dressed in fancy riding outfits and they all looked younger than me. I was surprised to see other girls of color in the group. I heard what sounded like foreign accents, too.

"Those two are from France," Susan said, nodding at the last two in the group, "and the cute little redhead is from Brazil."

"Really? Their parents sent them here?"

"A huh. They're part of our exchange program. They live with families here and the girls from those families live with their families in France and Brazil."

Mama would surely be as impressed as I am, I thought, but definitely satisfied she had done the right thing. If I wasn't safe here, where would I be safe? I thought there must be a gigantic protective glass bubble over all this. Everyone looked like she was untouched by unhappiness, poverty, crime and even illness. There were no Jerads walking these pathways, no graffiti on the walls, no one selling drugs on every corner.

"Right this way," Susan said opening the door for me. We entered the classroom building. The first thing I noticed was there wasn't even a shred of paper on the floors. Outside the classrooms there were bulletin boards with neatly placed announcements. It was well lit, glistening, airy and warm. The bell that had rung to announce the end of one period was followed by the one to announce the beginning of the next. Susan led me past clean classrooms with desks that looked like they had just arrived from the factories. When I passed a doorway, the girls who could see me looked out with interest. What shocked me was how few students were in each room.

"Where is everyone?" I asked Susan.

"Pardon?"

"There's only like ten girls in there and not more than eight or so in the last room."

"That's how big our classes are, honey. Mrs. Whitney doesn't like them to be much bigger than twelve."

"Twelve?" I shook my head. "That's how many were in my row at my old school. One of my classes had nearly fifty students in the room."

"Fifty? How can anyone teach that many at once?"

"They didn't," I said dryly.

"Here we are," she said. She knocked on the doorjamb. "Excuse me, Mr. Bufurd, Rain Arnold is here."

"Oh, fine, fine," I heard him say and walked around Susan to enter the classroom.

There were only eight students in this one and they all turned with one face toward me, a face full of curiosity. Mr. Bufurd looked like a man not much older than his mid twenties. He had long black hair, but trimmed and brushed neatly at the nape of his neck. What struck me was how green his eyes were. Even from the back of the room, I could see the vibrancy in them. They almost glowed because of the contrast to his dark complexion. He was just under six feet tall and I saw that his body was trim with a narrow waist and hips. He had a gentle smile on his soft, perfect lips.

Susan handed him my folder. He glanced at it while I waited and then looked up quickly.

"Welcome. Class," he said, "meet Rain Arnold. You can sit here for now, Rain," he said touching a vacant front row desk. I sat quickly. "I was just preparing the class for our study of *Hamlet.* You haven't read it yet, have you?" he inquired.

"Yes, I have read it," I told him, "but not as a class assignment. It was something I did on my own."

"On your own?" He looked at the others. "Did any of you ever hear of anything like that? Reading on your own? Raise your hand if you have," he added with a coy smile.

The girls giggled, but no one raised her hand. He turned to me.

"I've been trying to instill that idea in these bubbles all year," he told me, "but they just pop and pop and pop every time."

The girls giggled again.

Susan Hines lingered in the doorway for a moment, a look of longing on her face. She resembled someone who wished with all her heart that she could turn back time and be our age and in this classroom. After another moment, she retreated.

"What can you tell us about *Hamlet,* Ms. Arnold?" he continued.

The other girls took on looks of glee, hoping I would make a fool of myself, I was sure.

"What would you like to know?" I asked. "It takes place in Denmark and it's about a prince whose father is murdered and whose mother marries the murderer."

"Is that what it's about?" a thin girl with long blond hair who sat two desks across from me asked. "That doesn't sound so boring," she added.

"Oh," Mr. Bufurd said, "you're interested now, Maureen, now that you know it's about murder?"

The girls giggled again.

"It's about a great deal more than that though, isn't it, Ms. Arnold?" he challenged.

"I thought so," I said. "There are a great many questions about life and love in it."

"Love?" another girl piped up. She had short, dark brown hair with brown eyes as big as quarters in her pudgy face.

"And sex," Mr. Bufurd added nodding. "Don't forget the sex, Tamatha. Isn't that right, Ms. Arnold?"

"I don't think it's exactly what you would call R-rated," I replied and he really laughed.

All the girls looked perplexed. It was as if he and I had instantly embarked on a private conversation.

"Okay," he said. "Can you remember any line that impressed you, aside from the obvious 'To be or not to be?' "

I looked at the other girls and then at him. He waited with one hand still pressing the chalk to the board and the other on his hip.

"To thine own self be true," I said.

His smile widened in tiny increments like the ripples in a pool of water and then he bowed his head and said, "Welcome to Dogwood, Rain."

As soon as English class ended, most of the other girls gathered around me to ask questions. They wanted to know where I was from and why I had entered Dogwood so late in the school year. Neither Grandmother Hudson nor my mother had really prepared me with the details of our fabrication, so I had to make it up as I went along, telling them I was part of a unique exchange program involving young people from the inner cities, a program sponsored by a private charity. They were so accustomed to their parents being involved in charities, no one challenged it. Rather, they were fascinated with my background and fired question after question at me about life in a so-called ghetto community. They were intrigued with crime and gangs, but I knew that to them the details of my former life seemed like something from a television program. No matter what I said, they didn't seem to think of it as real.

One girl, Audrey Stempelton, dark-haired and a little dumpy because of her wide hips and short legs, remained in the background listening attentively, but not speaking whenever conversations with me erupted. I saw from the look in her eyes that she wanted to join in our conversations, but was shy. After lunch, she worked up enough courage to approach me in the hallway as I walked to class with the others.

"I live near you," she said. "We have the house just south of the Hudsons."

She said it all quickly and walked faster as if she was terrified I might continue the conversation.

"What's wrong with her?" I muttered.

"Audrey's a neurotic introvert," Maureen Knowland explained with the tone of an expert. "She's almost like an idiot savant because she's so good on the stage."

"On the stage? As what? A singer?"

"No, a thespian," Pauline Bogart said with a laugh. "She's in every one of Mr. Bufurd's productions."

"She has a mad crush on him," Maureen said gleefully.

"So do you," Tamatha Stevens accused. Before Maureen could deny it, Tamatha added, "So do I. So does everyone. You're so lucky to have him as your adviser, Rain," she told me. "If I had him, I'd have hundreds of problems to solve every day."

She laughed and the others joined her. They giggled almost all the way to the next class.

No wonder Mr. Bufurd referred to them as bubbles, I thought and laughed myself.

Was I too relaxed? Was this all too easy? Without girls like Nicole waiting to pounce on me in the bathroom, this school did seem safe.

Or was that all just an illusion? It's better to be cautious, I thought. Nothing has ever come to me easy in this life. There's no reason to believe it will now.

At the end of the day, I was scheduled to report to Mr. Bufurd to ask any questions and get some more information about the school, but he informed me after I entered the classroom that he had begun casting for his production of *Our Town.*

"I can't spend as much time with you today, but I can tomorrow during your study period. I have a free period that hour, too," he explained. "Are there any blatant problems we can solve quickly?"

"No," I said. "Everything is fine so far. I have a little more to catch up on in math, but I think I'll be all right."

"I like that," he said nodding and fixing those beautiful green orbs on me, "confidence without an air of arrogance. It's refreshing." He thought for a moment and then asked, "You haven't had an easy time of it, have you?"

"No, not an easy time," I said.

"I'll tell you a big secret," he said, "I come from a hard-working family. I'm still paying off education loans." He gathered his books into his briefcase and then paused to look at me. "Were you ever in any school plays?"

"No," I said.

"Why don't you hang around for tryouts?"

I started to shake my head.

"You've got nothing to lose. We don't penalize you if you're not cast. It's the best way to fit right into a new school, get involved in something," he advised. "You should listen to me. I'm your official adviser."

"My driver is supposed to pick me up in a half hour," I said looking at the clock.

"I'll put you up first," he said. "Walk with me to the theater and we'll continue our talk. Come on," he urged. "It's painless."

I laughed.

"Okay," I said.

I liked him because he didn't just ask questions. He continued to volunteer information about himself, how he came from a family with three sisters, grew up outside of Baltimore, vacillated between a career in the theater and education, and finally decided to be a teacher.

"You'd probably be a good actor," I told him.

"Maybe, but in the arts it takes more than just being good; it takes what I call bloodthirsty determination. You turn your head and neck into a battering ram and just keep going at the door until it opens a little and then you compete, learn how to sell yourself, trample over others until you get your name on that marquee. I guess I didn't have the stomach for the crusade, although getting my bubbles to care about Shakespeare is probably just as difficult a battle.

"It's nice to meet someone who has a little self-motivation," he added, and gestured toward the entrance to the theater. "Here we are."

I took a deep breath and walked in with him. The lobby was as clean and beautiful as the lobby of the administrative building. It had a ticket office, a coat room, a place for refreshments and display cases on the walls for play posters. The ones from the last production, *Anything Goes,* were still up.

He opened the doors to the theater.

"It's so big," I said.

"It seats 800. Nice size. Great stage, state of the art lighting and sound with a ceiling high enough to fly sets."

"Fly?"

He laughed.

"You know, draw them up and lower them to change settings in a show," he explained.

I saw a crowd of girls and boys had gathered at the front of the theater. Their laughter resounded through the auditorium. As soon as they saw Mr. Bufurd approaching, they all grew still and took seats, the boys moving as quickly as the girls.

"Good afternoon, everyone," he announced. "Thanks for coming."

A tall, strawberry blonde with eyes just a little lighter green than Mr. Bufurd's approached us. She wore a long skirt and a light-blue cashmere sweater that clung tightly to her firm bosom. She carried a clipboard and copies of scripts.

"Good afternoon, Colleen," Mr. Bufurd said. "This is Rain Arnold, a new student."

"Hi," she said, not wasting her eyes on me for long. "I have everyone's name in alphabetical order," she told him.

"That's great. Colleen is my P.A., production assistant," he told me. "She intends to pursue a career in the theater."

Colleen's face brightened with pride.

"Rain Arnold?" she asked me. I nodded.

"That puts her pretty much up front, doesn't it?" he asked her.

"There's an Atwell," she said looking at her list. "Martin."

"Looks like you're lead-off batter," Mr. Bufurd told me. "Just as I predicted. Colleen will show you the section I want read."

He moved to a seat in the center of the third row behind all the students. Colleen handed me a script and turned the pages, pointing to a section.

"He likes to hear candidates read cold," she said.

I gazed at the dialogue. It happened to be one of my favorite parts in the play, when Emily Webb says good-bye to life, to all the small but important things. I remember I cried when I read it.

"Where do I—"

"On the stage," Colleen said. "Where else? Just go on up there."

I looked at Mr. Bufurd. He had set himself up with his pad and pencil and suddenly looked very official and impersonal.

"Let's begin," he called.

How did I get myself into this? I wondered as I headed for the stage. All eyes were on me, some of the girls looking downright furious at the audacity of my bursting in on their turf my first day at their school.

When I stood on the stage, I looked into the audience, but the lights were on so I was blinded and couldn't quite see Mr. Bufurd.

"Start any time," he called when I stared. There was some laughter.

Here goes nothing, I thought and began. As I read the passage, I thought about Mama and our good-byes. It put tears into my words and nearly choked me before I finished. When I did, there was no applause, no sound, just some rustling.

"Thank you, Rain," I heard Mr. Bufurd say. "Next, please, Colleen."

"Atwell, Martin," she called.

I hurried down the steps and up the aisle, picking up my books. Mr. Bufurd smiled at me and then turned back to the stage as I continued up the aisle, fleeing into the courtyard and hurrying down the walkway to meet Jake. He was standing by the limousine talking to a groundskeeper.

"Hey there," he cried as I approached. "Where you coming from?"

"Theater building," I said. "I tried out for the school play."

"Wow." He opened the rear door and I practically dived into the seat. I simply wasn't comfortable with all this special treatment. It made me feel like a phony.

Jake was just as talkative on the way home. He asked dozens of questions, but sometimes, before I answered one, he told me about his own school experiences.

I really expected Grandmother Hudson would be waiting to cross-examine me on my first day at Dogwood, but Merilyn told me she was taking her afternoon nap and would probably not be down until dinner. I went right to work on my homework and my efforts to play catch-up. I hadn't been totally honest with Mr. Bufurd. The classes at Dogwood all seemed to be quite a bit ahead of where I had been in public school. I was too ashamed to admit how inferior my education had been.

When the telephone in my room rang, I just stared at it for a moment. I had forgotten it was there.

"Hello?"

"Rain, honey?"

"Mama!" I screamed. "Mama, I tried to call you, but they said the phone was disconnected."

"That happened the day you left, honey. Ken never sent in the last two payments and I forgot all about it. It didn't matter because I was packing up to go. I'm in North Carolina with my Aunt Sylvia. How you doing, baby?"

"Oh Mama. It's a big house and they're rich and everything and the school's beautiful, but I miss you something terrible and Roy, too. How is he? Where is he?" I rushed out my questions, starving for news.

"I haven't heard from him yet," she said. "You know Roy's not much for writing letters either, so if he doesn't get to a phone, it'll be a while. They making you feel at home there, Rain?"

I paused. If I told her anything terribly negative, she would only feel worse, I thought.

"It's all right, Mama. They're rich, but they're not as happy as you'd think."

"It's just for a little while, Rain, and then you'll be off to something wonderful, I'm sure."

She gave me her phone number and address and I promised to write regularly.

After we finished talking, I sat on the bed, sucking back my tears. I had such a deep ache in my heart. Life seemed so unfair. I threw myself back into my work to keep from thinking and then I got dressed for dinner. This time Grandmother Hudson was already in the dining room. For a moment I thought I was late. She was just as elegantly dressed as the night before, but she did look somewhat more tired.

I greeted her and took my seat. Just as Merilyn was beginning to serve, the phone rang.

"Should I get it, ma'am?" Merilyn asked.

"Yes, yes," Grandmother Hudson said petulantly. "Maybe it's your mother," she told me when Merilyn left the room. "She has yet to call me to see if you're alive or dead."

"She phoned me," I said. Her eyebrows went up.

"You'd think she'd have the courtesy to call me as well. Why do my children think everything is coming to them, that I owe them so much?"

I was about to offer an answer when Merilyn stepped back into the room to announce the phone call was for me.

"It's starting already?" my grandmother snapped. "Your girlfriends or boyfriends or—"

"Excuse me, Mrs. Hudson," Merilyn said with a tiny bow.

"Well?"

"It's not a girlfriend or boyfriend. It's her teacher, Mr. Bufurd."

"I told him she was at dinner and he said to give her this message."

"What message?" Grandmother Hudson demanded angrily.

"That she has the part of Emily Webb. Rehearsals start tomorrow."

# 13

# How the Mighty Fall

"What does that mean?" Grandmother Hudson asked.

As I explained who Emily Webb was in the play, her eyes widened and the way she looked at me changed from an expression of slight interest to a look of deeper appreciation.

"That's quite an achievement for someone on their first day at a new school," she remarked. It was the closest I had come to getting a sincere compliment from her.

"I don't know if I should do it," I made the mistake of saying.

"You don't know if you should do it?" She pulled her shoulders back and her face reddened. "Why? Because it entails some work, some effort? Was your family on welfare? Were you used to having everything simply given to you?"

"No," I said, my eyes stinging with angry tears. "Mama never went on welfare. Ken took advantage of everything he could, but Mama refused. And I am not afraid of hard work and making an effort. Do you actually think it was easy for me growing up in that neighborhood, trying to learn something in that school? My grades weren't gifts," I emphasized. "No, nothing's been handed to me on any silver platter."

I held my breath, expecting her to explode at my outburst. Her tight lips softened as she pulled the corners up gently and her eyes seemed to sparkle with pleasure. What a confusing woman, I thought.

"If, as you say, you've had to battle against such terrible odds to accomplish what you have accomplished, why does accepting the role in a school play look like such a Mount Olympus to climb? Why isn't it a piece of cake?" she added.

"Because . . . because I've never done this before," I stammered.

"So? Are you going to run away from every task you've never done before? What sort of grit and backbone does that exhibit? I'll say one thing for your mother," she continued, "I didn't approve of her activities in college, but she didn't shy away from challenges, even if it meant she had to suffer indignation and share poverty, things she never had to suffer and share before.

"Of course," she added, "you'd never know she was the same woman today."

"What about my father?" I dared to ask.

"What about him?"

"I don't know very much," I said.

"That makes two of us," she said, "and for my part, I'd like to keep it that way."

There would be no more discussion of that, I thought. When Grandmother Hudson slammed a door closed, it was closed.

The next day, the cast list was posted on Mr. Bufurd's door and everyone knew I had been given the coveted role of Emily Webb. The girls who were jealous of my having Mr. Bufurd for an adviser were absolutely erupting with envy. Most just gazed at me with green eyes, but Maureen Knowland put the first glass of ice water on my accomplishment when she said, "I wonder what Corbette Adams is going to do about this."

"What do you mean?" I asked. Corbette, who attended Sweet William, had been cast as George Gibbs opposite me. Emily and George are in love and marry in the play.

"I think what I mean is obvious," Maureen sailed in my direction as she entered the classroom. All the girls but Audrey followed like a tail of cans tied to the rear bumper of a car, bouncing their laughter along after her.

I looked at Audrey.

"Did you understand that remark?" I asked her.

She raised her eyes to me and then shifted them to the cast list. She had been cast as George Gibbs's mother.

"You're an African-American," she said. "You have a light complexion, but you're still—"

"What?" I demanded.

"Black to them, I guess," she said shrugging.

"Oh," I said looking at the cast list. What would Grandmother Hudson think of this? Would this make a mountain out of that molehill of Mount Olympus she accused me of falsely creating? "Do you know this Corbette Adams?" I asked Audrey.

"A huh," she said. "He was in a play with me last year, *Harvey.* He played Elwood and I played Elwood's sister."

"Well, what's he like?" I asked her.

"I don't know. We were only in a play together," she replied, as if I had asked her to reveal her deepest, darkest secrets. She looked down and then hurried into the classroom.

I stared at the cast list for a moment longer. If Mr. Bufurd thought I could play the part, he must not have been worrying about my being half African-American, I thought.

But that didn't keep me from worrying about it all day and trembling as I strolled over to the theater building after school to be in my first rehearsal in any play ever. I didn't walk like someone determined and excited. I was still a little indecisive. I told my pounding heart I could still back out.

All of the rest of the cast was already there when I arrived. They had the advantage of already knowing each other and needed no introductions. From the way they looked at me, I felt confident I was the subject of their conversation. After all, who was this girl who came charging through the venerable corridors of Dogwood to achieve such dramatic successes so quickly? Did I have political influence? Did I deserve the role? What was Mr. Bufurd thinking of? How would Corbette play lover to me?

I slowed as I approached them. Colleen Littlefield, Mr. Bufurd's production assistant, stepped out of the group.

"You're late," she pounced, wagging her head. "Mr. Bufurd insists we all be right on time. Being on time for an entrance is crucial to the theater," she continued in a lecture mode. The others froze their faces, their frightened eyes directed at me.

"I'm sorry," I said. "But I can't be very late."

"Late is late. That's like saying I'm not very pregnant," she added and there was a ripple of nervous laughter. "What does the rest of the cast do if someone misses her entrance?"

"Punt," one of the boys remarked and they all laughed so simultaneously and so hard it reverberated like a television sound track through the auditorium.

I gazed around.

"I don't even see Mr. Bufurd," I said.

"He'll be here shortly. I get things started every day. That's my job," she said smugly.

"So do it," I fired back at her. If she considered herself tough and nasty, she should meet Nicole, I thought. "You're just wasting more time with these histrionics."

The smiles on some of the faces vanished instantly. A few turned to Colleen to see what she would do. Audrey was the only one who looked happier, her smile widening.

"Good afternoon, gang," we heard Mr. Bufurd call from the rear of the theater before Colleen could get her jaw unlocked. "Sorry I'm a little late," he followed. He started down the aisle.

I walked up to Colleen.

"Doesn't he know better than to be late? What's the cast to do?"

A tall boy laughed loudly, his sapphire eyes brightening. He had broad shoulders and long legs. Under the spill of the stage lights, his dark brown, unruly hair held hints of copper. It reached the nape of his neck and curled upward, barely brushing the white collar of his thin shirt. No girl in her right mind would deny he was good looking, I thought. He tilted his head just a little to the right as if waiting to see what I would do or say next and our eyes met.

His didn't falter; they held as his strong lips opened slightly. He had a straight, Roman nose in perfect proportion to his other facial features. I saw a self-assurance in his eyes, a strength that was different from the strength I always saw in Roy's eyes. This strength came from a deep well of confidence and not from anger or pain. His eyes left mine first, but not to turn away. On the contrary, he took in the rest of my face slowly, moving to my throat, lingering at my bosom, and then traveling down to my waist, hips, legs and then back up again, just as slowly until he found my eyes, his now changing to reflect more curiosity and even appreciation, I thought with a small trembling beneath my breast.

"Good, so you've all met," Mr. Bufurd declared, dropping his briefcase on a chair. "Did you introduce Rain to everyone, Colleen?" he asked her.

"Not yet, Mr. Bufurd. She arrived only seconds before you did."

"Oh, okay," he said. "Gang, this is Rain Arnold, our newest discovery. I hope you'll all make her feel at home and quickly make her part of our little family. As some of you who have been in one or more of my productions know, it doesn't take long for all of us to bond in a special way, and if we don't have that bonding, the production suffers. From this day forward, we all pull hard for each other to be successful.

"Everyone have his or her script, Colleen?" he asked, turning to her.

"Everyone but Rain Arnold, Mr. Bufurd," she said with syrupy sweetness.

"Well let's get to it," he said clapping his hands.

She thrust a script at me as if she imagined it was a knife. Everyone sat.

"Let's begin with an introduction of players and then a read-through. Why don't you start, Gerald," he said.

"Gerald Longchamp," a stout boy with dark brown hair responded. "I play Mr. Webb." He looked over at me with a tight, crooked smile. "Emily's father."

Moments later, I discovered that the handsome boy was Corbette Adams, playing George Gibbs.

"For those of you who have never seen this play performed, I'll first describe the staging," Mr. Bufurd said.

"Mr. Bufurd," Maureen Knowland called out, her hand high. She was playing Rebecca Gibbs, George's sister.

"Yes, Maureen?"

"Before you arrived, we were all wondering how you were going to solve the problem," she said.

My heart, as though it was attached to rubber bands, felt like it bounced in my chest because of the way she pronounced "problem" and looked at me when she said it.

"Problem?" Mr. Bufurd said with a small smile of confusion. "Which problem? I've got about two hundred."

"The biggest one, Mr. Bufurd," she sang. "We all read *Our Town* in class of course, and we know it takes place in a small New England town. I don't think people had mixed marriages then, do you?"

You could hear the stillness, the holding of breath, the tightness in everyone's body, not a leg or arm moving, not even the wispy sound of clothes creasing. Mr. Bufurd stared at Maureen for a moment as if he was still trying to understand her question.

"Oh," he finally said as if he just realized it. He was a good actor himself, I decided. "You mean the fact that our George Gibbs and our Emily Webb are a little different from the traditional?"

"A little different?" She smirked and looked at the others, but most let their eyes drop except for Colleen Littlefield, who was standing beside Mr. Bufurd. She pulled the corner of her mouth into her cheek and gazed at me as if I was some smelly homeless person who had wandered in from the street.

"Well, that's a good question," he said. "I don't want to get into a lecture today, but you all know that America has always been what we call a melting pot. The great thing about *Our Town* is how well it lends itself to changing times. It's not a period piece, so put your mind at rest, Maureen. In fact, I was thinking of adding a line at the end to make the point that skin color is just another one of the 'layers of nonsense' in our lives.

"Anyone uncomfortable with that?" he concluded.

I couldn't help but glance at Corbette, who glanced at me and then stared forward.

"Good. So let's begin," Mr. Bufurd said and started the rehearsal.

We read through the first two acts with Mr. Bufurd stopping us occasionally to explain a line or what he envisioned would take place on the stage. While I read my lines to George Gibbs, I could feel Corbette Adams's eyes on me. I glanced up to see a small smile on his lips before he started his lines. Amazingly, he seemed to have his part already memorized. When the rehearsal ended, I couldn't help but ask him about it.

"I guess I always assumed I would get the role," he said, "so I took the chance and began memorizing. Are you a hard study?"

"Pardon me?"

Most of the students were leaving slowly, lingering to watch us talk, especially Maureen.

"Is it hard for you to memorize lines?" he explained with just enough of a condescending tone in his voice to make my spine stiffen.

"I don't know, but I don't think it will be. Of course, I never anticipated being cast as Emily Webb. The truth is, I never even expected to go out for the play. I just enrolled at Dogwood."

"I know," he said still holding that self-satisfied, impish grin. I felt like slapping it off him. He leaned closer to me. "You've stirred up Mr. Bufurd's melting pot. I think this is going to be lots of fun," he added and turned to catch up with the other boys from Sweet William.

When I turned around, I saw Colleen Littlefield glaring at me with eyes so full of fury again I imagined I was the most distasteful thing she had encountered. Rather than put fear in me, it lit a fire under my simmering sense of outrage. Maybe the Grandmother Hudson in me was awakening after a lifetime of hibernation. I walked right up to her.

"You and I got off to a very bad start today," I said, "but if you're really concerned about the play and helping Mr. Bufurd, you'll put aside your stupid prejudices and help me, too."

"I am not prejudiced," she wailed, looking toward Mr. Bufurd to be sure he hadn't heard. "Why is it you people always use that excuse whenever you're criticized?"

"Maybe because it's all we've experienced for the last two hundred years," I said. "I'm not leaving this play unless Mr. Bufurd decides I should, so get used to me," I told her. Remembering Nicole's aggressiveness, I put my face right up to hers and she nearly had heart failure. Then I screwed my eyes into hers and added, "Don't get me angry again."

Before she could blink twice, I turned and marched up the aisle, holding my breath and hoping she wouldn't challenge my threat. I burst out of the building into the late afternoon sunshine and let out my hot breath.

"You're good," I heard and turned to see Audrey lingering in the shadows.

"Thanks. So are you."

"No, I mean it," she said coming up to me slowly. "You read with feeling. Most of them just read. I can see why Mr. Bufurd cast you as Emily."

"Thanks," I said with more sincerity, but still a little cautious. The girls Mr. Bufurd called his bubbles had a way of hiding their true feelings behind a lot of sudsy smiles. Not one of them had come to my aid in there, and most looked like they enjoyed seeing me uncomfortable.

"Don't let Colleen bother you," she advised as we started down the pathway. "She's nasty to everyone."

"It doesn't excuse it and frankly, I don't let people like that push me around. My brother Roy always says if you act like sheep, they'll act like wolves," I told her.

She smiled.

"Where is your brother? Does he go to Sweet William?"

"No," I said laughing at the very thought of it. "He's joined the army."

"I'm an only child. Do you have any other brothers or sisters?"

"No. I had a sister but she was killed," I said.

"Killed? You mean like in a car accident?"

"No," I said. I hesitated. If I told her anything about myself and my other family, would she run to the others with stories? I wondered. "Are you just fishing for gossip?" I demanded. She looked terrified.

"No," she said quickly. "I was just . . . I was just . . ." She walked faster rather than finish her sentence. I felt sorry for her and the way I had snapped.

"Audrey," I called. She turned. "Wait up."

She did, but she still looked like she was trembling.

"I didn't mean to snap at you like that," I said. "It's not easy for me to talk about it and the girls here don't seem very sincere to me."

She nodded, her eyes softening.

"They're not," she said. After a beat she added, "I don't have a single friend here." Before I could say another word, she said, "There's my mother. I have to go."

I watched her practically run down the pathway toward a black Mercedes sedan. She rushed around to the passenger's side and got in quickly. A small woman with dark hair and sunglasses rolled down her window and looked my way. Then she rolled the window up and drove off.

Moments later, Jake pulled up and I was on my way home, too. Jake talked his usual blue streak, peppering his conversation with little questions. I just couldn't imagine Grandmother Hudson putting up with him. He was too much like real people, spontaneous and uncomplicated. Mama would like him, too, I thought.

When we approached the house, I saw another vehicle and Jake told me the doctor was there.

"What's wrong?" I asked quickly.

"Mrs. Hudson never told you she has a chronic heart problem?" he asked. "No," he answered for himself quickly, "I don't imagine she would share that with you. She doesn't acknowledge it herself."

"What sort of heart problem?"

"I don't know all the details, but from what I understand, she needs a pacemaker but keeps putting it off. That woman won't admit to any weaknesses or failings. It's not in her nature," he said, but he said it with admiration and not criticism. "Maybe you can get her to take better care of herself."

Me? I thought with a laugh. I would have as much influence on her as a girl living in China.

The doctor was just coming down the stairs when I entered the house. He was a tall, thin man with a reddish-brown mustache and dark brown hair.

"You must be Rain," he said. "I'm Doctor Lewis. Mrs. Hudson's daughter told me all about you."

"Hello," I said. "Is she all right?"

He paused at the bottom of the stairway and glanced up before turning back to me.

"I have never met anyone who confronts illness the way she does.

She treats it as if it were an insult, an affront to her good name and character. She practically defies disease, infection and malfunctions to show up in her body, and when they do, she declares them personae non gratae," he said with a laugh. "I'm sorry," he followed. "I shouldn't be light-hearted about this. It's just that every time I come here, I leave frustrated. Mrs. Hudson needs a pacemaker," he told me, "but no one in her family has ever had one so . . ." He reached into his inside pocket and produced a card. "Although she won't approve of this, I would like you to have my telephone number. Should she get weaker, please call. As I understand it, Mrs. Randolph wanted someone besides the maid to be in the house. I think that was a good idea. Well," he concluded, gazing up the stairway once more, "I'll be back in a week if I don't hear anything otherwise."

He started for the door, paused to smile at me, and then left.

I gazed at the card, noting the telephone number. How was I to know when she was sick or weaker? What an awesome responsibility, I thought. Why wasn't Victoria or my mother looking after her more?

I hurried up the stairs. When I reached the landing, I heard my grandmother call my name and went to her bedroom doorway. This was the first time I had actually seen her room. I had thought mine was big, but hers was at least three times the size with a part of it serving as a living room, containing two matching sofas, a reclining chair, a television set, tables and lamps. Her bed was a high post, dark maple wood with branches and leaves carved into the headboard. The room was thickly carpeted in light blue and the walls were painted a powder blue.

At first I didn't see Grandmother Hudson. I had anticipated her being in bed, but then I saw her sitting in a chair. She was in her velvet robe.

"So?" she said. "How was your rehearsal? Did you quit?" she asked with the corners of her mouth turned down.

"No, I didn't quit. The rehearsal went well after a few bumps," I said.

"Bumps?"

I told her what concerned some of the students. She listened with interest and then nodded.

"I was waiting for something like that to happen," she said. "Megan spends most of her time with her head in the sand. For someone who wanted to change the world, she has a remarkable ability to avoid reality."

"Maybe it's inherited," I suggested. Her eyebrows went up as if they were hinged to the folds in her forehead.

"What is that supposed to mean?"

"Aren't you avoiding facing reality? You have a medical problem that needs attention," I said.

"You are a very forward young lady. Who do you think you are, speaking to me like that?" she demanded.

I stood my ground.

"Your granddaughter," I said calmly. "Where I come from family members care about each other and don't need special permission to look after each other," I told her. Her face softened, her eyebrows returning to their place.

"My doctor has a big mouth," she said rather than continue to challenge me.

"He's just worried and trying to do his job. He has a responsibility," I said. "You're lucky to have a doctor like that. In my neighborhood you had a better chance of being visited by a man from Mars than a real doctor and when you were sick and had to go to an emergency room. They treated you like numbers and not people. If you didn't listen to what they said, they couldn't care less."

"I don't need to hear a lecture from a teenager about how fortunate I am," she snapped.

"From what the doctor tells me, you do," I fired back.

She took a deep breath.

"I'm not coming down to dinner tonight. Send that excuse for a maid up here to see me," she commanded.

"Did you call my mother and tell her about the doctor's visit? Or Victoria?"

She started to laugh and then stopped and straightened herself up, tightening her hands on the arms of the chair.

"I have never, nor do I ever intend to, throw myself on the charity of my children. Or," she pronounced sharply, "my grandchildren. Now do as I say."

"Yes, ma'am," I said and did as she wished.

Was pride ever a good thing? I wondered. It was important to have self-confidence, but more often than not, it seemed, being proud got in the way of better things, especially love. Maybe Grandmother Hudson wasn't capable of loving her own daughters and grandchildren. Maybe it was wrong to simply assume they were the ones who failed. If I stood still, closed my eyes and thought about all this, I would sink into a whirlpool of mixed emotions. It was better to just move ahead, keep as narrow a view of my future as I could, and wait for a chance to escape.

What I didn't know then, but what I would know soon, was there was no escape. There was never a real escape because you would have to deny who you were and that was something I was discovering I could never do.

As if she had heard my thoughts, my mother called that night. She wanted to know how my first few days at Dogwood had gone. I told her about the play and my part and she sounded very happy and impressed. Then I told her about Grandmother Hudson and what the doctor had told me.

"I've tried the best I can, but Mother is a very stubborn woman. How is she?" she asked after a moment of silence.

"She was too tired to come down to dinner tonight," I said.

I had sat alone and felt silly being served my dinner. However, whether I was afraid she would find out if I didn't or whether I'd already gotten used to the custom, I dressed for dinner. Merilyn had little to say except that Grandmother Hudson complained her food was cool by the time she had brought it up to her.

"Maybe I should try to visit sooner," my mother mused. "I'll try to be there the weekend after next. I might bring Alison and Brody along. I guess it's time you met, although you must promise not to tell them the truth. Do you promise?"

"I promise," I said. I had to admit I was curious about them, but if it wasn't important that they know who I really was, then I wasn't going to lose sleep over it.

"You have my number if you need me," she said.

"Shouldn't I have Victoria's number, too? She's closer," I said.

"That's up to Victoria. I told her why I wanted you living there. She's smart enough when it comes to business. She should be smart enough to give you her telephone number," my mother said.

That ended our conversation. She obviously didn't want to discuss Victoria nor hear any more about her mother. I was hoping Mama would call. I sat down and wrote her a long letter, describing the school, the teachers and the students. I told her about the play, but I left out any of the conflicts and controversy. Mama would hear only good news from me, I decided. She was praying she had done the right thing.

I couldn't wait to hear from Roy. I decided to write a letter to him so I would have it ready whenever I did hear from him. In my letter, I told a little about my fears and problems. It was hard to keep it all inside myself. I had no real friends, no sister sharing a room, no one who had a sympathetic ear. Afterward, I sealed the letter and kept it in the dresser drawer, just waiting for the opportunity to send it on its way.

At school the next day, I discovered that Grandmother Hudson had made preparations for me to be outfitted for horseback riding. The first time I put on my riding clothes and looked in the mirror, I laughed at myself. I thought I looked so silly. Nothing terrified me more than having to get up on the horse, but my instructor, Mr. Drewitt, was patient and after a few lessons, I actually began to look forward to equestrian class.

I knew that some of the other girls who were far advanced in horseback riding were making fun of me, but I ignored them and after I began to improve, their smiles wilted. In fact, Mr. Drewitt said I was one of his best beginning students ever.

Rehearsals went well, too. Colleen either avoided me or spoke to me more respectfully, especially when she saw that Mr. Bufurd liked my performances more and more. Audrey grew bolder and talked to me more, but always retreated quickly if anyone else approached. Even when she was finished for the day, she would linger to watch my performance and then walk out with me, hurrying away as soon as she saw her mother pull up or waiting.

Gradually, the tension I had experienced on the first day dissipated and even Maureen withdrew into the background. She wasn't at as many rehearsals as I was, of course. I had to be there every day and so did Corbette.

On our tenth day, he slipped into the seat beside me as we both waited to go on stage. Up until now, except for some small talk, we had really only conversed through our lines in the play. Since our classes were held on different campuses, we didn't have many other opportunities to see each other.

"You're getting good," he said in a whisper. He kept his eyes on Mr. Bufurd and the stage activity.

"Thank you," I said.

"You pick up on everything quickly. I like that. Most of the girls from Dogwood that I've played with are dimwits."

"Played with?"

He turned, smiling.

"I mean been in plays with, of course."

"Of course," I said.

"I was thinking about all that we have to do in Act Two," he continued.

"Yes?"

"Anyway, if you're willing, I'm willing to put in some extra time."

"Extra time? What do you mean? We rehearse every day after school," I said.

"I mean a weekend day, maybe this coming Saturday, for example."

"Mr. Bufurd wants to work on Saturdays?"

"No, not with Mr. Bufurd. Just us," he said. "We don't need him to go over stuff and if we come in prepared, he'll be very happy. I could pick you up Saturday, say about two, and we'll go rehearse in my barn."

"Barn?"

"We have this farm and I took over a barn we don't use. It's sort of my private home away from home, know what I mean?"

"No," I said shaking my head. I was lucky to have a home *in* a home, I thought. "Doesn't it smell?"

"No," he said laughing. "We have a farm, but we don't have any animals."

"What kind of a farm is that?"

He shrugged.

"It's what my parents wanted. I guess you could call it a movie-set home," he added. "Anyway, should I pick you up?"

"I'll have to ask Mrs. Hudson. I think her daughter is coming to visit and I might have to be there."

"Why do you have to be there? Can't you do what you want?"

"No. I'm under her supervision," I said.

"Okay," he said. "Let me know if you're free." He got up. "Oh," he added, "just keep it between us for now. I don't want any of those dimwits spreading stories."

"What kind of stories?" I shot back. What was he ashamed of?

"Who knows? You give them an idea and they'll run wild with it." He saw the disapproval on my face. "Look, you want Maureen talking about you behind your back?"

"No," I admitted.

"Neither do I," he said. He smiled. "I hope your supervisor gives you permission."

Why do the best looking boys have to be so infuriating? I wondered, but I did want to meet with him. At dinner that night I asked Grandmother Hudson if my mother had called to say she was coming on the weekend.

"She made some vague reference to it earlier this week, but today she informed me she had to attend a black-tie affair with Grant. He sees himself as a rising star on the political scene," she muttered.

"Then she's not coming?" I was both disappointed and relieved. Meeting my half-brother and half-sister would surely prove to be a traumatic experience. Would they look at me and see resemblances, sense them?

"She's threatening to show up during midweek," my grandmother mumbled. "Unless, of course, I die before that. Then she'll come sooner."

"That's a horrible thing to say. I'm sure she's worried about you."

She stared at me for a moment and then shook her head softly, her lips gently curling.

"For a girl who was brought up in what is sometimes referred to as Hell's Kitchen, you appear rather naive and trusting. I don't lie to myself, Rain. My children were spoiled and are self-centered. If anything is too inconvenient, they don't do it, even if it means not visiting a sick mother. *Especially* if it means not visiting a sick mother," she added.

"I don't lie to myself," I said, "but I don't want to stop believing in people."

"That's because you're still young enough to suffer disappointments," she remarked. "I don't have the luxury of time to waste."

She patted her lips, looked up at the ceiling and then dipped her spoon into her soup. I stared at her, feeling sorrier for her at the moment than I did for myself and Mama. She caught the look in my eyes and slammed her spoon down.

"Don't you dare look at me that way. Who do you think you are, pitying me? I don't need anyone's pity, thank you."

"I'm sorry," I said looking away quickly. "I didn't mean anything."

"Now you've gone and ruined my appetite," she said. "Not that this tastes like anything."

"I'm sorry," I moaned, tears stinging my eyes.

"And don't start that self-pity, either. It's just as annoying."

"Well, what do you want?" I wailed. Merilyn had just come through the kitchen door. She paused and retreated.

"What do I want?" She laughed to herself. "What do I want? I want my youth back and the chance to avoid the mistakes I made in love and marriage. That's what I want," she declared. "Is there any possibility of my getting my wish? Well? Is there?"

"No," I said.

"Right, no. So, I'll tell you what I want. I want the strength to endure."

She pressed her palm to her breast.

"Are you all right?"

"Yes," she said. "Just a little out of breath. Finish your dinner. I'm going up to rest."

"But you didn't eat much," I said.

"I'll have Merilyn make me some tea and toast." She rose slowly and started out. At the doorway, she wavered. I jumped up and went to her side, taking her arm. She tried to pull away.

"I'm fine," she said.

"You're terrific. We'll go horseback riding tomorrow," I mumbled, but I didn't let go.

She looked at me with surprise.

"I'm helping you upstairs, Mrs. Hudson," I said firmly. "Either with your approval or not."

"Very nice," she said walking, "showing such disrespect."

When we reached the stairway, she paused to catch her breath and then we started up. Although she seemed all right, I didn't let go of her arm.

"I'll be all right from here," she said when we reached the landing. "Go back and finish your dinner. You don't seem to mind the mediocre food."

I smiled and shook my head. She glanced at me, her eyes filling with a humorous twinkle.

"You're a lot like me, Rain," she said, "or like I was when I was your age. Be careful that you don't fall into the same traps."

"Traps? What traps?"

"Sex and love," she said. "That's all they are, traps."

She continued toward her room, her back more humped, her gait more clumsy. She looked like she had aged years. I was happy she didn't look back. She would have seen the look of pity in my eyes again and she would have been even more outraged.

I returned to the dining room to finish my meal.

"Where's Mrs. Hudson?" Merilyn asked.

"She's not feeling well. Bring her some tea and toast in about a half hour," I said.

"Great. Either I'll get fired or she'll die and I'll be out of a job," she muttered.

"That's a horrible, selfish thing to say," I snapped. Her eyes nearly popped. "If she's sick and suffering, you should show some compassion."

"What . . . why do you care about her so much? She treats you like a servant, too. I hear the way she speaks to you sometimes. She's a rich old white lady. You're just getting a handout."

"That's my business," I said. "I don't want to hear you talk against her again."

"Everyone gets so snotty here," she moaned.

"You shouldn't worry anyway," I told her. "You have another choice. You don't have to wait to get fired. You can quit."

"Maybe I will."

"Maybe you should," I said sternly.

She spun on her heels and retreated to the kitchen. I sat there fuming about it and wondering why my mother and my aunt didn't take more interest in who worked for my grandmother. I ate what I could and then I went into the kitchen myself and began to fix her tea and toast.

"What are you doing that for?" Merilyn asked.

"I thought I'd make it easier for you," I told her sharply. She didn't catch my sarcasm.

"Thanks," she said and went to clean up the dinner dishes.

I brought up the tea and toast. My grandmother was in bed, nearly asleep.

"Why are you doing that?" she demanded.

"She always manages to burn the toast," I replied.

My grandmother looked at it and then smiled.

"You're right," she said, "but I'm still not hungry."

"You'd better eat something anyway and you always need some liquid."

"Is everyone around here a frustrated doctor or nurse?" she cried toward the ceiling.

I sat beside the bed.

"And just what do you think you're doing?"

"I'm staying until you eat and drink something," I threatened.

She glared at me, dropped her head to the pillow and closed her eyes. I rose and held the tea cup. She opened her eyes, looked at it and then sipped some when I offered it. I gave her some toast and she took a bite, glaring at me the whole time.

"Satisfied?" she said.

"Yes."

"Good. Then let me sleep."

"The doctor should see you again," I told her. "You look too pale."

"Oh . . ." she moaned.

"All right. I'm leaving. Good night," I said and headed for the doorway.

"Good night," I heard her say. It wasn't a reluctant good night. It was warm.

I turned back and saw her close her eyes and made up my mind to call the doctor first thing in the morning no matter how angry it would make her.

# 14

# On My Own

Doctor Lewis didn't come to see Grandmother Hudson until after I had gone to school. I decided not to warn her that he was coming. I looked in on her before I left; she was awake, propped up in her bed and looked a little more rested, but still weak, her voice not as strong.

"How are you this morning?" I asked her.

"Fine," she said. "Just go on about your business," she said, waving me out before I could even suggest having the doctor come to see her. It was more bothersome to her that I saw her unwell than her being unwell. Her pride kept her a lonely woman, I decided.

On the way to school, I told Jake what I had done.

"Good for you," he said. "At least someone had the guts to make her do the right thing once. Of course, you may find yourself sleeping in the garage from now on," he joked.

"I don't care," I said. He gazed at me through the rear view mirror and smiled.

"Looks like she got more than she bargained for when she decided to do one more charitable thing and take you in, huh?" He stared at me for a few moments longer as if he knew more and was waiting for me to confirm it. I remained silent most of the way to school. Pretending to be someone I wasn't made me sick inside. I longed to open the window and scream out as we passed these fancy homes and people.

"I'm Mrs. Hudson's granddaughter. My mother is Megan Hudson Randolph. And if you didn't hear me, I'll shout a little louder. I'm Mrs. Hudson's granddaughter . . ."

For a moment I thought I might have actually done it. Jake had such a strange look on his face.

"You okay?" he asked.

"Yes," I said. I felt like bursting out in tears, but I repeated, "Yes, I'm fine."

I was on pins and needles all day, imagining Grandmother Hudson's wrath like a dark cloud ready to burst cold rain on my head the moment I walked into the house. Jake knew what I was anticipating. When he picked me up after the rehearsal, I could see he was more excited than usual.

"How's Mrs. Hudson?" I asked as soon as I could.

"Well, you must have had some effect on her," he replied. "She's agreed to having the pacemaker put in."

"Really? When?" I asked.

"Tomorrow morning. Doctor Lewis isn't taking any chances with her changing her mind. Good work," he added, and I got into the car quickly, more anxious than ever to get back to see what she would say.

As soon as I entered the house, Merilyn rushed out of the kitchen to greet me. She had obviously been lingering near the doorway, listening for my arrival. The look on her face told me she was under some strain and angry at me, too. I suspected Grandmother Hudson took out her frustration and rage on her, whipping her more with criticism and commands.

"Mrs. Hudson wants to see you immediately," she proclaimed with satisfaction. "It looks like you've caused a lot of trouble in the short time you've been here. I'm not surprised," she muttered.

I imagined that she was hoping I would be thrown out now. I didn't respond. I ran up the stairs and to my grandmother's bedroom. She was exactly where I had left her propped up with pillows. I tapped on the open door.

"Come in, come in," she said quickly.

"Hi."

"Hi? Don't put on that sweetness and innocent look your mother has made a classic. You know what you did. I hope you're satisfied now," she began. "You called Doctor Lewis without telling me and he is insisting I get that damn pacemaker or not call him anymore. It's so infuriating. You can't control what happens to your own body these days," she complained. She fixed her eyes on me. "Everyone sticks her two cents in. Even those you think you can trust."

"I was worried about you," I said, "so I called the doctor."

"Nonsense."

"It's not nonsense. It's prudent behavior. Adult behavior," I added.

She sucked in her cheeks and tightened her lips as she looked at me.

"You think you're wise enough already to know what's adult behavior for someone else and what isn't?"

"Yes," I insisted.

She shook her head, but her expression softened from one of annoyance and petulance to one of reluctant approval.

"Your Mama, as you call her, must have done a very good job of raising you and your brother and sister, under those dreadful circumstances. Very well, what's done is done. Let's not argue about it. Whatever happens, happens."

"What time are they doing it?" I asked.

"Tomorrow at ten. I have been assured it's a simple procedure nowadays, but that's just a doctor's propaganda. I don't know anything that's simple these days, except some of the people who come to work for me, and, even some who come to live with me," she added looking like a spoiled child.

"I'll stay home from school and go along," I said.

Her head jerked up.

"You will not. That's ridiculous."

"But—"

"Think about it, Miss Prudent Behavior, Miss Adult Behavior. Why would you? You're just a guest here," she reminded me sharply.

I swallowed my disappointment. I had been hoping she had come to see me differently, but holding onto our secret was still important to her. Family name remained the highest priority to be guarded at all costs. I might always be a stranger in this home and family. It was a hard lump to swallow.

"What about my mother and Victoria?"

"Reluctantly, I phoned them. Victoria will be here shortly. Megan says she'll be at the hospital tomorrow. I'd be better off if neither of them showed up," she added.

"Why? They're your daughters. They should be at your side."

"Holding my hand?" She laughed. "They'll only make everyone nervous and Victoria will argue with the doctors and the hospital administrator about the cost of an aspirin," she said.

I had to laugh, envisioning just what she described. She calmed down and asked me to tell her about school, my riding lessons and the play rehearsals. I showed her some of my test scores and grades on essays and she lifted her eyebrows, impressed.

"I must confess," she said, "that when Megan told me about you and it was decided you would attend Dogwood, I didn't think it would be for long. I couldn't imagine anyone coming from where you come from and doing well in that school."

"Thank you," I said. "I think."

She laughed and then she told me to go see about dinner.

"That girl will be a slacker if we don't watch her," Grandmother Hudson said. I smiled to myself. For the first time since I had come, she had said, "we."

Merilyn was sullen, especially when she found out I wasn't in any serious trouble. I thought she had overcooked the roast beef and made the potatoes too greasy. I wasn't anxious about having her bring the food up to Grandmother Hudson, but she ignored my comments and acted as if I wasn't even in the same room. When I finished eating what I could, I went back up to Grandmother Hudson's bedroom and as I expected, discovered she had eaten little.

My Aunt Victoria arrived about an hour after dinner. Despite her mother's health crisis, she'd made sure she completed her business at work before she'd come. She as much as said so when she came up to Grandmother Hudson's room. I know she was surprised to see me there. She carried a briefcase and put it on the bed. Then she turned to me.

"I understand you were the one who called the doctor," she said to me.

"Yes."

"Why didn't you call me or my sister first?" she demanded.

"I thought it was important to get the doctor as quickly as possible and you never gave me your phone number," I said.

"Did my mother ask you to call the doctor?" she cross-examined.

"No."

"Stop treating the girl as if she is a common criminal, Victoria," Grandmother Hudson said.

Victoria glared at me for a moment and then turned away, mumbling.

"It was still a nervy thing to do. She's only a guest in this house."

"I did what I thought was right and the doctor apparently agrees," I fired back at her.

She ignored me and opened the briefcase.

"We have a few papers to review, Mother, and documents you must sign," she said taking out one folder after another and laying them at Grandmother Hudson's feet.

"Now?"

"I didn't get much warning about all this," she complained. "You're going to have a serious procedure on your heart, Mother. There are some loose ends to close with the estate," she told her.

I nearly gasped aloud. This is what concerned her? Loose ends with the estate? She had yet to ask a single question about the medical procedure or the diagnosis. She saw my mouth fall open and smirked at me.

"Could you excuse us, please," she commanded. "This is personal."

I looked at my grandmother and then stood up.

"There's no reason to chase her away, Victoria. You know I don't sign anything or do anything without my accountant. Just bring it all to him. Go on," Grandmother Hudson said waving at the papers as if they were annoying flies, "put it all away."

"But Mother—"

"Whatever it is, I'm sure it can wait," Grandmother Hudson asserted.

"Not if something should happen to you," Victoria pursued. "Then we'll just have bigger problems."

"That's a terrible thing to put into her head. Nothing's going to happen to her, and the doctor said she shouldn't be disturbed, especially tonight. He's given her something to keep her calm," I interjected.

Victoria spun on me so fast, I nearly fell over from the wind.

"I thought I asked you to leave. This is a family matter. Your opinions are not of any importance to me."

Through the corners of my eyes, I saw my grandmother watching me with interest. She actually looked invigorated by the exchange between me and Victoria.

"Your mother's health is the most important family matter. I promised the doctor I would see that she was relaxed tonight. Rather than yell at me, you should be grateful," I charged.

Her face turned a dark shade of crimson as the veins in her neck strained.

Grandmother Hudson was smiling.

"I've never had so many people look after my interests," she said. She looked at Victoria. "It makes me want to live forever."

Victoria looked like she was choking on a peach pit.

"I'm just trying to do the right thing," she whined. "Daddy would have expected me to."

Reluctantly, she put the folders back and closed her briefcase. A few moments later she decided she had to go downstairs to get herself something cold to drink and make some very important phone calls. I never saw anyone as busy as she was and told Grandmother Hudson so.

"I suspect that half of what she does is really unnecessary," she said. "My husband accomplished a great deal more with far less effort."

Her eyelids looked heavier and heavier. I took the cup of tea from her hand and puffed up her pillows. Whatever the doctor had given her to calm her was having its desired effect, I thought. I told her good night and left to do my homework.

A half hour or so later, I heard Victoria come back upstairs and I opened my door a crack to watch her look in on Grandmother Hudson. She stood in the bedroom doorway. I knew Grandmother Hudson was already fast asleep. After a few moments, Victoria went stomping toward the stairway, casting a rapid glance at my door, her eyes red with fury.

I took the sight of them to sleep with me and fretted in and out of nightmares, seeing Victoria everywhere, even back in D.C., running along with Jerad and his pack, who were after me. She carried that damn briefcase and clutched it like a mallet, eager to pound me over the head with it.

Doctor Lewis had arranged for an ambulance to transport Grandmother Hudson to the hospital. She was angry about that, demanding to know why she just couldn't have Jake drive her there in the Rolls.

"An ambulance," she declared, "isn't going to be any more comfortable and will just attract a lot of unnecessary attention."

I began to understand that Grandmother Hudson thought of illness as weakness, something to be ashamed of, and not something beyond one's control. She wanted to keep her pacemaker procedure secret, go in and out of the hospital without any fanfare, and never tell another soul what had been done.

Once again I tried to get her to give me permission to go along, but she was even more insistent that I didn't. Just when I got into the Rolls to go to school, the ambulance arrived. Jake watched the attendants rush up the stairs.

"Wait until they meet her," he said. "She'll slow them down." He glanced at me. "Don't worry about her. She's not going to die until she's good and ready."

I nodded. He might not be all wrong about that, I thought. She had the grit to stand up to the Grim Reaper and tell him to go back outside and wait to be properly introduced.

For most of the day, I found it difficult to give my classes my complete attention. My eyes were continually drawn to the clock. Some of my teachers probably thought I was bored with their classes and was looking forward to the bell. The lunch hour came and went and my afternoon classes began. I had half-expected and hoped that my mother would call the school and have someone give me an update on Grandmother's surgery, but no one called.

My horse, Flagler, seemed to sense my distraction and continually wagged her head and challenged the reins during my lesson. For no reason she broke into a trot and I bounced like a rubber doll in the saddle, bringing laughter to Mr. Drewitt's lips. When I dismounted, he told me I was walking like a bowlegged drunken sailor.

I was terrible at rehearsal, missing lines, forgetting stage positions and moves, speaking with a voice barely audible from the first row. Maureen was at this rehearsal and sat with a smile of satisfaction on her face every time Mr. Bufurd had to remind me of something or ask me to project more.

"Aren't you feeling well?" Audrey asked me in a whisper when we were both in the wings.

"Yes, I'm just worried about Mrs. Hudson. She went in for a pacemaker this morning."

"Oh. Well, if she died, someone would come to tell you, wouldn't they?" she asked without much feeling.

"I don't know," I said. I really didn't.

"If she dies, will you go back to Washington, D.C.?"

"I don't know." I shook my head. "I don't know, but that's not why I'm worrying."

She took another look at me and bit down on her lower lip.

"Oh, I hope you don't get sent back," she said. "You're doing so well in the play."

"I think Mrs. Hudson's life is a little more important than this play, don't you?" I snapped at her.

"What? Oh yes, I didn't mean . . . I mean . . . yes," she said and walked quickly toward the back of the stage.

I felt sorry for her; she was just trying to find a way to become friends, but I didn't have the patience for it at the moment. Mercifully, the rehearsal came to an end.

Corbette seized my arm at the elbow to hold me back when I went for my books and hurriedly started up the aisle.

"Well?" he asked.

"Well what?"

"What about tomorrow?"

"Oh. I . . . forgot all about it. I'm sorry," I said and quickly told him what was happening.

"She'll be all right," he assured me. "My grandfather had that done last year. I'll call you tonight, okay? Okay?" he repeated when I didn't reply.

"What? Yes, okay," I said, more to get free than anything else. I practically ran out of the theater and toward the car. Jake was waiting beside it, the smile on his face giving me some instant relief.

"Everything's fine," Jake said quickly. "She's doing very well. The doctors will let her come home in a day or so."

"Really? That's great," I said.

"Yeah." He smiled. "Now they need you in that house more than ever."

On the way home, I thought about what he had said and how he had said it. That was what Audrey thought I was worried about, and surely Victoria did, too. Did everyone think I was only concerned with myself? Why shouldn't they? I realized. They knew nothing else about me.

When I arrived at the house, I discovered my mother and Aunt Victoria in the living room. They were both sipping wine and talking.

"How's Mrs. Hudson?" I asked from the doorway. Aunt Victoria smirked, but my mother smiled warmly.

"She's doing well, Rain. Thank you for getting her to do the right thing, finally. I've been after her to have a real examination and get this problem solved for nearly a year now. Doctor Lewis told me about your call." She turned her head from Victoria and winked. "How are you doing?"

"Good," I said.

"I understand you're getting good grades."

Victoria grunted.

"And you have the lead in the school play?"

"Yes."

"This is one amazing ghetto child," Victoria quipped and sipped her wine. With her eyes narrowing suspiciously, she looked at Megan. "It's just lucky the one you had assigned to you and Mother was so talented. You could have gotten a drug addict or something." She turned to me again. "Not that we know all there is to know about Rain. Police files on juveniles are usually kept under wraps."

"I don't have a police record," I snapped.

"Rain has a good reputation and a good school record," my mother said calmly. "She deserves a chance to make something of herself."

"You and your altruistic little endeavors, Megan. What does Grant think of all this?" Aunt Victoria asked.

"He's very supportive of my charity work, Victoria."

"What people will do to make a place for themselves in the political scheme of things," Aunt Victoria said, shaking her head.

"That's not why I do it," my mother said sharply.

"I know. I know," Victoria said in a tired voice. "Did you ever think of putting some of that energy into work that would earn your family something more than pats on the back, Megan? You still have that silly idealistic streak that got you into loads of trouble all those years ago."

"We do well enough without me having to find ways to create more income, Victoria. And it's not silly idealism to want to help people who aren't as well off as you are."

"You never can do well enough," Aunt Victoria insisted. "You have your own children to worry over."

My mother shot me a quick worried look.

"Are your children here, too, Mrs. Randolph?" I asked, expecting they might be in some other part of the house. I took a deep breath. It was time to meet them, I knew.

"No, I didn't want to take them out of school with such short notice," she replied.

I simply stared for a moment. She didn't want to take them out of school? Their grandmother might have died on the operating table and they didn't insist on coming here?

"They'll visit sometime in the near future," she added, seeing the look on my face.

"Oh. Are you staying awhile?" I asked, hoping she was. I wanted so to spend more time with her.

"That's what Victoria and I were discussing. We've decided to hire a nurse for a few weeks. Victoria's too busy to spend a great deal of time here and I'm too far away. And," she continued, "the awesome responsibility will be taken off your shoulders, not that you're incapable of handling it. However, you have to be in school, too, and I didn't make arrangements for you to be here to baby-sit," she concluded.

Victoria shook her head and finished her wine.

"I've got to get back to the office," she said rising. "You'll see that Grant looks over those papers I sent along last week?"

"Yes," my mother promised her.

"It's not an insignificant matter, Megan."

"I promise. I'll see to it," she emphasized, but Aunt Victoria didn't look placated.

"I'll be calling him," she threatened and started out of the living room. She paused beside me in the doorway. "I've left numbers on the bulletin board in the kitchen if for some reason you need something important, although I expect the nurse to keep me informed as to my mother's condition." She glanced back at my mother. "At least you won't have to call my sister and drag her all that distance back. Understand?" she pumped at me.

"Yes, ma'am," I said. I nearly saluted.

She pressed her lips together and left. When I saw her go out the front door, I turned to my mother, who put her finger to her lips before I could speak.

"Merilyn is nearby," she whispered. She pointed to the chair in front of her and I sat. "So how is it really going for you here?"

I told her again about my grades, how much I enjoyed the horseback riding lessons and the play.

"But are you able to get along with my mother? I know how trying she can be. Her ideas are planted in cement."

"We have a truce between us," I said. "She pretends to be a lot harder than she really is, although she's always complaining about the way young people are brought up today," I said, which made me think about Grandmother Hudson's other grandchildren. "I was hoping you would bring Brody and Alison."

"It really was such a big effort for them to get out of their activities. Alison had a test to study for; Brody had a big game. I decided it would be better to bring them another time. Don't worry," she said. "You'll meet eventually. Have you heard from your mother and brother?"

"Just Mama," I said and told her where she was living now and what Roy had done with himself.

"You should call her and let her know things are still going well here. I'm sure she's worried about you."

"I will," I said.

She gazed around, a soft smile replacing her tired, worried look.

"This is quite a house, isn't it? You're in my old room, right? I used to sit by the window late in the afternoon and watch the day darken." She embraced herself. "I felt so safe here. It was as if these were castle walls and there was a moat around the house. Nothing bad could happen to me. My father wouldn't permit it. He would run home if he heard there was a tear streaking my cheek. I don't know how many times I sat on his lap in his den and listened to him weave his dreams for me, all of them like little fairy tales.

"But," she said with a deep sigh, "you can't dream for other people. Once I went to school and made friends and saw the world that was on the other side of that moat, a world where people didn't live in fairy tales, things changed. I disappointed him in so many ways," she said sadly, "but it had to be."

"You and Victoria are so different. It's hard to believe you're related," I said.

She laughed.

"She's two years younger, but she acts like she's ten or twenty years older, I know. She's too serious. She always was. My father didn't pay as much attention to her as he did to me as she grew up, but later he seemed more comfortable around her than he was with me. She never challenged his preconceived ideas about people and business and the purpose to life. Still . . ." she said with hesitation.

"What?"

"I can count on my fingers how many times I saw him kiss her with any fatherly affection, while he rained kisses on me in torrents of love that left me giggling." She paused, recalling, her face filling with the pleasure of those memories. Then she grew sad. "No matter how content and self-sufficient Victoria portrays herself to be, I believe she felt cheated as a child. I really feel sorry for her."

"She'd hate to know it," I said.

My mother nodded and laughed.

"Still, I think she's jealous of me even though she calls my life all fluff. Well," she said standing, "I'd better start back. You can call me if anything happens or you need anything. Mother will be home by Sunday and the nurse, a Mrs. Griffin, will be with her."

I stood up and she beamed a smile full of sunshine at me.

"Somehow, just after meeting you for a short time, I was confident you would do well here. It didn't take you long to make the transition to a better life, to a world of opportunity. I guess your Mama was right. You can't deny the demands of blood. You're too much like me, like my mother, like my father, like the Hudsons."

"I'm not like Victoria," I insisted.

"Somehow I think that makes Victoria happy, too," she said and laughed. She hugged me once, and started out.

I hated to see her leave. I felt so unfulfilled. After the door closed behind her, I stood in the entryway for a moment. The silence in the great house surrounded me. I was even grateful for Merilyn's footsteps and whiny little voice asking me if I wanted the poached salmon or leftover turkey for dinner.

"Take a night off, Merilyn," I replied.

"What?"

"You can take the night off. I'll fix my own supper," I said.

"But I'm the cook and . . ."

"There's just little old me," I said with a smile.

"Very well. Do what you like," she said, "only be sure you clean up your mess, too."

She spun around and retreated to her quarters. I hurried upstairs to call Mama. She was happy to hear from me and happy to hear about the good things that were happening to me. I told her about Grandmother Hudson's operation and explained that the prognosis was good.

"I'm glad of that," she said. "I don't think your real mother would take you home with her if that woman died."

"It'll be all right, Mama," I said. For some reason now, I didn't want to be critical of my mother, even though I had every reason to be, even though I would *always* have every reason to be.

After a moment of silence, Mama told me about Ken. I sensed she had been debating keeping it a secret from me.

"Ken's in trouble again," she said.

"What is it this time?"

"He was arrested a few days ago for trying to rob a liquor store with another man. He tracked me down to see if I could help him, but what can I do? I don't have money for lawyers."

"I'm sorry, Mama."

"I know, honey, but this makes me even happier I got you away from there. Don't you think about it. I'm sorry I told you."

"Have you heard from Roy yet? Does he know?"

"He called, yes. I told him but you know how he and Ken got along. He wasn't as upset as you. He asked about you. He said he was doing fine."

"Do you have his address?"

She read it to me over the phone. After we talked a little more, I took out the letter I had written to Roy and addressed the envelope. It would go out tomorrow.

Afterward, I actually enjoyed my solitude and making my own meal. I cooked the fish the way Mama and I cooked it and made mashed potatoes that were creamy and rich, not greasy like Merilyn's. It was the best meal I had since coming here and it made me feel like I was back with my family and we were all sitting around the table during happier times. Beni would be complaining about something as usual and Roy would tease her. Ken would be bragging about the wonderful things he was going to do and Mama would hum at the stove. Why didn't I know then that happy moments were really only illusions?

Merilyn walked through the kitchen once as I worked, glanced disapprovingly at what I was doing, and then left. I sat alone in the dining room, imagining Grandmother Hudson's critical eyes watching my table manners. It brought a smile to my lips.

While I was cleaning up, the phone rang. Remembering Corbette was calling, I got to it before Merilyn, but it was a nurse from the hospital.

"One moment please," she said and then Grandmother Hudson got on.

"I'm calling to see how my house is," she said.

"It's still here," I told her. "Everything's fine. How are you?"

"I should have stayed home. They've turned me into some sort of electrical machine. Have my daughters come and gone?"

"Yes," I said.

"Did they divide up my estate just in case this contraption explodes in my chest?"

"Not that I know of," I said laughing.

"This nurse wants me off the line. I had to threaten a lawsuit to get them to let me make a call. They're holding me a prisoner until Sunday, but don't let that good-for-nothing Merilyn slack off. I expect to see a clean house when I arrive."

"I'll tell her," I said gleefully.

"Thank you," she said. "And don't you slack off either," she warned.

"Feel better," I said laughing.

I heard her hang up. When Merilyn came by to check on the condition of the kitchen, I told her what Grandmother Hudson had said.

"I do a pretty damn good job here," she said. "She's got no reason to complain."

"You have nothing to worry about then," I reassured her. She inspected the kitchen and left. I went upstairs to change into something more casual so I could relax, read and watch some television. The emotional roller coaster that had taken me through the day had really left me exhausted. I was sure I'd fall asleep early.

Just as I entered my bedroom, the phone rang again. This time it was Corbette.

"Can I come by at two o'clock tomorrow then?" he asked quickly. It was as if he was making the call from some secret phone and didn't want to be overheard.

"I guess," I said, "but shouldn't we have told Mr. Bufurd what we're doing?" I asked still worried about meeting Corbette outside of school. Maybe we would learn our lines the wrong way.

"Naw," he said. "Let's surprise him."

I thought about disagreeing more, but I didn't. I had to admit I was curious about Corbette. That's all I was prepared to admit to.

However, after I hung up, I gazed at my window and imagined Roy's face reflected on the glass.

He looked back at me with scornful disapproval and concern, his eyes filled with that dark worry I often saw.

It put a chill in my spine and for a moment, I wondered if I wasn't better off just living like my real mother had: behind these castle walls, protected by that imaginary moat.

At least until I had to go forth and make my way.

The answer wasn't long in coming.

# 15

# Fact or Fiction?

My mother called me late in the morning to tell me she had spoken with Grandmother Hudson and she was doing fine. She would definitely be home the next day. Then she added, "I'm bringing Brody and Alison to visit her next weekend. I was hoping Grant would come, too, but he has a political function he has to attend."

"Have you told them anything about me?" I asked her.

"Nothing more than Mother and I have told anyone else," she said. "With all that's happened, I don't think this is a good time to throw anything else at them. It will be difficult enough for them to learn the truth when the time comes," she said.

When the time comes? I thought. When would that be? How will they be told? Was it any less difficult for me to learn the truth?

"For now, let's just keep things the way they are. Everything seems to be working out, right?" she asked. It sounded more like a plea.

"Yes," I said gazing around at my big room. How ironic it was that I felt like I was just as much a prisoner here as I had been in the Projects. Only instead of bars on the windows, I was caged in behind secrets and lies.

My mother concluded our conversation with only vague promises thrown my way. Some time in the future, we would become a real family. I suddenly felt as if I had been turned into an orphan, someone without a history. All the adults in my life were like prism lights, changing colors constantly, confusing my thoughts. Was I just a foolish, gullible girl clinging to false hope? The weight of it all began to put me into a pool of depression, sadness rippling around me.

However, the sunlight brightening my curtains quickly washed away the gloom. Anyone would call this a nearly perfect day, I thought when I gazed out at the turquoise sky with small puffs of marshmallow clouds barely moving through it. All of the greenery, the flowers, the fountains and even the stone pathways glittered with a vibrancy. It lifted my spirits and I remembered that Corbette was coming by to pick me up at two.

I sifted through my wardrobe and chose the boot cut heather gray pants and a creamy silk blouse. I put on lipstick, brushed my hair until it gleamed and then I studied myself in the mirror wondering what the boys of Sweet William really saw when they gazed at me. Of course there would always be those who wouldn't get past my darker skin and judge me alone on that, but what about those who did? Did they see me as someone exotic or as simply someone who was the product of mixing races? To some I might even be a mistake.

Was I really as attractive as Mama used to say? Wasn't my forehead too wide and my nose too big? And my shoulders . . . weren't they too narrow?

As I gazed at myself, it suddenly occurred to me that soon I would be standing on that stage in the school's theater and performing before hundreds of people, all with their eyes on me. Every imperfection would be out there for the world to see. What had I done? What fantasy world had I been in when I agreed to do this? I was sure to get stage fright. How could I back out of it now? To desert the play at this point would be unforgivable and a terrible way to start at a new school. Somehow, I had to get through it, and maybe working with Corbette like this would help, I hoped.

When it was nearly two o'clock, I lingered near the front door. I hadn't told Merilyn where I was going. It was none of her business, I thought, and yet, what if she needed me or what if Grandmother Hudson called? Reluctantly, I searched her out and found her reading a magazine in the den-office. She nearly jumped out of her dress when I appeared.

"Why are you sneaking up on me like that?" she demanded.

"I was hardly sneaking up on you. I thought you said Mrs. Hudson didn't want anyone in here."

"I have to come in here to clean, don't I?"

"Look, I don't care if you're in here or not. I just came to tell you that if anyone needs me, I'm going to study my play lines with Corbette Adams for a few hours."

"And I suppose you're making your own dinner again?"

"Yes, as a matter of fact, I am."

"Then I might as well take tonight off. I'm owed a night extra," she said petulantly.

"You don't have to have my permission," I said.

"I know that. I'm just telling you in case someone calls for me," she whined.

I heard a car horn and hurried back to the front door. Corbette had driven up in a sporty, late model red Corvette convertible.

"Not the sort of car George Gibbs would have, but it's all *I* have," he called to me.

He wore a light blue button-down oxford shirt and jeans, and his hair was a little wild from blowing in the wind.

"Got your script?" he asked as I approached the car.

"Yes," I said patting my black leather bag.

"You have the lines memorized though, I bet," he said as I got into his car.

"Maybe."

He laughed and accelerated so hard and fast, I was thrown back against the seat. I screamed and he roared with glee as he spun around and out of the driveway.

Except for my ride to school and back in the Rolls, I really hadn't seen much of the countryside. Corbette seemed to take the least traveled roads, narrow and bumpy and then cutting over one that wasn't even well paved.

"Short cut," he said as we bounced over the ruts. We had yet to pass any houses or stores.

"Is this always how you get to your house?" I asked with teeth chattering from the vibrations.

"From yours," he said but looked away quickly. I suspected he wasn't eager to have anyone see me riding in his car. "How do you like Dogwood?"

"I like it a lot," I said.

"It's a big change from where you were I bet, huh?"

"No, not big," I said. "Gigantic."

He smiled, those white teeth gleaming. With the sun in his face and the wind playing in his hair, he looked like a movie star. He never had to question his good looks, I thought, but he also didn't show any signs of modesty. Roy would call him a white boy sweet on himself, I thought, and turned away to laugh at the thought.

We passed a farm where there were cows and a half dozen horses grazing. After another long section of overgrown fields and some woods, his family's farm came into view.

"Home sweet home," he declared nodding toward the house. It was a large house, covered in fieldstone and I had to admit I had never seen a home quite like it.

"My grandfather built it after he returned from the First World War, or at least, that's what I've been told. It's French Eclectic and you're right, there are few like it around here."

Behind the house was a large, freshly painted gray barn with glossy black trim on its doors and windows. The property was all fenced in, the grounds mowed and trimmed. There was a cobblestone circular driveway leading up to the house with lanterns on pewter colored metal poles. Corbette turned abruptly off the driveway and followed a dirt road toward the barn.

"When were there animals here?" I asked.

"When my grandfather lived here, but not for real farming. He had some riding horses and some prize bulls. It was more like a hobby."

"What does your father do?" I asked, impressed with the size of the house and the beautiful grounds. A pool and a tennis court were behind the house with a gazebo and a rock garden nearby. I saw at least a half dozen pretty fountains and stone benches.

"He's a lawyer, contract law, even some international work," he said. "My mother is the president of a half dozen charities. She's busier than my father. At least, that's what he says."

We stopped in front of the barn. It was so quiet, not a living soul was in sight.

"Is your mother home?"

"No, she's at a board meeting for one of the charity events she's planning. And my father had to go to his office. Come on," he said hopping over his door rather than opening it. I got out and he opened the door to the barn. "My hideaway," he announced and stepped back as I approached.

Part of the barn had been sectioned off and what looked like a living room in an apartment had been constructed. There was an oatmeal colored rug on the floor, furniture that included a curved sofa, two overstuffed chairs, side tables, a large coffee table, an entertainment center with a television set and a stereo unit that included a CD player. Above us, track lighting ran along the unpainted beams. He flipped a switch and lit up the room. Some of the walls had movie and rock posters on them. There was a mirror and a book case as well as a cabinet on the right wall.

"I can't believe this is in a barn," I said.

"Anyway, you see there's no smell. No hay or manure. You want something to drink?" he asked going to a small refrigerator on the left. He opened the door and looked into it. "I have beer, soda, bottled water, and some cranberry juice. Goes good with vodka," he said turning and smiling my way. "And I've got that too."

"Just some water, thanks," I said.

He took out a small bottle and poured me some and then he opened a bottle of beer for himself.

"Relax," he said nodding at the sofa when he handed me my water.

"How much time do you spend here?" I asked.

There were some magazines on the table, packages of CDs and tapes on the floor beside the entertainment center, and a small garbage can filled with beer bottles. On a counter near the refrigerator was an old open pizza box with some crust visible.

"Most of my time when I'm home. I go over to the main house for my meals and to sleep, but I've slept here many nights too."

"Your parents don't mind?"

"Mind? I'm out of their hair," he said. "My father had the carpenter build it for me and they bought me all the furniture and let me take the stereo and the television set out of the house."

How strange, I thought, that parents would want to avoid their child so much they would actually create another home away from home for him.

Corbette sat beside me, sipped his beer, and gazed at me as if he was waiting for me to say or do something mind-shattering. I glanced around again and then I opened my bag and took out my script.

"Should we just read through it first?"

"I have it memorized," he bragged. I put the script down.

"I think I do, too."

He smiled that smile full of confidence again.

"Thought so." He turned serious. "You know, you're driving everyone crazy."

"I am? Why? What have I done?"

"You're the first ghetto girl to attend Dogwood and the other girls have been expecting you to fall flat on your face. You keep surprising and disappointing them, especially Colleen," he said.

"Did you expect me to fall on my face, too?"

"Yeah," he confessed, "but I'm enjoying your success because I don't like most of those snobby bitches. It's refreshing to meet someone like you, a girl who knows the score, who's been around and yet can hold her own with them. They're jealous and they're afraid of you. I like that. Rehearsals have never been more fun for me."

He put his beer down and moved closer.

"Let's start, because I have to get back in a few hours," I said. "My guardian will be calling from the hospital and the maid isn't exactly a fan of mine."

"Sure, but we should get to know each other better first. That way we'll relate to each other better on the stage. I know about these things. I've been in dozens of plays," he said nodding.

"I don't think that's as important as getting to know the people we're supposed to be on stage," I countered. "It's easy to see they're both pretty shy. That might give you the most trouble," I added.

He stared for a moment and then laughed.

"You're pretty funny," he said. He reached under the sofa and came up with a small plastic bag. "I've got some good stuff," he said.

"What is that?"

"I'm sure you recognize good pot," he said.

"No."

"Come on. It's probably more common than cigarettes where you live."

"It's not more common for me," I said.

"You mean you don't smoke?"

"No," I said.

"Hey, it will relax you and you'll do better. Take my word for it."

He inched closer and brought his face so close to mine, we were nearly kissing.

I leaned back.

"I'd rather not," I said. "Is this why you brought me here? I thought we were really going to work on the play."

"I just want to get to know you better," he said. "Don't you want to get to know me?"

He put his left hand around my waist and urged me to lean into him. I resisted.

"Stop it, Corbette," I said putting my right palm against his chest. "I don't know what you expected, but I'm not here for anything but practicing our parts."

"We're supposed to be getting married in the play."

"So?" I asked.

"And Emily dies in childbirth. She has to get pregnant first," he said with a wide smile.

"I'll skip that part, thank you."

"You're tough."

"I'm not anything, Corbette, except disappointed in you. Is this what happens with all the girls you bring here?"

"Most," he admitted without any shame.

"I'm not most," I said. I stood up. "Maybe you should just take me back and we'll leave practicing our lines for rehearsals at school."

"Hey, don't get so bitchy. I didn't mean anything bad," he said looking down. He tossed the plastic bag of pot under the sofa and looked repentant.

"I don't just jump into a boy's arms," I said. "I get to know people."

He looked up at me skeptically.

"I don't know what you think or have been told, but not everyone from my neighborhood is the same. People should judge each other as individuals and not as some stereotype," I lectured down at him. I felt the blood fill my face and the heat go into my eyes. He looked impressed.

"Boy, you can get mad," he said. "But you know what, you just get prettier."

It was something Roy had said to me often. I relaxed, but I didn't sit on the sofa again.

"I don't understand the way you live," I said gazing around again.

"Why?"

"How come you want to be away from your parents so much?" I asked.

He gazed up at me and then down at the floor.

"It's been hard in my house ever since my baby brother died of a blood disease," he said. "My mother keeps herself busy just so she doesn't have to think about him. My father is the same way and I think when they do things with me, they're forced to remember and it hurts. It's easier for me to be alone and leave them alone. It doesn't stir up the grief."

"Oh, I'm sorry," I said.

He sat back, looking as if he was about to cry. I sat next to him.

"How old was he when he died?"

"Four," he said.

"That's terrible. I lost my sister this year. I can appreciate what you're going through."

"What happened to her?"

"She was murdered by gang members."

"Wow. I guess you have seen a lot more real life."

"It's not real life, Corbette; it's real low life."

"It must be hard for you living without family," he said. He leaned toward me and twirled some strands of my hair in his fingers. "It's hard for me even though I pretend it isn't. You think I have everything because I drive a fancy car and live in a big house and my parents are rich, right? You even resent me because of it. Right?"

"No."

"That's why you're so . . . cold to me."

"No, that's ridiculous," I said. "I don't resent you and I'm not cold to you."

He smiled.

"Good. I really do like you, Rain. You're an exciting girl," he said. He held my hair firmly so I couldn't back away as he brought his lips closer and closer until he touched mine. I didn't resist and he kissed me harder.

"You're right. It's so lonely here for me," he whispered. He kissed my cheek and then my neck. "Everyone is jealous because I have my own little place, but it's really lonely, just as lonely as it is for you. But neither of us really have to stay lonely."

His lips moved around my neck, to the other side and then up my cheek to my lips. This kiss was longer, harder, his body pressing against me until I fell back. He kissed the base of my throat and undid a button to kiss me lower until he was at my collar bone and then he undid another button and another. His lips nudged one breast and then the other and his tongue dipped into my cleavage. I felt my heart pounding. I wanted to turn away and yet, I felt as if my body was in rebellion, demanding I stay.

"Corbette," I pleaded. "Please, don't . . ."

"Rain, oh Rain. How warm and exciting you are," he whispered.

Another button went undone. His hands were inside my blouse and around to unfasten my bra. He undid it with expertise and then lifted the material away from my breasts. His lips were on one nipple and then the other and his body was down on me so that I couldn't get my hands around to stop him.

I tried to protest, but he filled my lips with another long passionate kiss and managed at the same time to unzip my pants. In seconds, his fingers were under my panties, exploring. I thought I would explode with excitement. I was surprised at the part of me that didn't want to resist.

"I knew you would be more mature than the other girls. I knew it," he muttered in my ear.

"Corbette, wait," I said weakly. "I'm not who you think I am."

"I want you. I want to know you so much," he said. I felt his fingers fumbling with his own pants. Panic began to do battle with the waves of erotic pleasure that rose from my loins into my stomach to meet the tingling coming from my breasts. I felt as if I was sinking into the sofa and every attempt to bring it to a stop was blocked by a darker side of my own self.

He started to jerk my pants down and when I pulled up to get away, I only aided his efforts. They were down to my knees and his hands were tugging at the rear of my panties. I felt his penis hardening between my legs.

I shook my head. This can't be happening so fast. It can't, I thought.

"Wait, no, wait," I pleaded. "This is too fast." My head was actually spinning.

"Not for you," he said. "Come on."

With one final burst of strength, putting all my resistance into it, I shoved him far enough to the left to have him roll off the sofa. The moment he was off me, I pulled up my panties and my pants and sat up, buttoning my blouse. He lay stunned on the floor.

"What's wrong?" he asked.

"I told you I don't just jump into bed with someone," I said. "I'm not saying I don't like you, Corbette, or I couldn't get to like you a lot, but I can't just do this the first time we're together. I just can't."

He stared at me and then he smiled.

"Okay," he said. "We'll take our time, get to know each other a little better. See?" He said buttoning himself, "I'm easy to get along with."

"Let's do some of the lines," I said, "or take me back."

"Okay, okay. The lines." He stood up, brushed back his hair, took a sip of his beer and after he regained his composure, we began.

We practiced for nearly an hour, with his interrupting every once in a while to kiss me and then, pull back with his hands up, claiming he was just trying to get to know me better. I had to laugh, even though I had just come the closest I had ever come in my life to making love. He didn't know it, but he had been only seconds away. I had nearly lost control of myself and even felt some regret that I hadn't, but that was something I wasn't going to let him know.

I told him I had to get back home and I insisted. He was disappointed, but we left.

He took me home the same way, over the back roads. At the house he kissed me long and hard again, running his hand over my breasts and down my stomach to my thighs before I pulled away and got out.

"What about tomorrow?" he asked. "Same time?"

"No. My guardian is coming home and I should be here to help out," I said.

"Maybe one night after school this week?"

"Maybe," I said.

"You're going to make me work hard for you, huh?" he asked, half-jokingly.

"Won't that be a big change for you," I said and he laughed.

"Good-bye, Emily Webb."

I watched him drive away, a part of me relieved, but an even bigger part of me sulking at my self-control. Yes, he was rich and arrogant, but he was so handsome and as he showed me by telling me about his family, he could be very sensitive, too. I couldn't help but wonder what Grandmother Hudson would think about all this, especially if Corbette and I actually became an item.

As I was going up the stairs, Merilyn called to me.

"You had a phone call," she said. "Someone named Roy."

"Roy?" I hurried back down. "Oh when?"

"An hour ago."

"Is he calling me back?"

"He didn't say."

"Did he leave a phone number for me?" peppering her with questions.

"No."

"What did he say?"

"He just asked for you. I told him you were studying lines from a play with a boy from school and he said to tell you he called. That's all. I wasn't hired to take messages for you," she added and marched away.

Disappointed, I walked slowly up the stairway and threw myself on my bed, my heart feeling jumbled. Pictures and sounds ran up and down, back and forth across the screen of my memory. Corbette's eyes faded into Roy's and Roy's voice was overtaken with Corbette's. Their kisses, their caresses nudged that part of me that had awoken with each small explosion of passion Corbette and Roy had created.

I lay on my back with my eyes closed and moaned softly, wondering if I should have surrendered myself, wondering what it would have been like, wondering what danger and what ecstasy waited on the other side of that door, a door I had nearly opened.

Merilyn had left before I went down to prepare myself some supper. I was standing in the kitchen, looking through the pantry and the refrigerator, reviewing what my menu choices would be when the phone rang. I lunged at it, snatching it off the cradle, hoping it was Roy, but it was Audrey.

"Hi," she said in a tiny voice. "I'm sorry to bother you, but I wanted to call to see how Mrs. Hudson was doing."

"Oh, she's doing fine, Audrey," I said, not able to hide my disappointment. I felt bad about it and quickly added, "but it's nice that you called."

Her voice grew stronger, bolder.

"I was worried about you too," she said. "The play's coming along really good, isn't it?"

"I guess so. It's my first so I really have no way to judge."

"Oh it is. Believe me. I've been in a few and none of them was as good as this is already. It has a lot to do with you, Rain. You're really very good."

"Thank you, Audrey. When you're as scared about it as I am, you appreciate that."

"A huh," she said.

She was quiet for a moment.

"What are you doing tonight?" I asked her. "If you'd like, you could come over here and have some dinner with me."

"Really? Let me ask my mother," she said jumping at the invitation. I heard the receiver drop to a table and laughed to myself. Moments later, she was back on line. "She said okay. We're just staying at your house though, right?"

"Yes," I said.

"I'll be right there," she said. She didn't even say good-bye.

I couldn't help but marvel at how easy it was to make friends and even become involved in a relationship with these rich white kids. Loneliness knew no boundaries after all. It doesn't care about the color of your skin or the numbers in your bank account. It just waits for its opportunity to crawl inside you and put a shadow over your heart.

Less than fifteen minutes later, I heard the door chimes and greeted Audrey just as her mother drove away.

"Hi," she said. "Thanks for inviting me."

"Come on in. I'll show you around, if you like."

"Oh, you don't have to. I've been in this house before," she said as I closed the door. "It's very nice. The last time I was here, I met Mrs. Hudson's granddaughter and grandson."

"Really? Tell me about them," I urged.

"You've never met them?"

"No. Come on. We'll talk in the kitchen. You can help me cook."

"Cook? You're making your own supper?"

"Yes," I said laughing. She still looked amazed. "It's not brain surgery."

"My mother never lets me make anything—except brownies once when I was very little."

"I often cooked for my family because Mama was working late or she'd come home tired," I said as we entered the kitchen.

"What are you making tonight?" she asked, looking at the bowls I had out on the counter. She was obviously telling the truth, I thought. Anyone with just the smallest amount of experience in the kitchen would know what I was doing.

"Fried chicken. First, I beat the egg, then I dip the chicken in the egg, the flour and seasoned bread crumbs."

I showed her how to prepare a few pieces.

"What do we do next?"

"We put it in the deep fryer."

On the stove I had some black-eyed peas.

"You can mash the potatoes. They're already boiled."

She looked like she was in heaven helping me.

"I've got to watch the biscuits," I told her. "Roy says I always bake them an inch from burning."

"Roy is your brother?"

"Yes," I said. "Tell me about Mrs. Hudson's grandchildren."

"I didn't spend that much time with them. Alison wasn't very interested in anything I had to say. Brody was nice. He's very good looking, as good looking as Corbette Adams."

I smiled.

"What?"

"Corbette picked me up earlier today and we went to his place to study lines."

"Oh," she said. She sounded disappointed. I imagined she, like most of the girls I knew at Dogwood, had a crush on him and dreamed she would be the object of his attention.

"Did you know he has his own little apartment in the barn?"

"Yes. It's famous," she said.

"Excuse me? What do you mean, famous?"

"Lots of girls have seen it. I never have," she added quickly. She mashed the potatoes harder. "But Corbette doesn't stay with one girl too long. I don't have any experience when it comes to boys, but I feel safe warning you to watch out. I wouldn't go there even if he invited me," she assured me.

I smiled to myself. This sounded like the fable of the fox and the grapes. Mama used to quote it all the time: The fox tried to reach the grapes, but they were too high. After repeated attempts, he declared they were sour anyway.

"He's not as bad as he makes out to be," I said.

I took out pieces of chicken and put them on a plate. They looked and smelled wonderful.

"He has a reputation. The other boys call him King Cherry Picker."

"What? Why?"

"He brags about how many virgins he's ruined," she said with her face turning crimson.

I smiled at her and shook my head.

"That's probably just all rumor. Boys brag a lot in the locker room. He's actually a very sensitive person. It hasn't been easy for him since his little brother's death. He opened his heart a little and told me."

"What?"

"About his younger brother dying from a blood disease," I said. "He was only four."

She stared at me for a moment. I turned off the fire under the black-eyed peas and put them into a serving bowl. When I looked back at Audrey, she was still staring at me with the same strange expression on her face. She looked like she had just swallowed her chewing gum.

"What is it?" I asked. "You look so funny all of a sudden. Still think cooking is so difficult?"

"No, I was thinking about what you just said about Corbette's little brother."

"So?"

"I didn't know he had died."

"Oh. Very sad. Only four years old," I said. "You take the potatoes and the peas in. I'll take the chicken. The table is set and . . ."

"Four years old? No, he's about eight. I know because my mother is on the same charity board of directors as Corbette's and she asks about him all the time."

I paused, tilting my head.

"I don't understand what you're saying, Audrey."

"Corbette's little brother isn't suffering from a blood disease. Well, I suppose technically it might be called that. It has to do with chromosomes and stuff. He has Down Syndrome. You know what that is?"

"Yes," I said, "but I thought it was a different sort of blood disease, maybe even a cancer."

She shook her head.

"He died when he was four," I repeated. "I'm positive he said that."

"We can call my mother and ask her," Audrey said, "if you don't believe me. Corbette's mother didn't have his younger brother until she was in her late thirties. She's already in her mid forties, so you can't be remembering it right."

"I know what he told me," I said.

"Why would he tell you that?" she wondered aloud. Her face brightened with the answer. "Maybe he was trying to get you to feel sorry for him so you would let down your guard and become another victim of the King Cherry Picker."

I stared at her.

"Rain?"

There was a disturbing smell.

"Oh no," I screamed rushing to the stove, "the biscuits!"

They were almost burned; just like I had almost been.

# 16

# Who Can I Trust?

Jake came by in the morning to pick up the Rolls so he could bring Grandmother Hudson back from the hospital. I saw him drive up in his car and went out to speak to him. I was thinking about going along, but I was afraid to suggest it, afraid it might upset Grandmother Hudson.

"Mornin', your ladyship," Jake quipped, tipping his hat and bowing as I approached.

"Good morning, Jake. What time will you be bringing Mrs. Hudson home?"

"They told me to be at the hospital by ten. It won't be more than a forty minute ride today. No real traffic." He gazed at the house. "How do you like livin' in that big house all by yourself?"

"I had a girlfriend over for dinner," I said as an answer. "I told her about your ghosts."

Jake laughed.

"Did it scare her?"

"A little, I think. You really believe in ghosts, Jake? My mama does."

"Something lingers in a house like this one, Rain," he said, taking his cap off and scratching his head. "There's too much history. There's nothing here that'll hurt you, though," he promised.

"How can you be so sure, Jake?" I challenged.

He shrugged.

"Nothing here has ever hurt me," he replied. He opened the car door and looked at me. "Did you want to come along for the ride?"

I was tempted. I actually took a step forward and then stopped.

"No, I'd better wait here," I said. "I have some homework left to do and I want to be free to do whatever I can for Mrs. Hudson."

"You know she's bringing a live-in nurse home with her, right?"

"Yes and I heard how Victoria thought she was too expensive."

He laughed and then shook his head.

"Well, I suppose there's nothing wrong with keeping your eye on your stash," he said getting into the car. "You can learn a lot from Victoria if you'll listen."

"When you're with Victoria, that's all you can do is listen," I muttered. I probably shouldn't have said it even though I didn't for one moment think Jake would tell anyone what I had said. I just didn't like sounding mean and ungrateful.

He lowered his sunglasses and gazed at me with a half-smile on his face and then he started the engine, waved and drove off. I watched until the car disappeared. Then I turned and slowly walked back into the house.

Merilyn was just starting her dusting and vacuuming. She had come home very late the night before and hadn't bothered getting up early enough to prepare my breakfast. She knew I would make my own and leave the kitchen in better condition than she usually did, so she wasn't worried.

I really didn't have any homework left to do, just a little studying for a possible history quiz. Audrey and I had done all our homework after dinner the night before. We had talked and talked until her mother had come for her. She had confessed that the one thing she longed for more than anything, more than the best grades, the best part in the school play, was a real boyfriend, and she told me about the one and only time she had almost had a relationship. Bizarre didn't even begin to describe it.

"His name was Charles Princeton," she had begun, "and he was in this special advanced French class that combined girls from Dogwood and boys from Sweet William. It was part of an experimental college satellite program run by the nearby community college. We were the only ninth graders in the class at the time, both having done well on the entrance exam. All the rest were juniors and seniors.

"Charles was just an inch or so taller than me and chubby, but I thought he had the most beautiful blue eyes, Rain. When he looked at me, he really looked at me. He would stare right into my eyes as if daring me to stare back into his. You know how some boys will always be staring at your breasts and make you feel as if you are naked. He didn't. He just kept his eyes on mine. I always gazed right back at him.

I wasn't intimidated like most of the other girls. Not that he was very popular with other girls. He wasn't, but he didn't seem to care. I used to watch him when the other boys in the class stared at one of the prettier senior girls. Charles really wasn't a gawker. At first I thought he just wasn't interested in girls yet. You know, some boys are so immature, they'd rather collect baseball cards."

I laughed.

"I didn't know many like that," I said. "Where I come from, you grow up fast. Twelve girls in my eighth grade class got pregnant."

"Really?" Audrey said impressed, her eyes wide with excitement. Rich white kids, I thought. What I told them about my life wasn't real to them, nowhere near as real as it had been to me.

"Have you . . . almost gotten pregnant or anything?" Audrey asked. It was her way of trying to find out just how sexually active I was.

"No, have you?" I countered. It brought a wide smile to her face.

"Me? The only thing I've ever done is kiss Charles a few times and let his hand rest here," she said indicating her right breast.

"That was all? How did you stop him?" I asked, just as curious about the intimacies of these rich girls as they were about mine.

"I didn't have to. When he touched me, he acted as if he had put his hand on a hot stove. He was more frightened than I was by what he had done."

I started to shake my head skeptically.

"No, really," she emphasized. "It was his mother's fault."

"Mother's fault? What do you mean? She wasn't there, too, was she?"

She looked down for a long moment and then said, "I swore to him I would never tell anyone."

"Then maybe you shouldn't," I said.

She looked up quickly. When someone is just bursting to tell you something, the best way to get them to do it quickly is to tell them not to, I thought.

"No, Charles is gone. His family moved away over a year ago and I suppose it's all right to tell you."

"Why is it all right to tell me?" I questioned.

"You're different," she said with a thin, nervous laugh that sounded like tiny china cups shattering. "And I don't just mean because you're African-American. You're easier to talk to," she said with sincerity in her eyes.

I gave her a small smile and waited.

"He told me how his mother warned him about sex. She made him think of his penis as if it was a little animal with a separate mind of its own living between his legs."

"He said that?"

"A huh. She told him it would get him into big trouble if he let it do what it wanted. So to stop it . . ."

"What?" I asked, finding myself more intrigued than I had anticipated.

"She made him wear tight rubber underpants. He said sometimes he was actually in pain down there. He told me that was why he was afraid to look at girls or think about them."

I had heard and seen some very ugly things in my life and I had grown up thinking this was the way it was with poor, oppressed people. Distortions, promiscuity, pornography, all of it was natural to the world I'd lived in and grew like fungus in our dark, dirty neighborhoods.

But the twisted and ugly avenues people's thoughts traveled apparently knew no money barriers. Charles's mother had tortured and abused him in a different way, but the result was the same, I concluded.

"How horrible," I muttered. "Didn't his father have anything to say about it?"

"No. His father had left them soon after he was born."

"I don't blame him," I muttered. I thought for a moment. "Was he still wearing those confining rubber underpants when you knew him? When you kissed him?"

She nodded and then turned crimson with a memory.

"What?"

"Swear you'll never tell a soul," she said.

"I don't gossip, but I swear."

"He . . . made me stand on one side of the room and he stood on the other and he took down his pants to show me the rubber underpants and then he lowered them to show me how quickly it—"

"What?" I practically shouted. She swallowed hard.

"How quickly it grew and grew and then erupted when he touched it."

I sat with my mouth open for a moment.

"He did that in front of you?"

She nodded.

"That's so weird."

"I ran away," she admitted. "It frightened me."

"I think I would have run too." I grimaced at the images. "He was your only boyfriend?"

"Sort of," she said. "After that, we didn't see each other much. I had the feeling he had told his mother what had happened and she had forbidden him to see me."

She looked so devastated because she had told me the story that I immediately changed the subject and got her to talk about other things like television and movies, books she had read and places she had been. The story had actually made me sick to my stomach and I wanted to forget it as well.

When she asked me questions about my life in the Projects, I found myself exaggerating the good things. It almost sounded as if I had left a wonderful world to come suffer in this big house with all these rich people and go to a private school. She left looking at me enviously and I felt as if the house and my new life was corrupting me, turning me into another one of those who stored secrets and lies in her heart.

Late in the morning, Grandmother Hudson arrived like a storm. I heard her voice rattling the walls as soon as the front door opened. The nurse, Mrs. Griffin, stood at her side and tried to hold her arm. She was a tall, dark-haired woman who looked strong enough, but Grandmother Hudson refused to lean on anyone or anything.

"Where is everyone?" she cried.

I rushed out of my room and hurried down the stairs. Merilyn came running from the kitchen.

"Welcome home, Mrs. Hudson," I said.

"Ma'am," Merilyn said with a nod.

Grandmother Hudson gazed around with furious eyes, glanced into the living room and then started down the hallway toward the dining room.

"Mrs. Hudson. I want you upstairs and in bed," Mrs. Griffin said.

"In a moment," Grandmother Hudson replied, waving her away. Mrs. Griffin looked at me and then at Jake, who beamed a wide smile and shook his head.

"Did you wash down that dining table once since I've been gone?" Grandmother Hudson demanded of Merilyn.

"Yes, ma'am."

"It doesn't look it. There's dust on those window casings. You need to vacuum them, not just wave a feather brush at them. All that does is move the dust to another spot. I think I've told you that about one thousand times, if I told it to you once."

"I did vacuum," Merilyn asserted.

Grandmother Hudson made a gruff noise in her throat and then looked into the kitchen.

"If there's anything wrong in there, it isn't my fault, Mrs. Hudson. Rain used the kitchen too. She even had a guest for dinner last night and cooked their dinner herself," Merilyn revealed.

Grandmother Hudson raised her eyebrows and gazed my way.

"And who might that have been?"

"Audrey Stempelton," I said.

"Mrs. Hudson, if you're not going to pay any attention to my orders, I might as well not be here," Mrs. Griffin said sharply.

Grandmother Hudson looked at her the way she would look at an annoying house fly, but then headed back toward the stairway.

"Bring me some tea and biscuits," she commanded Merilyn and started up the stairs. She turned to me. "Come to my room in twenty minutes," she ordered.

"Yes, Mrs. Hudson," I said as I stood beside Jake and watched her and her nurse go up the stairs.

"I give that nurse forty-eight hours," Jake said. "See you in the morning," he added and backed out as if he was happy he was able to escape, closing the door quickly behind him.

Merilyn gave me a fiery look.

"I thought you washed down that dining room table last night," she whined and pivoted like a toy soldier to go into the kitchen and prepare Grandmother Hudson's tea.

After Grandmother Hudson was settled in, I went to her room. She was propped up in her bed, looking comfortable. Mrs. Griffin had just finished taking her blood pressure.

"You can go get yourself some lunch now," Grandmother Hudson told her.

"I think I can decide for myself when I want to have lunch, Mrs. Hudson," the nurse replied dryly. "If you want me to leave the room, just ask for privacy."

Grandmother Hudson gazed up at her with a look that could burn a hole through the Washington Monument. Mrs. Griffin turned away, took her time, and left the bedroom.

"A most annoying, impudent, arrogant person, just like all those medical people. There's no better reason to stay healthy and well than avoiding those self-anointed saints. The doctors act like they walk on water. The nurses treat you as if you were interrupting their coffee breaks. I refuse to ever go back there. I'll live and die in this bed if I have to," she vowed.

I couldn't wipe the smile off my face.

"And what is so funny, might I ask?"

"The operation obviously hasn't slowed you down, Mrs. Hudson," I said.

"Of course not. It was unnecessary and it's quite annoying having this . . . this *thing* in my chest. Now what's been going on here?"

"Not much," I said shrugging.

"I realize that from one superficial look at the house. It doesn't look as if she was in this room once since I've been gone. I hate to go into the bathroom and see what condition it is in. Why is it so difficult to find reliable help?"

"Maybe you should try to relax for a day or so, Grandmother," I said in a lower voice. "Get your strength back."

"Everyone's got advice. Get my hairbrush off the vanity table. I look a fright," she said.

I found it and brought it to her.

"Just brush it down, please," she said. I smiled and began. She closed her eyes. "How's your school going? The play?"

"Very good," I said.

"And your mother? Have we heard a word from that country?"

She opened her eyes to see the expression on my face as I answered.

"She said she's coming this weekend with Alison and Brody, but not with Grant."

"One of her and her children's duty calls. I hate them. Keep brushing. What about Victoria?"

"She hasn't been here since you went to the hospital," I said. Her eyebrows rose.

"That's surprising." She was quiet for a moment and then put her hand on mine to stop me from brushing her hair. "There's something I want you to get for me," she said after taking a deep breath. "It's in the den in the safe. The safe is behind the desk, behind the picture of my husband.

"I'm going to trust you with the combination. I never make mistakes when I evaluate someone and I don't expect I'm making one about you now. Has this minor imperfection turned me into a fool?" she asked.

"I told you before and I'll tell you again, Grandmother Hudson, I am not a thief."

She made that small smile on her lips again.

"We'll see. Turn to the right twice and stop on ten. Then go back to two and to the right to twelve. On the very top of the pile of papers there is a document in a pale yellow folder. Bring it to me before Victoria gets here. And I don't want anyone to know about it. Do you understand?"

"Yes."

Merilyn came in with the tray carrying tea and biscuits.

"What did you do, send to Richmond for that? I asked for it hours ago."

"It hasn't been twenty minutes, Mrs. Hudson."

"Hmm," Grandmother Hudson said. "Put it here. Come on."

Merilyn hurriedly did so and stepped back. Grandmother Hudson felt the teapot.

"It's not hot enough," she said.

"It was scalding, ma'am."

"Maybe twenty minutes ago. Get me hot water."

"Yes, ma'am," she said directing her angry look at me.

"Well?" Grandmother Hudson said, turning to me. "What are you waiting for?"

I hurried out of the bedroom and down the stairs to the safe. Was it my imagination, or had Grandmother Hudson returned from the hospital even more crabby than before she had gone in? I thought she was supposed to feel better. I really felt sorry for Merilyn.

As I walked past the kitchen, I gazed in and saw Mrs. Griffin making herself a sandwich and some coffee. She looked like she was mumbling to herself. After I entered the den, I closed the door softly and then went to the portrait of Mr. Hudson. I carefully removed it from the wall and started to turn the knob on the safe. It clicked and I opened it and reached in. I could see there were some jewels, papers and what looked like a birth certificate. I found the document she wanted and closed the safe, carefully placed the portrait back and left the den. I didn't look at the document. It was very thick. As I approached the stairway, the front door opened and Victoria entered. Instinctively, I lowered the document and held it close to my side so it wasn't visible in my hand.

"How is my mother?" she demanded without a hello.

"She looks fine," I said. "The nurse settled her in and she's having tea and biscuits."

"Where's the nurse?"

"Having lunch," I said.

"That's probably what she'll do most of the time. I don't know why we needed a fully licensed nurse. A nurse's aide would have been quite sufficient." She started up the stairs.

Grandmother Hudson had wanted me to bring her the document before Victoria had arrived, so I was sure she didn't want me bringing it to her now. I went up to my room instead. I closed the door softly and sat at my desk, my heart thumping. All these intrigues made me nervous. Despite my efforts to fight them back, curious cat's eyes slowly replaced my own and I gazed at the folder, slipping the papers out. Carefully, I unfolded the document and read.

It was my grandmother's last will and testament.

I shoved it back as neatly as I could and put it aside. Then I opened my door enough to hear anyone walking by and waited until I heard Victoria leave. As soon as she left, I grabbed the folder and returned to Grandmother Hudson's bedroom.

She looked up expectantly and I held out the document.

"Did Victoria see you get this?"

"No."

"Good," she said. "Give me the phone."

"Shouldn't you be resting now, Grandmother?"

"What this whole thing has told me is I will be resting soon enough," she said firmly. "And I'm not the sort who would relish leaving something undone. Give me the phone."

I did as she asked. She waved me off as she made her call.

Rich people are too complicated, I thought, and for a while I actually longed to be back in the Projects, sitting in my room, worrying about nothing more than what I would make us all for dinner.

I didn't see Corbette the next day until the rehearsal. Despite our rendezvous on Saturday, he didn't behave any differently toward me. No one would guess we had kissed and been intimate. Whatever he had hoped would be between us, he wanted to keep secret. He did have an impish grin on his face when we performed, however, and that annoyed me. Mr. Bufurd stopped us continually to tell me I should try to be softer, more wide-eyed about life. The other girls had big grins on their faces and laughed together. I could almost hear them whisper, "Can she be softer? How can a girl like this ever be innocent and sweet?"

"You've had no trouble getting this before, Rain. Concentrate, relax, take a deep breath and try again," Mr. Bufurd urged.

I looked away, swallowed back my tears, sucked in my breath and turned again to face Corbette and say my lines. I tried to look past him, to really not think of him as Corbette Adams, but as the character in the play, as George Gibbs, who was just as sweet and innocent as I was supposed to be. Finally, it worked well enough to please Mr. Bufurd.

"That's it. That's more like it," he declared.

I was grateful when rehearsal ended; it had been the most exhausting yet.

"I told you we should practice more," Corbette whispered in my ear. "I'll call you later." He started after his buddies from Sweet William. I watched him go up the aisle and then I called to him.

"What's up?" he asked.

"Can I see you a minute, please?" I asked. He grinned at his friends, said something that made them all laugh, and then came sauntering down the aisle toward me.

Audrey looked my way and then quickly turned and hurried out. Corbette and I were the only ones left in the theater.

"You want to meet tonight?" he asked quickly.

"No. I want to know why you told me that terrible lie," I said.

"What terrible lie?"

"About your younger brother," I said.

He stared at me, his eyes blinking rapidly for a moment.

"It wasn't a lie," he insisted. He did it with such sincerity, I wondered if Audrey had been wrong after all.

"You said he had died when he was four from a blood disease. Isn't he still alive?"

"You went and asked people about it?" he asked, grimacing with pain.

"No, but someone told me he was in an institution and he was still alive and he had Down Syndrome. Isn't your mother on the charity board raising money for treatment and research?"

He looked back up the aisle and then he looked at me and sat with his head down, his hands clutched between his knees. He spoke slowly and toward the floor.

"When my little brother was four, they decided to institutionalize him. They treated it as if he had died. We had a big argument about it. Yes," he said looking up at me with angry red eyes, "my mother is an executive in that charity, but she's an executive in a number of charities, I told you. She does it to ease her own conscience and cover the fact that she couldn't stand people seeing him in our home, people knowing she had a child with Down Syndrome, and it does come from blood. It has to do with chromosomes and they're in the blood, so whoever opened their big mouth, doesn't know anything."

He looked down again.

"Maybe we didn't have a funeral for him, but he's gone, and that's no lie," he added as he rose and started away.

I tried to call to him, but my tongue stuck to the roof of my mouth. I felt like I was shrinking right where I stood. A numbness washed over me. Had I been unfair, insensitive, after all? Was I wrong to assume he was full of deception just because he tried to make love to me? Beni used to accuse me of thinking so much of myself I wouldn't permit a boy to get too close. Had I done what she accused me of doing? Had I been so overly self-protective that I was just as unsophisticated and inexperienced when it came to boys as Audrey Stempelton was?

Why was it all so complicated? Why couldn't people be who they seemed to be? I felt like I lived in a world full of mirrors and lights, all of them deceiving.

Audrey was waiting for me when I stepped out of the theater. Everyone else was gone.

"Are you all right?" she asked.

I told her what Corbette had told me when I accused him of lying.

"I knew I was right," she said as if the veracity of the information was the issue.

"That's not important, Audrey. I felt terrible forcing him to tell me about his fight with his parents and his mother's attitude. It was as if I had invaded his very soul. He couldn't wait to get away from me."

"He still lied to you," she insisted. "Besides, he's got a reputation."

"Maybe. Or maybe it's just a lot of rumor and innuendo spread by jealous girls."

"You said he almost raped you!"

"I never said that. See what I mean? People don't listen and then they exaggerate. Who's to say it hasn't happened many times before?"

"Well, I still think you'd be foolish to trust him," she said. She had been so happy when I was angry at Corbette. Now she looked sad and depressed again.

"I don't know who or what to trust anymore," I complained. "And I'm tired. I'll see you tomorrow."

I started for the car. Jake was leaning against it, reading a copy of the magazine from the American Association of Retired Persons.

"You're not retired. Why are you reading that, Jake?" I asked and he folded it and laughed.

"For as much as I do these days, I can qualify, princess. How's it look?" he asked nodding at the theater. "Should I buy a ticket?"

"I don't know," I said.

"You're looking a bit glum this afternoon. Miss some lines?"

"I miss a lot of things, Jake, like my mama and my brother and the miserable life I once had."

He laughed.

"Come on," he said opening the door, "I'll take you home a different way and show you something special."

I got into the car and sat back with my eyes closed. I had a terrible headache, probably caused by tension and nerves. Jake babbled about the weather, his lumbago, and the stock market. He had told me he had a little money invested and he was doing better than he had expected. He called it his scrambled nest egg.

"Here we are," he announced and I opened my eyes.

We were on an unfamiliar side road. He slowed down and pulled to the side near a corral.

"Step out a moment," he urged.

I did as he asked and we looked over the fence. In the center of the field was a mare with a beautiful glossy brown colt. It had a white streak between its eyes and down to its nose and stood close to its mother, whose tail seemed to be waving flies off the colt. It looked our way curiously.

"It was born just a week ago," Jake said.

"It's beautiful. Whose place is this?"

"Oh, a friend of mine. That's my colt," Jake said.

"What?"

"I invested a little in horses. His father was a successful trotter, Fallsburg. He raced in Yonkers, New York, for years and did the circuit. It's a gamble, but the worst thing that'll happen is I'll have a beautiful animal, huh?"

"He is beautiful, Jake."

"Whenever I get a little sad or depressed now, I just take a ride out here and watch them for a while," he said.

I nodded, smiling.

"Thanks, Jake. Thanks for sharing."

He shrugged.

"Better get you home before we both are put in the dungeon," he said.

I laughed and looked out the window as we drove away. The colt was still gazing in our direction.

There was an ominous quiet in the house when I entered. I listened for sounds of Merilyn preparing dinner and then I started up the stairs. Mrs. Griffin came out of the bedroom as I approached the landing. She was carrying her small satchel.

"That woman is impossible," she said.

"What's going on?"

"She fired her maid late this morning and has been arguing with me about everything ever since. I wasn't hired to be a cook and a maid. I've so informed her daughter. I've phoned for a taxi."

She walked past me and down the stairs.

"But . . ."

She never turned back. I threw my books down in my room and hurried to Grandmother Hudson's bedroom.

"Where have you been?" she demanded.

"I just . . . Jake stopped to show me his horse," I said.

"That horse? What a ridiculous investment. Men can be so foolish with their money, investing in dreams."

"What happened to Merilyn?"

"What happened was she left a ring around the tub, burned my toast and brought me a cup of coffee that you could use to grease a tractor. When I told her of all these transgressions, she resigned her position. I told her she had never truly filled it so she couldn't resign. She could just go and go she did.

"And as for that nurse—"

"But Grandmother, you can't stay here alone now."

"Of course I can. I've done it before." She paused. "From what you tell me, you'll probably do just as well if not far better making dinner."

I shook my head. "What does Victoria say about it all?"

"She's delighted. Look at all the money I'm saving. Of course, now she anticipates more will be going to her when I'm gone." She propped herself up. "I'd be satisfied with a bowl of soup and a toasted cheese sandwich. Don't burn the bread," she added.

"All right, Grandmother," I said and went down to the kitchen. I didn't mind preparing her dinner at all. I put a little butter and sweet pickle in her sandwich with a slice of tomato and onion even though she didn't ask for it. It was how Mama used to dress a cheese sandwich for me.

When Grandmother Hudson took a bite, she looked up surprised. I held my breath. She took another bite and then looked at the sandwich.

"This is excellent," she said. "Something coming out of my kitchen with taste. What a surprise. Now go eat your own dinner and do your homework. No one is going to blame me for any of her own failings," she declared.

I laughed and returned to the kitchen. Before I started to do anything, the phone rang. It was Corbette.

"Hi," he said. "I'm sorry I was so nasty."

"It's all right. I understand."

"Good. I was seriously thinking that you and I should get together again."

"I don't think so, Corbette. Not for a while at least. Let's wait until the play is over. It's just too emotional for me and I've suddenly been given new responsibilities here."

"Oh," he said dripping with disappointment. "You're still angry at me."

"No," I protested. I took a deep breath. "I can't hide what I feel when I'm on the stage as well as you can. We have only a few more weeks of rehearsal."

He was silent for a moment and then he asked, "Will you celebrate at our private cast party afterward? Just you and me," he said. "We'll sneak off to my place, okay?"

There was Roy whispering warnings in my ear and there was Beni whispering in the other ear.

"Okay," I said. Beni's voice was louder because it came from a deeper place inside me, a part of me that wouldn't be denied, the part that said, "It's time to know fully what it means to be a woman."

No matter how I tried for the rest of the evening, I couldn't stop my mind from wandering, my thoughts from weaving their way back to Corbette's hideaway. He was waiting for me, drawing me to him. Every time I imagined myself in his arms, I pushed the thoughts away and turned back to my math or science homework.

I stayed up as late as I could, reading and studying, but not because I wanted to do better in school.

I was just afraid to dream that night.

# 17

# Family Matters

During the days that followed, Grandmother Hudson got stronger and stronger. Even she had to admit finally that the pacemaker improved her circulation and her energy. Doctor Lewis visited her on Tuesday while I was in school, but she relished telling me how angry he was about the way she had treated Mrs. Griffin, bawling her out for chasing away the nurse he wanted to help her recuperate and monitor her progress.

" 'She's one of the best cardiac nurses I know,' he told me, but I told him even though she might be good with one organ, she's not good with the whole person."

I laughed, imagining the doctor's face. He tried to get her to hire another nurse, but she refused. The nurse could have been Florence Nightingale herself and Grandmother Hudson would have sent her packing. A nurse just called attention to her condition and she wouldn't stand for it. She did call the agency to find a new maid, however. They sent over two candidates whom she interviewed while I was in school. She rejected them both, one because she didn't believe she was strong enough to clean a big house.

"The girl was just skin and bones. She'd be gasping for breath after cleaning just one room," Grandmother Hudson told me. She just didn't like the second woman's face.

"Too sour. She looks like she has a constant toothache."

Because Grandmother Hudson paid so well, the agency promised to submit new candidates until she found one that pleased her. In the meantime, I did as much cleaning as I could and I prepared our dinners. Her compliments were less and less reluctant until she was finally lavishing praise on me and on Mama for teaching me so well. One night at dinner she talked about the cook her parents had. From the way she described her and her relationship with her, it sounded like Scarlett O'Hara and Mammy in *Gone With the Wind.*

My mother had phoned twice to see how we were doing and reconfirmed her intention to bring Alison and Brody down on Saturday. I grew more and more nervous about it as the weekend drew closer. Victoria, who had been out of town on business, popped in on us toward the end of the week. I should rather say invaded, because when she came bursting into the house, we were just sitting down to dinner and she barged into the dining room, her black raincoat flying up around her as she swung her arms, her hair wild, her eyes blazing.

At first I thought she was angry about Grandmother Hudson firing another servant and driving out the nurse, but that was nothing compared to what truly had enraged her.

"Well," she said pacing alongside our dining room table. "Don't the two of you look cozy."

"Hello to you, too, Victoria," Grandmother Hudson said. "And yes, thank you, I'm feeling better."

"I know how you're doing, Mother. I am in direct contact on a regular basis with Doctor Lewis."

"Oh? He never mentioned it," Grandmother Hudson said. "Would you like to eat with us, Victoria? Rain has prepared a rather delicious stuffed veal loin, sweet potatoes, string beans and corn bread."

"No thank you. I'm not here to eat, Mother."

"Well, do you mind very much then if we begin, Victoria? You know how I detest it when my food is served cold."

She began to eat. Victoria stood there fuming for a moment and then, reluctantly, sat across from me and reached for a piece of corn bread.

"So where have you been, Victoria?" Grandmother Hudson said casually.

I was holding my breath because I knew something more significant was about to happen. I also knew Grandmother enjoyed baiting and teasing Victoria. Her attitude made me laugh, but I hid my smiles behind my drinks of water and behind chewing my food.

"I've been in Richmond on the Snowden Project, Mother. I told you all about that, but you never listen to me when I discuss business."

"It's usually so boring, Victoria. How can you enjoy all that work with profit and loss statements, receivables, ledgers and workman's compensation? It's more suited to men."

Victoria pulled herself up in her seat. She looked like she had a spine that unfolded like a telescope, raising her neck and head higher and higher as she reached down for her words.

"It's not only old fashioned, it's insulting to conclude that a woman can't succeed and enjoy herself in the business world today, Mother. Women are not only equal to men; they're superior in many instances, and men are beginning to realize it," Victoria bragged through thin lips and clenched teeth.

Grandmother shrugged.

"It's always been my experience that when you make a man feel inferior, you close down his heart and you lose your feminine advantage."

"That's your experience, Mother. That's passé."

"Not for me," Grandmother insisted, which only further infuriated Victoria.

"I didn't come here to debate equality between the sexes, Mother."

"Oh, how I hate that terminology. Equality between the sexes. It's so . . . impersonal," Grandmother Hudson said looking to me. "Makes us all sound like lumps of coal being balanced on a scale." I risked a small smile and she turned back to Victoria. "This is delicious, Victoria. Are you sure you won't have some of the veal?"

"Yes."

"When do you eat?" Grandmother Hudson pursued. She chewed her food and stared at Victoria as if she was interviewing some other form of human species.

"I eat when I need to eat," Victoria replied impatiently. "Not because someone ordains a time for dinner."

"How pedestrian," Grandmother Hudson said.

Victoria's eyes widened. She took a deep breath.

"I'm not here to discuss my eating habits."

"Well now that we know a couple of reasons why you are *not* here, why don't you tell us just why you are here, Victoria? I'm glad to see you, of course, but you look like you have a hive of angry bees buzzing around in your head." Grandmother sipped some water and held her nondescript expression.

Victoria placed her long hands on the table, palms down, the fingers curling up slightly. She began, looking down at her hands as she spoke.

"This morning I called our attorney, Mother, on a business matter and I learned you've made a change in your will."

Grandmother Hudson lowered her fork, gazed at me and sat back.

"He had no right to discuss that."

"He didn't actually discuss it. It came up in a convoluted way because of some trust changes I was suggesting. Fortunately, it came up," she added and looked up at Grandmother Hudson. "Does Megan know about the changes you've made?"

"No, it's not any of her business, either."

"Can you explain to me why or how a complete stranger gets included in your legacy?" Victoria demanded, glancing at me.

I stopped chewing, nearly choked on what I had in my throat, and gulped some water. Grandmother Hudson had put me in her will?

"I don't care to discuss that right now," Grandmother Hudson said. "It's not a topic conducive to dining."

"I don't think it's a topic conducive to anything. It's maddening and bizarre. What has this . . . this girl," she said gesturing emphatically at me, "done beside cooking you a good meal to deserve being included in our family fortunes?"

"It's what I wish," Grandmother Hudson said. "And it's my decision."

"It's not a rational decision. It's not the action of a woman who has all her faculties."

"How dare you," Grandmother Hudson said, slamming down her fork. Her face turned a bright shade of crimson and her eyes widened.

"Mrs. Hudson really shouldn't be disturbed at dinner," I said.

"What?" Victoria spit at me with her eyes like two hot coals.

"If you are in direct contact with Doctor Lewis, you'd know that," I continued.

Victoria's mouth opened and closed, her rage reaching such a peak she strained the veins in her neck and her very vocal cords. Her face turned so red, I thought blood would come shooting out of the top of her head like a geyser.

Grandmother Hudson looked at me, relaxed, and then continued eating calmly.

"How did you get this flavor into the string beans, Rain?" she asked as she held up a forkful.

"I think it's because of the almonds," I replied.

"Oh yes." She laughed. "You know I didn't even realize. Victoria, you must try some of this."

"I said I wasn't hungry." She rose as if a fire had been lit under her chair. "I'll be back on the weekend when Megan arrives. The three of us should have a family meeting."

"Yes, we should. It's been . . . what, ten years or so since the last one?" Grandmother Hudson asked.

Victoria looked like she would swallow her tongue. She glanced at me and then mumbled something indiscernible and marched out. We heard the door slam.

"So?" Grandmother Hudson said as if she never noticed Victoria had come and gone. "What surprise do you have for dessert tonight?"

I didn't ask her about the will nor did I mention it again for fear it would make her angry, but I couldn't stop wondering, just like Victoria, why Grandmother Hudson had suddenly decided to include me. Did that mean she was preparing to acknowledge me as part of the family? What would my mother say or do?

I didn't have long to wait. On Saturday, just as she had promised, my mother drove up with Alison and Brody. After breakfast, I had done some straightening up. Grandmother Hudson hadn't settled on a new maid yet. Since we didn't use all that much of the big house, there was just some light dusting to do and washing the dishes and silverware we used. I volunteered to prepare a lunch for us all and put together a shrimp salad. Jake had gone to the supermarket for us and brought back a few loaves of French bread, too. I was happy to keep busy and my mind off meeting my half-brother and half-sister for the first time.

Afterward, I went up to my room to shower and dress, putting on a casual navy blue dress with my matching shoes. Despite her blustering about so-called duty visits and such, Grandmother Hudson chose a very nice print dress and did her hair up with some very pretty combs. I joined her in the living room to wait. She was listening to one of her favorite Saturday talk shows on the radio and doing a needlepoint. She looked up at me when I entered and took me in from head to foot in a single visual gulp.

"You look very nice," she said.

I thanked her and sat where I had a view of the driveway.

"It's almost time for them to be here," I said.

"I wouldn't count on Megan being on time. The clock might as well not have hands as far as that girl is concerned."

"Victoria strikes me as being the exact opposite," I said.

"Oh, she is. She hates it when someone is late. She was always bawling Megan out for being tardy."

"Why are they so different?" I asked.

She stared at me for a moment, looking as if she was about to reveal her theory. I was really expecting an explanation when she turned off the radio, but before she could reply I saw my mother drive up.

"They're here!" I cried and my heart began to pound.

"You'd better go let them in. I'm sure Megan's forgotten her key," Grandmother Hudson said.

Let them in? Me?

"Well?" Grandmother Hudson emphasized with her eyes wide.

I rose slowly and went to the door, opening it just as my mother and Alison were reaching the first step.

"There she is. How are you, dear?" my mother called.

Alison squinted when she looked at me and scrunched her nose up so that little wrinkles rippled along the top of it. She had hair almost as black as mine, but snipped short and brushed up in front exposing far too much forehead. Rounder faced with just a little pouch under her chin, she looked indulgent, spoiled, fifteen or so pounds overweight with most of it on her waist and hips so that her light blue dress clung too tightly there. She looked very uncomfortable in it, and I imagined it was something she didn't really want to wear. Her shoes didn't match the dress. They were more like military boots with thick heels. Both of her ears had tiny jeweled crosses filling the pierced lobes, and she wore all sorts of silver rings on every finger. A stack of silver bracelets adorned her right wrist and a shiny steel-banded watch was on her left. When she opened her lips a little more, I had a good view of a treasure chest of orthodontia work.

After she drew closer, I saw we had the same color eyes, only mine weren't as round, and hopefully, not as dull.

"This is my daughter Alison," my mother said. "Alison, I'd like you to meet Rain."

"Rain?" She pulled the corners of her mouth in so tightly, it made the crests of her cheeks balloon. "Is that *really* your name?"

"Yes, it is," I said. "Is Alison really yours?" I countered quickly.

She smirked.

"You're so funny, I'm hysterical," she said.

I looked past her as Brody came up the steps with a beautiful flower arrangement in his arms. He was tall, six feet two or more and his shoulders were so wide, they could almost fill the doorway. He wore his maroon and gold varsity jacket and a pair of black slacks with soft looking black leather loafers. His hair was also ebony and his eyes were more green than brown, although I saw hazel specks in them. He had a mouth like mine but a very firm, tight jawbone. His complexion was vibrant, athletic, with a rosy tint in his cheeks and full, dark crimson lips. There was something very assured about him, only a step or two away from pure arrogance.

"Hi, I'm Brody Randolph," he said extending his hand while he held the flowers in his arms. I quickly shook his hand and was the first to let go. His grip surprised me and for a moment we just gazed into each other's eyes.

"We're not going to stand out here all day, are we? Where's my grandmother?" Alison demanded impatiently.

"She's in the living room."

She nudged by me. My mother smiled and followed but Brody waited for me to turn and go in first.

"How do you like Dogwood?" he asked. "I hear the girls can be very snobby."

"Let's just say I've seen more nostrils than a nose and throat specialist," I replied and he laughed so hard, Alison turned before entering the living room. She wore a look of surprise and annoyance.

"Hi Granny," she sang as she entered.

"How are you, Mother?" my mother asked following on her heels.

Brody and I came up behind them.

"We hope you're feeling better, Grandma," Brody said handing Grandmother Hudson the flowers. She held them out stiff-armed as if she were preventing an allergic reaction from starting and then looked to me.

"Rain, please find a vase for these."

"Yes, ma'am," I said and hurriedly did so.

Alison gazed at me with delight.

"Is that what Rain is, your new maid, Granny?"

"Temporarily, she is my new maid and a new cook, yes," Grandmother Hudson said. "And you know how I dislike being called Granny, Alison. I'm not some backwoods, pipe-smoking old hag in a rocking chair."

"Sorry, Grandmother," Alison said, dropping the corners of her mouth and then plopping herself onto the sofa.

"Megan, haven't you ever shown this girl how to sit properly? What good was all that charm school?" Grandmother Hudson asked.

"I hated it," Alison said.

"It shows," Grandmother Hudson said.

Alison turned away in a sulk. I looked at Brody and noticed how hard he was looking at me. He smiled and I smiled back.

"Victoria called me," my mother said. "She said she would be here today, too. She said there were important matters to discuss."

"I wonder what," Grandmother Hudson said stealing a glance my way. There was that small, impish smile on her lips. "What is Grant up to today?" she asked.

"He's at a luncheon with our ambassador to the United Nations and our Attorney General," my mother bragged. "How have you been feeling?"

"Fine."

"You didn't need the nurse?"

"Will everyone stop harping on the nurse? I'm not quite the invalid yet."

My mother forced a smile and looked at me and then around the room.

"How have you managed to keep up the house without a full-time maid, Mother?"

"Rain has been doing a little and we're not very messy people. Once you see how easy the job is, you wonder why it's so hard to find someone adequate."

"Is that what you used to do before?" Alison asked me. "Maid's work?"

"I cleaned the house for my mama, if that's what you mean," I said.

"Your *mama*?" She looked to Brody, but he didn't smile or laugh with her.

"Rain has the lead in the school play," Grandmother bragged.

"Really?" Brody said. "What play?"

"*Our Town.* I play Emily."

"Is George Gibbs a black boy?" Alison immediately asked.

"No. He's actually . . . quite white," I said and Brody laughed hard. Grandmother Hudson let her small smile explode into a big grin and then chuckled.

I saw the look of pleased surprise on my mother's face.

"I'm impressed, Alison. I didn't know you knew the main characters in that play," my mother said.

"Our school did it last year," she said in a singsong manner.

"I'm sure it was better than ours will be," I said.

"So am I."

"Can we take you all to lunch today, Mother?" my mother asked.

"No. Rain has prepared some shrimp salad and fresh lemonade."

"Who has been doing your shopping, Mother?"

"Jake fills the list Rain gives him," Grandmother Hudson said, "and twice she went along. We're surviving. I'm not settling on another incompetent just to fill the position quickly," Grandmother Hudson emphasized. "How is everyone's school work?" she asked gazing at Alison. Alison looked away.

"Brody is in contention for valedictorian next year," my mother said.

"And Alison?"

"She has a few things to catch up on."

"Like math, science, English and social studies," Brody quipped.

"Shut up," Alison snapped.

"Alison!"

"He's such a dork." She looked at me. "I suppose you like hip-hop music the most."

"Actually no. I like Mozart. Your grandmother has a great collection of classical music."

"Oh pleeeeze. Classical music," Alison complained with a sour face.

"Why don't we all go for a walk down to the lake?" Brody suggested.

"Too many bugs," Alison said.

He looked at me and I glanced at Grandmother Hudson. She wore an expression of deep concern, but I didn't want to appear as rude as Alison.

"Sure," I said. "We'll have lunch in an hour, if that's all right, Mrs. Hudson."

"We should wait for my business adviser, my other daughter," she said, "but yes, an hour's fine."

"Can I watch television?" Alison asked.

"You came all the way here to watch television? Why don't you go with Brody and Rain?" my mother asked. "It's so beautiful today."

Alison folded her arms and stared down in a sulk.

"I'm tired," she said.

"Do what you want," my mother said.

We heard the front door open and moments later, Victoria appeared.

"Hello, Aunt Victoria," Brody said. "How have you been?"

"Busy," she said looking at Grandmother Hudson.

Alison looked up and greeted her, sounding like a tape recorder.

"Can the three of us spend a few minutes together, Mother?" Victoria asked.

"We're just going for a walk before lunch," Brody told her.

Alison jumped up.

"And I'm going to watch television."

Brody and I left the house.

"My sister's a little bitch these days," he offered as an explanation. "I guess it's just a phase girls go through."

"I never did," I said. "Where I come from you don't have the luxury of going through a phase."

"Tell me about where you come from," he said as we walked.

"What do you want to know?"

"Everything." He smiled. "That is, everything you're willing to tell a complete stranger."

Yes, I thought, we are complete strangers. The blood going through your body is similar to mine. If you looked closely at me, you might see resemblances you never expected. We have the same mother, and yet, here we are, strolling down this beautiful walkway toward a lake that glittered like a new dime, hearing each other's voices for the first time.

I told him about my family, about school life in the city, about Beni's horrible death. He listened with interest, not saying a word. I didn't realize how much I had been talking until we were standing on the dock, looking at the rowboat.

"Alison should have heard some of this, just so she learns how lucky she is. I swear, she's more spoiled than year-old apples. The complaints start flowing out of her mouth before she opens her eyes in the morning. You get along well with your brother?"

"Yes, very well," I said. "He always looks out for me."

"Yeah, well, Alison throws a fit every time I try to do anything for her." He stared at me for a moment. "I bet you're really good in the play. You have a really nice speaking voice."

"Thank you," I said and looked away quickly. His intense gaze was making me feel very self-conscious.

"You think we have time to row across the lake and back?"

"No. I have to set out the luncheon," I said.

"You really are helping my grandmother a lot."

"Well, she's helping me, too."

"My family's finally done something I can appreciate," he said. He continued to stare and then he nodded. "Maybe I'll come see the play."

"Oh, it's not going to be anything," I said.

"Hey, don't be so negative. Think positive about the things you do. That's what I do. Besides, I'm a critic. Leave it up to me to decide how good it is or isn't," he said laughing. "Come on. I'll show you my favorite place on the lake. We have time at least for that, don't we?"

I hesitated and looked back at the house.

"Come on," he urged taking my hand. He tugged me hard and I fell toward him. He embraced me to keep me from falling into the water. "Sorry," he said gazing into my eyes and still holding me close to him. "Sometimes, I don't know my own strength."

I pulled away quickly.

"No, you don't."

He laughed again, but he didn't let go of my hand. I had to follow him along the shoreline until we reached a place where there were half a dozen large rocks.

"Whenever I come down here, I always sit on one of these rocks and watch the water. You can see the fish clearly here. Come on, try it," he urged. He guided me onto a rock and we sat looking down. Sure enough, some catfish appeared. I cried out at the sight of them. "Haven't you been down to the lake before?" he asked, astounded at my surprise at the fish.

"Yes, but only when I first arrived. I've been too busy."

"Well, then I'm glad I came along. After lunch, we'll take another walk," he said. "I'll show you where I once built a tree house and you can recite some lines from the play. Too bad we just can't leave them all in there and have a picnic by ourselves."

"I don't think . . ."

"I'm just kidding. I should spend some time with my grandmother, too. Tell you what," he offered before I could disagree, "I'll even help clean up after lunch and force Alison to pitch in. If she doesn't, I'll threaten to tell my mother about her smoking pot at a friend's house. What do you say? Okay?"

I looked away, unable to fight back a smile. I felt so strange. On one hand I was thrilled by the attention my new brother was lavishing on me, but on the other, I was a little frightened about what he would do and say once he learned the truth.

Lies, I thought again, are like termites weakening the foundation of your very soul.

Brody wasn't exaggerating about Alison's flair for complaints. At lunch they flowed out of her mouth faster than freshly sprayed roaches in any of the apartments in the Projects. She thought it was too hot in the dining room. She complained about the seasoning in the shrimp salad being too spicy. The lemonade was too bitter; she'd rather have a Coke, but Grandmother Hudson didn't have any Cokes. Wasn't there any normal bread? The crust was too hard on the French bread. It was stale. She spotted a smudge on her glass. The dishes weren't that clean. Why didn't we go to a fancy restaurant?

Our mother tried to please her. Brody told her to stuff it and Victoria simply glared sullenly. Apparently, she hadn't been satisfied with their so-called family meeting, and the way she was staring at me from time to time made me feel very uncomfortable. This wasn't turning out to be as good as I had hoped our first get-together would be. Where was the love that was supposed to flow among members of the same family? What did family really mean to these people? I wondered. Did I even want them to ever know we were related?

Just as he promised, when the meal ended Brody volunteered to help clear the dishes and told Alison to help, too.

"Why? I'm not the maid. She is," she whined.

"Rain wasn't brought here to be my maid," Grandmother Hudson said sharply.

"I still don't understand why she was brought here, Grandmother. Why is your house suddenly a foster home?"

"I didn't come here as a foster child," I snapped at her.

"Why did you then?"

I looked at my mother.

"We've been through this already, Alison. I explained what the Save a Child Foundation's purpose was."

"Yeah, you know about that," Brody said. "Just last night you and Rachel Sanders were talking about it at Rachel's, right?" he said with a wry smile. He gave me a side glance. "Billy Crammer told me all about it."

Alison shot darts at him from her eyes, but he held his smile.

"Don't you remember what you did just last night?"

"Shut up, Brody."

"You want to help clean up, right?" he emphasized.

She looked at Grandmother Hudson and then at me. Without comment, she picked up her own dishes and silverware and headed for the kitchen.

Brody smiled at me.

Alison really wasn't much help and in fact, when she went to hand me a bowl, she deliberately let go before I had my fingers around it and it shattered at our feet.

"You're so clumsy!" she cried.

I stared at her. Boy, I thought, would Beni make mincemeat out of you.

"That was your fault, Alison," Brody said. "I saw it."

"It was not."

"What's going on in here?" Grandmother Hudson asked from the doorway.

"She dropped a bowl," Alison said pointing to me scraping up the pieces.

"No, she didn't, Grandmother. It was Alison's fault," Brody said.

Grandmother paused for a moment when she looked at him. Then she turned to me.

"Just clean it up," she said.

"Why are you such a bitch, Alison?" Brody asked as soon as Grandmother left.

"How come you're taking her side?" Her round eyes became oval and cold. "What, do you like her? She's black, Brody."

"Shut your mouth," he said through clenched teeth.

Alison smiled.

"You do like her. I'll tell Mother how successful her charity work is," she said, glanced down at me, and left the kitchen.

"I'm sorry about her," Brody said.

"Forget about it. I've heard a lot worse."

"I know you have. It's not fair," Brody said.

"Fair? That's a word that was removed from my vocabulary a long time ago," I said bitterly. "I'd better get the mop."

"I'll finish bringing stuff in," he said and went out to the dining room.

He and I put away the leftovers, put the dishes into the dishwasher and cleaned up the sink and counters. When we were finished, we discovered everyone had gone back to the living room to talk. Alison had been upstairs and learned I had been given what was supposedly her guest room. As we walked down the corridor, we could hear her grumbling about it.

"Suppose I want to stay over one weekend," she whined. "Where do I stay?"

"I only have four other bedrooms available, Alison," Grandmother Hudson said.

"It's not the same. That was my room. It will always have a smell now. I don't ever want to stay in it again," she declared and stomped out. She paused when she confronted us in the hallway.

"We heard what you said, Alison. You're pathetic," Brody told her.

"I'm pathetic?" She looked from him to me and then to him. Her smile was like a slice in her face, but wide enough to show some silver braces. "I'm ashamed I'm related to you," she told him and charged off. Imagine, I thought, what she would say to me.

As we reached the living room doorway, my mother appeared.

"Where are you going, Brody?" she asked, looking quickly from him to me.

"I was going to show Rain where I used to have a tree house."

"I'm afraid we have to leave soon, Brody," she said.

"I thought we weren't going until four."

"We have to leave earlier," she said again looking at me, "and you should be spending more time with your grandmother."

"It's all right. I have some studying to do," I said.

Brody looked very disappointed.

"All right," he said. "You know what, Ma," he said, "I think I'll come down to see Grandmother next weekend, and I'd like to go to Rain's play."

I could almost hear my mother suck in her breath. Her eyes lit with absolute fear.

"You can't come down next weekend, Brody. We're having the Samsons for dinner and Daddy wants you and Alison to be there because they're bringing their children."

"But their children are years younger."

"We'll discuss it later, Brody," my mother said with fear in her eyes.

"Okay, okay. But I'm coming to the play so don't plan on me being anywhere else that weekend."

"It's not going to be that great, Brody," I said.

"What did I tell you about being negative?" he said with a smile.

"Please come in and spend some time with Grandmother," my mother pleaded in a softer voice.

Brody nodded.

"Should I say good-bye now?" he asked me.

"Yes," I said. "Good-bye." I turned to my mother. "Have a nice trip home, Mrs. Randolph."

"Thank you," she said.

We held each other's glance for a moment and then I walked quickly to the stairway. I didn't look back.

When I got to my room, I closed the door and sat by the window gazing out at the thin line of gauze-like clouds that stretched lazily across the horizon. These people will always feel like strangers to me, I thought. What did Mama hope would happen? I never missed her as much as I did this very moment. I went to the phone to call her at Aunt Sylvia's. It rang and rang with no one answering. Disappointed, I sprawled on my bed and closed my eyes. Memories of Mama, Roy and Beni began to unspool across the screen of my mind. Some of them brought a smile. Sometimes, it's easier to dwell in the past, I thought. If we didn't have our memories, we wouldn't have a doorway of escape.

Just then there was a soft knock on my door. I sat up. What if Brody had snuck upstairs?

"Yes?"

My mother opened the door and stepped in.

"I just came up quickly to talk to you. I'm sorry about being so abrupt downstairs before, but . . . what happened between you and Brody?"

"Nothing," I said warily, beginning to understand why she'd acted so strangely. "I certainly didn't encourage him, if that's what you think."

She looked relieved.

"Of course I don't believe that. It's just that for now . . . it's a bit of a delicate situation. Please discourage him from coming to your play, should he call you," she said.

"I'll try, but he seems to be a very determined person."

She smiled and nodded.

"It didn't take long for you to see that. Anyway, I'm glad you're getting along so well with my mother."

"Victoria is not so glad," I said.

"I know."

"Have you told her the truth?" I asked.

"No, not yet. Mother's doing a good job of holding that eventuality off."

"Why is that necessary?" I pursued.

"Victoria won't . . . handle it well," she admitted. "I told you. We haven't been as close as sisters should be. I think I was seven years old the last time I told her something secret and she went and told my father immediately to try to get me into trouble.

"Don't worry about it," she continued. "You're doing so well here. I'm proud of you."

I looked at her with surprise.

"I know I can't show it as much as I would like, but I am," she insisted. "Good luck with the play," she said. She smiled and backed out, closing the door softly.

Loneliness made my stomach feel so hollow inside. My heart ached, but I wouldn't let my tears rise to the surface. I swallowed them back, pressing them down into the well and pouring in anger to seal them tightly.

I should take what I can from these people, I thought. Mama was right about that. I should be just like Alison, self-centered and spoiled, and fill my pockets. Then, when I was satisfied, I would go running back to Mama and we would have a good laugh.

All of us together, laughing at the rich white family that was choking on its secrets and lies.

I should, I should, I chanted, but in my secret heart of hearts, I knew I couldn't be like Alison.

I could only be myself. I really was like Emily Webb, innocent and trusting.

Maybe if I threw myself into Corbette's arms, I could change.

And then maybe, I could survive in this new world.

# 18

# The Big Night

Grandmother Hudson finally found a new maid she believed was qualified and not too soon either, for as the play's opening drew closer, Mr. Bufurd wanted to work more and more with Corbette and me, sometimes spending whole rehearsals just on us. Exams were coming up as well and I had more than enough to study because I had so much catching up to do. I had tried to think of meals that didn't require a great deal of preparation time, and I fell behind on dusting and cleaning. Grandmother Hudson had seen me scurrying about and realized how busy I was.

Fortunately, an African-American woman named Sissy Williams made an excellent first impression. She was tall and stocky with a small bosom and long arms. She claimed to be forty-one, but Grandmother Hudson believed her to be closer to fifty, maybe even fifty-five.

"I don't care if she lies about her age," she told me, "as long as she can do the work we need done."

Sissy had a pleasant disposition with a melodious, happy voice, but she was serious and efficient about the housework, which Grandmother Hudson liked. She took great pride in her work, especially her meal preparation. It only took one dinner to realize she was a very good cook who made a delicious sweet potato pie. She had been born in South Carolina and had worked once in her uncle's restaurant as a chef. She had never been married, but she talked about her nieces and nephews as if they were her own children. I liked her from the start because she had many of Mama's sayings in her book of wisdom. What I especially admired about her was her self-confidence. If I did anything in the kitchen or helped her prepare something, she didn't feel threatened as Merilyn had.

Jake liked her too, and he enjoyed handicapping Grandmother Hudson's newly hired servants.

"This one might last," he told me. "She's just old-fashioned enough to please the queen."

I laughed and then asked him if Mrs. Hudson knew how often and how much he made fun of her.

"Oh, I don't make fun of her, princess. I kid her a bit now and then, but she knows I admire her. She knows," he said, his voice trailing off as his eyes grew distant and misty.

"You knew her when she was younger, Jake. Was she always so strong and independent?"

"Yes," he said without hesitation. He gazed at me and smiled. "She was always someone who knew what she wanted and got what she wanted when she wanted it. Defeat and disappointment just aren't in her vocabulary. I pity the fool who gets in her way," he added. "Why?" he asked, suddenly thinking about my question. "Is she threatening to put you in the dungeon again?"

"No," I said. I smiled to myself. If Jake only knew that Grandmother Hudson had put me in her will, wouldn't he be shocked? Or would he? I wondered. He seemed to know a lot more about everyone in this family than I'd expect a chauffeur to know.

He stared at me for a long moment and then shook his head with a smile. On the way home from school, we stopped to look at his horse. There was such a sense of contentment about him when he looked at the colt. Surely he would have been a wonderful husband and father, I thought.

"How come you never married and settled down, Jake?" I asked him.

"I don't know, princess," he said. "It just wasn't in the cards, I guess."

"You think things happen because they're destined to happen, Jake?"

He turned to me with that half smile on his face again.

"I know you're a pretty smart young lady and you read a lot and think a lot, Rain, but I just don't think about it all that much. I take it as it comes, sort of like that leaf there blowin' in the wind," he said nodding at a leaf that had leaped off a branch and danced its way toward the tall grass. "Wherever I land, that's where I am."

"Maybe that's the best way to be," I said.

He shrugged.

"Don't know. Like I said. I don't think about it," he told me and with his eyes filled with awe and amusement, he continued gazing at his beautiful horse.

I really didn't know how old Jake was, but from what he had told me and from what he had described, I figured him to be as old or even a little older than Grandmother Hudson. They were so different and yet, when they looked at each other, I saw something between them, some little acknowledgment, some special exchange of understanding that only they could hear. How I wished I could someday tell Jake the truth about myself and this family and listen to what he had to tell me about it all. Perhaps I was looking at him as I wished I was able to look upon the father I never had.

Just another dream, I thought. Just another dream. I put it away and went on with my days and nights, concentrating on what was real and what had to be.

Toward the end of the week, I was surprised by a phone call from Brody. Since I hadn't heard from him or heard Grandmother Hudson mention him, I forgot about his possible visit. He phoned early in the evening. As soon as I heard his voice, my heart began a mad pitter-patter. He sounded very nervous, too.

"How's the terrible play going?" he kidded.

"Terrible. Everyone, including our director, is getting anxious about it. Some of the actors still don't know their lines well enough," I told him, which wasn't a lie.

"At least you don't have to worry about scenery, right?"

"Yes, but Mr. Bufurd is trying to do some special things with lighting and it's not working as well as he'd hoped it would," I said. "I really don't think you should bother coming. It's not worth the trip."

"I'm really coming to see my grandmother," he offered. "She's getting along in her years and after this recent scare, I feel guilty about not being there more often. I mean, I've got my own car. It's not a problem."

"Don't you have studying to do too? Your mother said you were battling to be the valedictorian next year."

"I don't really care about it. I've been offered a full scholarship to play football at U.S.C. after I graduate next year if I want," he said. "You know where that is, right?"

I was too nervous to think.

"No."

"That's Los Angeles."

"Oh."

"Pretty far away. Where do you think you'll end up going to school?"

"I don't know. I haven't really thought about going to college."

"From what I see, you shouldn't have any trouble getting into a good college. When the time comes, why don't you think about U.S.C., too?" he asked.

"I'm afraid to plan anything," I said.

"I understand. All this opportunity is so new for you. Have you been down to my special spot at the lake to look at the fish?" he asked.

"No," I said.

"See? I've got to get there or you'll never appreciate that place. Get me a good house seat."

"Pardon?"

"The star of the show should be able to reserve the best seat in the theater for me," he explained. "They call them house seats."

I didn't know what to say. If I went ahead and reserved a seat for him, my mother would surely think I was encouraging his coming.

"Really, you shouldn't bother," I said.

"It's a done deal, Rain. When that curtain opens, I'll be looking up at you," he insisted.

"Does your mother know?" I asked softly. Throughout this conversation, I felt like I was tiptoeing over a floor of shattered glass.

"Not yet, but she'll know later today. Don't forget to get me the seat and oh, if you're free afterward, maybe I can take you for something to eat."

My heart felt as if it had fallen into my stomach.

"I can't," I said. "I promised to be at a cast party."

"Oh." His voice dropped. Now maybe he won't come, I thought. "Well . . . maybe I'll crash," he added with a rebound. "After all, I know the star."

I just gave him a nervous, little laugh. How was I supposed to discourage him? Every obstacle I put up, he either leaped or smashed aside.

We talked a little about Grandmother and her new maid and he told me how he and Alison had been giving each other the silent treatment ever since their visit.

"I hate to be the cause of trouble between you and your sister," I said.

"You're not. She's just a brat."

When we finally ended the conversation, I felt as if I had backed myself into a dark alley with only one way out. Every time I heard the phone ring in the house after that, I expected it would be my mother wanting to know why I didn't try harder to keep Brody from coming to spend a weekend. She didn't call, but she drove down by herself to talk to me and to Grandmother Hudson about it and that was the beginning of a terrible new crisis.

When Jake drove me up to the house after school the next day, he said, "Uh-oh."

My mother's car was parked in front and right behind it was Victoria's.

"What?" I asked.

"Big family confab goin' on," he said. "Those two don't get together that often here. Something's up."

I felt my heart stop and start as I stepped out of the car.

"Be careful in there," Jake joked. "You don't want to get hit by anything they throw at each other."

I flashed him a quick smile and approached the house. My jittery nerves made me move like a burglar, turning the doorknob softly and opening the door as if I believed Jake's joke was more a prophecy than a jest and I might open it on a battle scene. Instead, I was greeted by total silence. I entered and then stopped dead in my tracks.

Aunt Victoria had apparently not heard the door open. She was too glued to the doorway of the living room, standing just outside. It was clear what she was doing: she was eavesdropping on Grandmother Hudson and my mother. I was afraid to move, afraid to reveal my presence and my knowledge of her sneaky behavior. For a long moment, I held my breath and didn't take a step. When I finally did, the floor board creaked and Victoria's head nearly made a full turn. Her eyes were wide and her mouth grotesquely twisted. Before I could speak, she entered the living room with a loud, "Why didn't you tell me you were coming to see Mother today, Megan?"

I let out my hot breath and debated going directly to my room or greeting everyone. Grandmother Hudson would know I had come home and not been polite, I thought. I really had no choice but to go to the living room doorway and poke my head in for a quick hello.

My mother and Grandmother Hudson were seated on the sofa. Victoria had just sat on the settee across from them and the three of them looked up at me.

"Hello, Mrs. Randolph," I said. Victoria's lips went into a tight, cold smile. I nodded at her and said, "Ms. Hudson," emphasizing the "Ms" part just the way Grandmother Hudson often did.

"Is everything all right?" my grandmother asked with one of her scrutinizing gazes.

"Yes. I've just got to get right to my school work. They always pile it on toward the end of the year," I said.

"Maybe you're just not capable of doing as much as you think," Victoria commented. Her eyes narrowed. "It's wiser to face up to your limitations."

"How would she know her limitations? She's never been given any opportunities," Grandmother Hudson said. "I'm surprised hearing such a remark from you, Victoria. I thought you believe women are capable of anything men can do."

"Most women," she muttered.

"I'm running an A average in all my subjects," I said with hot tears under my eyelids. "So far, I haven't broken any speed limits."

Grandmother Hudson's eyes filled with glee. My mother tilted her head with a tiny smile and Victoria looked away quickly. I left them and went up the stairs to begin my work. Teachers were the same everywhere, I thought. They suddenly realized the school year was ending and they had fallen behind on their objectives, so they assigned even more homework.

I worked, but I expected to hear my mother's footsteps in the hall and then the knock on the door at any time. I had left it slightly open. She surely had come down here to bawl me out for permitting Brody to plan a trip to see me. My biggest worry was what Victoria had heard during her eavesdropping and what would result?

After an agonizing twenty-five minutes, the silence in the house was broken by loud voices coming from the entryway. Now curious and becoming the eavesdropper myself, I rose from my chair and went to the door. I could only make out a word or two, so I went to the top of the stairway. The front door was open and my mother and Victoria were standing on the portico shouting at each other.

"Why should we have to bear the cost of your sins, Megan? Why should you dump your mistakes on our doorsteps? How dare you take advantage of Mother like this?"

"I'm not taking advantage of her and I'm not dumping anything on your doorstep, Victoria."

"Somehow, that . . . that illegitimate child has wormed her way into Mother's last will and testament. What Mother gives her, she takes from me and I won't stand for it. If anyone is to leave her anything, it should be you and you alone. If you don't get those changes out of the document, I'll call Grant."

"You're so spiteful, Victoria. You've always been cruel to me and I don't know what I've ever done to you to deserve it," my mother wailed back at her.

Victoria laughed a chilling cold laugh. I took a few steps and sat down on the stairway.

"You don't know?" she spit at my mother. "Of course, that's always been the face you've worn. Innocent, precious little Megan doesn't understand what she's doing. She can't be blamed for anything. She's too perfect. We always have to forgive Megan or cover up for Megan's mistakes. We're still doing it!"

"I've never asked you to do anything for me," my mother said.

"No, of course not. It's not your style to ask, Megan. You just screw up and then come around with your big, innocent eyes. Father was always giving in to you. I had to make up for anything I wasted or anything I failed to do, but not Megan, oh no, not little Megan.

"Well, Father's gone and I'm the one who runs the business now. I'm not covering up your disgusting sexual blunders, and with a black man, too. How dare you bring that girl into this house and permit her to be a part of this family and our business? Haven't you any pride at all? I don't understand how you do these things with a husband as devoted as Grant is to you, and what about his goals and his career? Don't you realize what you are risking or don't you even care about him?"

"You're twisting everything and making it look uglier than it is, Victoria, and since when is Grant's career so important to you?"

They were both silent for a moment, glaring at each other. I could see my mother's face take on a cold smile too suddenly.

"You're jealous, aren't you, Victoria? You've always been jealous of me and Grant."

"That's ridiculous."

"Is it?"

"Think what you like, only remember what I'm saying to you, Megan. If Mother doesn't take that girl's name out of her will soon, I'll expose you. That's a promise," she vowed and marched down the steps.

My mother stood there watching her get into her vehicle and then she turned and with her head down, re-entered the house. I stood and she looked up at me.

"You heard all that?" she asked.

"Most of it, I guess. Where's Grandmother?"

"She's in the office, thank God. She would surely have a heart attack if she had heard that venom spill out of my sister's mouth."

"What are you going to do?" I asked.

"I don't know."

"Should I leave? I can go to Mama."

"Of course not," she said. "It's just that I'm worried about Brody. He talked a great deal about you on the way home from our last visit; he was very taken with you. He thinks you're fresh and honest and someone special. I was trapped. I couldn't disagree with him, but I couldn't join in his lavish praise. Now he's determined to come down to see your play performance. He called Mother to tell her he was coming and she called me. She's worried about it, too."

"Maybe you should tell him the truth, then," I said.

She shook her head.

"I just can't do that yet."

"You can keep the secret forever and ever?"

She looked up at me and then gazed toward the door.

"Not if Victoria has her way."

"Just get Grandmother to take me out of the will," I suggested.

"If my mother even imagined that Victoria was blackmailing us, she would take her and me and everyone else out of the will and leave everything to you just for spite," my mother said with a nod and a smile. "I've got to think of something else."

"Mama used to tell us that lies are like rabbits: they beget offspring so fast, they'll make your head spin and before long, you won't remember which lie started it all."

"She's right, of course, but for now . . ."

How I hated that expression: *for now*. It was simply another way to bury your head in the sand, I thought.

She straightened up and looked as firm as Grandmother Hudson did most of the time.

"I'm going to say things to Brody that I don't really believe, Rain, but please remember that I'm trying to discourage him," she said.

"What sort of things?"

"Nasty things . . . about you," she added.

"What if he doesn't believe you?"

"He will. Just be understanding, all right?" she pleaded.

I looked away. Wasn't there any other solution? It was unfair for me to have to be the one bearing the blame and the sin. Then I thought, why was it suddenly so important to me what Brody thought of me anyway? My mother was right. He would just go off to college and never think of me again. Everyone's precious little world of deceit would be protected.

"Do what you want," I said, turned and marched back up the stairs.

"Rain . . ." she called.

I turned at the top of the stairway.

"I'm sorry. I really hoped you would have nothing but happiness here."

"Why should I?" I asked. "You didn't."

She looked at me with such surprise and awe for a moment, and then she nodded softly, turned and headed into the house to talk to Grandmother Hudson before leaving for home.

It wasn't until a day before the play that I decided I had better reserve a seat for Brody as well as for Grandmother Hudson. Even though I didn't hear from him since my mother's visit, I didn't want him to be embarrassed if he did come. Grandmother Hudson surprised me one morning by telling me Jake would be accompanying her to the play and not just driving, so I had to have three seats reserved.

"He has taken a liking to you," she confessed, "and it would be stupid for him to drive us there and wait outside."

It was as if she had to explain and justify his attendance.

"I'm glad," I said, "but I just don't want everyone to be disappointed. Don't expect too much. It's my first play and I'm so nervous, I don't know if I'll remember my lines."

"Stop that," she snapped at me. "You sound like your mother, making excuses before she even tries. I don't want to hear that. I want to hear confidence. Believe in yourself and let everyone know you do," she commanded. "Who on that stage is better than you?"

"No one," I replied angrily.

"Precisely my point. You will not do poorly and don't let anyone make you think otherwise."

She said it with such power, I wondered if she could stop the rain. I smiled at her.

"Okay," I said.

"Good. Now let's not talk about it anymore. If you dwell too long on something, it does seem more like an impossible task. Just walk in there and do what has to be done. Sissy," she said turning to the new maid, "what have you done to my roast chicken?"

"Ma'am?"

"It's absolutely delicious. Whatever you did, do it again," she said.

Sissy's eyebrows rose and she looked at me with a little smile on her face.

"I will try, ma'am. That I will do." She winked and went into the kitchen.

As the countdown to the performance continued, Corbette continually reminded me in little ways and with little remarks of my promise to celebrate afterward with him.

"I'm cleaning the place up," he told me. "It'll be our special night."

"Won't your parents want to do something with you after the play?" I asked.

He grimaced.

"My parents won't be here. They have an engagement they can't get out of," he said.

"They won't be at the play?"

"They've only been to one that I've been in," he revealed. "It's all right. I'm not doing it for them. I'm doing it for myself."

He did seem like a tenant in his own home. I didn't know if he had intended to win me over with pity or not, but he was certainly doing a good job of it. He was as nice to me as could be, too, often taking blame for any mistakes made between us. When I looked at the other girls to see what they were thinking about us, I thought they looked pleased. Most had become friendlier and in fact, Maureen looked like she was alone in her skepticism and criticism of Mr. Bufurd casting me as Emily. Audrey, of course, thought I was great, and after dress rehearsal, most of the cast congratulated me on my performance. I was beginning to fill up with that confidence Grandmother Hudson demanded.

Since I hadn't heard from Brody all week, I assumed my mother had accomplished what she had set out to do: discourage him about me. Grandmother Hudson didn't mention his coming either. I breathed relief, but I couldn't help a tang of regret slipping into my thoughts. I really did like Brody and wished we could be friends, actually more than friends, a real brother and sister. I would surely be a better sister to him than Alison was. But then again, almost any girl would be, I thought.

The day of the play, all my teachers wished me luck and promised they would be at the performance. So many people were talking about it, I couldn't help but have a stomach filled with butterflies. Their delicate wings tickled the inside of me all day and made it impossible to eat, to concentrate, to even sit still. I was a total wreck by the day's end and when Jake brought me home, I went upstairs immediately and threw myself on the bed, burying my face in the pillow and vowing never to leave the room.

It was at a time like this when I needed to hear Mama's voice the most, so I went to the phone and called Aunt Sylvia's again. Again, the phone rang and rang and no one picked up. Where were they? If they were going on a trip, Mama should have told me, I thought. Why hadn't Roy tried to call me again? It was so frustrating not knowing how to reach him. The tension, the excitement, all the pressure and worry made me feel as limp as a busted balloon.

I decided to soak in a hot tub and try to relax and not think about anything but my first line in the play. After that, it would either all roll off my tongue or get stuck in my throat and quickly end my career in the theater.

After the applause, I remember thinking maybe Grandmother Hudson had been right about me. Maybe I didn't know my own capabilities because I had never been given the opportunity. I shook so much when I walked out on that stage for the first time with an audience present that I thought my chattering teeth would distort all my words and bring the roof down with the audience's thunderous laughter.

Instead, something entirely unexpected happened to me. I felt as if I had really fallen into another place and another time. My Emily Webb persona seized my very body and soul. The sound of my own voice was even different to me, and when I moved, I moved with the innocence and grace Mr. Bufurd had envisioned. What helped was not really being able to see much of the audience. The lights created a wall of illumination that washed out faces. It was almost as if I was alone, practicing the lines in front of my mirror.

And when Corbette and I looked at each other and spoke to each other, I didn't see him as Corbette either. He and I bounced off each other's performances, each of us reaching higher and higher to match the other for sincerity, credibility and dramatic impact.

When Corbette knelt at my grave and spoke his lines, I felt the tears build in my eyes, and when I did my famous good-bye speech and looked at him standing in the wings, I saw the amazement and appreciation in his eyes. I felt as if the effort couldn't be stopped. I was flying, reaching for the stars. The applause after the stage manager's final lines was thunderous, and when we came out for our bows, the audience rose to its feet.

I couldn't stop myself from crying. Suddenly, someone ran to the stage and thrust a bouquet of beautiful red roses up at me. I looked down and for a moment was unable to move.

"It's for you," Corbette shouted over the continuous ovation.

I stepped forward.

Brody was holding the flowers up, his face enveloped in glee. He had been there after all.

"Thank you," I said and took them quickly.

When the curtain came down, everyone in the cast and crew let out a nearly simultaneous roar. Corbette embraced me in the dim light and kissed my cheek.

"You were fabulous," he whispered. "It's our night!"

I was spun around by the adulation. Mr. Bufurd looked so proud. I thought his face seemed positively luminous. Other cast members and stage crew members waited for their opportunity to squeeze my hand or hug me. Even Maureen had to choke on her words of approval.

People began to stream backstage. I wanted to get the make-up off, but my teachers and other people in the audience kept me busy accepting their accolades. I saw Jake, Brody and Grandmother Hudson talking to people in the wings and made my way toward them.

"Some terrible play," Brody said with a smirk and then a smile. "This made the one at our school look like a jcke. You were fantastic. I'm impressed and I'm glad I decided to come," he said quickly.

He held onto my hand and looked into my face so intently, I couldn't just push him away. I had to smile and thank him even though I saw Grandmother Hudson watching us with concern darkening her eyes. Fortunately, Jake interrupted us.

"I have to get Mrs. Hudson home," he said. "You were great, princess. Proud of you," he said.

"Thank you, Jake."

I hurried over to Grandmother Hudson.

"Very nicely done, Rain," she said. "It's difficult to believe this was your first time on the stage. I'd like you to meet Conor MacWaine," she added nodding at the tall, thin gentleman with auburn hair beside her. He wore a tweed jacket and cravat. "Mr. MacWaine is a drama instructor from London, a friend of my sister Leonora."

"A very impressive premiere," he told me.

"Thank you."

"Don't stay out too late," Grandmother Hudson warned. The small tight smile on her lips and the gleam in her eye told me she was very proud.

"So where is this cast party?" Brody asked quickly.

"It's at someone's home," I said. "I really can't invite people. I'm sorry," I said quickly.

His eyes turned bleak so quickly, I felt a shaft of pain in my chest.

Corbette was at my side, slipping his hand into mine.

"Let's get out of here," he said loud enough for Brody to hear.

Brody and he gazed at each other for a moment.

"I see why you can't invite anyone," Brody said with a cold smile.

"I told you not to come," I replied, feeling just terrible.

Corbette tugged at me.

"I'll see you at the house," I offered as we retreated.

Brody just gazed after us looking shattered.

"Who was that?" Corbette asked as we hurried toward the rear entrance of the theater.

"Mrs. Hudson's grandson," I said.

"He's the one who gave you the roses."

"Yes."

"I've got roses for you too," Corbette said.

We got into his convertible.

"What a night!" he screamed back at the building and shifted quickly to speed us away before too many people had noticed.

There was a cast party at a local pizza parlor. Mr. Bufurd was paying for it himself.

"Shouldn't we at least make an appearance?" I asked Corbette as he drove.

"Later," he said. "Stars are always supposed to arrive fashionably late."

His laughter trailed behind us in the wind that lifted my hair and washed away all caution and care.

I didn't believe him, but I was in their world of lies. What difference did one more make?

Corbette wasn't lying about the flowers, however. When we entered his hideaway, I saw roses everywhere: a half dozen on a table here, another on the desk, another on the television set and even a vase filled at the center of the floor.

"You must have spent a small fortune," I said laughing.

"How often do we have a hit play? Guess what else I have for us," he said going to his little refrigerator. I shook my head. He opened it and produced a bottle of champagne in a silver bucket. "You know what this is, right?"

"I do, but I never really drank any," I said.

"Tonight's a night for firsts. It's a premiere!"

He opened the bottle and the champagne ran out the opening and streamed foam down the neck. He poured me a glass and one for himself.

"To the most talented, most beautiful, and most charming new girl at Dogwood," he toasted. We clicked glasses and sipped. "Like it?"

"Yes."

He poured me some more and we performed another toast, this one to Mr. Bufurd for casting me. Then he put on some music, loosened the tie he had been wearing, and sat on the sofa. He patted the spot beside him.

"Let's take a few minutes to relax. I feel like I've been running for miles," he said.

"Me too. I just can't believe I did it." The excitement inside me bubbled as much as the champagne Corbette continued to pour in my glass.

"I knew from the first day that you would be something special."

"Sure," I said skeptically. "I saw how you were laughing at me that first day."

"I was laughing at the other girls who were hoping you would fail and fail quickly."

"You really think that's what they wanted?"

"Don't tell me about Dogwood girls. I know Dogwood girls. They have rich chocolate running through their veins instead of blood."

He made me laugh. I sipped the wonderful champagne and we joked about some of the others in the cast, especially Maureen.

"I'm still wearing my make-up!" I realized.

"So am I. Hey," he said, "that means we're still Emily and George." He put down his glass and took mine from my hand to place beside his before turning back to me. "That means we're married."

I laughed. I was laughing at everything he said and my head that had been taking my thoughts on a merry-go-round began to spin even more. I didn't even realize he was kissing my neck and my face. His fingers undid my blouse so quickly, I was surprised to look down and discover it was completely undone and his hands were in and around my ribs, moving up to my bra. It seemed to fly away from my breasts and when he pressed his lips to mine, I didn't resist as he slipped my blouse over my shoulders and down my arms. In seconds I was naked from the waist up and his mouth was on my neck, my breasts, his lips and tongue over my nipples.

When my head fell back, I felt as if I was falling, falling, falling and I clung to him to keep from hitting the floor. Vaguely, I remember moaning some small protest, but his hands were over my thighs and his lips were on mine again. He tasted so good and this was so wonderful a night and I had secretly committed myself to a special night, a night full of pleasure and ecstasy, defiance and abandon.

When I felt his hardness moving between my legs, I tightened for a moment and then, as if casting my soul off like a ship into an undulating sea, I relaxed and accepted him. I rose and fell with his thrusts and barely heard his moans of pleasure over my own. He mumbled mad promises, vowed love and said all the things people say in movies and books when they surrender themselves fully and ultimately to each other. I was on stage again. He kept calling me Emily, interspersing his own words with words from the play. I half expected to hear an audience applauding when we were both spent and exhausted, clinging to each other for a long moment.

I think I passed out for a few seconds at least. When I opened my eyes, he was lying back with his eyes closed and a smirk of contentment on his lips. I groped about for my clothes and, still dizzy, began to dress myself.

"I feel a little queasy," I said suddenly sensing a wave of nausea rising.

His eyes snapped open and then he looked terrified.

"Jeeze, you're turning white!"

He jumped up and fetched a garbage can.

"Don't throw up on my furniture," he pleaded.

He made it just in time.

"I guess it's all just too much excitement for you," he commented as I groaned.

"I'm sorry," I said.

"Hey, I've done it plenty of times," he declared with pride.

My head started to pound. I groaned again and lay back.

"I'll get you a cold rag. Just relax," he said and put one hand on my forehead.

I either passed out again or just fell into an exhausted sleep, for when I opened my eyes, I found the lights were dim and he was sprawled on the other sofa. I glanced at the clock. It was nearly two-thirty in the morning!

"Corbette!" I cried, sitting up. He didn't open his eyes. I put on my shoes and stood up. I did it so quickly, I was dizzy for a moment. As soon as that passed, I went to him and shook him hard.

"Whaaaa." He opened his eyes. "What's the matter?"

"It's nearly two-thirty in the morning. Why didn't you wake me up?"

"It is?" He wiped his eyes and looked at the clock. "Oh yeah, it is."

"It's not funny. I'm sure they're worried about me."

"Why? It's a big night," he said casually. He looked like he wasn't going to get up.

"You've got to take me home right now, Corbette. We missed the cast party, too! This is terrible."

He opened his eyes and smiled.

"Not all of it," he said.

"Take me home, Corbette," I demanded.

"Okay, okay. Jeeze, for a dead wife, you sure are pushy," he quipped, but I wasn't in the mood for any jokes.

He took me over that bumpy back road route again. By the time we arrived at the house, I was feeling nauseous and sick.

"Thanks for a nice time," he said.

"Good night, Corbette."

" 'Night," he said without promising to call me. He drove off before I even reached the steps. It was so dark and quiet. It felt ominous as I opened the door. As I started for the stairs, Sissy came out of the kitchen. She was in her robe.

"Why are you still awake, Sissy?" I asked.

"I promised Mrs. Hudson I would be until you came home," she explained.

"Oh."

"And I have a message for you from Mr. Brody," she added. "He waited until about one o'clock."

"He left?" I asked surprised.

"Yes, he did. He told me to tell you he should have listened to his mother."

It felt like I had stepped into a cold shower. It shook the weariness out of me and woke me to the wintry reality of where I was and who I was supposed to be. Something shattered inside me like thin ice.

I was turning into the very thing I despised: a liar. I felt sorry for Brody, driving through the night, fueled by the disillusionment he had hoped to defeat.

A long time ago, my mother gave herself to someone while she was living a life of her own fantasies, dooming me, I was afraid, to live the same false way, moving from one illusion to the next until I was left with nothing but the memory of myself.

# 19

# Joy and Pain

The impact of the play and my performance continued well into the following week. All of my teachers who had attended repeated their congratulations, and Mrs. Whitney made a special trip over from the administrative building to see me in Mr. Bufurd's class and offer her congratulations in person. And then Grandmother Hudson surprised me one day with the news that Conor MacWaine was coming to dinner especially to talk to me about my future. I had no idea what that meant until he sat across from me in the dining room that night and said, "I think you could have an acting career."

"Really?"

I looked at Grandmother Hudson, who remained stone-faced and serious.

"I really don't think I'm good enough," I said.

Grandmother Hudson nearly growled.

"I think Mr. MacWaine has a little more experience and a little more insight about that, Rain. He is the director of a prestigious drama school and for your information, students at his school must audition and most are turned down. Isn't that so, Conor?"

"Yes."

I looked at him again.

"Some people have a natural inclination for it," he continued. "Let's call that talent, for want of a better word. They have an instinctive sense about timing, poise, and attitude. Of course, they must have the natural gifts of voice and appearance. They must have something to develop.

"When I learned that this was actually your first and only experience on the stage, I was impressed. I will tell you that you have a certain look that I believe can be a remarkable strong point if you're guided and developed properly.

"Most actors and actresses today don't have the training to do deep and complex parts. They should be schooled in the classics and they should all begin with the theater. The difference between theater and film is the theater relies on the spoken word. You have good diction and excellent expression. In my school you learn how to make your body a true vehicle of communication. Every gesture, every look, every word spoken has a purpose and is directed toward that purpose.

"Popular American film stars are merely products for exploitation. They don't have lasting qualities and will be replaced as soon as the next Hollywood product is introduced. They are merchandised as if they were a new brand of toothpaste and not developed as talent.

"Our school is serious and full of substance. It also requires, therefore, that you be a student, a good student. Which you are. For all these reasons, I think I could do something significant with you."

I looked at Grandmother Hudson again.

"What Mr. MacWaine is saying, Rain, is he wants you to attend his school of drama in London as soon as you are finished with school here this year."

My mouth stayed open, but my tongue wouldn't move.

Me? I almost said, but I was happy I hadn't. Grandmother Hudson might have thrown a fit about self-confidence again.

"Live in London?" I finally managed to ask.

"It won't be a problem. I have spoken with my sister and she is very excited about the possibility of your going there to live with her while you study the arts. I might even make the trip over with you and stay until you are settled," she added. "It's been some time since I've been to London."

"And since you've seen our school," Mr. MacWaine said, "we've added a new dance facility and sound stage."

"Yes. Mr. MacWaine's school also develops your ability to sing and to dance."

"Dance?"

"You'll be trained in ballet as well as modern interpretative dance," he explained. "Our teachers are world renowned."

I remained tongue-tied.

"Doesn't this sound exciting to you?" Grandmother Hudson finally asked, impatient with my lack of reaction.

"Yes, but . . . I never really thought of acting as a career for myself."

"What did you expect you would do with yourself, Rain?" she followed with her lips tightening, "marry and raise a herd of children?"

"No, I thought maybe I'd become a teacher," I said.

"One can always fall back on that if she should fail or get discouraged," Mr. MacWaine said. "Frankly, I don't think that will be the case for you. I haven't made many errors of judgment when it comes to candidates. I have some rather well-known former students on the London stage at present and a number in film and television."

"Well?" Grandmother Hudson pursued, thumping the table with her fingers.

"I guess, I suppose, I . . ."

"I understand. It's a great deal to have thrust on you like this," Mr. MacWaine said, smiling.

"Nonsense," Grandmother Hudson said. "It's the only way for it to happen. Either she does it with a full heart and determination, diving right in, or she doesn't attempt it at all."

"Can't I think about it for a while?" I begged.

"How many applicants do you have applying and on a waiting list at present, Conor?" Grandmother Hudson asked him.

He sat back and thought for a moment.

"About four hundred," he said.

"And how many will you take?" she followed.

"Not more than ten new students," he replied.

She looked at me.

"I'm just so surprised by all this," I moaned.

She softened and turned back to Mr. MacWaine.

"The truth is the girl has rarely had any good fortune in her life and when it appears, she is skeptical and afraid," she explained. "I'll call you tomorrow with her decision," she promised him.

He turned back to me.

"I won't disappoint you, Rain. You will benefit from your experiences at my school and with Mrs. Hudson as your benefactor, you will have great advantages," he said.

I nodded. I didn't want to appear ungrateful. It was just the idea of going to another country and being so far away from Mama while I attempted to do something people only dream about doing. What would Roy say? And Mama?

I couldn't wait to get Mama on the phone and tell her all about it. I went upstairs after dinner and tried to call again, and again, the phone rang and rang with no one picking up. Why hadn't Mama tried to call me all this time? I wondered. Maybe she had decided in the end to go see what she could do for Ken, after all. No matter how bad he was, she still had her memories and she wasn't the kind of person who could just write someone off forever, I thought. I decided I would call every night until I spoke with her.

I wanted to get right to studying for my finals, but my mind drifted back to the discussion at dinner. Was I really that good? Why was Grandmother Hudson determined that I do it, and so determined that she volunteered to go to England with me and see that I was well situated?

Maybe all she was really hoping to do was get rid of me, I thought. Maybe she and my mother had concluded that this would satisfy Victoria and would certainly keep me away from Brody. If I was as far off as England, they could keep the secret of my identity locked away. It really wasn't that I had talent. It was just a convenient solution. Was I wrong to think this? What a horrible thing to do to me: send me off to try to become something I could never become. They couldn't do that, could they, and yet how could I believe in anyone who was comfortable sleeping on a bed of lies?

I wanted desperately to trust Grandmother Hudson, to believe she really did care about me now. She had put me into her will, hadn't she? I asked myself.

Or was that a phony thing, too? Was all this designed to win my confidence and then to send me away full of false hope? Beni always accused me of being too naive, believing in people too much. Was she right? Was I a fool and an easy mark without someone like Roy looking over me?

The questions bounced around in my head like ping-pong balls. Questioning my own weaknesses when it came to people made me think about Corbette. He hadn't called me since our private celebration. He didn't even call to see how I was the day after. Every day after school, I expected to see him, but he never came over from Sweet William. Had he taken advantage of me? Maybe I was a fool. It made me think that I should not agree to anything too quickly, even a supposed golden opportunity.

Before she retired for the evening, Grandmother Hudson stopped at my room. I was working on math and didn't even hear her knock and then open the door.

"Rain," she said and I turned.

"Oh, I'm sorry. I was struggling with a problem."

"So am I," she said. "I was disappointed in you at dinner. Mr. MacWaine was doing me a great favor by attending your play and auditioning you for his school. It's no exaggeration to say that there are probably thousands of young people who would love to have this chance presented to them. You've never seemed ungrateful before, but tonight . . ."

"I appreciate it. I'm just . . . I'd like to talk to Mama about it, first. Please," I begged.

"I see. Yes, I suppose that would be right," she admitted. "After all, the woman was a mother to you all your life. All right, call her immediately and discuss it with her."

"I've been calling, but there's no answer," I said. "I'm starting to worry. She might have gone back to help my stepfather, who was arrested for armed robbery."

"Arrested?" She thought for a moment. "All right. Give me the phone number and the address and I'll see to it that your mama is contacted tomorrow, wherever she is."

"You will?"

"I said I would. When I decide to do something, I do it. I don't waste time wondering should I or shouldn't I? What if this, what if that? I do what has to be done," she assured me.

I wrote down the number and the address with Aunt Sylvia's name.

"Fine. Go back to your homework problem," she said, "and solve it."

I watched her leave and then I smiled and shook my head. There were flashes of Victoria in her, but not as much of my mother. What, I wondered, had I inherited from her?

At school the next day, I was surprised to see Corbette and some of his friends watching me riding in equestrian class. They had come over from Sweet William and were all standing by the fence. When I made a circle, I rode closer and then stopped.

"Hi," I said. "What are you doing here?"

"We had a break between classes and I thought we'd come over to see how you ride. You sit in that saddle a lot better now," he said and his friends all laughed. What was so funny?

"Practice," I said, "pays."

"Is that an invitation?" he asked and again, the clump of boys beside him roared.

"What's wrong with you?" I asked. He seemed so different. "You never called me."

"I've been busy." He smiled at his buddies who all wore sly smiles and who all watched my reactions. "Teddy here is not as busy, however."

"I'm free tonight," the tall, brown-haired boy said.

"I imagine you're free every night," I told him and his friends laughed, some pounding him on the back.

"Very funny," he cried, reddening.

"What happened to George Gibbs?" I asked Corbette.

He shrugged.

"He went on and married someone else. Now he's stuck in a marriage and has more diapers to change," he quipped. They were all flashing their smiles.

"At least he has a family," I said sharply, "and a reason to get up in the morning. Why do you?" I shot at him and turned the horse.

I didn't look back. I went into a gallop and despite my teacher's admonitions, jumped a gate to catch up with my class. He bawled me out for it afterward, but I barely heard him. I was so angry, I could hear only a buzz of rage in my ears. The first thing I did when I saw Audrey afterward was tell her she had been right about Corbette.

"Boys," she said with an ugly grimace as if they were some sort of disease that infected girls. "I'm not getting married. I'm going to be a career woman."

Maybe, I thought, she was right.

It was on my mind for the remainder of the day and even during my ride home. Jake kept talking and asking me questions. He could see I was terribly annoyed about something. As we approached the house, I recalled Grandmother Hudson's promise to reach Mama. At least I had something to look forward to, I thought, and hurried out of the car and up the stairs. I burst into the house and looked for Grandmother Hudson in the living room. She wasn't there. I charged through the dining room into the kitchen where Sissy was working on the evening's dinner.

"Do you know where Mrs. Hudson is, Sissy?"

"Last I saw she was sitting in the office at her desk," she told me and I hurried to her.

Grandmother Hudson had just put down the telephone receiver when I appeared.

"Hi. Did you locate Mama?" I asked, too anxious to spend time on small talk.

"I did, Rain. Sit down," she said firmly and nodded at the leather sofa.

Grandmother Hudson's face was more often than not an open

book. Her thoughts were usually under glass, easy to read. She had too much self-confidence to be subtle or indirect. She looked terribly serious at the moment and that put a coat of ice around my heart. It thumped like a small hammer trying to break out.

"What's wrong?" I asked after sitting.

"I was hoping to have a longer period of time before having this conversation with you, Rain. Why it was left to me to be the one to have it is just another example of my daughter's lack of responsibility. I can't tell you how many times over the years I have been put in a similar position, but . . . what's done is done. Her father kept me from building her backbone."

"What's wrong?" I demanded more firmly, now the impatient one.

She leaned forward, clasping her hands and resting her forearms on the desk.

"When Megan came to me to ask if you could live here and go to Dogwood, I was naturally reluctant. Even after you first arrived, I thought this was possibly a big mistake. Then, about two weeks afterward, Megan called to tell me she had spoken with your mama and learned more about the situation."

"What situation?"

"Your mama's health. It seems," Grandmother Hudson said leaning back with a deep sigh, "that beyond her good intentions to get you out of that environment and all the danger, she was looking ahead to what she would be able to do and not do for you. She knew how sick she was."

"Sick? What's the matter with her?" I cried.

"She's . . . suffering from a cancer that has spread rapidly through her body and she's presently in the hospital. The prognosis is not good. In fact," she said, "the doctor told me she goes in and out of a coma. Your Aunt Sylvia has been staying with a friend near the hospital. That's why you haven't been able to reach anyone on the phone."

My heart shrank and closed like a tiny fist in my chest. Suddenly, the room felt like an oven.

"Does my brother Roy know about all this?"

"Yes. I believe he is on his way to the hospital on special leave," she said.

"I've got to go, too," I said.

"I know you do. I've made all the arrangements for you," she said. "Jake will be taking you to the airport in two hours. When you arrive, there will be a car waiting for you. The driver will hold up a card with your name on it. I have made arrangements for you to stay at a nearby hotel. Here," she said, opening a drawer and taking out an envelope, "is some money for your expenses."

It was all happening so fast, I was too stunned to accept it. I shook my head.

"It can't be true. I can't believe Mama kept all this secret."

"She probably knew you wouldn't have agreed to come here if she told you the truth. She was a brave woman," Grandmother Hudson said.

Was? I thought. Mama . . . Mama . . .

"I've spoken to Mrs. Whitney at the school. You're not to worry about your exams. They'll provide makeups for you if need be."

I gazed at her, truly in awe. She was a woman of action, always in control.

"Take the envelope," she ordered and I did so.

"Thank you," I said.

"I'm sorry that you'll have to make this trip by yourself on top of the shock, but . . ."

"I'll be all right." I was anxious to get started and get to Mama.

"I know you will, and I want you to know that I expect you to return, Rain. No matter what, I expect you to come back here and fulfill your life."

I nodded and then rose and left the office like a sleepwalker, barely realizing where I was going and what I was doing. I felt that numb.

Grandmother Hudson had told Jake why I was going to the airport. He was caring and concerned and made sure I got to the correct gate. He waited with me until they called for the passengers to board.

"This is never an easy thing to do, Rain," he said. "I didn't get a chance to say good-bye to my mother. I was overseas, but that didn't make the pain any less. You be strong, hear?"

"I will, Jake."

"See you soon," he said and then he hugged me and held me a moment before turning and hurrying away through the terminal. Moments later, I was strapping myself into a seat, feeling like I had been caught up in a whirlwind of disaster.

Just as Grandmother Hudson had promised, there was a limo driver waiting for me at the airport. He told me that he had been assigned to me for as long as I needed him and the car. He wanted to take me to the hotel first, but I insisted on going to the hospital. From the way Grandmother Hudson had described the situation, every moment counted.

"I'll be right here waiting for you," the driver told me when we arrived.

I hurried out and to the information desk. The elderly woman volunteer sent me to the fourth floor. When I stepped out, I immediately saw Roy sitting in a small waiting room, his head down, his elbows on his legs, his hands against his forehead. He was in uniform. I walked up to him slowly. There was no one else in the waiting room. He seemed to sense my presence and lifted his head. His eyes were bloodshot from spilled tears. He blinked as though not believing what he saw and then he smiled.

"Rain," he said standing. "Rain." He threw his arms around me and held me.

I had forgotten how good it felt to be held in his strong arms, to lay my head against his chest and feel his hand stroke my hair while he comforted me and promised to always be there to protect me.

"How is she?" I asked stepping back.

He shook his head.

"She's real bad, Rain. She can't even open her eyes anymore. It's like watching a clock tick down. I'm happy you're here," he said, "and I'm sure she will be too. She'll know you're there. You just hold her hand and talk to her like I've been doing and she'll know.

"You look good," he said with a soft smile. "Like you're all grown or something."

"It hasn't been that long, Roy."

"Oh, it's been long for me, Rain."

"You look good, too," I said. He did. He looked more mature, even stronger and firmer.

"How's it been, living with the rich white folks?"

"Not easy, Roy," I said smiling. "Not easy." I looked toward the doorway. "Where's Aunt Sylvia?"

"She's at her friend's house. She was here all morning," he said.

"I want to see Mama right away, Roy."

"I'll take you there," he said. He put his arm around my shoulders. "How'd you get here and all?" he asked.

I told him what Grandmother Hudson had arranged.

"A limo, too? They are rich, huh?"

"They have money, Roy, but I wouldn't call them rich, not the way I want to be rich," I said.

He didn't understand, but I thought there would be more time later to explain.

No matter what had been told to me, there was no way to anticipate what I would find when I entered the intensive care unit and Roy led me to Mama's bedside. She looked so much smaller and so much thinner. The bones in her face seemed to be rising out of her skin. Her eyes were shut tight. I thought she was already gone and a panic seized my heart.

"Roy."

"She's still with us," he assured me and nodded toward the monitors.

I took Mama's hand in mine and held it tightly, held it as if I was holding her from falling into the grave itself. She didn't stir.

"Mama," I found strength enough to say, "it's me, Rain. I'm here, Mama, with Roy. Don't die, Mama. Please don't die," I pleaded.

The tears that streaked down my face felt like drops of boiling water.

"You'd be proud of me, Mama. I'm doing so well at school and I was in this play. I had the starring role and people think I can be an actress, Mama. Mama . . ."

Roy put his hand on my shoulder when I lowered my head to catch a breath. My chest was so tight, I could barely get enough air into my lungs. A nurse came over to the bed and looked at Mama. She checked an I.V. line and then glanced quickly at us as if the truth in her eyes would destroy us. I looked up at Roy and he looked down.

"Mama," I chanted as I stroked her hand and then stood to touch her hair and kiss her face. "Why didn't you tell me the truth, Mama? I would have stayed with you."

"That's why she didn't," Roy muttered.

I stood there, my hand on her hair, gazing down at her quiet face, recalling the sound of her laughter, the way she held me and spoke so hopefully to me, always hopefully, dreaming my dreams, urging me to have more confidence in myself, telling me I was beautiful and special.

"Is she in any pain, Roy?"

"They say no," he replied. He gazed at her. "She doesn't look like she is."

I sat again and buried my face against her shoulder and the bed. Roy stood by me patiently. After a while, he touched my hair.

"Maybe we should go down to the cafeteria and get something to eat, Rain. What do you say?"

"I'm not hungry, but I'll go with you," I told him. I kissed Mama's cheek and we left the intensive care unit.

I let him buy me some coffee. He got himself a ham and cheese sandwich and we sat alone at a table near the window. There were mostly hospital employees in the cafeteria, all of them chatting away and looking through us or past us as if we were invisible. I supposed the sight of troubled relatives was common enough to them.

"Tell me about what you've been up to," Roy urged. I knew he wanted to keep me talking because while I was talking, I couldn't cry.

I described everyone and what I had been doing in school.

"Horses?" he said with a smile. "You, riding horses?"

"My teacher says I'm good, too."

He laughed.

"Why didn't you call me more often, Roy?" I asked. "Didn't you get my letter?"

"Yeah, but for a while it wasn't easy to make a call and then, when I called and heard how you were so busy and involved, I figured you didn't want to hear from me."

"That was stupid, Roy," I snapped.

He looked sorry so fast I felt bad for getting angry.

"I was waiting for you to call again. I was very worried about you."

"I figured I'd see you soon enough," he said with a deep sigh.

"You knew about this, then? You knew from the start?"

"No, Rain, I didn't. She didn't tell me until you were gone from D.C.," he said, "and she made me promise on her life that I wouldn't tell you. That's the truth, Rain. I swear."

"When I first left," I began, "I was so heartbroken because I thought Mama couldn't have loved me as much as I thought if she could just let me go like that. I was even angry and thought I wouldn't call her, but when I heard her voice, I knew she loved me just as much and what she was doing, she was doing for me, putting me first. No one's ever going to do that for me again, Roy. Not these people, not this side of my blood, no one."

"I will," he promised, his eyes narrowing with determination and assurance. "I always will."

"I know, but you've got your own life to live."

"I want you to be a part of it, Rain. You know that," he said.

I looked down, sipped some coffee, closed my eyes and sat back.

"It all happened so fast, Roy," I said with my eyes still closed. I could see Beni laughing and Mama singing in the kitchen.

"Yeah, seems like it," he said.

"Let's go back upstairs, Roy," I told him.

"You sure you don't want anything to eat?"

"I couldn't hold anything down," I said and he nodded.

He gulped some coffee, cleared the table and then we went to the elevator.

"Where are you staying? With Aunt Sylvia?"

"Yeah, and I'm sure you're welcome, too."

"I've got this hotel room already booked," I explained.

"Oh yeah," he said.

When the elevator door opened, we saw Aunt Sylvia in the hallway. Her friend was embracing her.

My heart stopped and started. Roy looked at me fearfully.

"Oh children," Aunt Sylvia cried as we approached. "I'm so sorry. She's gone."

"Mama!" I screamed. "No. We were just with her. No!"

I pulled away and charged through the door. They were just putting the sheet over her. I rushed to the bed and pulled it down.

"She can't be dead," I screamed at the nurse.

"I'm sorry, dear," she said.

Roy took my hand and then embraced me as we both gazed at Mama. She didn't look any different from the way she was before. Maybe she wasn't dead.

"Please," I cried. "Are you sure?"

"She's passed on, dear," the nurse said softly. "The doctor was here and pronounced her."

I pressed my face against Roy's chest and he held me tightly. I could feel him sobbing inside, struggling to hold his tears from flowing.

"She waited for you, Rain," he whispered. "She waited for you."

Mama's funeral was simple. We decided she should be buried near the other members of her family. Roy called our Aunt Alana in Texas to tell her, but she said she was sick herself and didn't have the money to make the trip. She had no idea where Mama's brother Lamar was. She hadn't heard from him for nearly two years. So, aside from Aunt Sylvia and her friends, Roy, myself, some members of Aunt Sylvia's church, there was no one else at the funeral. Roy didn't want to call the prison to tell Ken. He didn't think he would care, and they certainly weren't going to fly him down to the funeral. In the end, I made the call and left the message for him.

Grandmother Hudson sent beautiful flowers. She and I spoke once on the phone, but my mother never called, nor did she send anything. Later, she would tell me that she had asked Grandmother Hudson to send flowers for her as well. I laughed to myself, thinking Grandmother Hudson was right: my mother always relied on her to do the right things, the necessary things.

After the funeral we all returned to Aunt Sylvia's house. Roy was supposed to leave that afternoon and return to his base camp. With everyone comforting us and trying to get us to eat, we didn't have much time alone. Finally, he took me aside and asked me to walk outside with him.

Aunt Sylvia had a small house with a little patch of grass for a backyard. She had a portion of it set aside for a vegetable garden and some chairs with a redwood picnic table. The day was partly cloudy with a warm breeze. Aunt Sylvia's flowers filled the air with a perfumed aroma. In the distance over the row of houses to our right, we could see a commercial jet begin its climb into the soft white patches of clouds.

"I can't think of her as dead, Roy," I said. "I just can't believe she's gone."

He nodded.

"It takes time to settle in."

He held his hat in his hand, turning it around and around with his thick fingers. Dressed in his uniform, he looked handsome, I thought. He looked heroic, the hero I always imagined him to be.

"Where are they going to send you?" I asked him.

"Germany is what I hear, but I can't be absolutely sure yet. You going to finish at that school?"

"Yes," I said.

"I was thinking . . . there's just the two of us now. I mean, I never think of Ken as part of us anymore. It was hard to think of him that way even when we were all living in D.C. When you finish at the school, you could . . . I mean, we could be together again.

"I'd make you happy, Rain, and I'd watch over you," he quickly continued. "We could get married. There's no reason why we can't. We don't have shared blood. I can't give you a big, fancy home, but we'll make out fine. I know other guys in the army who are married, and some with kids, too."

It was tempting, I thought, to leave the world of lies finally, to curl up in Roy's strong arms and be his wife and live like we had no other life before.

"Mama would probably want it," he said and nodded.

"Would she, Roy?" I asked with a small smile.

"I don't know. Yeah," he said. "She would."

I laughed.

"You don't want to go back to living with those rich white folks who don't even want you, who never really wanted you," he argued. "What kind of life is that going to be for you, Rain?"

"I don't know, Roy. I really don't know."

"But you're going back?" he asked angrily.

I took a deep breath.

Who am I? I wondered again and again.

"For a while," I said. "I have some questions that I have to answer."

"Questions? What questions?"

"Questions about myself," I said. "If I ran off with you, Roy, and never answered them, I would always be troubled. Can you understand that?"

"No," he said. Then he looked down and shook his head the way he always did when he knew he was wrong or had to face some fact reluctantly. "Yeah, maybe," he said.

"Just call me often and write to me," I said.

"You know I don't write much. What are you going to do after school is out?" he asked. "You going to go to England and be in that acting school?"

"I might," I said.

"You're becoming a fancy little lady, huh?"

"No, not fancy. I don't know what I'm becoming, Roy, but if I don't explore a little, I'll always be wondering if I should have. I wouldn't be any good to you like that, Roy."

"I have to get going," he said after a moment.

"You know I love you, Roy," I said.

"Yeah, but not the way I love you," he said.

"No, not now, but maybe someday."

He looked up with some hope in his eyes.

"Only, don't wait for it to happen, Roy. If someone else comes along, don't drive her off," I warned him.

"Yeah, the girls are just flocking to me."

He stared at me and then he smiled and we hugged. He never held me as tight. I thought he wasn't going to let go. Finally, he did.

"You be good," he said. "No," he added, "you be better than them. You're really Latisha Carrol's girl, hear? You always remember that, Rain. No matter what they tell you, that's who you are."

I nodded.

He reached out and touched my face and then started away. I didn't want to see him leave. I waited in the yard for a while, having my private little cry. Then I went into the house, said my farewells to Aunt Sylvia and her good friends before leaving myself.

I told the limo driver to take me to the cemetery again. I wanted to say my private good-bye to Mama. I stood by her grave and closed my eyes and heard her voice.

"Good-bye Mama," I whispered. "Thank you for loving me more than you loved yourself even though you didn't give birth to me. There will always be a place for you in my heart. No one will ever take that place."

I said a little prayer, touched the fresh earth after my tears fell to it, and then I rose, took a deep breath, turned and walked away to the waiting limousine and the future that dangled its promises before me.

# Epilogue

Jake was waiting for me at the airport gate. He took my bag and gave me a hug.

"I'm sorry," he said. "How you doing?"

"I'm all right, Jake. How's Mrs. Hudson?"

"Feisty as ever, even more so since you left," he said laughing.

When I arrived, Grandmother Hudson was waiting for me in the living room. I paused in the doorway.

"Thank you for sending the flowers," I told her. "They were beautiful."

She nodded, looking embarrassed as usual by any show of emotion.

"You should soak in a warm bath, relax and then come down for dinner. I have spoken with Mrs. Whitney and she wants you to know that you can postpone your exams for a week, if you like."

"I'd rather not," I said.

"Are you sure?"

"Yes. I'd rather keep busy," I said.

"That's very wise," she told me.

I picked up my bag and started to turn away.

"I've asked Sissy to make stuffed pork chops. Your favorite, I believe."

"Thank you," I said. She looked away quickly and then went back to her needlework.

I took her advice and soaked in a warm bath. While I was lying in the warm water, I suddenly began to cry. I couldn't stop myself. The tears poured out so fast, I thought I might fill the tub to the brim and let it spill over. Then, just as suddenly as they had come, they stopped. I scrubbed my face, dried myself and got dressed for dinner.

After I ran a brush through my hair quickly, I rose and stood by the window, gazing out at the sky. A knock on my door pulled me from my reverie. It was Grandmother Hudson, dressed for dinner and looking as elegant as ever.

"I was hoping you were ready to go down," she said.

Go down together? I thought. I had always been there before or right after her, but we had never gone together.

"I'm not all that hungry," I said.

"When you smell Sissy's cooking, your stomach will change your mind," she insisted.

She might be right, I thought.

We started down the stairs.

"Your mother called to see how you were, but you hadn't arrived yet. I'm to give you her sympathies and best wishes because she was on her way to a political ball. Your friend Audrey called to see how you were, too. There were a few other calls from students. I left the list in my office. I'll give it to you after dinner. I've done nothing but man the phones on your behalf," she added.

"Thank you," I said hiding a small smile.

"I don't know why I told her to make those pork chops. They really don't agree with me," she continued as we rounded the stairway and headed toward the dining room.

"Maybe Sissy can make you something else," I suggested.

"Of course not. What do you think this is, a restaurant? I swear, all you young people today are so spoiled."

She took her seat at the table and I took mine. Sissy served the meal and it was as delicious as ever. Grandmother Hudson was right. I hadn't realized how hungry I was. Nevertheless, I felt guilty eating, guilty enjoying. How long does the sadness last? I wondered.

Grandmother Hudson saw how melancholy I was. I had made little conversation. Toward the end of the meal, she put her silverware aside, and her elbows on the table as she clasped her hands and turned to me.

"I never met the woman you called Mama, of course, but from what I have learned and from what I have seen, she made remarkable sacrifices for you. She would want you to take advantage of every opportunity you were offered. That's all I will say on the subject," she declared, then took the napkin off her lap, placed it on the table, rose and left the room.

I sat for a few moments listening to my own heartbeat. Then I started to help Sissy clear the table.

"Oh you don't have to do that, honey," she said.

"I want to, Sissy," I insisted.

After the table was cleared, I went outside and sat on a bench. It was a night of blazing stars, but no moon. I heard an owl way off in the darkness of the woods. It sounded so mournful.

Was Mama with Beni somewhere now? Were the two of them looking down at me and waiting?

I looked up at the mansion with its magnificent stone columns. Could this ever be home to me?

Where is home? Home has to be someplace in your heart, too. Could I ever be a part of this world, really a part of it? Or should I have told Roy to come and get me as soon as he could? At least with him, I would never be afraid.

Or would I be afraid of the worst thing of all . . . never knowing who I really was.

I want my name, Mama, I whispered. I want my Mama.

As if I was still on stage, I imagined the audience's applause. It was loud and overwhelming and somehow, if I pretended this was just a terribly emotional scene I was acting in, maybe I could pretend my pain wasn't real.

Actors are always being someone they are not, and that was what I have been, I thought. They move through personalities and characters like someone without a face, searching for the right identity, waiting for that applause and wondering if the applause was for them or for someone they imagined themselves to be.

Who am I?

The answer was out there waiting to be discovered. I would do what Grandmother Hudson said I should do: I would take advantage of every opportunity and open every door until one day, I looked at the truth.

Then, I could come home.

